"I'm harmless."

Somehow Allison doubted that.

"Oh, darn! I forgot my purse. The bartender put it behind the bar for me."

"No problem." His bordering-on-cocky smile turned Good Samaritan. "I'll get it for you."

"Thank you," she said. And then she made mondo mistake numero uno as her fingers spontaneously curled into the front of that warm, snug t-shirt and she pulled him down to kiss his sexy five o'clock-shadowed cheek. "You're such a gentleman."

Mondo mistake numero two came when, caught up in his warm masculine scent that oozed with sexual promise, she allowed her lips to linger on that cheek.

Lightning flashed in his sexy baby blues, and before she could say, "Holy hotstuff, Batman," his big hand covered hers and he lowered his head.

In her experience, kisses could easily be judged on a sliding scale from "meh" to "za-zing." When Jesse's mouth met hers, she struggled to hang onto the tail of the skyrocket he ignited.

Smooth masculine lips. Firm yet soft. Possessive but not aggressive. Sexy and . . . yeah. *Really* sexy.

And dangerous.

By Candis Terry

SOMETHING SWEETER
SWEETEST MISTAKE
ANYTHING BUT SWEET
SOMEBODY LIKE YOU
ANY GIVEN CHRISTMAS
SECOND CHANCE AT THE SUGAR SHACK

Short Stories
HOME SWEET HOME
(appears in FOR LOVE AND HONOR
and CRAZY SWEET FINE)
SWEET FORTUNE
(appears in CONFESSIONS OF A SECRET
ADMIRER—A VALENTINE'S DAY ANTHOLOGY)

CANDIS TERRY

Something
SWEETER

AVON
An Imprint of HarperCollinsPublishers

AVON BOOKS
An Imprint of HarperCollins*Publishers*
195 Broadway
New York, New York 10007

Copyright © 2014 by Candis Terry
ISBN 978-0-06-223726-2
www.avonromance.com

First Avon Books mass market printing: July 2014

10 9 8 7 6 5 4 3 2 1

For the amazing and beautiful Lisa Filipe.
Because sometimes people come into our lives
and we are just thankful.
XOXO

Acknowledgments

$\mathcal{M}$y sincerest thanks and appreciation to the incredibly talented geniuses at Avon Books for helping me put my best foot forward and for making me look good even on a bad hair day: my editor, Amanda Bergeron; Pam, Jessie, Caroline, and Abigail in Publicity; Shawn, Dana, and Julie in Marketing; Tom and his incredible team in the art department for my amazing book covers; and all those who put their hands on my books to produce such an incredible outcome. Thank you so very, very much.

Over-the-moon gratitude to award-winning photographer Greg Lumley, and Ronald and Jennifer Anne Vleggaar for their generosity in allowing me to use their gorgeous wedding photo for this book cover. The moment I saw it I knew it was perfect to represent the romance, fun, and joyfulness I wanted to convey for this story.

Also, thank you to Lisa Jaramillo and "Earl."

Chapter 1

Jesse Wilder prided himself on two things: his dedication to his family and that he was the best damned veterinarian in Sweet, Texas.

Everything else was up in the air.

Including the fact that in a sticky situation, minding his own business was a total shot in the dark.

Up until a couple minutes ago, everything in his little world had been stable and serene. But as he cut a glare across Seven Devils Saloon dance floor to the woman who had just dragged his soon-to-be-married older brother out for a little country swing dance, all bets were off.

It was obvious the petite brunette had no clue how to execute the lively dance steps. It was equally obvious that as a former Marine, Reno could handle himself. His brother had been drowning in grief until he met his vivacious fiancée Charlotte Brooks. There wasn't a chance in hell he'd do anything to risk the relationship.

Still, somehow, the evening had gone haywire.

Initially, Jesse had agreed to meet up for a quick beer, so Reno could avoid the flurry of females and the wedding-detail crunch going on at his house. Then the brunette fluff ball blew in and dragged Reno right out onto the dance floor.

Reno's Southern gentleman manners prevented him from walking away.

Jesse had no such problem.

He might be the best damn vet in town, but protecting his family was his number one job. Therefore, he wouldn't allow her and her dazzling, flirtatious smile to threaten his brother's happiness. As the middle child in a family of five boys, he'd struggled his whole life to figure out where he fit within the circle. In the past few years, tragedy had hit their family hard. With each heartbreak, Jesse had been shown not only where he belonged but also the duties he needed to accomplish. After the deaths of his big brother, then their father, he'd vowed to make sure each of his family members found happiness.

Reno was currently tops on his radar.

The woman in question was sexy and hot in a compact package. But she was clearly *not* local. And she had no idea you didn't mess with Texas—or an engaged Wilder brother.

Not while Jesse was around.

Her long, wavy hair looked to be a shade of rich caramel with a toffee-colored streak that dangled near her exquisite face like a satin ribbon. At this distance, Jesse couldn't tell the color of her eyes.

He only knew the deep hue drew him in and made him think of making love on a lazy, rainy morning. Definitely one of his favorite pastimes. And definitely something he'd gone too long without.

Something about the woman's energy told him she'd have to be taught to take things at a leisurely pace. Not that he minded playing teacher to a willing student, but there was something about the expression on her face, the way she moved, that said she could be more than a handful of trouble.

For his tastes, she was a bit on the short side, but a man would have to be dead not to notice the way she filled out a pair of jeans. And he, most certainly, was not dead.

She wore a ruffled little nothing of a top he was sure he could see through if he looked close enough.

Or maybe that was just wishful thinking.

He ignored the way her arms and feet kept getting tangled up. Instead, he studied the playful smile tilting the corners of her perfectly bowed top lip and succulent bottom lip. A clear indication she was having way too much fun.

A groan of frustration rumbled through his chest. While he sat on the barstool playing Fashion Police, his brother needed a rescue.

The powerful rhythm of Miranda Lambert's "Kerosene" vibrated the dance floor, and the overhead red and amber lights shone down in a hazy inferno. Resigned, Jesse set his bottle of Shiner Bock down on the bar and turned to the bartender. "How about you save these stools for me?"

Rory McIntire—Irish by blood, Texan by choice—grinned. "You coming back with Reno or the hot-bodied brunette?"

Jesse considered the female in question and had to agree, she had one smokin' body he wouldn't mind taking his time to get to know. And those killer high heels at the bottom of her nicely toned legs? Totally shooting his testosterone level over the red line.

"Hard to say," he responded.

"Don't know why I even bothered asking." Rory shook his head. "This is *you* we're talking about."

Jesse gave him a tight smile.

Years back, he and his brothers had developed quite a wild reputation. Though they'd never spent a single night in jail for their sometimes risky antics, they had spent a lot of time with the ladies. As much as folks liked to think boys talked, it was the girls, then later, the women in Sweet who'd spun the gossip into a firestorm that was often exaggerated beyond imagination. He was pretty sure he'd never had sex in a tree or on top of a horse before, but he also didn't bother to squash the rumors.

It never hurt to be known as a good lover.

Of course, if he'd done even half the women whose favors he'd been rumored to have partaken of, he'd never get out of bed. The older he and his brothers became, the faster the rumors flew—most of them courtesy of a very bored community.

With Reno and Jackson now off the market and Jake in Afghanistan, *he'd* become the main focus for the hotbed of gossip, the poster child for play-boys everywhere. Didn't matter that he'd served honorable time in the Marines, or maintained his status as a good son, or had become a trustworthy caretaker of poodles and potbellied pigs alike. All anyone in this ranching community cared about was who he slept with and how long it would last. The going bets ranged anywhere from one night to a week. Apparently, a monthlong relationship took imagination past its limits.

Everyone would be disappointed to learn that the rumors were far-fetched, and he was far from the town *manwhore*. Yeah, it was his bad that he let them think what they wanted. Under normal circumstances, he'd never let that happen. Instead, the rumors worked in his favor. As long as everyone believed he was a confirmed bachelor, it kept the serious-minded women looking elsewhere. This allowed him the time and focus he needed to help his family.

The gossip didn't make a difference to him or the business he ran, and he supposed there were worse reputations to be had. Of course, his mother didn't feel that way, and he'd often have to run interference and assure her that no, he didn't sleep with every woman he met. And no, the reason he couldn't keep his vet assistants employed wasn't because he was sleeping with all of them but because the job paid low wages. And often the commute to their little town was too far.

He'd swear that on a stack of King James's.

When everyone in his family was settled, he'd have time to focus on his own future. His own happiness.

Although, at the moment . . . he tilted his head as the brunette on the dance floor did a sexy hip wiggle . . . he wouldn't mind putting his bad-boy reputation to good use.

A last sip of beer cooled his throat before he headed toward the dance floor. When he came up behind the brunette, Reno speared him with a "What the hell took you so long?" glare.

In a smooth maneuver they'd perfected back in the day, Reno handed her off. Jesse took her in his arms and spun her off to a corner so his big brother could escape. On the way off the dance floor, Reno gave him an "I'm outta here" signal.

Jesse nodded.

He was on his own.

With a hot little brunette.

Who looked up at him with "Who the hell are you?" sparks shooting out of what he could see now were smoky gray eyes with flecks of fools gold and whiskey brown flashing in their depths.

In a blatant disregard of the lively dance steps, he slowed down, pulled her close, and watched a tiny wrinkle appear between her perfectly arched brows. Over the twang of guitars and vocals, he smiled and poured on the Southern charm.

"Hey there, darlin'."

She glanced toward Reno's retreating backside, then at him again. "What are you, some kind of tag team?"

He kept his smile in place as he enjoyed the way she fit against him. "Just didn't want you to waste any more of your time in his direction. In case you didn't notice, the man has *taken* written all over him."

"I didn't see a ring."

"Women wear the engagement ring. Not the men."

"Ah." She glanced back at the exit, where the exterior neon light shrunk to a sliver as the big door closed behind Reno. Then those smoky eyes came back up with a hint of amusement. "So you're what . . . his rescue party?"

"His brother."

Her nod was as slight as the way her hand felt captured within his own. "Duly noted."

Those fingers with the sexy red nails slipped away, and he had to wonder why that felt like such a loss. In response, and because missing a display of such sexuality would be a sin, he watched her walk away. As she moved across the dance floor, her hips swayed in an easy fashion that spoke of confidence, not arrogance. Sensuality, not desperation. Unlike Lila Ridenbaugh, who'd cornered poor Brian Doolittle and was trying to convince him to be baby daddy number five or six or whatever position she was currently trying to fill.

As the brunette sashayed back to the bar, he had no choice but to follow. Because really, his mama didn't raise any dummies. Five crazy-ass Southern boys? That'd be a big hell yeah. Dumb? Not a single one.

As they approached, Rory the bartender looked up, grinned at Jesse and his choice of returning company, and set out two fresh bottles of Shiner.

Judging by her abrupt withdrawal, Jesse hated to admit it would probably take more than an icy bottle of beer to get her to stay put. After all, she'd chosen Reno to dance with, not him. Still, he was willing to give it his best shot.

As she reached that scarred pine bar, she surprised him by leaning a curvy hip on the barstool and lifting the fresh bottle to her lips. At the sight of that seductive mouth pressed to the rim of the amber glass, a hot and naked image of her pressing her lips to his body leaped into his head. He barely suppressed a groan as he lifted his own bottle and took a soothing drink of the mellow ale.

She gave a little smile like she knew what he was thinking. And if she was looking anywhere south of his belt buckle, then, yep, his thoughts were probably pretty transparent at this point.

"So . . ." She turned toward him and leaned her elbows back on the bar, which thrust her ample breasts into the ruffled little nothing of a top for him to appreciate. She flashed a playful smile. "Come here often?"

"Worst pickup line ever." He grinned, appreciating the playfulness for what it was. Even if it led nowhere. He raised his bottle of Shiner in a salute. "In this case, it just might work."

"Oh, I've got a million pickup lines." A low, sexy chuckle rumbled from that long, delicate throat. "Some I've even stockpiled for when I need a good laugh."

"Try me."

As if preparing for an improvisational monologue, she stepped back, rolled her neck, and cracked her knuckles.

He chuckled until she jumped into character. Those smoky gray eyes took a slow ride down his body, then inched back up. When she leaned in closer, everything inside him tightened. He breathed in the warm feminine scent that hinted of something sweet and tasty like cotton candy.

"Do you believe in love at first sight," she purred. "Or should I walk by again?"

He was starting to believe.

"Or how about . . . Are you a parking ticket? Because you've got FINE written all over you."

Back atcha, gorgeous.

"And then there's always the classic . . ." She slowly dragged her finger down the buttons on his shirt. "If I could rearrange the alphabet, I'd put U and I together."

"Nicely done." He gave her a small applause.

"But . . ."

Uh-oh.

"Going back to my first line? It wasn't meant as a pickup."

Color him disappointed.

"Obviously, in a town this size, you've realized I'm not from around here." Her head tilted as she studied him once more. "I'm looking for a place to have breakfast in the morning."

"Since I'm guessing you're not going to follow up with 'your place or mine,' it's just your luck I'm born and raised in this area."

As she took a quick sip of beer, he leaned an elbow on the bar and did a visual slow ride down her body just to keep things even. "I've got everything you need."

Her lips parted, and her tongue darted out to swipe away a drop of ale. "I'll bet you do."

The air between them shifted into the hot-and-heavy zone before he realized he was getting mixed signals. Her words were flirty. Her long hot gazes definitely showed interest. But something deep in those smoky eyes said she wasn't a hundred percent on board. And since he'd been brought up to always wait for an invitation, he wasn't quite sure which way to rock this . . . encounter.

"Nothing finer," he said.

She laughed. "And you're confident, too."

He sipped his beer and watched her over the lip of the bottle. When he set the bottle down, he clarified, "Bud's Nothing Finer Diner. Best place in Sweet for breakfast. They serve up a killer fresh strawberry banana French toast with whipped cream that'll make you want to lick the plate clean."

"Sounds like you've enjoyed that once or twice."

"Consider me an expert licker."

She grinned. "Are we talking about breakfast?"

"I don't know." He grinned back. "Are we?"

The hesitant half laugh she gave him told him two things. One: She wondered just how good he'd make on his innuendo. And two: She was definitely thinking it over.

"Well, Mr. . . ."

"Just Jesse. Folks around here don't call me mister. And you are?"

"Just Allie. Folks don't call me mister either."

He laughed and extended his hand. "Pleasure to meet you."

The warmth of her skin settled against his palm, and he felt like he'd been hit with a thousand volts. The electricity she threw off sizzled from his hand, zipped through his heart, and rocketed down into his crotch. He couldn't help wonder. If she had that much energy balled up in just one little handshake, what could she do with the rest of that curvaceous body?

"Well . . . Jesse, I thank you for the beer." She glanced down at the rhinestone watch on her wrist. "But I really need to be on my way."

"Where you headed?"

One slim shoulder lifted in a careless shrug. "Just passing through."

"And yet you asked about a good place to have breakfast?" He searched her eyes. Even though he found himself drawn in by the flashes of silver and gold, he still found no invitation.

Her lovely shoulder came up in another shrug, and all he could think was how badly he wanted to lower his nose right into the soft curve of her neck and inhale her delicious, mouthwatering scent.

When Blake Shelton's ballad "Who Are You When I'm Not Looking" came over the sound system, Jesse saw perhaps his last opportunity before she blew through the door and back to wherever it was she came from.

His mother taught him how to be a gentleman. His now-deceased father had taught him how to treat a lady with respect. His older brothers had taught him how to get laid.

The brothers were winning on this one.

He held out his hand. "Then maybe you'll do me the honor of a full dance before you go?"

$\mathcal{A}$llison glanced out across the dance floor, then swung her gaze back to the man in front of her, who held out his hand and gave her a smile. She pulled a breath of stale air into her lungs while she considered her choice and *him.*

Judging by the less-than-conspicuous stares, she wasn't the only female in the bar who found his tall, muscular body a bit on the tasty side. In well-worn cowboy boots, a snug pair of jeans, and a baby blue Henley shirt that hugged some impressive pecs and biceps, he also possessed a roller coaster of six-pack abs.

She, for one, had always been a thrill-seeker.

The glitter in his deep blue eyes was mesmerizing. His dark blond hair was on the long side and pulled back into a ponytail. She imagined that if he let it go, he'd resemble some mythological deity like Thor.

Okay, so maybe he didn't look like Marvin the Masher, and maybe several people in the place seemed to acknowledge their friendly acquaintance by the tip of a cowboy hat or bottle of beer. But he was far from what she'd deem as *safe.*

Yet that wasn't what tipped her *uh-oh* meter.

Jesse—as he called himself—was one hundred percent the kind of guy she'd always been attracted to and equally the kind who always wound up breaking her heart. Not that she ever planned to look for a forever guy. She just wanted any temporary one to quietly go away instead of ripping out her favorite organ and taking it with him when he left.

Jesse looked like a bona fide heart ripper.

Several seconds ticked off the clock before her pulsating girl parts won the coin toss, and she put her hand in his. His smile was not quite wolfish and not quite Boy Scout as he led her onto the dance floor. But when he took her into his arms and drew her up against that super yummy chest, any question of his intent took a leave of absence.

The warm male scent of him filled her head as he held her close. And the heat from his hard, strong body radiated through layers of cotton. The lyrics of the song they danced to asked "Who are you when I'm not looking?" *She* was just looking for her bones—which seemed to have gone missing.

With their height difference and his leg moving between her thighs, some really interesting friction started going on in all the right places. Dangerously so.

Get a grip, girl.

Grasping for control, she briefly closed her eyes as he led her across the dance floor in smooth, seductive steps. As a distraction from what was going on in the rest of her body, she worked really hard to recite something other than "I want him" inside her head.

A deep chuckle rumbled from his chest, and she looked up.

Big mistake.

The look he'd angled her way suggested he knew exactly what was going on in her twisted noggin.

"Something funny?" she asked.

Slowly, he shook his head, and his hand slipped down to the small of her back to pull her in closer. "Just thinking that those high heels must be pretty uncomfortable to dance in."

She cocked her head. "You're thinking about my shoes?"

"I'm thinking about you taking *off* your shoes."

The rest he left unsaid. But she could guarantee the remainder of that sentence included her blouse, pants, and underwear. And because she started thinking along the same lines, she gave him a friendly pat on the chest and eased from his arms.

"Thanks for the dance. Time for me to head on down the road." If her shoes had been made of rubber, she would have left a burn mark heading for the door. But as she reached for the iron handle, his big hand was already there. She glanced up and found him smiling.

"Wouldn't be gentlemanly of me to let you walk to your car alone."

"Like there might be lions, and tigers, and bears out there ready to eat me?"

He flashed a smile. "Or something." He pushed open the door and held it while she ducked beneath his arm and headed out into the dirt and gravel parking lot.

She could put her legs in gear and run like hell,

but that would seem too desperate. Somehow, she managed a controlled pace that didn't scream *"Get me out of here before I jump this guy."*

"Where are you parked?"

A spring storm crackled across the sky, and the wind lifted the ends of her hair as she pointed to the silver economy car she'd rented at a lunch-box-sized place near the San Antonio airport. The pebbles embedded in the dirt made a serious attempt to twist her ankles as she hurried across the lot.

"You know," he said, following at a leisurely pace behind, "I can't help but wonder why a woman like you would choose to come to a less-than-reputable honky-tonk all by herself."

"Beats sitting in a motel room."

"True. But since Sweet doesn't have any motel rooms . . ."

"I'm staying at a bed-and-breakfast," she said quickly, unwilling to reveal anything about herself. Though *Jesse* had *good time guaranteed* written all over him, she hadn't come to Sweet looking for romance. Or to get laid.

Unfortunately.

It was time she refocused on her purpose for flying in all the way from Washington State.

"Paige and Aiden's place?"

As she reached the little silver car, she turned and looked up at him. "Who?"

"The Honey Hill B&B?"

"You don't expect me to give out that information, do you? We just met. You could be Ted Bundy Jr. for all I know."

"I'm harmless."

She doubted that.

She pulled the key from her front pocket and thumbed the fob to unlock the door. To his credit, he didn't try to corral her against the car or lean in for a kiss. With the storm flashing at his back, he just stood there as if waiting for her to make a move.

She did.

It just wasn't the one he was probably hoping for.

"Oh, darn," she said with a dramatic look back at the glowing neon lights of the saloon. "I forgot my purse. The bartender put it behind the bar for me."

"No problem." His bordering-on-cocky smile turned Good Samaritan. "I'll get it for you."

"Thank you," she said. And then she made mondo mistake numero uno as her fingers spontaneously curled into the front of that warm, snug shirt, and she pulled him down to kiss his sexy, beard-shadowed cheek. "You're such a gentleman."

Mondo mistake number two came when, caught up in his warm masculine scent that oozed with sexual promise, she allowed her lips to linger on that cheek.

Lightning flashed in his sexy eyes, and before she could say "Holy hot stuff, Batman," his big hand covered hers and he lowered his head.

In her experience, kisses could easily be judged on a sliding scale from "meh" to "za-zing." When Jesse's mouth met hers, she struggled to hang on to the tail of the skyrocket he ignited.

Smooth masculine lips. Firm yet soft. Possessive but not aggressive. Sexy and . . . yeah. *Really* sexy.

And dangerous.

Really dangerous.

And because *she* certainly didn't have the power to back away, she was oddly disappointed and yet relieved when he raised his head and looked up at the tempestuous sky.

"Better get in the car and out of this storm." That deep "Come here, baby" voice rumbled against her chest. "I'll be right back with your purse." He let go of her hand and turned. The neon red of the overhead sign shone down on his hair and gave him a devilish allure as those long, muscular legs jogged toward the bar.

With an appreciative "Mmm mmmm mmmmm," Allison watched until his ultra-fine backside disappeared inside the bar.

*J*esse pulled open the saloon door and went inside just as another bolt of lightning streaked across the sky and thunder rolled overhead. He was glad he'd told her to get inside her car. No sense taking any chances. Though brief, that kiss she'd given him had definitely been an invitation. He'd had no choice but to respond.

Well, his head had given him a choice.

His body?

Uh-uh.

Even now, as the taste of her lingered on his lips, he made plans for her that included his hot tub and the bottle of Malbec he'd bought on a tour down the Texas Wine Trail a few weeks ago.

With a rowdy outlaw song raising the roof, the

sound level inside the bar had become unbearable. Dodging folks bent on having a good time, he made his way across the room to find Smitty Johnson, not Rory, tending bar.

"You got a purse back there?" he shouted over the music.

"When did you start batting for the other team?"

"Ha-ha." Everybody had to be a comedian. "Just look will you?"

Smitty wiped his hands on a towel and bent at his beer belly to do a quick search. He came up with a shake of his head. "Got a carton of Marlboros and a box of Trojans but no purse."

"You sure?"

He checked again. "Yep."

Shit.

Suspicion dropped over him like a net as he crossed the bar, pushed open the door, and stepped back out onto the old-fashioned boardwalk crossing the front of the building.

A bolt of lightning lit up the sky, revealing the now-vacant parking space where Allie's little silver car had sat just moments ago.

Empty.

Gone.

Message received.

Invitation revoked.

Chapter 2

With all the hustle and bustle going on at Wilder Ranch, one would think a huge event was about to take place. But as Jesse pulled down the gravel road and parked in the shade of the barn, he knew that Reno and Charli's wedding was still a few weeks off, Jackson and Abby were waiting to get married until they finished building their new house, and his mother and her new beau hadn't yet set a date. So the reason for all the hoopla in the courtyard that had everyone scrambling left him scratching his head.

True, his mother and her usual last-minute hectic flair were no surprise. The woman had been known to throw together a carnival-sized event in only a few hours. She also couldn't keep a secret to save her life. Yet somehow she'd managed to keep the purpose for this little shindig hush-hush. No doubt she had another bombshell up her sleeve like the one she'd sprung on them a few months ago when she'd announced she was marrying a man she barely knew.

In the past few years, their family had been to hell and back. First, his oldest brother had been killed in Afghanistan. Less than a year later, their father unexpectedly died. And when Reno's former fiancée was killed in a head-on collision just days before their wedding, it seemed the rest of them would never survive their heart-crushing grief. With the worry of his littlest brother Jake—or maybe since the subject stood close to six-foot-four he should say youngest brother—still fighting with the Marines in the sandpit, maybe they all deserved a little fun.

Whatever the reason.

As Jesse sat in his truck for a moment, watching the flurry of activity just beyond his windshield, he realized life had recently begun to turn around. Reno had met the beautiful and vivacious Charli and was about to be married. Jackson and Abby, the girl he'd loved nearly his whole life, had finally found their way back to each other. And now his mother had seemed to find someone. Thankfully, it seemed as though things were settling down.

He switched off the ignition and swiped a hand over his eyes, fighting the exhaustion that had settled deep in his bones.

After he'd shaken off the encounter with the gorgeous yet quick-footed brunette named Allie, he'd gone straight home from Seven Devils. He'd barely crawled into bed when he'd received the call from a frantic Francine Meyers about her favor-

ite mare. Seemed the onetime champion cutting
horse was about to foal, and Ms. Meyers didn't
believe all was going well. As the only veterinarian within a thirty-mile radius, he'd ended up sitting on a bed of hay all night. Though he believed
the mare would do fine, he'd stayed because he
couldn't bear to know Ms. Meyers would wring
those arthritic hands all alone as she watched
over her beloved pet.

She'd kept him company all those long hours,
bringing him hot cups of tea and amusing him
with stories of the days she'd competed in the cir-
cuit. His father had also competed, and Reno still
rode the man's champion cutter.

After the mare delivered a pretty buckskin
filly just fine, Jesse made it home just as the sun
came up. He'd barely had time to shower before
heading straight to the clinic for his Saturday appointments. Luckily, his vet assistant and future
sister-in-law, Abby, had only scheduled him for a
few well-pet visits and vaccinations, and they'd
made it out of there in time for his mother's . . .
mysterious celebration.

"All y'all quit your dillydallying," his mother
shouted with a swipe of an arm across her forehead to sweep back the bangs of her big blond
Texas-sized hairdo. "The surprise will be here
soon."

Message received, Jesse slid from his truck to
jump in and help. He made it as far as the picnic
tables where Charli, Abby, and Annie—Abby's
younger sister who was pregnant and had been
abandoned by the baby's jackass father—spread

out calico-print tablecloths. Fiona, Jackson's ex-wife, kept busy popping fresh-cut daisies into galvanized watering cans and arranging the colorful Fiesta Ware. His brothers were setting out bowls of side dishes, including Jesse's favorite fried green tomatoes and fried okra. Jackson and Fiona's three-year-old daughter, Izzy, made a running leap for Jesse. He caught her, swung her up into his arms, and was rewarded with a sticky kiss on the cheek.

"Hi, Unca Jethe."

"Hey, little darlin'." He gave her a loud smooch on the forehead. "What have you been eating?"

Her little Cupid's bow of a mouth curled up in a red-stained grin. "Gwanma's jam."

"Ah." He kissed her again, avoiding the sticky spots, then turned to the remainder of the crew. "What the . . . heck's going on?" he asked everyone.

Reno looked up with a shake of his head. "Mom won't even tell me this time."

"Oooh. And you're the favorite," Jesse joked, knowing it would set off Jackson. His little brother didn't disappoint.

"He is not. *I'm* Mom's favorite."

"Nuh-uh, Daddy." Izzy, having learned somewhere in her infancy that everything in the Wilder household was a competition, jumped in with her two cents. "*I'm* Gwanma's favvit."

Jesse laughed and gave her another kiss on the cheek. When she squirmed, he set her down to go visit Miss Giddy, their mother's pet goat. Today, the fashion-conscious farm animal sported a flashy neon pink satin ribbon around her long brown neck.

"So how'd it go with your girl last night?" Reno asked.

"His girl?" the four adult females within hearing range echoed.

"Not open for discussion." Jesse shook his head and turned to go help his mother.

Jackson hooted. "Guess that means no additional notches on the bedpost."

Jesse raised his middle finger and left his brothers cackling like old hens. In the distance, the big grill he and those same pain-in-the-ass siblings had constructed several years back, awaited his arrival.

When they'd all still been together, Jared, the oldest and by far the wisest, had come up with the idea to build the barbecue monstrosity. Together, he and Reno came up with the design. The five of them had then donned welding masks and gloves to make it happen. The creation ended up much larger than the original design, and some jokingly called it a military tank. But with the blowout community barbecue the Wilder family hosted once a year, not to mention their ever-growing brood, the structure grilled some amazing meals.

The memory of creating that steel contraption sent a bone-deep ache through his chest. Jared had loved to sit in the nearby shade of the oak trees with a cold bottle of beer, tending the brisket or ribs or whatever he'd thrown on the fire. The day of Jared's funeral, the grill had sat cold and empty.

Jake, the baby of the family, had a scar down his

right arm from tearing it on the sheet metal they'd used. His remedy had been to cover it up with a tribal tattoo the Marine Corp didn't much appreciate. Jake was currently deployed to Afghanistan, and it had been over a year since any of them had seen him. Jesse missed him like hell, and he spent many sleepless nights worrying about Jake's safety.

He smiled, thinking of the bundle of trouble their mom and dad had brought home almost thirty years ago.

Being the youngest hadn't slowed Jake down. He gave as good as he got when it came to whatever his big brothers were up to. Which usually meant trouble in the form of two or more weeks of restriction. When it came to the military, no one had any doubt Jake was a lifer. He'd quickly moved up in the ranks and still gave the rest of them shit for bailing out when their contracts expired. They'd all made excuses, but after Jared's death, most of them just didn't have the heart to fight anymore.

Jake? He had a score to settle with the enemy. But like a true, dedicated soldier, he pushed his personal beliefs aside to do his job, and he did it extremely well. Jesse figured that one of these days, all that pent-up emotion would blow like Mount St. Helens.

Providing his little brother came home at all.

"Hey, Mom." Smoke billowed out of the grill in a tangy-sweet aroma that made his mouth water. "How about you sit over there in the shade while the rest of us finish putting things together?"

"Oh." She looked up at him with blue eyes that

matched his own and patted his cheek. "Y'all are just so thoughtful. Sometimes it makes my heart want to leap clean out of my chest."

Whatever the reason for the party, his mother had been in a tizzy since her new beau, Martin Lane, had asked for her hand in marriage. And though Jesse and his brothers weren't quite yet sold on the man their mother planned to marry, it was only because they didn't know him well enough. Then there was the issue that all of them were still, and maybe always would be, mourning the loss of their father. While no one would re-place the man who'd taught them the ways of the world, they all wanted to see their mother happy.

Cheeks flushed, she plopped down on a nearby bench beneath the shade of an ancient live oak. He lifted the lid of the grill, stepped back from the wave of smoke, and slathered the brisket with another splash of sauce.

"So you want to let me in on the reason for the party?"

"No." A grin spread across her face. "And don't you keep asking, or it will ruin the surprise."

He laughed. "I'm not sure my heart can take any more of your surprises."

"It's all going to work out just fine, son. Martin's a good man, and he'll take good care of me."

"Hope so. I'd hate to have to break his legs."

"I'll admit . . ." She chuckled. "He is a little in-timidated by all you boys."

"Good. At least we'll keep him honest."

"I have no doubt." She brushed a leaf from her shoulder. "How are things going with you?"

He closed the lid on the grill. "The clinic has been pretty busy. Spent last night waiting with Ms. Meyers for Dandelion to foal. Got herself a pretty little filly."

"Well, that's nice." She looked up and squinted against the late-afternoon sunshine. "But I'm not talking about your work."

"Then what?" As if he didn't know.

"You've got two brothers getting married. Figured your time should be coming up soon. Any prospects?"

He didn't stop the laughter that rumbled from his chest. "I think you need to admit that I'm probably going to be the eternal bachelor." He couldn't resist the opportunity to tease her even though he knew someday he hoped to be lucky enough to have a wife and family. "You know, like Chester Banks?"

"You are nothing like Chester!" Her face flushed, and her eyes sparked. "That man's been married too many times to recall. Don't even know how he made it into his eighties without one of those wives shooting him right through the heart."

"Yeah." He gave an exaggerated shudder. "Don't sign me up for that."

"Love is out there for everyone." She stood and gave him a hug. "I never thought I'd find it again after your daddy passed. He was the love of my life. Always will be. But I don't want to go through the rest of my days alone and lonely. Martin and I have a lot in common, and we have a healthy respect for each other. And for marriage."

"I just want you to be happy."

She reached up and gently patted his cheek.

"Right back atcha, my beautiful boy." Then she tugged his ponytail. "Which reminds me. Maybe you should get a haircut before I have to start calling you, my beautiful girl."

He chuckled, knowing he'd been long past due for a haircut. Amongst other reasons, the long hair was just one of those little things he did to keep his family fussing at him instead of each other.

At the sound of tires on gravel they both turned to see Martin Lane's big blue dually truck pull up in the shade of the barn.

"Oh goody!" His mother's high-toned enthusiasm shot Jesse's curiosity into WTF mode. "The surprise is here!"

He shaded his eyes with a raised hand to get a better look until his mom grabbed him and pulled him toward the truck. "Come on."

Everyone halted the party preparations as the truck idled, and the passenger-side door opened. One heavy boot stepped out onto the gravel drive. A big man dressed in desert camo followed. And a collective gasp rolled throughout those gathered.

"I didn't fly halfway across the world for all y'all to stand there gawking at me." A familiar smile broke across the man's face, and he opened his arms wide. "Bring on the hugs."

A rush of exhilaration shot through Jesse's heart, and he smiled.

Little brother Jake was home.

With the exception of Annie, everyone rushed to gather him back into the fold, including Charli, who'd never even met him before. After an animated round of "Oh my Gods" and "It's so good to see yous" they stepped back to give him air and allow their mother to touch his face, make sure he was okay, and shed a few happy tears. In the midst of the joyful reunion, the slam of two truck doors closing was barely noticed.

When the dust settled, Jesse looked up to thank Martin Lane for bringing his brother home. The smile on his lips died.

Standing beside Martin was none other than the hot little brunette who last night had turned the *tease* dial up to full volume just before she set her sexy red high heels on *sprint*.

Reno leaned in, and murmured, "Isn't that the—"

"Yep." Jesse folded his arms and tried not to laugh when her eyes met his in startled recognition.

"What the hell is she doing here?" Reno asked, echoing Jesse's own thoughts.

"Looks like we're about to find out."

"Everyone?" Martin's voice filled with pride as he announced, "I'd like you to meet my youngest daughter, Allison."

Daughter?

As Martin began the individual introductions, Jesse and Reno looked at each other, eyes wide.

In unspoken words, *holy shit*, became the understatement of the year.

*B*reathe.

Beyond the huge ranch-style home, the enormous barn, and the tall oak shade trees, Allison didn't have far to look to find the source for her sudden racing heart. He stood about ten feet away—tall, blond, and stunning with his hair pulled back into an untidy ponytail and a hint of beard stubble dusting his masculine jaw. He wore a plaid shirt with the sleeves rolled up to his elbows and a pair of jeans with specific and infinitely interesting areas worn to a faded blue. His muscular arms were folded across what she knew was a rock-solid, mind-blowing, want-to-lick-it-up-one-side-and-down-the-other chest. And the boots on his big feet were planted in the soil as if claiming his territory.

Though it seemed impossible, the man looked even tastier in the daylight.

Unfortunately, the steady scowl on his face was a clear sign that while all her girl parts might be buzzing at the mere sight of him, anything male inside of him—and she guessed there was a whole lot—was still a bit miffed that she'd pulled a fast one on him in that parking lot last night.

She'd had no choice.

She wasn't usually a woman who had trouble saying no. But if she'd have leaned into his kiss a bit further, tasted him a little more, inhaled his warm, male scent just a smidge longer? She'd have been toast. There hadn't been a possibility in hell that her lips would have formed the letters *n* and *o*.

Dragging her gaze from the blue-eyed glare shooting bullets in her direction, Allison took a quick glance at her surroundings. The large ranch-style home's open veranda had been made inviting by the addition of wooden rocking chairs and colorful pots of red geraniums with trailing purple and white alyssum.

The huge, weathered barn and the horses moseying about in a nearby corral finished off the reality that this was an authentic working ranch. Beneath the canopy of a large tree, extralong picnic tables had been set with colorful cloths and dishes in a fashion she could imagine on the cover of a country-lifestyle magazine.

Maybe the goat and the little orange poodle playing tag was a bit unusual, but other than that, the entire place had a welcoming atmosphere.

Except perhaps for the firing squad of Wilders waiting to make her acquaintance.

With one of her more professionally affable smiles, she tuned her ears in to her father's enthusiastic introductions.

"Sweetheart," he said to her, wrapping an arm around the most seasoned female in the crowd. "*This* is Jana."

What the woman lacked in actual height, she made up for in big blond hair, bright blue eyes, and a warm smile. Her simple jeans and button-down floral blouse were a complete 360 from anything Allison's own mother would wear. A woman who, with her five consecutive marriages *and* divorces to men each more wealthy than the last, refused to wear anything unless it bore a designer tag from Nordstrom or Neiman Marcus. A woman who depleted vast portions of her divorce settlements for the series of nips and tucks she believed would keep her young.

Jana Wilder had pleasant, soft features that

hadn't been subjected to needle or scalpel. The crow's-feet at the corners of the blue eyes said she laughed often.

Allison extended a polite and friendly hand for a formal greeting to her potentially future stepmother and let out a squeak when the woman pulled her into a tight embrace.

"Welcome to Texas, sugarplum."

Allison wished she could share in the excitement of her father's recent engagement. But she couldn't. Not yet.

Once she unraveled from Jana's enthusiastic greeting, her dad guided her down the reception line while she tried to figure out how to avoid the man at the very end.

"You've already met Jake," her father said.

Like the rest of the men gathered, Jake Wilder was mouthwatering. And, as she'd learned on the thirty-mile ride from the airport to Wilder Ranch, he was always ready with a flirtatious smile and a humorous story.

With a hand firmly grasping her elbow as if given the chance she'd run, her dad continued down the really long line of really good-looking people. "This is Jackson, a firefighter in San Antonio. His fiancée Abby, who's recently opened an animal-rescue center. And Fiona who was once married to Jackson. She's moving to Sweet soon and plans to open a cupcake shop."

While the women all gave her a friendly hello, Allison couldn't help but be fascinated. Ex-wife *and* current fiancée? Interesting.

"And this cute little muffin . . ." Her father

picked up an adorable little girl with golden ringlets and a shy smile. "Is Jackson and Fiona's daughter, Isabella. Or, as we call her, Izzy."

Allison adored children. While part of her wanted to run off with Izzy and play dolls just to get away from the awkwardness of meeting potentially new family members, she managed a simple hello.

A quick glance between Fiona the *ex* and Abby the *new* told Allison that any obvious animosity was absent. Hopefully, that worked well for little Izzy. Being the child of combative, dissociated parents sucked. Allison knew that sad story only too well both in her personal and her professional life.

Her father then gave a hug to a beautiful and very pregnant young woman. "This is Abby's sister Annie, who just moved back to Sweet from Seattle." Farther down the line, her father said, "And this is Reno and his fiancée Charli. You might recognize Charli from *My New Town*, the cable TV show she hosted."

Allison didn't have much time for boob-tube viewing, but Charli's smile was infectious and did a lot to put Allison at temporary ease. The slight frown on Reno's handsome face tempted her to say they'd already met, but she would never be one to instigate ill will between an engaged couple. Even if she believed that the marriage in which they were about to embark had a slim chance of survival.

A quick glance at the three sets of happy couples, all of whom appeared to be utterly in love, gave her pause. She'd been witness to too many "happily ever afters" that were doomed from the start. And she wondered how many—if any—of these pairs would actually make it for the long haul. Thus her entire reason for coming to Sweet in the first place. Her dad had already suffered one devastating end to a relationship; she didn't want to see him have to endure another.

She'd made the trip to Texas to figure out the specifics of his sudden push to tie himself to a woman he'd just met. Allison might not have been around to pull back on the reins of his disastrous engagement to her own mother, but she darned well wouldn't stand by now and let him make another grievous error.

The end of the greeting line came up way too fast, and she found herself face-to-face with Mr. Gorgeous.

"This is Jesse," her father announced. "Our resident veterinarian. And like the other boys, a Marine."

"Former Marine," Jesse politely corrected her father.

The intensity of his blue eyes flipped her stomach as she extended her hand. "Nice to meet you."

A smile brushed those chiseled lips as their palms met midair. The instant heat felt like she'd been zinged by a bolt of lightning. Electricity snapped between them, and her mind went right back to last night when she'd had to crawl inside her rental car so she didn't crawl all over his big, muscular body.

"A handshake instead of a hug?" One sexy slash of brow lifted. "That's not how we do it here in the Lone Star State, darlin'."

With the ease of a man who knew exactly what he was doing, he gathered her in, and both of those strong, muscular arms went around her. Flashes of dancing within those arms and against that chest the night before zoomed back. And just like the night before, unwanted desire pinged through her system.

In that brief moment, with their bodies pressed together, she knew she'd have to put up every guard, every fence, every barrier she could find to keep her hands off the merchandise and her heart locked up nice and tight.

"Award-winning performance," he whispered against her ear. "You always that good at faking it?"

The innuendo hit its mark.

Sometimes, when a girl met a new guy, she knew immediately whether she'd have to fake it or whether she'd get the real deal. Everything about Jesse Wilder shouted "satisfaction guaranteed."

With as little fanfare as possible, she extracted herself from his hold. "In Seattle, we usually just say hello with a cup of coffee or a flying fish."

"Proof that everything's bigger and better in Texas," he drawled.

"Would you like a tour of the ranch?" her father asked.

She tore her gaze from the challenge in Jesse's eyes and snapped her head around to look at her dad. "What?"

"Perhaps Jesse could give you a tour while the rest of us finish getting things together," her dad clarified.

"Oh. No. That's okay, I—"

"It would be my pleasure," Jesse interjected.

"I wouldn't want to impose."

"Nonsense," her father said. "Southern hospitality. Right, Jesse?"

"Absolutely, Mr. Lane."

"Martin." Her father's smile drooped a little at the corners as though that hadn't been the first time he'd had to remind the handsome Mr. Wilder to address him in a more informal manner.

She took a closer look at Jesse and recognized a hint of stubbornness in the dark blue depth of his eyes. Maybe she wasn't alone in the not being jump-up-and-down-happy department at her father and Jana Wilder's sudden engagement announcement.

Sensing that any argument she might want to broach would land on deaf ears, she raised the proverbial white flag.

"Before I do anything, I need to let my dog out of the car." She turned toward the gas-guzzling blue truck her dad had bought to replace the Prius he'd driven in Seattle. Jesse, of course, followed.

"Your dog?"

She nodded. "Wee Man."

He stopped in his tracks and a puff of dirt kicked up from beneath his well-worn cowboy boots. "Your dog's name is *Wee Man*?"

She stopped too and jammed her fists on her hips. "What's so funny about that?"

"I'm sure it's not funny to your dog." He came closer, and she had to look way up. God, she hated being short.

"Were you trying to give him a complex?" he

asked. "Or do you just have a problem with men in general?"

Was that fire filtering from her nose? Because she certainly felt some dragon spikes popping out on her fingers. Too bad she had an audience and most likely wouldn't get away with sinking those nails in his strong, tanned throat.

"He's a *little* dog. There was no diss intended."

"Then shouldn't you have called him something like Brutus, or Kong, or Maximus?"

She yanked open the truck door. As if he wore springs on the bottom of his paws, her energetic Jack Russell terrier jumped out and trotted off toward the closest tree. When he lifted his leg, she could almost hear his *Ahhhhhhhh*. "Does he look like a Maximus to you?"

"No." Jesse smiled. "But he is cute."

Somehow, the word *cute* coming from such a masculine mouth just seemed odd.

"And a little overweight," he said. "You might want to change his food."

"My dog is *not* overweight."

"So you're the expert?"

"No."

"Well, too many years of college and several degrees tells me he's got some pudge on."

"Thanks, Mr. Smarty Pants. I'll make a note of it."

He laughed as he bent at the knees and made a kissy sound toward her dog. She smirked. Wee Man wouldn't have anything to do with strangers. He was a one-person dog. Dedicated. Loyal. He'd never . . .

Allison refrained from dropping an F-bomb

when Wee Man took one look at Jesse and ran right to him, smiling and acting all wiggle-butt happy as if the man were a lifelong pal. She expected them to do the whole high-five, knuckles-to-paws bump thing, but Jesse simply picked up her dog and held him against his broad chest. Wee Man, disappointingly, slurped the shadow of a beard dusting his chin.

"That's odd. He usually doesn't like people he doesn't know."

"I'm a vet." Jesse grinned up at her.

"He *hates* his vet."

"Then you're taking him to the wrong person." He gave Wee Man a little rub across the top of his head, then set him down. Her dog took off like he owned the place—sniffing here, whizzing there. And then he spotted the poodle. Yikes.

"Wee Man! Come back here."

"Pumpkin's safe." Jesse laughed. "He'll be fine."

"What about the goat?"

"No worries. Miss Giddy's more of a lover than a fighter."

"The goat has a name?"

"Of course. The goat is Mom's pet. Mom has also been known to name the lizards and hummingbirds too, so—"

Dear God, what kind of crazy woman was her father marrying? "She names the hummingbirds?"

He nodded. "But they all get the same name because, obviously, they're so fast, it's hard to tell who's who."

"And that name would be?"

"Pete."

"And the lizards?"

"Larry." He sighed. "They're all Larry. And the snakes are Earl."

"She names the snakes?"

"Sure," he said, like it was totally normal to name slithery reptiles with fangs. "So when she goes out on the property and sees one, she won't get freaked out because it's just Earl taking a walk."

"I . . . ummm . . ."

"Don't worry," he said. "Mom's harmless. Just likes to have a little fun."

Fun definitely had a different meaning in Texas.

"Well, it looks like your dog's getting to know the place," he said. "So how about you?"

"Lead the way."

Before he did, he looked down at her feet. "You always wear those?"

She glanced down at her strappy mile-high wedges and remembered how cute she thought they were when she'd got them on sale at DSW. Although she had to admit they were designed for smooth concrete and carpet instead of gravel-pitted dirt. "What's wrong with them?"

"In general, not a damn thing. Around a ranch? Dangerous. You planning on an extended visit?"

Not if she could help it. "Not sure."

"Well, you might want to consider a pair of boots." His big hand went to the small of her back and sent a tingle to other places on her body as he guided her through the big barn doors. "Or at least a pair of tennis shoes. Although if you plan to ride, you need boots. Tennis shoes would be dangerous."

"You sure have a lot of rules around here."

"And they're always made to be broken." He flashed that smile again—the one that said his thoughts were a thousand steps ahead of her. "So feel free."

Yep. She'd get right on that.

"*This* is the barn." His bite of sarcasm didn't go unnoticed as he led her inside, where honey brown chickens clucked and scattered at their sudden appearance.

"Interesting." She looked around at the empty stalls, saddles, and big stack of hay bales. It was neat and tidy and looked like something she'd seen in a Western movie. Which was as close as she'd ever been to a horse. Or a cow. Or live chickens. Or a goat named Miss Giddy.

"Equally interesting is why you were at Seven Devils last night . . ." Jesse's smile disappeared, and a frown wrinkled between those blue eyes. "Seemed to zero right in on my brother. Then failed to mention who you were."

"I didn't *fail* to do anything. I didn't know who you were. I just went in to check things out."

"Right."

"You don't believe me?"

"Darlin', I don't know you. So why would I believe you?"

Good point.

"I'll just assume that you make a habit of kissing strange men in dark parking lots before sending them off on a wild-goose chase to get rid of them."

"I do not—"

One slash of brow lifted, and she couldn't tell if

it was raised in amusement or regret. "All you had to do was say no."

And that was the problem.

She wouldn't have.

She'd been on a sexual dry spell longer than the drought in the Southern states, and he was just way too tempting. Not that she was the kind to sleep around with every hot guy she met, but for him, she might have made an exception. No way in hell would she let him know that little tidbit of insanity. Especially now that she knew he was the son of the woman her father planned to marry.

Whoo boy, what a mess.

"Look," she said. "No offense, but I don't date guys like you."

"Wasn't exactly looking for a *date*. If you remember, you said you were just passing through." Those thick-muscled arms folded across his chest. "And what exactly do you mean by *guys like me*?"

Oh, so now he'd gotten his feelings hurt?

"I thought you were assigned to show me around," she said. "So how about we get to it?"

He studied her for a moment. Those incredible eyes moved down her body as if recording her assets and deficits for his own personal gain.

"Ah," he said as though he'd discovered a box of treasures. "I get it now."

"You get *what*, exactly?" Her shoulders came up as she tried to make herself look big and bad though she didn't know why other than she didn't like his tone.

"You know, it's not fair that you women look like *that* and only play for the other team."

"Look like what?"

"A man's walking sexual fantasy."

She looked like a man's walking sexual fantasy? Sweet.

"Who says I play for the *other* team?"

"Come on." He shook his head. "It's obvious you don't like men. Starting with the pathetic name you gave your dog and ending with the way you ran out last night."

"For your information . . ." She stuck a finger in his chest. "I *love* men. Just not *players* who are too pretty for their own good and assume every woman around will fall at their cowboy boots."

"See. There you go again," he said. "Men aren't *pretty*."

"Looked in the mirror lately?"

His surprised expression nearly made her laugh.

"And I noticed you didn't bother to deny the *player* part," she added.

"I just have a fine appreciation of women."

"Uh-huh." She patted that amazing chest and seemed to have some trouble removing her hand from the skin-warmed cotton. "You keep telling yourself that, bucko."

"*Bucko?*"

Time for diversionary tactics. "So what's that up there?" she asked, pointing to the door above the stairs.

"Nice try, *buckette*. But I don't think this conversation is over." His squared chin jutted out, making him look even more tenacious if that was even possible.

"Really?" She gave him a fluttery bat of her eye-lashes.

"Really." His gaze dropped to her mouth, then came back up.

"Well, since you don't know me, and—"

"Darlin', last night I had my mouth on yours and my hands on your ass. That's a damned good start of getting to know you, don't you think?"

What she thought was that in her business, she met a lot of men. But she was almost one hundred percent sure she'd never met a man as exasperat-ing as him. Or as sexy. Or . . . oh yeah. She needed some distance.

And a cold drink.

Preferably one with a little kick.

"What I think is . . . I would appreciate it if you would please pretend to be the hospitable tour guide my father obviously believes you are and finish our little excursion. Then, I'd like to collect my dog and get back to getting to know the rest of you *Wilders* with the hopes that they won't be quite as unbearable as you."

With a swift turn, she headed toward the open barn doors, cursing as her wedge slipped. Her ankle twisted on a small rock and forced her shoe to land in something . . . gross. She didn't even want to know what that was.

As she disregarded the sound of male hilar-ity, she couldn't help wonder why anyone would choose to live where animals just pooped wher-ever they wanted.

And where men were far too tempting to ignore.

Chapter 3

"Something's not right about her," Jackson said from the picnic table where Jesse and Jackson sat long after dark and watched Allison Lane. Jackson sipped his fresh bottle of Shiner. "Can't put my finger on it though."

Allison currently stood near the blazing fire pit, talking to Jake, who was having a hell of a good time putting on the flirt.

Who could blame him?

Baby brother had been tromping across the sands of Afghanistan for too long, dodging bullets, IEDs, and figuring out how to stay alive. The hot brunette was probably the first pretty sight Jake had seen in a long time. Which was *not* a slight against women in camo. Women in the military were more likely to be focused on flying F-15s, defining logistics, or honing their lifesaving medical skills than the newest brand of lash-lengthening mascara.

Didn't mean Jesse had to like the attention his little brother was pouring on the newcomer. Though he'd have a hard time explaining why that bothered him so much. It wasn't like *he'd* been the one relatively quarantined from the fairer sex for so long. Maybe he wasn't the manwhore everyone in town thought he was, but he still didn't do too shabby when it came to his own share of female admiration. In fact, Allison might be the first to shy *away* from his attention.

Scratch that.

She didn't shy away, she ran like hell.

Which opened the door for all kinds of whys and whats and how comes.

"What do you mean something's not right?" he asked, as Jackson's frown tightened.

"See the way she keeps watching Mom? Like she thinks she's sneaking a glance. Why would she do that?"

Jesse shrugged. "Maybe she's just trying to figure things out. Maybe she's just as surprised as the rest of us that our parents decided to get married after such a short time of knowing each other. Maybe—"

"Stop! You're making my brain hurt."

Jesse took a drink from his beer and watched as Allison sipped from an ice-filled Mason jar full of his mother's specially blended watermelon cooler. And . . . yep . . . she snuck a glance in their mother's direction.

While she pretended to be interested in whatever line of BS Jake was tossing her way, she clutched her poor dog with the emasculating name against her like he would protect her from the big bad Marine. At least she hadn't forced the terrier to wear a rhinestone collar or those humiliating dog clothes.

Judging by all that heavy panting—the dog's, not Jake's—all the pooch really wanted was to be let loose so he could hang out with Charli's equally energetic poodle, Pumpkin. Another ridiculous moniker. What was it with pet owners and the crazy names they chose? In his business, he'd pretty much heard them all—from Zeus to Peanut and everything in between. Wee Man, however, might top the list.

The rest of the family began to congregate around the fire pit, pulling up chairs and blankets or whatever they needed to be comfortable. They'd always been a family who liked to gather, often sitting around a campfire or the kitchen table for hours discussing everything from cattle branding to whether Steven Seagal could actually be considered a movie star. No need to change that for some out-of-towner who would most likely only stay a day or two.

Sadly, as the out-of-towner pretended to be interested in what Jake had to say and pretended not to be covertly watching every move his mother made, Jesse couldn't stop watching *her*. Or the way she moved in those tight jeans. Or the smile that flashed perfect white teeth. Or the way she tilted her head back just a little when she laughed. Or the way her silky hair fell down her back in a cascade of loose waves.

At some point in his life, he might have been

more sexually aware of a woman, but damned if he could remember who or when.

Snap. Snap. "Earth to Jesse."

Amid the current fire-pit conversation of how many tattoos were too many—himself possessing only two at that point in time—he glanced up to find Jackson grinning like a damned fool. "What?"

"I heard you and Reno had a little *encounter* last night at Seven Devils." The grin widened. "Anything I need to know about?"

"Nope."

"Really?"

"Really."

"Caught you staring."

"At what?" Like he didn't know.

Jackson gave a nod in Allison's direction.

"What are you, five?" Jesse held back an eye roll. "I'm just appreciating the package."

"Never noticed the package."

"Right."

Jackson shook his head. "I've got Abby. I've always wanted Abby. Why would I look elsewhere?"

"Guys look."

"Not guys who are crazy in love and not afraid to admit it."

"You are so whipped."

"No shit. And damned happy to be." Gingerly, Jackson stood up from the picnic bench, favoring the leg he'd broken in a firefighting accident a few months before. He pointed at Jesse with his bottle of Shiner. "You will be too someday."

"Uh-uh." Jesse held up his hand. "Established bachelor here."

"Oh how the mighty will fall."

"Not gonna happen, jackass."

Jackson just grinned as he walked away.

And so the game played on.

As Jesse glanced at the couples gathered, he couldn't fight the twinge that settled in his heart. He, probably more than most, believed in commitment. The relationship with his last serious girlfriend had ended over two years ago. Since then, he'd pretended to have an aversion to the holy sanctity of relationships. And while he'd been the inventor of the game in order to see everyone else's happiness secured before he could even think about his own, he'd sadly become pretty good at playing by the rules. He cleverly continued to come up with a thousand excuses for not looking for his own Ms. Right. But eventually, he had to run out. Hopefully, by then, everyone would be settled and wouldn't notice that he'd been feeding them a line of bullshit a mile long.

From the moment their oldest and wisest brother had been killed, he'd pulled up his big-boy pants and found a way to help everyone else carry on. He hadn't always succeeded, and in his eyes, that was unacceptable.

Only two people would understand the passion behind his reasons for being so committed to this task. Neither was still alive. So Jesse was on his own, to keep his reasons confidential, to uphold a promise, and to do what he could to help his family find peace.

When Reno found Charli and almost let her slip through his foolish fingers, Jesse had needed to insert a little brotherly advice. Just as he had when Jackson had almost lost Abby. The only brother left to take care of was Jake. With Jake's exuberant personality and spirited outlook, Jesse figured he'd be the easiest to handle when the time came.

Then again, who knew? Life was often unpredictable.

He stole a glance across the fire to where Allison sat within the glow of the dancing flames that only enhanced her mystique.

It wasn't his turn at a chance for happiness.

Not even when he might have met a woman he was wildly and inexplicably attracted to.

He was the last to join the group circling the fire. For a moment, he just stood there looking at the lucky couples, the sweet little girl curled up on her daddy's lap, the contented animals— including Miss Giddy, who'd stretched out by his mother's feet.

Something hit him in the center of his chest that took his breath away.

He couldn't claim to be the creator or the glue that held everything together. And he'd be a fool not to believe the man who'd set the wheel spinning wasn't trying to help from the other side. But sometimes he needed to just take a moment to breathe and feel the love. Because sure as shit, something would pop up and threaten to put the kibosh on utopia.

"So what is it you do in Seattle, Allison?" Charli asked as she snuggled closer to Reno.

"I own and operate Happiest Day Events."

"You're a wedding planner?"

"An event planner," Allison said quietly as though she was uncomfortable talking about herself. "We do equal amounts of birthdays, anniversaries, and weddings."

Jesse noted that last night she'd been animated and funny. In the barn earlier, she'd been outspoken. So here was yet another side of the woman he'd discovered in a short period of time. Curiosity forced him into the empty Adirondack between Reno and Abby.

"She's in high demand," Martin said proudly. "Puts together all sorts of incredible parties. Threw one for the retirement of an Alaska Airlines bigwig just last month on a luxury yacht."

"Oh, I wish I'd known. I've been driving everyone crazy with our wedding plans," Charli said, tossing Reno an apologetic look.

"I've seen your creativity," Allison said. "I'm sure it will turn out beautiful."

"Charli's always watching those wedding shows," Reno said. "It shocks me how much people pay just for a dress."

"And now the new photography trend is to set the dress on fire." Allison shook her head. "They're calling it 'trash the dress.' Not something I'd ever recommend. Aside from its being dangerous, it makes no sense. Our mission is to provide economical, personalized events. We believe the greater amount of the budget should be spent in areas where the memories are more tangible and long-lasting. No one remembers if the plastic forks were clear or white or if the party favors were bottles of bubbles or containers of candy, but when they look at a photo, they remember exactly how they felt at that moment."

"How many people do you employ?" Jesse asked. Though he knew nothing of the event-planning business, he did understand the details and significance of being an employer. Taking on the challenge of that level of responsibility said a lot about a person. Whether he liked it or not.

"I have a staff of three including my sister. I'd like to hire more as soon as the economy picks up."

"How did you get into party-planning?" his mother asked.

Jesse watched Allison settle back a little more, cross her ankles, then tuck her feet beneath the chair. She looked anything but relaxed. The *hot seat* was an uncomfortable place to sit. He knew. He'd been there a few times himself.

"My dad actually got me into the business." She smiled at him. "I'm sure you're familiar with his chain of party stores."

"Oh, you know your father. He doesn't like to talk about himself much." His mom looked up at her new fiancé and affectionately patted his arm. "I knew he operated a few stores, but I had no idea he created such a prominent business. I'm not surprised though. With all the things he's done to help out at the senior center, I know he's more than just a handsome face."

If his mother hadn't been aware that her fiancé had built a party-store empire, Jesse wondered what else she didn't know about the man. Unsettled, Jesse glanced across the fire at Allison and noted the same concern darkening her expression.

"Daddy. You should be proud of your accomplishments," Allison admonished. "Not try to hide them."

"I'm not, sweetheart. But the past is past."

"Hmm." Allison's brows pulled together. "Well, hesitant as he might be to talk about himself, my dad created Party Lane party stores. He expanded the business to four states and eventually established online shopping before he sold it all and moved here last year."

"I've been in those stores," Charli said. "I threw a heck of a New Year's Eve celebration for my production crew one time. Party Lane had everything I needed under one roof. Including the rental of the chocolate fountain *and* the chocolate to go in it. Boy, I wish we had one of those here. It would have made planning the wedding much easier."

"Aren't the stores wonderful?" Allison lifted her little dog onto her lap and stroked the top of his head. "I started working at the original Seattle location after school and during the summer. Eventually, I moved my way up to manager. There were so many people who came in not knowing how to put things together for their parties, so I started helping them. Eventually I put together a little side business, and it expanded to Happiest Day Events. I've done everything from a pirate birthday party to a park wedding in several feet of snow."

"You love what you do," his mother said.

"I love seeing people happy," Allison responded.

Something they had in common, Jesse thought. One more point to add to her assets.

His list of questions about her, however, left far more to be uncovered.

$\mathcal{B}$y the time Allison and her dad arrived back at his sprawling ranch-style home, exhaustion had seeped into her bones. All she wanted was to climb into the guest-room bed and forget about the past two nights' events.

Before she'd left Seattle, she'd had to juggle the items on her project list and finalize several more. Before she'd boarded the plane, she'd put the responsibilities of the Cramer wedding and little Jenny Curran's princess party in the hands of her capable assistants, who happened to include her big sister Danielle. The temporary passing of the torch meant she could stay a few days in Sweet and spend some time with her dad while trying to decode what was really going on behind his sudden engagement.

While she waited outside until Wee Man took whiz number three thousand of the night, she glanced around at the surrounding landscape. The area was the complete opposite from the lush green of Seattle. Texas had its own rugged kind of beauty.

Much like the man who'd captured her attention.

As the dust had kicked up beneath her tires in that saloon parking lot, she'd thought that would be the last she'd ever see of him. That he would just be future fodder for her nighttime fantasies. But nooooo. He had to go and be her possible future stepmother's son. Which meant if she intended to get to know Jana Wilder better, she might also be seeing a whole lot more of Mr. Hot Stuff.

Whoo boy.

She wondered what deity she'd pissed off to be slapped with *that* penalty. Not that *seeing* him was a hardship, just the whole *being around him* part.

Her dad poked his head out the back door. "You coming in, sweetheart?"

"Give me a sec." She whistled for Wee Man, who trotted off to the next tree like he hadn't heard. "Seriously, dog?" she muttered under her breath. First, her pooch revealed his fickle self by latching onto Jesse, now he had the audacity to ignore her? "Get it in gear, or no more Scooby Snacks for you . . . *Pudgy*." Finally, after another two quick spins around the yard, he made a dash for the back door like the idea to go into the house had been all his own.

Allison stepped inside a kitchen that, while it could use a few upgrades, like dumping the avocado green stove, the white cabinetry, and simple farm-style decorations, made for a friendly atmosphere. Far different from the impersonal Seattle town house her father had moved into eight years ago.

"Wee Man giving you trouble?" her dad asked as he pulled a glass pitcher from the refrigerator.

"He's just not used to having so much room to run."

"The open space out here is good for everybody."

Allison gave her dad a quick once-over, noting the color in his cheeks and that he'd lost the excess weight he'd put on after the divorce. He looked healthy. And happy.

The *happy* part worried her.

She needed to make sure it was real.

"You want a glass of sweet tea?" he asked.

"Before bed? The sugar and caffeine would keep me up all night."

"Well, you could always sleep in tomorrow. Nothing to do around here but take in the atmosphere and everything Sweet has to offer. Enjoy the slower lifestyle. The hospitality." His smile hinted that he'd like her to consider staying on a permanent basis.

"I don't know if I could ever get used to that," she said. "It's so quiet around here. I swear you can hear birds chirping from a mile away. I don't even know how you're coping since you've always been a go-get-'em kind of man." She filled a bowl with fresh water for Wee Man and set it on the floor. "Out of so many cities in America, how did you choose Sweet anyway?"

He sat down at the big kitchen table, patted the chair next to him, and sipped his tea. She joined him even though her brain had already gone into shutdown mode.

"Years ago, I met a sales rep who told me he was from the Texas Hill Country. I started asking questions. The place sounded perfect. So when I decided to get out of Seattle, I came out to see if reality lived up to what I'd pictured in my mind. I took my time looking around. Sweet immediately felt like home."

"It's just so different," she said although she could definitely see the advantages and the allure. "It's so . . . laid-back."

"There's more to life than running on the hamster wheel," he said. "I've been working since I was a young boy. Figured it was time to enjoy myself a little before I got too old to appreciate it. Or before some wicked disease got me."

Her heart gave a hard knock. She'd been so busy getting her business off the ground and keeping it afloat in a down economy, she'd never really noticed that her parents were getting older. With her mother, it was hard to tell behind all the Botox. Still, she'd never considered either of them being stricken with a life-threatening illness.

She reached out and laid her hand over the top of his, noticing the age spots on his skin. "But you're healthy, right?"

"Far as I know."

"Maybe you should see about getting a complete physical."

"I'm fine, sweetheart." He chuckled. "Happier than I've been in a long time and looking forward to the future."

"Daddy, you're not getting married just because you're getting older and afraid to be alone, are you?"

His hesitation lifted her eyebrows.

"Don't be silly," he said.

"I'm not. I love you. And I worry about you."

She leaned over and kissed his cheek. "I want you to be happy, but I also want you to give things careful consideration. You'd want me to be careful about something as important as tying myself to one person for supposedly the rest of my life, wouldn't you?"

He leaned back. "What are you trying to say?"

"Well . . ." She knew the *what*, just not *how* to say it without sounding bitchy. "Jana hardly knows anything about the business you built from the ground up. In fact, she doesn't seem to know much about you or your past. So what does that really say about how much the two of you know each other?"

"Doesn't matter where I've been in life, sweetheart. It only matters where I'm going."

"But why keep something like your accomplishments a secret?"

"Not keeping it a secret. Just never really came up much in conversation."

"The fact that you created a party-supply empire never came up?"

"If you're worried about your inheritance—"

"No! Dad!" She gave him a cross look. "I don't give a damn about your money. You taught me how to make my own way in life. And for that I'm grateful. I just don't want you to wake up one morning and find out you've married another Mom."

"You have nothing to worry about. Jana isn't anything like your mother."

"How do you know?"

"You really think I'd make that kind of error in judgment a second time?"

"Some people do. Even when they think they've got it all together. Sometimes people just get lonely."

"I promise you," he said. "I'm not just lonely."

Allison sighed.

"That's quite the heavy unspoken thought slipping out there," he said. "Why don't you just say what's on your mind?"

"Because I'll sound mean."

"Sweetheart, I'm your dad." He patted her hand. "You can say anything to me."

"Promise you won't be offended?"

He shook his head, and the glow of the overhead light caught in the silver of his hair.

"For years, I wondered why you'd ever married Mom. And then . . ." She glanced away, then back at him again. "I wondered why you stayed married to her for so long. She was always so selfish, and demanding, and mean and . . . you're such a nice guy."

The smile that formed on his lips was slow to find its place. When it appeared, it was more grim than cheery.

"I didn't know your mother very long before we got married. I was young and not very experienced. I guess you could say I was bedazzled by her beauty and oblivious to the fact that she was nothing like me. While I was content with the simple things in life, she wanted more. She wanted the parties and the social events. The expensive dresses and shoes. A live-in maid and a fancy car. I didn't have the social status to please her, so I set out to try to accomplish what I could to give her the life she wanted."

Allison's heart tightened. "But she was never satisfied."

Her father said nothing. He'd never been the type to slam her mother even when he had every right.

"When you realized she was that way, why didn't you leave?"

His head shook slowly. "Because she'd gotten pregnant with Danielle. After your sister was born, your mother didn't like the focus of the attention being torn away from her. And I . . ."

"What, Daddy? You can tell me." Anything he had to say she already knew. She'd grown up with the woman, and her egocentric behavior was no secret.

"She thought if she had a second child, the baby spotlight would dim, and everyone would again focus on her. So we had you. I don't regret that for a moment. Not even when she threatened to take you and Dani away and never let me see you again if I left."

"I don't understand why she'd care if she thought she wanted more than what she had."

"I suppose because I was better than nothing until something better rolled around."

"I'm so sorry." Allison wrapped her arms around him. "I never knew."

"And you shouldn't know now." He hugged her. "All I can say is that while living with your mother was a challenge, I never regretted one single day since you girls came into my life. You've been my everything. The reason I got up every morning and went to work. I wanted you to have the best life I could provide."

"You are an amazing dad."

"I just try to do my best. And I want you to know that I gave it a lot of thought before I asked Jana to marry me."

"Dad?" Allison sighed again. "A second ago, you said you didn't know Mom very long before you were married. You haven't known Jana very long either."

"But I also said your mother wasn't anything like me. We had nothing in common. Jana and I . . ." A smile brightened his face. "We have everything in common."

"But how do you know that's enough to last forever? There are no guarantees."

He took a long, contemplative drink of tea. "*Life* doesn't come with guarantees, sweetheart. That's a fact."

"Then I guess some people are just lucky. Like they were born under the perfect alignment of the moon and stars."

He chuckled. "A lasting relationship doesn't have anything to do with astronomy. It has to do with finding your soul mate."

"Soul mate! That's pure fantasy."

"How so?"

"Because it doesn't make sense."

"What about your sister?"

"She and Andrew might be the one in a million."

"Why do you think that is?"

She shrugged. "Because there's a strong possibility Danielle might be the only one of us Lanes who has the appropriately adjusted DNA to make it happen. She's always been different. It's like from the moment she was born, she had the maternal instinct in her blood that gave her more patience, more understanding, and just . . . more."

"Your sister wasn't born with that—she had to develop it so she could take care of you when your mother and I failed. I take the blame. I should never have allowed either of you to be put in that position."

"In case you've forgotten, Dani volunteered for that stuff. I think she's always known deep inside that she'd excel at being a wife and mother. All she had to do was wait for Andrew to pop into her life and voila! He's a strong man with a soft heart. They complement each other like bacon and eggs."

"Yes. They do. And I know you and she are very close. Which is why I want you to take a look at her and what she has and realize–"

"Dad. I'm lucky to have her as a big sister. She did great with me all those years." She laughed. "Otherwise, I might have gone to school with the whole mismatched Pippi Longstockings thing going on. But that doesn't mean I ever expect to have what she does. I'm more like Mom than Dani."

"That's where you're wrong. You are the total opposite of your mom." A frown tugged at the corners of his mouth. "And just because your mother hasn't found the right one doesn't mean you won't."

"Eh." She waved a hand. "I call BS on the whole 'right one' thing."

"You have to keep the possibility alive."

"Can't." Feeling sure of herself, she locked her fingers together on the tabletop.

"Because?"

"Because . . . if there's just *one* person—a soul mate—for everyone, what happens if your person dies? Like Jana and Reno. They found their soul mates, and they lost them. So do you get a do-over or something?"

Silver brows lifted over his dark gray eyes. "A do-over?"

"Yeah. And what if you think you found *the one*, and you're wrong? What if you stick with the wrong *one* forever, and you miss the real *one*?"

The silence in the room hung heavy as her dad considered her concerns, so she filled the void with more of her trepidations.

"As an event planner, I've heard dozens and dozens of brides say they've found their *soul mate*. Out of curiosity, I started to mentally log how many of those marriages actually worked out. More of them fell apart than lasted. Even when the bride or the groom was sure they'd found *the one*. Sure, some seemed doomed from the start. I mean, when the groom is flirting with the maid of honor, it's pretty clear he's not thinking of *the one*. He's thinking of *the next one*. But, Dad, some of the marriages that fell apart took me completely by surprise. There's just no good way to predict whether something will work out."

"A lot of people go into marriage thinking it

will be easy," he said. "Sometimes it's hard to find a person who will put up with you for the rest of your life. Sometimes people change. They fall out of love. A relationship isn't like what you see in the movies. It's hard work."

She leaned back in her chair and folded her arms. "The bottom line is if *forever* really worked, the divorce rate wouldn't be so high."

Her father cupped her cheek in his hand. "The divorce rate is so high because it takes *two* people who truly love each other and who will work hard for something that isn't always easy."

"And that's you and Jana Wilder?"

"Yes."

"You sound so sure."

"I am."

"Daddy, no offense, but everyone thinks they've got the magic. They think they have what it takes to make it for the long haul. And then wham! Next thing they know, they're fighting over who gets to keep the Chihuahua and the china."

"When did you get so cynical?"

"I'm not cynical. I'm a realist."

"Then how about you send the realist on vacation." He patted her cheek. "Reach down deep inside and rediscover that little girl who spent hours in her room dressing up like a princess and dreaming of her Prince Charming."

"Prince Charming doesn't exist."

"I beg your pardon." He leaned back and grinned. "Don't *I* fit that description?"

"You're a prince, all right." She laughed, then let go a long sigh. "Dad? I'm really not trying to be a naysayer, but I can still remember the sadness and the hurt I saw in your eyes when you were married to Mom and when you went through the divorce. It gave me nightmares."

"I'm very sorry about that."

"No need to be sorry. It wasn't all your fault," she said. "I really do just want you to be happy."

"Then how about you quit worrying about me and focus on rediscovering that little girl who used to believe that fairy tales came true and that everyone got a happy ending. If you can do that, I promise you'll find your own Prince Charming," he said in such a positive way she almost believed him.

She shook her head. "I'm not looking for one."

"Doesn't matter. He'll find *you*."

Later, in the guest bedroom, Allison settled in on the lodgepole-style bed, which had been nicely decorated with a cozy, handmade quilt. She pushed aside the fact that her dad and his visions of sugarplums currently resided in La La Land and picked up her phone to call Danielle. While she tapped her sister's name in her contact list, Wee Man jumped up onto the quilt and curled into a ball in the center of her pillow. Moments later, he proved once again that little dogs snored big.

Though it was late, she knew that Danielle would still be up waiting for her Seattle detective husband to finish his swing shift and come home. Dialing the number, Allison sighed. She wondered if her father had given the same Prince

Charming speech to Danielle. Because her sister truly seemed to have the fairy-tale marriage.

Danielle and Andrew had dated all through high school and college. Somehow, Danielle seemed to have miraculously overcome their mother's flighty and undependable genes. She was the one female role model Allison had always been able to count on. The only one to offer a little consistency in her life. Dani had nurturing down to an art. Which was why it seemed so right once Andrew had established himself with the SPD, that they'd gotten married and set up shop in their own Camelot.

They now had two beautiful little princesses, Lily and Angeline, and they seemed happier than ever. They were a close-knit, do-everything-together family unit Allison both admired and envied.

In the past year, Andrew had been assigned to undercover work, which was scary and dangerous, and only one of the reasons Danielle never went to bed until he came home safe and sound.

If Allison ever dreamed of having a long-term relationship of her own, her sister's was the ideal model. Danielle and Andrew's picture-perfect union was truly rare and, honestly, her one hope to be proven wrong about her doubtful nature.

After the sixth ring, Danielle finally picked up and without a hello said, "Everything is under control. Stop worrying."

Part of being the younger sister was that the older sister thought she knew you too well. Of course, she usually did. Not only did Dani balance being a wife and motherhood like a pro,

Allison wasn't sure she could manage the whole event-planning business without her. She was a rock. And as the little sister, Allison didn't mind admitting Dani had always been a beautiful tower of strength in her sometimes wobbly world.

"Hi, Sis," Allison said in an overly cheerful tone. "I hope you had a spectacular day. I know you did an awesome job making those calls to find a white horse we can turn into a unicorn for little Jenny Curran's princess party. I just called to say thank you."

"You're such a bullshitter." Dani laughed. "How's Dad? You're not getting extra points for being there while I'm stuck here, are you?"

"Ringing up extra points as we speak." She lay back on the queen-size bed and kicked her feet up. "Seriously. How are things going?"

"Seriously? Fine."

In the background, Allison heard Dani's hand cover the phone and her murmured threat of "Get back to bed or no SpongeBob tomorrow."

"Sooo . . ." Danielle said when she came back. "Have you met her yet?"

"Yes. I've met *her* and her entire family." Including one extremely hot veterinarian. "She seems very nice. Completely different than Mom."

"In what way?"

"Real. Totally the non plastic-surgery-queen type. She actually has laugh lines."

"Well, that's a good sign."

"She also has a huge family that's expanding as we speak. Two more weddings are in the mix. There was a young pregnant woman too. And dogs. Oh, and a goat named Miss Giddy who favors satin bows as a fashion accessory."

"Crap." Dani sighed. "I'm missing all the fun."

"And the barbecued brisket."

"I *love* barbecued brisket."

"Don't worry. I'll be back in a couple of days and fill you in on all the details."

"Will you bring me brisket?"

"How about a whole cow? The Wilders have plenty. I'm sure they have one they could spare."

"Ha-ha."

"How are Andrew and the girls?"

"Andrew is amazing as always. He's still working undercover in the massage-parlor investigation. Actually . . ." she whispered, "it's a prostitution ring. Meanwhile, the girls have discovered the Fancy Nancy books and have been hounding me to buy every single one."

"Tell them Auntie Allie will buy them the collection." Her nieces were adorable, and feisty, and Allison couldn't imagine her life without them. That she tended to spoil them whenever possible couldn't be a bad thing.

"Every single one?"

"You know how I feel about reading." Getting lost in a story had been her escape while her parents battled it out in another room. Or sometimes in the same room. After she'd discovered that horrific events and the unknown were much more tolerable between the pages than in real life, her favorite books quickly became R. L. Stine's Goosebumps series. Mummies and ghosts she'd been able to handle. A shrieking mom and dad? Not so much.

"I'll tell the girls as soon as we hang up," Danielle said. "Maybe that will settle them down so they'll *go to sleep.*" Earsplitting emphasis was put on the last three words and was obviously meant for her nieces. "So . . . Jana Wilder really seems nice?"

Allison pictured the woman and mentally replayed the past few hours. Pushing aside the truth that she'd been totally distracted most of time by Jana's charismatic son, she said, "Yeah. She seems really nice."

"Then if there's no boogeyman or *woman* to uncover, you should be able to come home faster and take over the planning of Blair Rutherford's Carnival of Delights Sweet Sixteen."

"Maybe." An image of Jesse's flirtatious smile flashed through her mind. Replacing that likeness with some spoiled rich girl's overzealous frothy pink party seemed wrong in too many ways to count. "I finagled a lunch date with just Jana and me tomorrow. Something tells me there's a lot more here to discover than I initially thought."

"Like what?" Danielle sounded worried.

"Like . . ." *A hot guy in cowboy boots and a tight T-shirt.* "When I figure it out, I'll let you know."

With a promise to check in after the lunch date, she disconnected the call, tossed the cell phone on the dresser, and pulled her computer onto her lap.

Event planning wasn't the only way Allison spent her time. Even her sister would be surprised to know she had a secret life as a blogger. *Project Happy Ending* was a postparental divorce and often cynical blog she'd created as a place to voice her frustrations, relationship observations, and maybe—hopefully—find proof that everlasting love truly existed.

The latter had yet to transpire.

After twenty years of a dreadful marriage, her father had finally stuck a fork in it and walked away. Most children would be disappointed. Allison had been grateful. Her father was an amazing, special man who deserved to be happy. Her mother ranked much lower on the deserved-to-be-happy scale.

For years, Allison and Danielle had tried to ignore the shrieking, mostly one-sided, arguments. The temper tantrums. The late-night slamming of doors that often meant their mother would be gone for days.

In her absence, their father made a valiant effort to keep his daughters happy and give them as normal a life as possible. They'd cook silly dinners together like mac and cheese and potato chip sandwiches. They'd take walks on the beach—even in the rain. They'd tell stories in a round-robin fashion that often added a hilarious element. And sometimes she and Danielle would fall asleep on the sofa with their father in the middle stroking their hair softly while he hummed an Irish lullaby.

While their dad had worked hard to build his party empire, their mother worked hard at blowing his money. Their father had been ultrasupportive, always telling them that through hard work and determination, they had every opportunity to rise to the top of anything they chose to do. Their mother insisted nothing lasted forever, and it was always better to find a way to have things given to you instead of working for them, so you had time to move on to the next best thing. Hard work made a person look and act old, she'd say. According to her, it was more important to keep the *package* looking good.

Allison had dreamed her mother was someone else—Mrs. Cochran down the street, who sacrificed fixing her hair so she could play in the sprinklers with her four children. Or Mrs. Lorenzen, who lived across the street and invited Allison and Danielle over to eat cinnamon toast and play with her weenie dog Dutchie. Or even Mrs. Jerry who often helped her and Danielle with their homework while their mother spent the day at the beauty parlor.

Allison supposed she loved her mother. At least, she continued to try. But most of the warm, loving moments in her life had come from her dad. Of her two parents, *he'd* been the nurturer. The caretaker. The one she and Danielle ran to when their mother blew out of the house like the Wicked Witch of the West.

Her blog, as pointless as it might seem to some, allowed her to let go of her bottled-up emotions and also to keep a miniscule grain of hope alive that some people were meant to be together forever. Then again, it could be more than likely that she'd just plopped down on her sofa to watch *The*

Notebook one too many times. Because it didn't take a genius to know a relationship like the one depicted in the movie was only Tinsel Town trickery.

She flipped open the lid of her laptop and pushed the power button. When the program opened, she typed her new blog heading.

Picture-Perfect? Or Too Good to Be True?

An hour later, after conveying her thoughts on all she'd observed that night at Wilder Ranch, her eyes grew bleary, and she powered off her computer. She flopped down on the bed beside her dog and stared up at the outdated popcorn ceiling. For several minutes, she lay there stroking Wee Man's soft fur and listening to the crickets and cicadas outside her window. She thought of the evening's events and the Southern hospitality that had been extended to her. Amid a yawn, she had to remind herself—again—of why she'd come to Sweet.

And though she was intrigued as hell, her reason had absolutely nothing to do with Jesse Wilder.

Chapter 4

Sundays were all about sleeping in. Relaxing. Getting rid of the week's stress so you could prepare for the coming week's bucket of troubles. Yet even as Jesse sat shoulder deep in the swirling waters of his hot tub, he couldn't get a break from all the bits and pieces that jumped around in his head, like his brain was a custom-made trampoline.

Last night, he'd spent sleepless hours tossing, turning, and staring at the ceiling. Though he enjoyed the time spent at his mother's house amongst family, friends, and beautiful women, he didn't know if he'd ever get over the absence of his father and brother. Equally, he didn't know if he'd ever be able to let go of the promise he'd made before everything went south.

The *secret* often converged on his mind like a dark cloud, hovering there until a ray of sunshine broke through. For him, that usually came in the form of his niece's infectious giggle or something as simple as holding a puppy and getting a whiff of puppy breath. Common sense told him he'd feel relief if he just told someone. Loyalty prevented that from happening.

Unable to close his eyes and let his mind go, he searched for the small things in life that momentarily pushed away the weight of the responsibility and made him smile.

This morning, his spa-side entertainment came courtesy of his dog Dinks, who chased the slobbery tennis ball Jesse tossed over and over. An added source of amusement was provided by the look of utter disgust on his cat Rango's face as he observed the drooling mess of black Lab from his perch on the outdoor kitchen bar.

Though the clock had barely reached 8 A.M., the sound of a truck coming up his driveway told Jesse he was about to have company. Which meant it would either be Jackson or Jake. Chances on either were fifty-fifty.

He lifted the cup of coffee to his lips, sank deeper into the water, and waited for whoever it was to make an appearance.

"Holy shit. When did you put all this in?"

Through his Ray-Bans, Jesse looked up at his youngest brother's sudden arrival, which sent the cat scampering and the dog leaping around like it was Christmas Day.

"Over the past year," Jesse said. "Finished up about two months ago. Thought about waiting for you to come help but figured you'd get more enjoyment if it was already done."

"Dude. This is fucking party central," Jake said as he petted the drooling canine, then chucked the slobbery tennis ball out into the yard. Casually, he strolled the perimeter of the backyard to check it all out.

Since he'd been about ten years old, Jake loved to landscape. He loved to get his hands in the dirt. He'd learned to appreciate stone, wood, water, and any other natural element he could get his hands on besides a woman's body.

The hint of envy in Jake's eyes was obvious.

"Outdoor kitchen, built-in grill, pool, spa, fire pit, freaking waterfall." Jake's hands dropped onto his hips. "Bet it's even easier to get the chicks over here now, right?"

Jesse grinned his response. Although, like the others, baby bro might be sorely disappointed to know that not a single female other than their mother, their future and former sisters-in-law, or little Izzy had stepped foot on this portion of Wilder Ranch.

"Damn." Jake came full circle to where Jesse sat neck deep in the spa. "All you need to go with that Stetson and smirk is a cigar and a whiskey neat."

God, what a ridiculous reputation he'd managed to build for himself. "Little early for alcohol consumption."

Party Central as his little brother called it was actually the piece of paradise he'd carved out for himself with his own two hands, plus a lot of sweat, blisters, and sore muscles. The several hundred acres of Wilder Ranch had been divided up amongst all of them. Reno had built his home first. Jesse had been second. And now Jackson had broken ground for his own place.

Jesse figured he'd live here forever, and he'd planned the entire concept of the house and the yard so he'd have somewhere to relax and host numerous family gatherings with the ever-increasing Wilder brood. He loved his family and loved having them around. So he'd created a space for their enjoyment as well as his own.

"Until last night, I hadn't had a beer in eight months," Jake said. "Damn thing tasted so good. Sometimes you just want to wash the taste of sand out of your mouth with a good ale. Know what I mean?"

"I do." Jesse nodded, remembering all the months he'd spent living in a tent with a bunch of other guys. No privacy. Always on edge. No comforts of home. No good old American ale. "There's an extra pair of board shorts in the bathroom off the patio if you want to take a swim."

"I'll pass on that for now." Jake rolled his head, relieving the obvious tension in his neck. "Got things to do. People to visit."

"Such as?"

Jake grinned. "Jessica Holt."

"On a Sunday morning? Doesn't she sing in the church choir?"

"It's been a long dry spell. She stayed home to put together something tasty."

"Breakfast?"

Jake's laughter floated across the yard. "I was hoping more for scented oil and lingerie."

"Lucky you."

"Yeah." Jake did another quick scan of the landscape. "I'll take a quick cup of coffee and be back later for a dip if that's okay."

"Door's always open." Jesse got out of the spa and dripped water over the rock surface as he reached for the towel he'd dropped near the edge. "Hang on. I'll get that coffee for you."

"Bullshit. Nobody waits on me."

Jesse shook his head and chuckled at the streak of stubborn independence that ran through all of them. He joined Jake at the outdoor kitchen island. Eager for a little catch-up, he freshened his own cup. "So how's it going over there in good old Camp Leatherneck?"

"Same shit, different day."

"Still think you're making a difference?"

"Keeping the faith."

Jesse sipped his coffee and, with tremendous respect, studied the little brother who'd once struggled to keep up with the rest of them. What he saw was a leader. A man who took stick-to-it to the max. And though Jesse knew he'd had nothing to do with the man Jake had become, he was damned proud.

"You sure about that?" he asked, noting the exhaustion in his brother's eyes.

"You've always been the most intuitive brother," Jake said.

"It's a gift."

"Or a curse, depending on which of us you're dealing with." A chuckle rumbled in Jake's chest before he looked up, and the bright morning sun washed out the vivid blue of his eyes. "I don't know. I'm just . . ."

"Tired of fighting?"

"Yeah. In the beginning, I thought maybe I could be a lifer. Now, I'm not so sure."

"Takes a lot out of a man to fight that battle every day. To be on guard twenty-four/seven and then some."

Jake nodded. "I'm only twenty- nine, and I feel fucking old."

"So don't sign another contract. No one is going to think any less of you if you walk away. Hell, you've put in more time than any of us. When we lost Jared . . ." Jesse paused to sip his coffee and swallow down that harsh memory. "I was done. Not that I was afraid. I lost the heart. The drive. I couldn't sleep nights worrying about the rest of you. And I realized that I just fucking missed home."

"I think about him all the time," Jake said. No name needed to be mentioned to know whom he meant. "Hard not to when they send you through that same area, and your boots hit the dirt where his blood was spilled."

"He was the best," Jesse said. Still, Jared had been damned good at hiding important issues.

Jake gave a silent nod that reaffirmed he'd not yet fully dealt with Jared's death. When he finally did, Jesse knew it would be tough. But Jesse also knew that, as he had for the others, he'd be there to help Jake pick up the pieces.

"So what brings you over to my side of the ranch at such an early hour?" he asked because it became obvious a change of subject was needed.

"Early? You've grown soft, big brother. Looks like you've been out of the Marines so long you've forgotten what o-dark-hundred means."

"Yeah. I don't miss that."

While Jesse perched on a barstool, Jake rummaged through the refrigerator the same as he had when he'd been a teenager. Seemed like one or the other of them had always been hunting for something to eat. It was probably a miracle with five boys that the appliance even stayed cold or their parents hadn't gone broke from their healthy appetites.

"So what's next on your agenda?" Jesse asked. "Besides raiding my fridge and paying a visit to the fair maiden Jessica?"

"I've got a few weeks of leave, then I'm headed back to Cherry Point." Jake peeled open a package and took a bite of the string cheese Jesse kept on hand for Izzy.

"You going to be able to stay there a while?"

"They told me not to bother unpacking, so I'm guessing that's a no. Which leads me to what's up with mom getting engaged so quick? I mean, Mr. Lane seems like a nice enough man, but what's the deal? And if this is really going to happen, when's the big day? Because I don't have long and—"

"Whoa. Back up the tractor. Take a breath."

"Sorry." Jake shook his head as if to clear it. "I just feel out of sync, you know?"

Jesse could relate. After he'd completed his last tour of duty, it had taken him a long time to unwind and get back into the real world. The short furloughs the Marines allowed were never long enough to quite get a grasp on all that had happened in everyone else's everyday life. Sadly, it was easy to get out of touch with that reality and not feel whole until you were in uniform again.

That's when he'd known he had to get out.

He'd been losing his identity bit by bit and losing what mattered the most. His family, and the bond they shared.

"Like . . ." Jake pulled up a barstool and sat on the opposite side of the concrete island. "All these big events are going on, and I'm missing everything. Reno met Charli, and they're getting married. Jackson and Abby are engaged and building a house. Izzy's almost four years old. And now Mom . . ." He ran a hand over his buzz cut.

"You know, it's always been tough keeping up with the Wilders," Jesse said with a laugh meant to lighten his brother's load. "Maybe we should have our own reality TV show."

Jake scoffed. "Probably be the only way I can keep up with everything going on around here."

"My guess is that if Mom really intends to tie the knot, she won't let it happen unless we're all in attendance. In the meantime, I suggest we all sit back and let the adults figure it out."

"I carry a military assault rifle." Jake pointed his stick of string cheese. "You saying I'm not an adult?"

"Not in my eyes. I still see you as the little shithead pain in the ass who used to run around with crap in his diapers while trying to hang with the big boys."

"And I still see you as the guy who used to try to scam every female in Sweet High School."

"I never scammed any of them."

"Bullshit. You'd have a date with one on Friday and a different one on Saturday, and you'd tell both of them they were . . ." Jake placed his hand over his heart and raised his voice an octave. "The *only* one."

"Yeah." Jesse laughed. "Good times. And things you can only get away with when you're sixteen."

"I figured with the way you were looking at Allison last night, you were—"

"I wasn't looking at her in any way."

"Again, I call bullshit." Jake sipped his coffee, then grinned. "If eyes were hands, you'd have been peeling away her clothes slow and easy and savoring every moment."

Yeah. He'd probably done that. Wasn't going to admit it, though. "You've been letting that Afghani heat get to your brain, little bro."

"Still going to bet you're next in line."

"For what?"

Jake hummed out the "Wedding March."

"Get the fuck out of here. That's not in the cards." *At least for a very long time.*

Jake slurped down the rest of his coffee. "You keep fooling yourself about that, big brother. And I sure as hell hope I'm around to watch you take a dive right at those pretty high heels."

"I've got sturdy legs. Don't plan on falling anytime soon."

"Dude, you built a five-bedroom, three-bath house." Jake hitched a thumb over his shoulder at the Victorian farmhouse Jesse had designed and built with his own two hands and a little help from Rockview Construction. "Why the hell did you build such an enormous house if you didn't plan on sharing it with someone?"

"I like space to ramble."

"Ha!" Jake slapped his knee. "Good one."

"Have I told you lately how irritating you are?" *And how good it was to have him back.*

"Been hearing that all my life from you guys. Goes in one ear and out the other." Jake set down his empty coffee cup, shoved the last piece of string cheese in his mouth, and stood. "Just in case you're thinking about filling those extra bedrooms sometime soon, the lovely Ms. Lane is having lunch today with Mom. So I'd suggest y'all get on over there before I grab her up for myself."

Jesse tried to ignore the implication that for some reason jabbed at him like a well-delivered uppercut. "I like those bedrooms just the way they are," he said with a great big lie. "Big and empty."

"Uh-huh." Jake tossed him a wave as he headed for the door. "Save me a piece of the cobbler Mom made for lunch. See you later."

Once Jesse heard the front door close, he found himself looking at the clock over the sink of the outdoor kitchen. It was still early, but he couldn't help but wonder what time his mother planned to serve that cobbler.

*J*ana Wilder was a whirlwind of energy as she set a bowl of pasta salad on the kitchen table, currently covered by a sunflower tablecloth. In the center of the table sat a large white ceramic pitcher filled with fresh sunflowers. Also on the table were two place settings of colorful yellow Fiesta Ware, with sterling silverware and white cloth napkins tied up with little raffia bows. It was obvious Jana had gone to a lot of trouble this morning to make things perfect for their luncheon. As an event planner as well as the daughter of the man Jana was engaged to, Allison appreciated her efforts.

"I thought about inviting the other girls for lunch," she said. "But I really wanted a chance for the two of us to get to know each other. And once all those girls get in the same room, there's no telling which direction the conversation or the activities will go."

"In a bad way?"

"Oh. No." Jana laughed. "Not a single one of them has a mean bone in her body. But as an example, the first day Charli and I really got to know each other we made smoothies—or as she called them *high-octane margaritas*. Somehow, we ended up on the veranda dancing with Miss Giddy, and she had to call Reno to come pick her up."

"Good to know," Allison teased. "Just in case you haul out the blender."

The previous night had been a bit overwhelming, with all the probing questions and her careful responses. Not to mention the underlying pressure from Jesse, who watched her with a peculiar fire in his eyes. The times she'd looked his way, she honestly couldn't tell if he was the big bad wolf ready to take a bite out of her, or a kick-

backed pussycat prepared to take things as they
came.

A ridiculous thought.

In all the conversations they'd shared, *nothing*
led her to believe that there was anything laid-
back about him. The man had an intensity she
was positive ran on full power every minute of
every day.

A wise woman operated off her first instincts.

Her first instincts told her to run like hell.

"I wish my sister Danielle could have come
along," Allison said of her perfectly put-together
and always-on-her-toes sibling. "You'll love her."

"Why, sugarplum . . ." Jana turned with a
basket of steaming biscuits in her hand. "You say
that like you think I won't love *you*."

Allison would like to think she didn't care what
Jana or anyone else thought of her, but that would
be a lie. As the daughter of a woman she'd had to
work hard to please, and now with an occupation
that demanded she have an eager-to-please personality, she knew she cared a lot.

"People tell me I'm more . . . complicated."

"Nonsense." Jana set the basket on the table and
waved a hand like she was batting flies. "It's like
I always say . . . when you've got a locker room
full of players, everybody is different. Each player
has their own job. But when they start playing together as a team, things just fall into place."

"Was that a baseball or football analogy?"

"Football. This is Texas. And the only thing
closer to God than football is Pearl Ewing's hair."

Allison didn't know who Pearl Ewing was, but

she'd pay money to see that hair. Her stomach growled. She plucked a large black olive from the rooster-shaped bowl on the table and popped it into her mouth. "Obviously, I'm a Seahawks fan. Who's your team?"

"Houston Stallions, of course." Jana grinned. "It sure will be interesting when our teams play against each other. Though I'm afraid you'll have to cheer really loud to be heard over everyone else in this house."

With that huge grin on Jana's face, it was impossible to tell the woman that most likely she'd never be around to watch football. As soon as she declared the coast clear for her dad and his emotionally charged relationship decisions, she'd hightail it right back to safe-and-sound Seattle.

With the football banter complete, the kitchen became awkwardly quiet. While Allison sipped her sweet tea, she wondered the best way to approach the subject of the seemingly *spontaneous* engagement.

"Mrs. Wilder, I—"

"Please. Call me Jana. And don't worry, I'd never ask y'all to do something ridiculous like call me *Mom*. You already have one. I'd just like to be a friend."

"My mother prefers I call her Linda."

Blond eyebrows lifted. "Really?"

Allison nodded. "She's afraid if I call her *Mom*, people will try to calculate her age. And she's doing everything in the name of science to keep *that* little detail under wraps."

"No offense to your mother—because we all

have our own way of doing things—but if one of my boys called me *Jana*, I'd smack him upside the head. I put in a lot of sleepless nights to get them to behave like gentlemen and not the wild herd they aspired to be. I earned the title."

"I imagine they were quite a handful."

"I did have my hair-pulling moments." Jana chuckled. "One or the other of them was always getting into trouble. Often that required a trip to the ER for stitches or a cast. Never had any trouble with the law, though. My Joe wouldn't have tolerated that for a minute."

"You talk with such affection about your husband." Good lead-in, she thought. Jana seemed the type more than willing to open up. Maybe this discussion would present some cracks in Jana's seemingly flawless exterior. Not that she really hoped she'd find any.

"Joe was a wonderful man." Her father's fiancée refilled the glasses of sweet tea and sat down. "And though not perfect, we had a marriage most only dream about. He had a heart as big as the state we live in, and there wasn't a soul within fifty miles he didn't know or who didn't know him. He was always out helping someone build a barn, brand cattle, or work the land."

Allison worried her bottom lip. How could her easygoing father ever live up to Joe Wilder's memory?

"After our Jared was killed in Afghanistan, Joe sank deeper and deeper into grief and regrets. There wasn't a soul, including me and our boys, who could drag him out of his despair. One day, he sat down at his desk at the hardware store, and that generous heart of his just quit. The boys and I believe he died of a broken heart."

"I'm so sorry." Allison reached out and covered Jana's hand with her own. She couldn't imagine losing a husband or son, or anyone she loved. Thankfully, she'd never lost anyone in that manner. All her losses had come in the form of hope and the promise of a dream. Not the same to be sure, but devastating in their own right.

"There were a lot of years I took things for granted." Jana sipped her tea thoughtfully. "But with the loss of my husband and my firstborn, I learned a new appreciation for life. And I never forget it. With the girls, or I should say, the young women, my sons have introduced into our family, I find something special in each and every one. And I'm grateful for the joy they've brought to my life."

Allison leaned her chin on her palm and allowed Jana's soothing Southern drawl to settle into her soul.

"That includes your daddy." Jana leaned back in her chair. "I've been alone for a time now. Since I met him, your father has brought a smile to my face each and every day. And I'm grateful. So don't worry your pretty head, sugarplum. Because I plan to make him smile every day too. He's a good man. And he should be treated well."

In her profession, Allison had heard almost every line of BS known to the universe. Looking into the bright blue of Jana Wilder's eyes, she didn't sense an ounce of dishonesty.

Allison had come two thousand miles armed

with a bagful of questions. She'd come looking for answers and to determine whether marrying this woman was right for her father. She thought she'd either find a woman after his money or at least sufficient flaws in Jana's character to make a case to her father that he was making a huge mistake. Since Jana hadn't known he was wealthy, money wasn't an issue. Jana's armor was not only intact, it had been built with a double layer of strength, love, and character Allison couldn't help admire.

"Jana, I—"

The back door creaked open, and Allison looked up to find Jesse standing in the entry— long hair neatly pulled back, grin in place, and devil written all over him.

His eyes met hers, and his grin increased. "Am I too late?"

$\mathcal{J}$esse ignored the pair of smoky eyes glaring at him as though he'd intruded on some secret recipe exchange. He walked into the warm kitchen and inhaled the aroma of freshly baked sweet potato biscuits. Delicious as it might be, the food on the table didn't look nearly as appetizing as Allison, in a simple lightweight sweater that fell off one delectable shoulder and a pair of skintight black leggings. He couldn't see her feet, but he guessed she again wore a pair of high heels that added a few inches to her petite height.

"Late for what?" his mother asked, sounding cross yet grinning at the same time.

"Lunch."

"You weren't invited," Allison chimed in, obviously hoping he'd take the not-so-subtle hint and retreat.

"Well, lucky for you I made enough for an army," his mom said. "Pull up a chair, and I'll grab you a plate."

His mama didn't raise any fools, so of course he chose the chair next to Allison. And as he sat down, he caught a hint of the sweet scent of either her perfume, shampoo, or a tasty body lotion. He didn't know which, but he was willing to investigate further.

While she glared her obvious displeasure at his sudden and unannounced appearance, the house phone rang.

"Oh, darn," his mother said as she set a platter of moist, sliced roasted chicken down on the table. "I'll pick that up in the other room. You two go ahead and get started. I'll be right back."

Jesse watched her disappear through the door, then he turned to Allison and tried not to laugh at the less-than-amiable expression on her face. "Where's your dog?"

"You mean Wee Man?"

"I am *not* calling him that. It's disrespectful."

"I really don't think he gets that you think it's an insult. As a vet, you should know it's all about the tone of voice you use. In any case, I left him with my father so your mother and I could have a nice lunch without *interruption*."

"There's no such thing in this house. There's always somebody coming or going or the phone's ringing."

"Believe me, I'm starting to get that." She reached for the bowl of pasta salad that was just beyond her fingertips. He grabbed it and plopped a big spoonful onto her plate.

"Hey, I can serve myself."

"Southern hospitality," he responded, then reached for the platter of carved chicken breast. "One slice or two."

"One." She glared. "So why are you really here? Shouldn't you be out doing something like . . . getting a haircut?"

"You don't like long hair?"

"On girls. On men, it just looks like they're trying too hard." She stuck her fork in a curly noodle, lifted it to her luscious mouth, and chewed. "So what is it you're overcompensating for?"

"Obviously, you're an outsider who knows nothing about me, so I'll let that slide."

"Obviously, you're quick to cover, so I'm going to maintain you have something to hide."

He leaned in and stretched his arm along the back of her chair. "I'm willing to prove you wrong."

She didn't immediately reject the idea, and that sparked curiosity.

She took another forkful of pasta and chewed thoughtfully, meeting his eyes as if to show he didn't scare her one little bit.

"Is it going to be like this every time we're in the same room?" she asked.

"Like what?"

"Like a fuse has been lit, and we're just waiting for an explosion."

"God, I hope so."

"I didn't mean that in a sexual way."

He searched her face and found it even more appealing than the moment he'd first seen her at Seven Devils. Denial looked really good on her. "Didn't you?"

"No."

"Well, that's too bad." He dropped a spoonful of pasta on his own plate, then reached for the basket of biscuits. "So what brings you here?"

"Lunch." Sarcasm dripped from those pretty lips as she pointed to her plate.

"Eating aside . . ." Although she had plenty of soft places he wouldn't mind nibbling. "What brings you here to Sweet? And why did you keep it such a big secret when we met at the bar?"

"I didn't keep anything a secret. I didn't know you, so why would I give you any personal information?"

"You shared your best pickup lines."

"I hate to burst your bubble, but I've never used a pickup line in my life."

"Oh. That's right. You just grab strange men in bars and make them dance with you."

"I didn't know your brother was engaged."

"Which raises the question, what *were* you looking for in the bar that night?"

"Wasn't that obvious?" She leaned closer and gave him a flirtatious smile. Batted her eyelashes.

"Ummm . . ."

"Obviously, I had concerns about my father's sudden engagement to a woman neither my sister nor I had ever heard of," she said, bursting any hot-and-steamy fantasy he had brewing inside his head. "I wanted to check out the area, the people who live here, and try to figure out why my dad would sell off his business, move to someplace he'd never been before, and promptly ask a strange woman to marry him."

"My mother's not strange. She's a good person. I can validate her overwhelming generosity and helpful nature."

"Yes, but who's going to vouch for *you*?"

"Are you against your father's marrying my mother? Or just marriage in general?"

"I'm not necessarily against my father's marrying your mother. I just want to make sure it's the right thing for him."

"Understandable."

"As for marriage in general . . ." She shrugged. "The jury's still out."

"That's pretty pessimistic."

"Don't get me wrong. I think most people love the *idea* of the whole being-together-forever thing. They love the attention, the celebration, the lavish gifts. What comes after the honeymoon is when they seem to lose interest."

"So basically, it's safe to say you're against marriage," he said. Most people could hide their true feelings behind a mask of indifference. Allison's face was far too expressive to have that gift.

"Just not a real big believer that two specific people are destined to be together for the rest of their lives."

"Excuse me?" He couldn't believe what he'd just heard. "Aren't you a wedding planner?"

"I'm an *event* planner."

"Who plans weddings."

"Sometimes."

"And yet you don't believe in marriage."

"Half end in divorce. So you can't say that it's *me* who doesn't believe when it appears that most of those who say 'I do' don't believe. Or maybe they just don't have what it takes to make it for the long haul. I think it's more about the longevity of a relationship that's questionable than a legal document."

"So what you're saying is you don't believe in true love," he said.

"I'm highly suspicious that it exists."

"Wow." He leaned back in his chair. "It must be awful to walk around with so much cynicism."

"I'm not by nature a negative person."

"Aren't you?"

"No. I'm a realist."

"Darlin', you're something. I just haven't figured out what."

"You know," she said on a long sigh, "I came over here to get to know your mother. I didn't come to get in an argument with *you* about my beliefs or disbeliefs." She tossed her napkin on the table and pushed her chair back for a quick getaway.

He'd seen her run enough. And while he might enjoy a backside view, it didn't mean he wanted it—or her—to disappear. Not to mention if he chased her away, his mother would have his hide.

He curled his fingers around the soft skin of her wrist. "Sit down and stop being so prickly."

"Prickly?"

"Yes, like those cacti outside that stab you every time you brush up against them. In this family, we yell. We argue. We get to the bottom of things with a whole lot of emotion."

"Since my parents' divorce, we don't yell in our family."

"Ever?" he asked.

"Ever."

"Wow. That would just be . . . weird." He stretched his arm along the back of her chair. "So how do things get resolved?"

She remained silent for a minute, but he could see her wheels spinning. "I guess they don't. It's become unspoken knowledge that you don't discuss volatile issues."

"Like your parents' divorce?"

"Yes. Like that."

"You didn't see it coming, did you?"

"Oh I saw it coming. I prayed for it."

"That's terrible."

"Yes. It was."

"So what does your mother do now? Is she remarried?"

"She's currently seeking out husband number six."

"No shit?" No wonder she'd lost her faith.

"No. And I don't know why I'm letting you pull all this personal information out of me."

Jesse had some troubling thoughts dart through his head. He really hated to see anyone have such a strong disbelief in what he believed to be the ultimate highlight of a person's life. To find that one person you were meant to spend your life with. To share the joyous moments and support each other through the bad. It's the one thing he'd always looked forward to. After all, he'd had the best role models. Someday, he hoped to be lucky enough to find the same enduring kind of love his parents had shared. But it was not his time yet.

While Allison might truly be here just as she said—to get to know the woman to whom her father had proposed—she might also have other objectives that could put a damper on his mother's happiness. He couldn't let that happen. Best to dig a little deeper and see what she really had on her mind. And if that meant he had to stick to her like glue, well, that was a burden he'd be willing to bear.

"Don't get offended, darlin'," he said. "But I'm not pulling out the info. You're offering."

Her mouth opened to argue, and at that moment, his mother reappeared, unwittingly rescuing him.

"Everything okay?" he asked her, ignoring the daggers Allison shot him from behind her smoky eyes.

"Oh." His mom looked up. "Yes. That was Izzy. She wanted to sing me a new song she learned. I'm so sorry for the interruption. But it looks like y'all are enjoying the meal and . . . getting along?"

"Depends on who you ask," he said around a bite of homemade biscuit. "I'm sure Allison might have a different opinion than me."

"Everything's fine," Allison said, her tone defying the pleasantry of her words. "Please. Join us. You worked so hard to make everything just right. Besides, you must be hungry."

"I am that. It's been a busy couple of days." His mother sat down and dropped a few items onto her plate. "So what have y'all been discussing?"

Allison opened her mouth to respond.

Jesse beat her to the punch.

"Oh, just some little things. Like Allison's not believing in happily-ever-afters."

"What?" His mother's brows lifted.

Allison's brows pulled together.

"But don't worry," he said, stabbing his fork into the moist chicken. "I have just the plan to change her mind."

Chapter 5

How had she let herself get talked into this?

Allison stood in the guest bedroom of her father's house, trying to decide if jeans were the appropriate attire to murder someone, or if she should go all out and wear a dress.

Earlier that day, all she'd been trying to do was get to know Jana to find out if this engagement was a good thing or if something seemed haywire. She hadn't expected to be blindsided by a six-foot-three hunky pain in the ass.

During her brief conversation with Jana, she'd found out a little but not nearly as much as she'd planned thanks to the party crasher named Jesse. True, he could be irresistible when he turned on that good old Southern boy charm, but mostly he was a complete distraction to her goal. Now here she was, waiting for him to pick her up so he could try to prove to her that true love was more than just a cliché.

It wasn't that she didn't actually believe it existed, she just believed it was rare. And for someone like her, a person who inherited her mother's screwed-up DNA, the possibility of finding a lasting relationship would be like expecting to win the lottery the first time you played the game. Her sister had found it, which almost guaranteed *she* wouldn't. Lightning never struck twice in the same place.

She thought of Jesse, a playboy who obviously couldn't commit, and she couldn't imagine what he had up his sleeve, or why he cared what she felt or how she thought.

Oddly, she was intrigued enough to play along.

Beyond the closed bedroom door, she heard the doorbell ring and the low murmur of masculine voices.

A thought struck her, and panic set in.

Dear God, she hoped he didn't see this as some kind of date. Because it wasn't. She hadn't come to Texas for a *date*. She'd come to protect her dad and his best interest.

End of story.

She held up the yellow cotton dress again, one of the limited items of clothes she had packed for this brief trip. Because she didn't know what Jesse had planned, she decided something a little dressier might be in order.

As she slipped it over her head and smoothed out the wrinkles, her dad called out from the living room to ask if she was almost ready.

Tempted to take her time just to ruffle Jesse's feathers, she finally relented with a "Just a minute" response. With a few more fluffs of her hair, she grabbed her purse and stuffed in her lipstick and phone. At the last second, she tossed in a safety measure in the form of a can of hair spray.

A girl could never be too cautious.

Hating melodramatic appearances, she tried to join the two men chatting in the living room with as little fanfare as possible. Jesse made that impossible with the heated look he skimmed down her body when she entered the room.

Hopefully, no one noticed when her face flushed. And thankfully, the tingles that hot-blooded appraisal delivered straight to her girl parts were invisible.

"You look beautiful," her dad said.

Wee Man obviously thought so too as he leaped into the air, trying to steal a slurp. Knowing her dad would say the same thing even if she were dressed in her cat pajamas and frog slippers, she smiled.

"Thank you, Daddy. We shouldn't be long . . ." She turned toward Jesse. "Right?"

"Hard to say." His broad shoulders lifted. "Could prove to be a lively evening."

Unsure what *that* implied, she kissed her dad's cheek and followed Jesse to his enormous black truck, a vehicle far too flashy for a veterinarian yet completely apropos for an obvious player like him.

With a large masculine hand extended toward her, he held the truck door open. At her hesitation, one dark, sexy brow lifted.

"What's so funny?" he asked.

"Did I laugh?"

"It was more like a snicker."

"Oh." She settled her hand in his, placed her foot on the step bar, and hiked up onto the seat. "Well . . . I guess I just thought you'd be driving an animal ambulance. You know, something like the Ghostbusters drove? Maybe even with a big bobblehead dog on top."

He kept hold of her hand, and a slow grin spread across his handsome face. "Good one."

"I aim to please."

"Do you now?"

"Of course," she said. Before he let go, the grip on her hand changed from strictly accommodating to something that sent a tingle up her spine. "It's the biggest part of my job."

The grin never left his face as he stepped closer and moved between her and the door.

"Nice sidestep. You're pretty good at that, I've noticed." He reached across her lap, took hold of the seat belt, and clicked it in place. His big hands lingered at her side, and more tingles ensued. "But I'm not buying that that's what you meant."

"I'm not even going to ask what you *think* I meant because you'd be wrong."

"Uh-huh."

"I'm serious." She folded her arms beneath her breasts, and his eyes tracked the movement.

His grin flashed again. Sadly, instead of wanting to wipe it off his face, she'd prefer to kiss it off. Which raised the question: Why was she so attracted to this man who probably had women falling in his lap and following him home like good little cowgirl boot-wearing sheep?

If she'd been wearing blinders, she couldn't have stopped the pleasurable ride her gaze took up and down his lean, muscular body.

The answer to her question came in a woolly-sounding *Baaaaaaa*.

Although she didn't wear cowgirl boots and broke into hives at the sight of wool, apparently she wasn't immune.

So what did that say about her other than the fact that she hadn't gotten laid in a really, really, *really* long time?

"Darlin' . . ." His Texas drawl came out deep, smooth, and sexy as he propped his arm on the seat behind her and leaned in. "You can deny it till the cows come home, but you are as hot for me as I am for you."

She opened her mouth to protest, then clamped it shut because she'd never been a liar.

"But let's get one thing straight between us besides the obvious," he continued. "It's *not* going to happen."

"I know," she said, leaning away just so she wasn't tempted to close her eyes and play a game of *Pin the Lips on the Hot Guy*.

"Do you?" His head tilted just a smidge, and a silky strand of hair slipped from that loose ponytail. His gaze never left hers as he tucked it behind his ear. "Because, darlin', you aren't just sending signals, you are skyrocketing them."

"I'm tempted to laugh at your audacity to believe I'd just jump into bed with you. I'm not a jumper. Although that's what I'm sure you're used to with these small-town girls."

"Small-town girls are no different than big-city girls. They all want the same thing; just some of them go about it differently. Some are more open. And some are just . . . uptight."

Before she could snap out a comeback, he closed the truck door.

When he reappeared in the driver's seat, she planned to keep her lips zipped, get the evening over with, and refuse to rise further to any bait he might dangle. She tightened the lock on her folded arms and gave an imaginary *so there* nod.

"I'm not *uptight*," she said. Geez. What was with the mouth not listening to the brain?

"Uh-huh," was all he said as he turned the key in the ignition and pulled away from her father's house. Two seconds later, he broke the mental breather she'd been allowed and said, "But you *are* hot for me."

She glanced across the cab of the truck and considered his handsome face. The broad shoulders beneath that plaid shirt. The strength in the forearms bared by sleeves rolled to his elbows. The obviously nice package pressed between the legs of those jeans. Her gaze came back up and caught the smile playing across those masculine lips.

Hot for him?

Yeah.

Damn it.

She was *muy el fuego.*

A ten-minute drive had never taken so long.

As Jesse parked his truck at the curb in front of

Arlene Potter's little rock bungalow, he knew staying on track and getting through the evening unscathed would be a challenge. He couldn't name what it was about Allison that drew him in. He only knew he was a damned moth to her sweet-smelling flame.

And she was on fire.

Around her, every common sense thing he had in his head froze. And every stupid thing he thought flew from his mouth as if he were a dopey sixteen-year-old.

He'd meant it when he'd told her nothing between them could or would ever happen. He had a job to do. He'd helped out Reno in his time of need. Supported Jackson. Now it was time to take care of his mother. Jake's time would come too. Which meant that no matter how interesting, hot, funny, or promising Allison seemed, it was *not* time for him.

"Isn't that your brother's truck parked next door?" she asked.

"Good eye. That's Abby's house. Or at least the one she grew up in. Her parents moved to Florida, and she planned to put it up for sale for them. But now Annie and her baby will need a place to live. Abby and Jackson are staying there while they build their own house and to help Annie until after she delivers the baby."

"That's nice of them. Your brother's a firefighter, right?"

He nodded. "He's studying to move up in the ranks."

"I always thought my brother-in-law would

choose firefighting over law enforcement." A frown pulled her delicate brows together.

"Why's that?"

"Both jobs are dangerous. But in all the years I've known him, I've always thought he was more of a rescuer. He's often been my go-to guy for advice I was afraid to ask my dad. He's always been Johnny-on-the-spot when it comes to helping someone out.

"When we were in high school, he often included me in their activities—much to my sister's dismay."

"Sounds like a decent guy."

"He's great." She gave him a smile that revealed her deep admiration. "So what made you want to be a veterinarian?"

He hesitated. Only those closest to him knew the reason. It wasn't something he liked to share. Mostly because it made him look like a pansy ass.

"What's wrong?" she asked.

"Just trying to figure out a response that will earn me Brownie points with you."

She laughed. "Just tell me the truth."

"You'll take away my man card."

"Just tell me. I promise I won't laugh."

Time would tell.

"Blame it on a cat." He wrapped his hands around the steering wheel and sighed. "Since I was a kid, I've always been used to seeing things city kids don't see. Like branding, artificial insemination, castration."

"Eeew."

"Yeah. Definitely not for the weak-stomached."

He chuckled. "So you'd think not much would bother me. Not true. When I was about eight, I found this little gray kitten in the barn. The mother cat had pushed it aside for whatever reason, and I knew if I didn't do something, it would die. I got my dad and Jared, who knew the most about stuff like that. We made a makeshift bottle and milked one of the goats. Jared and I sat up all night trying to feed this little tiny thing and keep it warm and alive. I tucked her inside my shirt next to my heart. Somehow she survived. In fact, she lived to be old and crotchety. But that first night when I was trying so hard to keep her little heart pumping? That's when I knew I wanted to help as many animals as possible."

"Awwww." Her expression softened as she reached over and touched his arm. And that touched something deep inside him. "That's so sweet."

"Yeah. And if you tell anyone, I'll have to hurt you."

"I promise I won't say a word." She crossed two fingers across her chest. "Unless someone offers me a million dollars."

He pulled the keys from the ignition. "Good to know you can be bought off."

"But I don't come cheap." She glanced out the window. "So, where are your brother and Abby building a house?"

"Wilder Ranch."

Her perfect brows lifted. "You *all* live on Wilder Ranch?"

"Why would we want to be anywhere else?"

"It's a great big world out there," she said. "There are some fascinating places to choose from. In fact, I just had a friend, who's lived in Seattle all her life, move to Paris."

"Texas?"

"There's a Paris in Texas?"

"Yep. They even made a movie about it."

"Imagine that," she said. "My friend moved to Paris, *France*, to indulge herself in the lifestyle, the iconic landmarks, and the arts."

"Well, that must be nice for her if she wasn't content where she was at. Me? I'm happy looking at good old American soil, cattle, and barns as big as they come."

"So you'd never want to live anywhere else?"

"I've spent plenty of time on foreign soil. And if my boots never touch it again, I'm good." He expected a snappy comeback; instead, she surprised him.

"I guess I can understand that," she said. "Especially when you probably had to spend a lot of that time trying to stay alive."

"That is a fact."

"I always wonder if our soldiers understand how thankful we are."

"It sometimes gets lost in the heat of battle."

"Back in the States, I know it's easy to go on about your day and forget what's happening half a world away. To forget the sacrifices our soldiers and their families make. I can't imagine how difficult it might be. Especially when you suffer such a loss as your brother. So . . . thank you."

Jesse looked up and caught the sincerity in her

eyes. The sentiment touched him in a place he hadn't allowed to be touched in a long time. "I appreciate that."

Warm as honey, a smile lingered on her lips long enough for him to think about changing his mind and pulling her into his arms. But there was no time. He was on a mission. And personal satisfaction was not in his deck of cards.

"So what about you?" he asked. "You ever think of leaving Seattle?"

Her slender shoulders lifted beneath that pretty dress. "Never gave it much thought. I was born and raised there. Almost everyone I know lives there."

"Except your dad."

"Yeah." She sighed. "Except him."

"You miss him."

"I do. At first, I wondered what brought him here."

"Haven't you ever asked him?"

"I finally did last night. And now I realize it's not so much about what *brought* him here as it is what *drove* him here. He needed to find some peace in his life. He needed a change. And I'm sure there's more."

"Such as?"

"My mother." She gazed out the windshield. "She's gone through five husbands—all wealthy—and yet she can't stop trying to wring every last drop from my dad."

"Why?"

"Clearly she's selfish and greedy. And clearly I shouldn't be talking about her like this without her here to defend herself."

"So maybe the real question is *can* she defend herself?"

"Probably not." She sighed. "My dad was always the caregiver. He was the one Danielle and I ran to when we needed comfort. Which is why . . ."

"You feel the need to protect him."

"Yeah. No offense to your mom, but my dad has gone through some tough times. I just want him to be happy."

"That makes you a good daughter."

A smile quivered at the corners of her lips. "I try."

Something in this woman's past had really done a number on her. And since she'd be leaving in just a few days, there wouldn't be enough time to figure it all out. Which raised the question . . . why did he feel the need to know?

"Guess we should go on inside," he said, even while he knew he'd like nothing more than to sit right there all night and get to know her better.

"I can't wait to see what you've got up your sleeve."

It wasn't what was *up his sleeve* that she needed to worry about.

When she reached for the door handle, he said, "Wait." In a flash, he was out of the truck, opening her door, and holding out his hand.

She looked at him like he was ten kinds of crazy.

He'd bet on twenty.

Those intriguing gray eyes narrowed just slightly. "What are you doing?"

"Being the Southern gentleman my mother raised me to be so I don't get my ass kicked."

"I'm perfectly capable of opening my own door."

"Apparently you missed the ass-kicking part of what I just said."

"I promise. Your mother will never know."

"See that house behind me? The one we are about to walk into?"

"Yes."

"There are two people in that house who are right now spying through the lace curtains and watching every move we make. If I don't display every ounce of chivalry and Southern hospitality I was raised with, they will spread the word all over town. Without a doubt, that word will hit my mother's ears, and I will never hear the end of it." He moved his hand closer to her. "So please. Spare me the agony."

"Well . . ." She laughed and put her hand in his while he fought the desire to pull her in close. "Far be it from me to set you up for an ass-kicking. Although that might be fun to watch."

"No. It's ugly. Believe me."

As they walked up the sidewalk together, he fought the urge to reach down and take her hand. He didn't know what was wrong with him and why he was having all these touchy-feely urges. He only knew he'd have to get it under control now and figure it out later. Still, he couldn't help be aware of every gentle sway of her hips, the sweet scent that reached out to him, the lavender polish on her toes, the smoothness of her skin.

"Sounds like you have a lot of experience in the ass-kicking department," she said, looking up at him.

"You have no idea."

Before he could ring the bell, the door flew open, and there stood the two little blue-hairs who'd agreed to help him bring clarity to Allison's doubtful nature.

"Hello, hunkalicious!" Gladys Lewis, a fireball in orthopedic shoes, wore a slash of bright red lipstick that clashed with her silvery blue cotton-ball hair. She threw her arms around him and gave him a hug that stole his breath.

"My turn!" Arlene Potter, with her elderly girth hidden beneath a floral muumuu, shoved aside Gladys, wrapped her crepey arms around his middle, and squeezed. "God, I love a man in uniform."

"You crazy old broad," Gladys said, "He's not in a uniform."

Arlene gave him a wink. "Saw him once in those dress blues." She tapped her finger against her temple. "Still got the memory locked in right here."

Jesse didn't know what was more uncomfortable, that eighty-year-old Arlene thought of him like *that*, or the repulsed glare Allison shot at him. Like he had any kind of control over Arlene's wayward thoughts? Hardly.

For pure survival reasons, he prayed the remainder of the evening would go a whole lot smoother than the beginning.

"This is Allison, Martin's daughter," he said. "The one I told you about."

That little comment received a lift of Allison's perfectly arched brows before she was yanked into an exuberant hug by Gladys.

"Well, aren't you just a beauty," Gladys said. "Figured so, with your daddy being such a looker."

After pleasantries—or in this case, oddities— were exchanged, he and Allison followed the two golden girls inside the cozy little bungalow. They were ushered into the dining room, where a spread of cookies and cupcakes was laid out on the table. Apparently, the ladies had spent a lot of time baking that afternoon.

Although Jesse appreciated their caloric efforts, his main goal was for Arlene and Gladys to convince Allison that it would be to her benefit to believe, or at least consider, the fact that true love existed and relationships were meant to last. And that marriage was not an evil plan to strike terror in the hearts of those who chose to participate in the tradition.

"Have a seat, handsome." Gladys pulled out the chair next to hers.

Arlene had other ideas. "He's sitting by me."

To his surprise and delight, Allison jumped in and saved the day by plunking down in a seat across the table and patting the chair next to hers. "I apologize, ladies. Jesse promised to be my"— she flashed them a wink—"*escort* for the evening. I hope you don't mind."

"Oh, that's fine," Gladys said with a wave of her hand. "He's probably too young for either of us anyway."

Probably?

"Speak for yourself." Arlene folded her arms.

Ignoring her friend's pout, Gladys poured sweet tea with a clink of ice into tall glasses, then passed around the cupcake-and-cookie platters. Jesse, who hadn't eaten since breakfast, helped himself to probably more than was polite. Allison went the well-mannered course and only took one slightly overdone sugar cookie.

"So, Allison . . ." Gladys, the queen of mincing no words, jumped right into the matter at hand. "Jesse here tells us that you've got a bit of a problem with your father's getting married to Jana."

Allison speared him with a glare.

He shoved a cookie in his mouth to stay out of trouble.

"I think what he meant to say," Allison tried to politely explain, "was I have a problem with marriage overall. Statistics show—"

"Statistics?" Arlene gulped down a good amount of sweet tea, then returned the glass to the table with a thunk. "Horse pucky."

Jesse glanced across the table at Gladys and noted a peculiar pink to her cheeks. If he didn't know better, he'd think the two spry seniors had tipped the bottle a little earlier in the day.

"Harold—bless his heart—and I were married for more than forty-nine and a half years before he passed," Gladys said. "Missed our fiftieth anniversary by just two months."

"And Arnie and I were married for fifty-three years before he passed," Arlene said. "I was a child bride." She batted her eyelashes at Jesse.

Allison managed to keep her smirk at a minimum as she asked, "So how did you two manage to stay together for so long? What's the secret?"

"Oh, there's no secret." Arlene pushed the cookie

platter in Jesse's direction. "Have another cookie, handsome. We need to keep your energy up."

He didn't want to know for what. "I'm good. Thanks."

"You just need to be patient," Gladys explained. "Understanding. If you know going in that the man is going to walk around in his skivvies, make gross body noises, and growl every time the mortgage is due, you know what to expect. Then it's not a surprise, and you figure a way to work around it."

Gladys then leaned in closer. "Like once in a while, you just need to take a little sip from that bottle of cooking sherry."

Okay. *Not* the conversation Jesse had intended Allison to hear.

"Good sex," Arlene blurted out. "*That's* the secret. Otherwise, you got nothing. For every dirty pair of overalls I washed, Arnie knew he had to take care of me. If you know what I mean." Arlene winked at Jesse. "And I'm sure *you* do."

"Ladies!" Sweat dampened Jesse's forehead. "How about we get back to all those special things that made your relationships last for fifty years? You and your husbands surely loved each other and were close."

"Close?" Gladys glanced away. "Not really."

"Arnie and I were close when it counted." Arlene winked again. "If you know what I mean."

"Is sex all you ever think about?" Gladys huffed.

"What else is there?" Arlene took another slug of her sweet tea and coughed.

Jesse picked up his own untouched glass and sniffed. Yep. Spiked.

"You never complained," Arlene said, "but I'm guessing old Harold was a dud in the hay."

"Pfft." Gladys waved a hand. "He spent more time out on the range than he ever did with me. Always complained he was"—she made air quotes—"too tired. Isn't that supposed to be the woman's line?"

"You got to take care of yourself, Gladys. They got that *special* section in the back of the lingerie boutique." Arlene winked at Jesse again. "You know which one I'm talking about."

Okay, this conversation was going to hell on a racehorse.

Jesse glanced at Allison, who, guessing by the smile playing on her lips, was highly entertained. She even threw him a look that had *Seriously?* written all over it.

"Well, ladies." Jesse scooted his chair back and stood. "I apologize, but we've got to get going. I promised Allison I'd take her to dinner."

"Oh?" Gladys looked surprised.

"What's your hurry, handsome?" Arlene pushed his glass of sweet tea closer. "You didn't finish your drink."

He had a feeling that if he had even a few sips of whatever was in that glass, he'd be pounding back a hangover come morning.

"And it's just a darned shame we won't be able to stay," he said. "I know Allison really looked forward to just sitting back sipping and talking tonight. Weren't you?"

Luckily, she picked up on his *please rescue me* tone.

"Absolutely." She lifted her glass. Sipped. Then coughed so hard he had to whack her on the back, so she didn't choke to death.

She looked up at him with tears of laughter in her eyes. He reached down, took her arm, and helped her from the chair.

"We're meeting some friends at Sweet Pickens for dinner," he lied.

Allison looked up. "We are?"

He tossed her a look that begged her to go along.

"Oh." She rolled her eyes. "I forgot. Yes. Unfortunately, we really do need to get going."

"Well that's just too darned bad." Arlene looked truly disappointed, and, for a flash, Jesse felt guilty for lying. But then she ran her hand down his forearm and squeezed. "You come back anytime."

"We will." When the rivers in hell flowed with ice water.

"You don't be so hard on Jana, now," Gladys said to Allison. "She's a special woman."

"I understand." Allison gave them a compassionate smile. "It's not my intention to make anything personal."

"Well, that's your problem, honey." Gladys guffawed. "Everything's personal. Especially here in Sweet."

Jesse figured he should probably explain to Allison how things worked around there. But right now, all he wanted was to be gone.

With abbreviated good-byes, they finally climbed back up in his truck. He glanced at the clock. What had felt like a several-hour visit had actually only lasted a half hour.

Allison's chuckle turned into giggles. "Well that was fun."

"Fun?" He looked up from turning the key in the ignition. "That couldn't have been any more bizarre than if we'd dropped through the rabbit hole and discovered Alice brushing the Cheshire Cat's teeth."

"Maybe. But I'm sure if you're ever lonely and looking for a hot date, Arlene would be happy to help you out."

"Holy hell."

She giggled again. "I have to say, I do appreciate your efforts to educate me."

"Who knew? Between the two of them, they have a century of long-lasting relationships under their aprons. I figured they'd be the experts."

"Awww." She reached out and touched his arm. "Don't feel too bad. What they lacked in actual information, they gained scores in the entertainment value."

"Yeah, because *that* was entertaining as hell." He pulled the truck out onto the road. "When it wasn't scary as shit."

She laughed again, and he realized how good the sound felt washing over him. Then she glanced at her watch. "It's still early, and you promised me dinner."

"I didn't exactly *promise* you dinner. I was just using that as an excuse to get the hell out of there."

"'Too bad." Her smoky gaze slid over him. "I expect you to make good."

He allowed his gaze to roam her in the same way. "Oh, I'll make good all right." He turned the truck onto Main Street. "You up for a real taste of Sweet?"

"More barbecue?"

"Nope. I'm going to drop you right in the hub of all the activity and gossip within thirty miles. And you better be serious about having an appetite because where we're going they don't serve pansy-ass nouveau cuisine."

$\mathcal{S}$everal minutes later they pulled into a gravel parking lot next to a yellow concrete box of a restaurant with a big red neon sign that flashed BUD's NOTHING FINER DINER. Allison remembered this as the place Jesse had suggested served up the best breakfast in town. Apparently, dinner was recommended too.

The air surrounding the diner was scented with charbroiled burgers, crispy onion rings, and hot apple pie. Her stomach growled. Good thing she only planned to be in Sweet for a few days. Otherwise, she could easily pack on unwanted pounds with all the big heavy meals that were served.

As Jesse again opened her door, she looked around and had to admit that Sweet was a charming little town with ancient buildings, some of which had recently been renovated. And, thinking of Gladys and Arlene, she could see that it obviously had no lack of characters.

She glanced at the man who held out his hand to help her down from his ginormous truck.

No lack of hot men either.

Inside Bud's Diner, she discovered a lively place with old-time vinyl booths and big round tables in the center for easy conversations. The décor was all Texas all the time. Red, white, and blue stars and American flags highlighted the yellow walls. And while Allison knew she should be at her father's house working on her next blog, she decided to just appreciate all that Sweet had to offer.

Including the man beside her.

They grabbed a booth near the door and just as they sat down, a blond ponytailed waitress passed by. Her tray was piled high with double-decker burgers dripping with cheese, crispy golden onion rings stacked on a wooden dowel, and frosty milk shakes in old-fashioned glasses.

"Wow," she said in awe. "I want *that*."

"A Diablo burger?" He laughed. "Where would you put it?"

"I don't know, but I'll find room." Determined, she waited until the waitress came up to their table to place her order. But when the attractive young woman with the swinging ponytail showed up, she held a tray piled high with plates of chicken fried steak and thick country gravy. Allison promptly changed her mind.

"Hey, Jesse." Allison watched as the two exchanged brief small talk. Then, before Jesse could make the introductions, their waitress turned to her with a big grin.

"Hi. I'm Paige Marshall. Old family friend. I've got to deliver this order real quick, then I'll be back to take yours." She set a retro plastic menu in front of Allison but left Jesse's paper place mat empty.

"Doesn't *he* need one?"

Paige grinned. "*He* can probably recite the menu better than he ever could any of his school work."

"Or his little black book?" Allison asked.

"That too. Which I'm sure would break a lot of hearts that think they're the *only one.*"

"Hmmm." Allison picked up her menu and, tempted to order one of everything, did a quick scan.

"Hmmm?" Jesse took a drink of the ice water Paige had left behind. "What's hidden behind that little sound?"

Allison lowered her menu and looked at him. "Just wondering why a guy like you, who has a little black book he knows by heart, insists on proving to me that commitment and relationships can make it for the long haul."

Those broad shoulders lifted as he took another sip of water. "It's what I do."

She leaned in. "Exactly what is *it* that you do?"

"Take care of people."

"Meaning?"

"It would take far longer to explain than would hold your interest. And far be it from me to blow your whole idea of who I really am."

"So I'm wrong that you're very happy playing the field?"

"No."

"Or that you've slept your way from A to Z in that little black book?"

The smile he gave her sent a marching army of zips and zingles through her highly alert nervous system. A smile that told her he was trouble. Not because he was trying to make any kind of move but because she knew there was a lot more going on behind that gorgeous face and killer body. She had a feeling he was a man of a lot more substance than he'd ever let on.

Why?

Hard to say.

But wasn't it going to be interesting to find out.

"Apparently you're pleading the Fifth," she said.

"No one ever said women had sole ownership on being mysterious."

"You may be right."

"There's no maybe about it." He leaned in. "So tell me more about yourself."

"Oh, I'm not really all that fascinating."

"Why don't you let me be the judge of that? How about you start off telling me more about your event-planning business. Is it something you always wanted to do?"

"Truth? Not really. But I like helping people. And I like seeing them happy. So I guess my profession captures all of that."

He leaned back in the booth. "So what else is it you'd rather do?"

"Aside from being a character at Disneyland and eating cotton candy every day?"

An easy smile curved his mouth.

"When I was younger, I wanted to be a counselor. I thought helping people deal with the issues in their lives would be a gratifying and honest way to make a living."

"But?"

"But then I realized I was too screwed up to help anyone else."

"Looks like you turned out pretty okay to me. Except for the whole not believing in happily ever after thing."

His assessment moved her, but he was way off base. And she certainly didn't want to openly give him any ammunition.

"I've probably just become really good at hiding my crazy."

Before he could respond, Paige returned and took their orders. There were too many delicious choices, so Allison closed her eyes and dropped her finger to the menu. Her selection ended up a blue cheese burger—hold the grilled onions, with sweet potato fries and deep fried pickles. She added a toasted marshmallow milk shake, then smiled as Jesse's eyes widened.

The order would be an intestinal nightmare, and she didn't care. For the brief time she was in Sweet, she planned to forget that she usually stuck to a dull plate of grilled chicken and vegetables. And maybe she could even forget that the men she'd most recently selected to date had been predictable and generally non–*zingle* worthy.

Maybe it was time for a change.

Even if it was only for a brief time.

After Jesse placed his order for a mushroom cheeseburger, and Paige left the table with their orders, he leaned back and smiled. "I'm impressed."

"What, that I didn't order a salad?"

"Yeah."

"Unlike you, Mr. Mysterious, I don't have anything to hide."

"So says the girl who sent me to find her *purse* so she could disappear into the night."

"That was different."

"How so?"

"We're talking hamburgers versus the fact that you could have been dangerous."

"Who says I'm not?"

Certainly not her heart.

"Yeah, well, now I know who you are, and I'll tell your mother on you."

"You're an interesting woman, Allison Lane."

And you're a hot guy I want to put my hands all over.

"I'll tell my clients you said that," she said. "It will be good for business."

After Jesse's brief interrogation of the current list of events her business was working on, their food arrived, and she wondered what she'd gotten herself into. The plate overflowed with sweet potato fries, and the burger literally dripped with bleu cheese. Before she could get too deep into thoughts of plop-plop-fizz-fizz, she dipped a fried pickle in ranch dressing and bit into it. While she expected tartness, the taste was smooth and flavorful.

"You like?" Jesse asked.

She nodded. "I love."

"Welcome to the South, where if it isn't deep fried, it doesn't hit the plate."

"That's an exaggeration."

"I can prove it's not in just one day."

"How's that?"

"State fair. In just one food row, you can get chicken fried bacon, fried meat loaf, fried pecan pie, fried butter, and even a deep-fried margarita."

"How do they fry *that*?"

"It's magic."

"And deep-fried butter?"

He grinned. "Don't knock it till you've tried it."

"Not knocking it. Afraid I might fall in love with it."

"So you do believe in love."

"Of the crispy kind. If it's high-volume cholesterol, I'm your girl. Otherwise . . . She lifted her shoulders. "Eh."

He pointed at her with a fry. "I'm going to change your mind about that."

How could she explain it wasn't that she *didn't* believe but that she was *afraid* to?

For a few moments, they ate in silence. Mostly because she was too enthralled with the tasty meal. But that didn't last long.

Jesse licked the tips of his fingers. "When do you go back to Seattle?"

She tried to ignore the little kick low to her belly as she watched his tongue dart out and capture the juice from his burger.

"Day after tomorrow. My plane leaves at 10 A.M."

"Short visit."

"We're heading into our busiest time of the year. Danielle would kill me if I were gone longer. She's got two little girls who keep her busy plus a husband who often works odd hours."

"Which means he can't always watch the kids?"

She took a small bite of burger. "He might be an undercover detective, but he's also a great dad and husband. But criminals don't work on a regular time clock."

"So your sister has a good relationship with her husband?"

She shook her head. "I can see where this conversation is headed."

"Just a simple question."

"Nothing is simple about you," she said, and meant it.

"So . . . your sister has a good marriage?"

"My sister has a perfect marriage," she admitted. "In fact, they're my one hope that what you're trying to prove to me is real."

He smiled, picked up his messy burger, and took a bite. "Good to know."

"Just because Dani and Andrew might beat the odds, I have to warn you not to get your hopes up that I'll change my mind."

"So beautiful and yet so cynical."

She popped another fried pickle in her mouth, assuming a casual demeanor even though his words stung. "So handsome and yet so delusional."

Jesse Wilder smiled a lot. He didn't disappoint when those sensuously masculine lips curled again and added to the desire in her belly. His words sparked another round of curiosity.

"We'll see."

Too bad she'd only be in Sweet another twenty-fourish hours because she really wouldn't mind finding out exactly what "We'll see" meant.

Chapter 6

In a perfect world, dogs wouldn't have noses that were smashed into their faces and made it hard for them to breathe.

In Jesse's world, he had the never-ending task of explaining to their owners that pinched nostrils was a common problem with pugs and a few other breeds and that surgery was available to correct the problem. At a cost. To which their owners, like Mrs. Trambley, who was on a fixed income and currently sat across the desk from him, wept into their embroidered handkerchiefs because they couldn't afford the procedure for poor little Prissy. Or Petey. Or Princess.

Jesse knew he'd perform the intricate procedure, and Mrs. Trambley would take Prissy and her new snout home without paying a cent because *he* couldn't say no.

Especially today, when his mind was not on his work where it was supposed to be and instead was completely focused on a woman who was about to get on a plane and fly away.

Oh sure, he'd see her again.

Most likely at their parents' wedding, where she'd stand in the background frowning because she didn't believe the marriage would last.

No doubt he'd had his moments of negative thoughts too. But mostly those had been when his feet were planted in foreign soil and he'd been fighting a war where so many young lives were lost. His brother's included.

Big difference.

Bringing himself back around to the current issue of the day he helped Mrs. Trambley from her chair. "I don't want you to worry. You make an appointment at the front desk with Abby, and I'll make sure Prissy gets her new nose."

The elderly woman looked up at him with tears misting in her faded hazel eyes. "But I can't—"

He patted her wrinkled hands where she clutched her beloved dog to her chest. "It won't cost you a thing."

"Oh, Dr. Wilder." She reached up and patted his cheek. "I don't care what they say about you. I just think you're wonderful."

He knew what they said about him, and he didn't care, as long as nice people like Mrs. Trambley could go home a little happier. He escorted her to the front desk, where Abby wasn't at all surprised that he'd be doing the procedure for free. Once the reception area was clear of pets and their owners, he leaned into the reception desk and picked up the appointment calendar.

"You're going to go broke giving away everything," Abby said with a shake of her head.

"According to the entire town, I give it all away anyhow, so no big deal."

She turned in her chair and crossed her arms. "When are you going to squash the rumor that you are not the manwhore everyone thinks you are?"

"One of these days."

Abby leaked out a sigh. "Well, make it happen before Izzy gets older and has to explain to her friends about her uncle's *wild side*."

He lowered the calendar and looked at his future sister-in-law and future stepmom to his adorable niece. "I never thought about Izzy's having to deal with that."

"Apparently." Abby chuckled. "Because the look of shock on your face is priceless."

He hesitated to respond because, honestly, he'd never thought of what his overblown reputation might mean to the younger set in his family. He didn't necessarily care what his brothers thought, and his mom understood it was all BS.

Maybe.

He'd had a few serious relationships. One fairly recent though it seemed everyone except him had forgotten about that.

"Don't worry," Abby said with a patronizing pat on his back as she stood and stuffed Prissy's folder into the file cabinet. "I'm sure before that time comes, you'll have settled down and changed everyone's mind."

"Do I look like the *settling down* type to you?"

She pushed in the file drawer, turned, and gave

him a good hard look. "Yes. Not only do you *look* like the type, you *are* the type. All you Wilder boys think you have the market cornered on the whole badass-bachelor thing. And you can keep on thinking that . . . up until the moment the right woman walks into your life." She grinned. "I can say that because *I'm* the right woman for Jackson."

"Took him damn long enough to figure that out."

"Exactly." She pointed at him. "Reno's got Charli. Jackson has me. You're next."

He let go a cynical laugh. Not only was he *not* next, he wasn't even in line.

Unbidden, an image of Allison sitting across from him at Bud's last night popped into his head, and something funny happened in the center of his chest. At this moment, he didn't understand why he had the strongest desire to go to her father's house and stop her from driving to San Antonio and getting on that plane. And because she *was* leaving, he realized he didn't have the time to figure it out.

For some odd reason, that didn't settle well.

Ignoring the urge to further examine his feelings and the determined look on Abby's face, he waved the appointment calendar. "Why are the next three hours blocked out?"

"Because you and the boys have to go be fitted for tuxes. In case you forgot, Reno and Charli's wedding is coming up fast, and *you* are the best man."

"I haven't forgotten that. Just about the tuxes."

"Hmmm. Mind elsewhere?"

"What's that supposed to mean?" Dumb question. The smirk on her face said it all. God, she was worse than his brothers with the meddling business.

"Nothing." She glanced toward the door. "I think *they* can pick up where I left off."

He looked up just as the door opened and in walked Reno, Jackson, and Jake, slapping each other on the backs and laughing like they'd just shared the funniest joke. He had to admit they were a good-looking bunch, even as a pang hit him right in the heart.

Reno was about to be married, and one of the brothers would miss the ceremony. As would their father.

Jesse had to take a deep breath to clear the overwhelming sense of loss from his chest.

"You ready to go?" Reno asked him, while Jackson went around the desk and stole a kiss from his girl.

"Yeah," Jesse answered. "Why do you look so nervous? Second thoughts?"

"Hardly. I was about to ask you the same thing."

"What would I be having second thoughts about?"

"He meant . . ." Jake planted his feet and folded his arms, looking every bit the badass Marine. "Why the hell do *you* look so nervous?"

Behind him, Jesse heard a snicker and couldn't tell if it came from Abby, Jackson, or both. He didn't turn to look. "Because I'm about to get in a truck with a bunch of jackasses where I'll be stuck listening to you yammer on about nothing the whole ride to San Antonio."

"Uh-huh." Reno flashed his dimples. "Wouldn't

have anything to do with a certain brunette who's about to get on a plane and fly out of here, would it?"

Jesse tossed the scheduling calendar on the desk. "Don't know what you're talking about."

"Ooooh," Jackson hooted. "Paddling upstream on the River of Denial."

With a toss of his white jacket on the peg near the desk, Jesse turned and headed for the door. "Y'all coming?"

"Nope." Jake grinned. "Just breathing hard."

"Jesus." Jesse pushed open the door and headed out to the parking lot. His brothers followed, hooting laughter like drunken sailors. It was going to be a long haul to San Antonio. Because as much as he wanted to deny, deny, deny, there was something sweeter about Allison Lane than she was ready to reveal.

And damned if it didn't just pique his curiosity.

Allison shoved her laptop, which contained a new blog post about the possibility of failing to find *the one* because you might live in different regions, into her carry-on bag and closed the zipper. Wee Man leaped off the bed and did a little dance on his hind legs when her dad popped his head into the guest room.

"You about ready?" he asked.

"Yeah." She hiked the bag over her shoulder and looked up. His gloomy expression nearly buckled her knees. "Are you okay?"

"I'm gonna miss you, little girl."

Her heart crumpled at the endearment he'd

always called her, not because she was the youngest or the shortest, but because he always said no matter if she was 102, she'd still be his little girl. She dropped the bag on the bed and went to him. When she curled her arms around his waist and laid her head on his chest, she heard his heart thump a little out of time.

"I'll be back soon," she promised.

"Won't be the same as having you here every day." He leaned back, looked at her, and smiled. "I like your face."

She chuckled. "I like your face too."

"I wish I could talk you and your sister into moving here. But I know that could never happen." He embraced her again. A teensy bit tighter this time. "I want you to know how proud of you I am. Of both of you. As screwed up as we both are, I don't know how your mother and I ever made such spectacular children."

"Daddy, don't say that. You're as normal as they come." She leaned back and looked up into a face full of character that never failed to break into a smile as soon as he'd see her. "Mom, on the other hand . . ."

A chuckle rumbled in his chest. "Yes, they certainly broke the mold with her."

"Thank God." Allison had always tried to love her difficult, frenetic, and flighty mother. Most times it wasn't easy. Especially when her mother insisted, "You're just like me, Allie. You just don't have settling down in your DNA. Life should be a carnival of delicious treats, not a forced slab of the same humdrum meat loaf every day."

Her mother had said it enough times that Allison feared it might be true. She'd spent too many years beneath the tutelage of the woman whose narcissism couldn't help but seep into Allison's head. As a result, she tired of things—and people—quickly. She'd never kept a boyfriend longer than six months. Once they were ready to move in, she moved on. While her dad had always told her she could do anything and be anything, her mother tried to convince her that a new pair of shoes would keep her happy longer than any man.

Unfortunately, Allison had quite a shoe fetish.

She still wondered how her father had managed to stick it out for so long. Since the day her parents divorced, he'd been alone. But maybe that was nothing new. Even if her mother had been in the same room, it was like she wasn't there. She was a shell of a woman too wrapped up in glamour magazines to pay attention to what was going on in the real world.

Or the people who were right under her nose.

When Allison and Danielle became heavily involved in the event-planning business, she often went too long without seeing her dad, and she'd been eaten up with guilt. Though she hadn't quite gotten all her questions regarding Jana Wilder resolved, she would be as selfish as her mother if she didn't want him to be happy.

"Well." Her dad grabbed her bag up off the bed, turned, and gave her a wistful smile. "We'd best get going, so you don't miss that plane."

Emotion clogged her throat, and she simply nodded.

"Daddy?" On the way out the door, she touched his sleeve, and he stopped. "If you ever need me. For anything. And I truly mean *anything*. You call me, and I'll be on the next flight. Okay?"

He lifted his hand to her cheek and gave it an affectionate stroke. "How about if I just want to see your face?"

"Perfect."

$\mathcal{S}$omething was wrong.

When Allison, her dad, and Wee Man walked past a yellow ribbon wearing Miss Giddy on Jana's back veranda to say good-bye, Allison immediately sensed the gloom.

As soon as they entered the kitchen, they found Jana and Charli at the table with their heads in their hands, staring into cups of coffee Allison imagined had grown cold.

"Is everything okay?" she asked.

Both women looked up.

"Oh, nothing a little miracle won't fix." Jana popped up from her chair and went into Southern hospitality mode. "Coffee and biscuits before you head to the airport?"

"No thanks." Allison sat down beside Charli, noting the sheer panic in her brown eyes. "Anything I can do?"

"The wedding is in two weeks," Charli said. "I've heard something crazy always happens to put a wrench in the works. We just got pile-driven with *three* servings of crazy."

"Believe me, that's not a record," Allison said,

while Jana and her father murmured over by the coffeepot.

"Seriously?" Charli's eyes widened.

Allison nodded. "So what's going on?"

Charli held up her hand and began counting the events off with her fingers. "The local florist had a family tragedy and had to close down the shop until further notice. The reception venue had a water pipe burst, and the place was flooded. And the deejay we hired for the reception was just arrested on robbery charges. Like he couldn't wait until *after* our wedding to get stupid?"

Though it wasn't a funny situation, Allison chuckled. "Those are easy fixes."

"Maybe not." Jana set a steaming cup of coffee down in front of her. "This is Sweet. And it's the busiest time for weddings because midsummer is too hot. Trying to find replacements for everything will be—"

"Impossible," Charli said, sounding very much like Eeyore.

After meeting Charli the other night and witnessing her lively spirit, Allison knew this reaction was completely the opposite of her normal can-do personality.

Charli shook her head. "I don't know what's wrong with me. I used to deal with crises like this on the show all the time. But this . . ."

"Is different." Allison understood. "Because this is *your* crisis."

"I just don't want Reno to be disappointed."

"Sugarplum"—Jana sat on Charli's other side and rubbed a hand over her back—"as long as he gets to marry you, he doesn't care when, where, or how."

A timid smile touched the corners of Charli's mouth.

Though the airline ticket was burning a hole in her purse, Allison didn't hesitate to swan dive into the situation. "I can help."

Jana gave her a look of surprise.

Charli gave her a look of hope.

Her father smiled.

"How?" Charli asked. "I mean, I know you're a wedding planner. But you're getting on a plane. And you live in Seattle. And I couldn't impose. And I know you're busy. And—"

"I can help." Confident she could do just that, Allison leaned back in her chair and looked at her father. "Daddy? Would you mind calling the airlines for me?"

"I'm on it," he said, and away he went.

Jana put on a fresh pot of coffee, and heads came together over that sunflower tablecloth. Hours, and a plate of cinnamon rolls later, Allison stood up, notes in hand, prepared to wage war on the events that threatened Charli and Reno's chance at happiness.

Before she made it to the back door, Jana grabbed her in a hug.

"Thank you, sugarplum," Jana whispered, then leaned back and looked at her with complete gratitude in her bright blue eyes. "I can't tell you how much this means to us. Reno and Charli—"

"Deserve the very best," Allison said. Her father had told her of Reno's tragic past of losing his former fiancée to a head-on collision a week before their wedding. And he'd told her of the incredible love story that brought Charli and Reno together.

Allison took a deep breath. Sometimes a girl just had to do what was right. Even if that girl had a million doubts. These two wonderful people deserved the opportunity to find their forever together. And she'd do her best to make damned sure it happened.

Halfway out the door, Jana stopped her again.

"I know you need to get that rental car back, and I'm sure you don't want your daddy chauffeuring you around. You need transportation." Jana grabbed a set of keys off a brass-rooster key holder near the door and handed them to Allison. "Use Jared's truck."

A chill slipped up Allison's back. If Jana had kept her son's truck after all this time, it must be sacred. "Oh. I don't . . . I wouldn't . . ."

"It's perfectly okay. Jared would be thrilled to have a beauty like you behind the wheel. We've pretty much kept everything as he left it, but feel free to toss it all in the backseat."

No way. As Allison tentatively took the keys in her hand, she knew she'd do everything she could not to move a thing.

"It's got a full gas tank," Jana said. "Jackson always refills it whenever he takes it out and runs it low."

"I can call the car agency and just extend the rental. It wouldn't be a problem."

"Don't be silly. The truck's just sitting there. You might as well make good use of it."

"Well . . . thank you."

"Come on." Her dad tilted his head toward the door. "I'll show you where it's parked. Jana and I can return the loaner for you, so you can get started on the wedding stuff."

Allison followed him, her wedge shoes wobbling in the gravel drive. When he pulled open the big doors to a huge old shed, she peered from the sunlight into the darkness. Her dad flipped on the light. Inside, there were a couple of old cars that looked to have been restored. A turquoise one with red interior in particular caught her eye, and she hummed her appreciation.

"That's Jared's pride and joy." Her dad pointed to a green truck.

Holy schnikeys.

Apparently, everything *was* bigger in Texas.

*H*ours later, Allison pulled the mammoth truck to the side of the road. With darkness stealing away daylight, she knew she'd accomplished a lot since leaving Jana Wilder's warm and cozy kitchen. However, *a lot* wasn't enough with Charli and Reno's wedding day looming.

As she sat parked beneath a particularly large oak, she glanced around the cab of the truck and studied the belongings of the forever-lost Jared Wilder.

Before she'd hung it over the seat back so Wee Man didn't use it as a bed, there had been a gray USMC T-shirt on the passenger side. Dog tags dangled from the rearview mirror. And to verify Jared had been a smoker, a crumpled pack of Marlboros sat wedged between the dashboard and windshield. Tucked up into the sun visor, she'd found a photograph of all the handsome Wilder boys, with Abby tucked in the middle. The first time she'd turned the engine over, she'd had to turn down the volume on the CD player blasting Waylon Jennings's "I've Always Been Crazy."

She might never have met Jared, but from the items left in his truck, she could get a hint of the kind of man who'd led the band of Wilder brothers.

Sadness tugged at her heart as she reached up and touched the swinging metal tags with his name and info engraved on them. For a moment, she studied his image in the photo.

Such a loss.

She thought of Jana Wilder and had a newfound respect. The woman really had been through a lot. She deserved to be happy, just as her dad did. Though there were still questions to be answered, Allison's initial reserve was beginning to melt away.

Heart a little heavier, she tucked the photo up into the visor and got back to business. She plugged her cell phone battery cord into the cigarette lighter and began to read the numerous texts from Danielle she'd conveniently ignored until now. The news wasn't good. Case in point—Audrey Shackelford changed the entire color scheme of her wedding a month before the big day, and little Tommy Morgan's parents filed for divorce two weeks before little Tommy's first birthday. Apparently, now the parents were fighting over who would have custody of Tommy on the big day. Everything was on hold pending a court decision.

Over the years, Allison had learned to roll with the punches being an event planner threw at you. Sometimes those punches left you with a stomachache.

While Wee Man settled his paws on the windowsill and snapped at each passing car as if he thought he could catch it, she tapped out a few text replies to her sister. Disasters momentarily averted, she put the truck in motion.

Last chore of the day?

Taking a look at her final prospect for the misplaced reception.

She'd hit up everywhere in a ten-mile radius, and none had seemed right. They'd either been too small, too tacky, or just too awful. With any luck, this last place to see would miraculously be the one.

Several miles later, she parked and walked up to a large yellow Victorian farmhouse with crisp white trim and an inviting wraparound porch that included a bench swing at one end and two white rocking chairs side by side at the other. An assortment of colorful pots filled with daisies, alyssum, and geraniums bordered the red front door. And the welcome mat at her feet said "Howdy." The entire place oozed charm.

As the sun dipped low in the sky, and Wee Man tap-danced at her side, she rang the doorbell, then stepped back to wait. While butterflies did aerial acrobatics in her stomach, she looked down to her dog. "You behave yourself in here, mister."

Wee Man looked up at her with his big brown eyes as if to say "I will." But she knew him, and he tended to be a little ADD. Any command she gave to him now would be instantly forgotten once the door opened up into a new Adventureland.

With no response, she stepped forward and rang the bell again. While she still had her finger on the little brass button, the door opened, and there stood Jesse Wilder.

Wet and nearly naked.

Her gaze took an indulgent tour of all those exposed muscles and tanned skin. The rest of him was covered by a pair of blue board shorts that hung low on his lean hips. A wings-of-freedom tribal tattoo decorated his left biceps and another tattoo on the inside of his right forearm read NO REGRETS. Water dripped from his untied hair down his long, lean body and onto the slate floor tiles.

Allison swallowed.

Jesse Wilder had the kind of physique a woman wanted to run her mouth and hands all over.

She curled her fingers into her palms for safekeeping, as a slow smile spread across his gorgeous face.

"Hello, darlin'. I wondered when you'd show up at my door."

She rolled her tongue back up into her mouth and, without waiting for an actual invite, strolled inside. The house was accented with lots of stone and wood. The rich leather furnishings were sparse but tasteful. Yet other than a *Tombstone* movie poster and at least a sixty-inch flat-screen TV, there wasn't much else to the decor. Aside from the very inviting layout, the house was definitely a man cave.

Wee Man trotted inside like he owned the place, and Jesse greeted him with a "Hey, buddy."

"You were last on my list," she said.

Jesse shut the door and grinned. "What do I need to do to be first?"

Her eyes took another trip down his body.

Not much.

"You can show me your facilities," she managed to say without tripping over her tongue.

"I have to show you around before I can climb on top?"

Oh, and didn't that just create images in her head. "I need to see if what you have will fit the need."

"Darlin', if you have to do an inspection first, I'm doing it all wrong."

When laughter threatened, she pressed her lips together. "I know your mother called you and told you about the crisis. So I'm here to see if your *home* will accommodate the wedding reception of the brother you obviously love so much." Not that she needed to add that last part for emphasis. Jesse was the type of man who'd always try to do the right thing, even if sometimes he was a bit misguided.

"How many people are we talking about?" he asked.

"A hundred. Very doable."

The steamy look he gave her took *doable* in another direction.

"How about you come through and take a look," he said. "I don't have a clue about parties or how many people a place will hold."

"Really?" She followed him into the large home, watching his big, wet, bare feet leave prints on the floor. "I figured you'd be hosting all kinds of skinny-dipping extravaganzas for your lady friends."

"Ah. So who's been telling tales this time?"

"Tales? You mean you don't have a weekly bare-naked bash?"

"Hardly. I don't do half the things people say I do. But don't tell anybody. I wouldn't want to burst their bubble."

Though it was really none of her business, she wondered how that could be true. From the moment she'd arrived in Sweet, he'd played the part of a playboy. He looked the part. With her own eyes, she'd seen women's reactions to him. Heck, she'd experienced her own. And now she was supposed to believe he wasn't guilty as charged? That was quite a stretch.

Intrigued, she followed him through a huge dining area with an extended table and a chef's kitchen. Allison had to admit she'd always longed for a kitchen like his, with granite countertops and stainless appliances and an island where friends could gather around while she made a meal. She loved to cook, and Jesse's kitchen was a dream compared to her own dinky condo kitchen, where she barely had room to turn around.

A wall of glass including a set of glass doors

extended out to the back, where Jesse waved her through. When she stepped outside to the enormous stone patio, her jaw dropped.

The backyard stole her breath. Rolling green hills dotted with live oak were the backdrop for an expansive lawn. The rest of the yard was a masterful blend of a pool and spa with natural stonework and a rock waterfall. The outdoor kitchen and patio provided a comfortable gathering place for family and friends. There were plenty of trees for shade, and now at dusk, small white lights twinkled amongst their branches.

No need for wondering if this place would work for a wedding reception. It was perfect.

Allison was knocked over.

Literally.

When she looked around, she was ass on the ground looking up into the big slobbery face of a happily panting black Lab with a neon yellow tennis ball crunched between his teeth.

"Dinks!" Jesse sent a scolding look to the Lab, whose tail hadn't quit wagging.

Allison brushed off her hands and accepted Jesse's help getting up. "Your dog's name is *Dinks*?" she asked, when he pulled her upright, and they were almost chest to breast.

"That's right. And he's a *bad boy*," he said in a scorching tone that had the dog sitting back on his hindquarters. "And that"—he pointed to a fluffy striped cat hissing at Wee Man from a countertop—"is Rango."

"How can you make fun of Wee Man if your dog's name is *Dinks*?"

"Because I didn't name him. Or Rango. They were dropped off at the clinic long before Abby got her pet-rescue center going."

"Someone just abandoned them?"

"Happens all the time," Jesse said, as Dinks suddenly discovered Wee Man, and the two took off in a barking race across the lawn.

"That's horrible."

"I agree. But now Abby's center is helping to find forever homes for them."

"Well, I like her even more now."

"She's easy to like. Always has been."

"You've known her a long time?"

"Hell, she's been around since she and Jackson were in kindergarten."

"Wow. That's longer than most marriages last."

"Uh-huh. Mom said you were coming by to take a look at the place to see if it'd work for the reception." He gestured at the yard. "Go ahead. If you need anything, just call me."

"And where will you be?" she asked.

"Right over there on the lounger under the pergola with a cold beer in my hand."

"It's almost dark."

"Best time to lie out and relax after a hard day at work. No scorching sun. Bugs aren't out yet." He gave her a look that piqued her curiosity. "Care to join me? There's plenty of room for both of us."

"No thanks." A refusal she might very well regret the rest of her life. "I've got a job to do."

"Do you mind if I ask what made you change your mind to stay and help out with the wedding? I mean, you being all anti–wedded bliss and all."

"I'm not against people being happy. I just don't believe getting married has anything to do with making that happen."

"Sure it does. I see happy married people all the time." He walked to the pergola, flopped down on the lounger, and tucked his hands behind his head.

"That's not exactly the same thing."

"Depends on your perspective. Maybe now that you're going to be here a while longer, I can prove you wrong."

She stepped closer, giving herself a better look at that long, muscular body and those tight, rippling abs. "Maybe you should take your own advice and spend your time finding a woman to settle down with instead of wasting your time taking me on some kind of wild-goose chase."

"No can do, darlin'."

"Why?" She folded her arms and settled her weight on one hip. "To me it sounds like *you're* the one opposed to marriage."

"It's not that I'm against it," he argued. "It's just not right for me."

"What makes you think that?" she asked.

"Got my reasons. How about you?"

How many reasons did she really need to count out for him? "I just don't have the right DNA for it."

Brows pulled tight, he lifted his gorgeous head off the lounger. "Says who?"

"Says me."

"You know what I think?"

She looked up and down that phenomenal physique, and the last thing on her mind was what was on his. "I'm afraid to ask."

"Ha!" He pointed at her. "Key word."

"I didn't bring my supersecret decoder ring. So maybe you can help me out here and explain what the hell you're talking about."

"I think it's not that you don't believe." He leaned up on one elbow. "I think you're just afraid."

How was it that someone who barely knew her could get a read on her and be so on target?

Fearful of revealing too much, she honestly didn't know what to say. Silence drifted between them for an uncomfortable beat. When she finally found her voice, it came with a complete deterrent to their discussion. "I guess I should get back to business."

"Okay." Looking as relaxed as a man could get, he raised the bottle of ale to his lips.

"Okay?" She'd expected some kind of cocky comeback. "That's it?"

"Sure. You go ahead and take a look around to see if the place works for the reception. And I'll pick you up at seven tomorrow night."

"For what?"

A smile tipped his sexy mouth. "If I gave away all my secrets, it wouldn't be any fun, would it?"

Chapter 7

The following evening, Jesse let his truck idle in front of Martin Lane's house to keep the air conditioner going. The temperature had hit an unseasonable ninety-five degrees that day, and the last thing he wanted was for Allison to be hot and sweaty.

Well, at least without a little sexual recreation and him being involved in the cause.

A minute later, she opened the front door wearing tight jeans, a flirty little top, and the high heels she obviously felt she needed to make herself taller. He liked her height. He thought back to when they'd danced at Seven Devils. She'd fit nicely in his arms. All their important parts lined up perfectly. It was at that point he reminded himself that he was not here to pick her up for a date.

This was business.

Only business.

"You said dress casual," she said, quickly pulling the front door closed so her little dog didn't escape. "I hope this is all right."

If he'd been held at gunpoint, he could not have stopped his eyes from taking a luxury cruise down and back up her body. God. The woman would look good wearing a sack. "Looks great."

As they walked toward his truck, he had to resist taking her hand. When they reached the truck, he used the excuse that she needed help up into the vehicle and took her hand anyway. When he leaned across her warm body, inhaled her sweet scent, and latched her seat belt, he told himself it was all about safety. When her smooth eyebrows lifted, silently telling him she could have managed such a menial task on her own, he denied the attraction that tightened every muscle in his body and then some.

Not a date.

Not a date.

Not a date.

With regret, he reminded himself that at the end of the night, there would be no hot and heavy. No down and dirty. No doing the wild thing.

For his mother's happiness, this was just business.

He went around the front of the truck and got in. "All set?"

She looked over at him. Amusement brightened her eyes. "Whatever you've got going on . . . bring it."

He laughed. "Sounds like you're up for an adventure."

"Well, your last attempt was highly entertaining. So why deprive myself of a little levity?"

"At my expense."

She smiled. "Of course."

There were two things Jesse knew about himself to be true—he never kept a lady waiting, and he never left her hanging.

But tonight wouldn't be about laughter. Tonight he intended to show her the serious, heartfelt side of a relationship that kept couples together until death did them part.

Unfortunately for some, death came way too soon.

"*I*nteresting." Allison peered through the windshield at the Yellow Rose Cinema.

Jesse smiled.

He helped her down from the truck even knowing she'd been jumping in and out of Jared's even taller Chevy for two days. Just because they weren't on a date, there was no reason to stop being a gentleman.

Or, obviously, deny himself the opportunity to touch her as often as possible.

"We're going to the movies?" she asked, tucking a wavy lock of hair behind her ear. Her silver hoop earrings flashed in the fading sun as he placed his hand at the small of her back and guided her toward the theater entrance.

"Good guess."

"But it's closed."

"Says who?"

"The sign right there." She pointed. "It says CLOSED MONDAYS, TUESDAYS, WEDNESDAYS. Today is Tuesday so—"

"No worries. I've got an *in*."

"I don't think breaking and entering is your thing." She reached up and tugged his ponytail. "You might catch your pony on the broken glass."

"You got a comeback for everything?"

"I try my best."

Laughter tickled his chest as he opened the glass door to the theater. "Then I like your style."

As soon as the door opened, Gertrude Donovan, owner of the Yellow Rose for the past three decades, came toward them in her famous old-time usher uniform, red cap and all.

"Welcome, moviegoers." Mrs. Donovan clapped her hands. "Welcome."

Jesse caught Allison's enthusiastic smile from the corner of his eye. Yep. It was going to be an interesting night.

"Mrs. Donovan, this is Martin Lane's daughter, Allison."

"Indeed." Mrs. Donovan pursed her wrinkled lips, then took one of Allison's hands in her own and gave it a motherly pat. "Don't you go worrying your pretty little head. We'll get you fixed right up."

"I'm sorry?" Allison's head tilted and a ribbon of carefully tucked satiny hair fell out of place.

"Oh, now." Mrs. Donovan chuckled. "There's nothing to be sorry about. Like I said, we'll get you fixed right up. How about you two hit the concession stand. Grab anything you want. I just made a fresh batch of popcorn, and the butter dispenser's full."

With that, Mrs. Donovan wandered off toward the stairs that led to the projection room. Jesse knew this not only because he'd worked there for a summer but because he might have taken a young lady or two up there to impress her with his filmography skills. Or romance skills, whichever came first.

Allison looked at him with raised eyebrows. "What's she going to fix me up with?"

"She's on board with the whole true-love-matrimonial-denial thing you've got going on."

"So she's going to *fix* my way of thinking?"

"Exactly."

"Well this just gets more interesting by the minute."

They headed toward the concession stand and the glass case that displayed every kind of candy imaginable.

"Pick your poison," he said.

"Seriously?" Her dark eyes widened as they traveled over the sugar surplus.

"If you don't have a stomachache by the end of the movie, I'll feel as if I've failed."

She laughed. "So we're really going to do this? We're going to watch a movie in a theater that's closed because you batted those incredibly long, dark eyelashes at some nice old lady?"

"We're really going to do this because I used to work for that nice old lady who busted my can every Saturday afternoon by making me sweep up popcorn kernels and mop the sticky stuff up off the floor."

"Eeew."

"You have no idea." He leaned his hip against the glass counter. "So you like my eyelashes?" He batted them comically.

" 'Jealous' would be a better word."

"Guess I'll have to use them to my advantage more often." He pointed to the glass case. "I'm a Milk Duds, Junior Mints, Sugar Babies kind of guy. What kind of girl are you?" Besides knock-out gorgeous and incredibly cynical, he thought.

"I've been known to down a box of Milk Duds or a package of Red Vines in my day."

"Done." He moved around to the other side of the counter and reached into the display case. "Can we share the Milk Duds or do you want the whole box?"

"The last time I ate a whole box, I think I was sixteen, and I remember I *did* get a stomachache. I'm good with sharing. Can we share popcorn too?"

"Only if I can douse it in butter."

"The more the better."

"I knew you were my kind of girl." The words slipped before he could call them back. He covered up his error with, "Soda?"

"Diet." She laughed. "I know that sounds ridiculous when I'm about to gorge on a gazillion calories in one sitting. But I just like the taste better."

"Personal tastes often lead to interesting places." He poured two tall cups full of soda and ice, stuck everything in an easy-carry cardboard box, and gestured toward the retro vinyl swinging doors. "Shall we?"

"We shall." She swiped her soda from the box and took a sip from the long straw. He tried not to notice how amazing her lips looked pursed over that little plastic tube and failed.

"So we're seeing . . ." She glanced at the movie poster near the door. "*Hatchet III* to convince me of true love?"

"No, darlin'." He laughed. "That would probably be *your* choice as a representation. Mine is a bit on the gentler side." He opened the door and held it for her while she stepped inside the cool, darkened theater. Jesse remembered coming here on dates or hanging out with his brothers. The place held great memories. Tonight, he hoped to add to the list.

When she headed toward the center of the theater, he took her by the arm and led her to the center of the back row.

"Is this your special place?"

"Not mine exclusively." He handed her the popcorn. "But I've been known to plant my Levi's in these seats a time or two. Jared was the one who had his own seat. His initials are probably still there on the arm."

"You're kidding."

He shook his head and pointed to the seat in the corner. "Go check it out."

She handed him back the popcorn and, using her cell phone as a flashlight, got up to look. When she let out a laugh, he knew she'd found where in high school, his brother had carved his initials into the arm of the seat.

When Allison came back, she sat down, and their arms brushed against each other. Anticipation shot through his middle.

"Was your brother a legend or something?" she asked.

"Or something."

Her smile faltered. "You really miss him."

"Understatement of the century." He tossed a kernel of popcorn into his mouth and chewed.

"I'm sorry," she said, placing her warm hand over his forearm. "I didn't mean to bring up bad memories."

"On the contrary, thinking of Jared sitting in that seat and raising a little hell is a great memory. So don't be sorry."

She sat back, and the warmth of her hand slipped away to settle in her lap. "I've never lost anyone close."

"You're lucky." Jesse's chest lifted on a long intake of air meant to clear the clog that had settled there. "There's nothing worse."

"Want to talk about it?"

He tossed her a diversionary grin. "I'd rather watch the movie and share the popcorn before you eat it all."

"You're the one who's already started munching."

He held out the tub, and she scooped up a few kernels.

"This certainly isn't what I expected tonight," she said before she popped the corn into her mouth.

He handed her a napkin to wipe the excess butter from her fingers. She licked them instead, and his groin tightened. "What did you expect?"

"Another episode like the one with Arlene and Gladys." When she lifted her index finger to her mouth and sucked off the butter, he nearly groaned.

Light flickered on the giant screen and the dancing, cartoon, concession-stand snacks began to sing "Let's all go to the lobby."

"I've been told you have to change things up to keep a woman interested," he said.

She gave him a sideways glance. "I can't imagine you have any problem in that area."

"Is that a compliment?"

"You wish. What I meant to say is I can't imagine you have any problem in that area because you don't stick around long enough to have to change things up."

"Uh-oh. Who's been talking now?"

"Who hasn't been?" She munched another kernel. "Today, I had the pleasure of contacting several local ladies who do floral design on the side. They all had plenty to say. Mostly about how happy they were for Reno and what a devil *you* were."

He slapped a hand down on his knee. "What do I have to do to get a little respect around here?"

"Stop sleeping with every woman you meet. That might be a good start. Or at least choose to be a little more covert."

He stuffed a Milk Dud in his mouth and chewed thoughtfully. For years, he'd let the love 'em and leave 'em reputation propagate because it had been harmless entertainment. A chance for a good laugh upon hearing he'd had sex with a woman he'd never even been alone with. For a long time, the rumors had worked to his advantage. Lately, he'd grown tired of the game. Tired of being the bull's-eye for gossip. And for some reason, he cared what *this* particular woman thought.

"I don't," he said.

She turned her head and through the darkness studied his face. "You don't what?"

"Sleep with every woman I meet. I'm no angel, but I'm hardly the horny devil everyone paints me to be. I've had some long-term relationships."

Her gaze flicked over his face as if looking for visual proof of honesty or deception. "Really?"

He nodded. "Do you think even less of me now?"

"I don't know what to think of you."

On the screen, the giant, dancing hot dog disappeared, and the film started.

"Maybe you'll figure it out after the movie," he said.

"Doubtful." She turned her attention to the beautiful ruby sunset in the opening scene. "Uh-oh."

"What?"

"We're watching *The Notebook*?"

"Have you seen it?" he asked.

"Only about a hundred times."

"Then count this as a hundred and one."

"Why *The Notebook*?"

"Because . . ." He'd gotten sucked into seeing

the movie when he'd accidentally walked into a girl's movie night at his mom's house. And though he'd never admit it to his brothers, the film had touched him deeply. "This movie is a great example of true love. There's no better proof than when spouses are there for each other even when they can't remember they're spouses."

"Jesse? I hate to burst your eager bubble, but this is a movie. It's not real life."

Disappointment tightened his chest. "Do you truly believe those kinds of relationships don't really exist?"

When she snagged her bottom lip between her teeth and hesitated, he rolled on.

"I can walk you into Texas Rose Assisted Living right now and prove it to you. Margaret Whipple was my third-grade teacher. She's been in Texas Rose with dementia for the past ten years. Elmer Whipple has been married to Margaret for over sixty years. She can't remember him at all. But he goes there every day, has lunch with her, and reads her the newspaper. He once told me that it was just like having their first date over and over again."

"Well, that's very nice but I—"

Then there's Gus and Zelma Mortimer. They got married when they were sixteen years old. Had ten kids. And they're both so old, I quit counting the wrinkles. About five years ago, Gus had a stroke. He's still with it in the head, but his body isn't in sync, and he's been in a wheelchair ever since. Yet every once in a while when I go out to their ranch to vaccinate their calves, I catch them dancing on the front porch."

"How can they dance if he's in a wheelchair?"

"She sits on his lap, wraps her arms around his neck, and sings while she moves the wheelchair around with her feet. And she still looks at him like he's the strong, independent man she married all those years ago."

"That's so . . . sweet."

Jesse didn't miss that her words were spoken with admiration. "Open your eyes, darlin'. There's a whole big mushy in-love world out there to see. If you keep them closed, you're going to miss what's right in front of you."

For a long moment, she remained silent. Yet while he watched the movie screen, he could feel her gaze on him. Finally, she leaned in, and whispered insistently. "It's a movie."

"Fine." He turned, and in her eyes found an almost desperate need to hang on to her misguided beliefs. "Then if you won't look at those possibilities, think about the fact that maybe I just wanted to get you alone in the dark."

Two hours later, Allison had sobbed through several paper napkins plus the tissues she'd found crumpled up in the bottom of her purse. Without even looking, she knew her nose was red and her face blotchy. She'd consumed far too much buttered popcorn and way too many Milk Duds. And she could swear her stomach sloshed from all the soda.

On top of all that, she was still intrigued by Jesse's premovie *alone in the dark* comment.

After they thanked Mrs. Donovan for the private screening, they stepped outside the theater and into the warm night air. With the lingering emotions of the movie message, the older woman's generosity made Allison think about the connection Jesse had to the people in this town. She thought about the comments he'd made about his third-grade teacher and Gus and Zelma. She had to admit the idea of having someone to love her that way in her waning years made her pulse beat just a little faster. It made her question the reasons and excuses she used to deny that the possibility of that kind of love actually existed.

It made her wonder.

Surprisingly—and frighteningly—it created a warm little flutter of hope right in the middle of her heart.

"Care to walk off some of that popcorn?" Jesse asked as he stood beneath the marquee lights.

"I'd love to."

As they moved down the boardwalk, she realized that even though it was just after nine o'clock, the little town seemed nearly deserted. Only a few vehicles cruised down Main Street. The stores were all closed, and only the glow from their display windows and the old-fashioned streetlamps offered illumination. From somewhere down the street, the night came alive via some smooth rhythm and blues.

"Where's that music coming from?" she asked.

"The Blue Armadillo. They bring in bands from as far as Oklahoma, but usually not on a Tuesday night. Want to grab a beer and listen for a while?"

"I'd rather walk."

"Whatever you want to do."

What she wanted to do was figure him out.

The night she'd met him at Seven Devils, he'd seemed a total player ready to jump in her car and take her places she'd probably never gone except in her fantasies. His reckless love 'em and leave 'em reputation was the talk of the town. Yet he appeared quite the opposite. He seemed attentive to the needs of those around him. When they'd been at the bar and in Bud's busy diner, his eyes had been focused on *her*. Not once had his gaze wandered. And there had been plenty of places for those sexy blue eyes to travel.

He openly admitted monogamy and marriage weren't for him. Yet he seemed hell-bent on making sure she understood there was more to marriage than divorce. That relationships really did last.

Why?

So his mother and her father could find happiness together?

A typical playboy was self*fish*, not self*less*. Jesse appeared to be more the latter.

Walking beside him on the street, she looked up. Not for the first time, she found him unbelievably gorgeous. But there was more going on behind that pretty face. It seemed impossible to paint him as a stereotypical hunk. He was fun, easy to talk to, and family-oriented. He was a man of substance.

So why did he try to disguise that behind some reckless devil-may-care image?

"I have a confession," she said as they passed Goody Gum Drops' candy-bright window display.

A smile touched his masculine lips. "I hope it's something good, like you have a weakness for buying X-rated underwear."

She laughed. "Isn't it better to keep you wondering about stuff like that?"

"Hey, anytime you're ready, I'm willing to take on the challenge. Reality vs. fantasy is my kind of game."

"Sorry to disappoint you, but my confession has nothing to do with underwear."

"Damn." He snapped his fingers. "Just when I thought I was onto something good."

Allison was sure she'd never met a man who made her laugh more than him. She knew for a fact that she'd never met a man who turned her on more. And since *that* was never going to happen, those fantasies would have to remain in her twisted little imagination.

"I have to confess that although I'm not a fan of beer," she said, "I changed my mind, and I would like to go hear the band."

"Your wish is my command." He reached for her hand as they began to cross the street. "The Blue Armadillo also serves wine and a variety of coffees. I'm sure you can find something you like."

The tingle she got just from his holding her hand was a good start.

She wondered if just this small amount of skin-to-skin contact with him started her engine, what would it be like if he'd take off all his clothes?

With that totally fantastical thought swimming through her head, they walked hand in hand through the garden arbor and into the patio area of the Blue Armadillo. Set back beneath a small grapevine-covered gazebo, the four-piece band cruised into a new song. Dimly lit latticework surrounded the patio and provided a welcoming atmosphere that Allison also found romantic. Or maybe that was just more fantastically wishful thinking.

The patio area was packed with music and beer lovers. Jesse snagged them a table with two comfy wicker chairs back in a corner and far enough from the band where they could still converse without having to shout. As soon as they sat down, a college-aged guy with long hair and a tie-dyed apron showed up to take their order. While she settled for a locally made chardonnay, Jesse ordered a bottle of what she was getting to recognize as his standard ale.

When their drinks arrived, she leaned in, and said, "I really appreciate the efforts you put into setting up the private screening tonight."

He smiled and tilted his bottle of Shiner as if to toast her. "I'll make a believer out of you yet."

"I don't mind admitting your methods are fascinating. And fun. But I'm still not sure my opinions are going to budge anytime soon."

He lifted the bottle to his mouth, took a drink, then licked away a drop on his bottom lip. "You ever feel like you're just going in circles?"

"All the time."

"Maybe you should break that cycle."

She shrugged. "It seems to be working just fine."

"Is it?"

Before she could respond, one dark brow lifted and signaled his skepticism.

"Have you ever been in love, Allison?" He leaned in and draped his arm along the back of her chair. "I'm not talking about a crush or infatuation. I'm talking about where you'd do anything for someone. Can't stop thinking about them. Be there if they were sick or just needed a shoulder to lean on. Someone you wanted to wake up to every single day and couldn't wait until you saw them again at night. Someone who made you truly happy and magnified the good in you. Someone who made you feel like you're everything you've ever wanted to be."

Reality nose-dived right before her eyes.

Relationships had never been her biggest strength.

During high school, she'd had a fairly steady boyfriend who'd been handsome, on the football team, and a little possessive. She'd been relieved the day he'd gone off to college on the East Coast, and she'd stayed in Seattle to attend UW. After that, she'd been so busy putting her business first, she hadn't had time for more than a casual date here and there. Last year, she did go out with a nice construction worker she'd met when he'd built a gazebo for a lakeside wedding she'd planned. But he didn't like being second on her time-management list, and the relationship had ended after just a few months.

"Not really," she admitted.

A big sigh lifted his broad shoulders. "Not what I was expecting you to say."

"Which is?"

"That yes, you've been in love, but some jerk broke your heart. Or did something to rip away all your illusions of grandeur."

Oh, they had. Unfortunately, they'd been her parents. "In that case, *I* might be the jerk."

He studied her face. "Hard to imagine."

"Are you being sarcastic?"

He shook his head. "Honest."

As the band eased into the Otis Redding classic "I've Been Loving You Too Long," she took a deep breath.

"Just goes to show you appearances can be deceiving. Which proves my point."

"You know what I think?" He held out his hand.

As she looked at that large hand that earlier had felt so good holding hers, she expected him to call a truce.

Instead, he said, "I think we should dance."

"Dance?"

He nodded.

"That won't change my mind."

"Not trying to right now. Just want to dance."

Her gaze swept over that big masculine body, and everything inside her started to hum. "Sure. Why not."

She put her hand in his, and that familiar tingle started up again. Instead of leading her to the dance floor, he took her in his arms right there by their table in the shadows of the little white fairy lights and a bubbling three-tiered water fountain.

His arm went around her waist and drew her in close, so there was nothing between them but a thin layer of fabric. The heat of his embrace seeped through the cloth and into her skin. Her heart kicked up a notch as their bodies moved together to the seductive tune. A melody that was perfect for making love—slow, sweet, and tender.

Jesse's words played over again in her head, and she realized exactly how he viewed love. For him, the emotion was powerful and all-encompassing. Something that made you a better person and made you desire to be a better person. It was selfless and honest. She knew in Jesse's heart and mind, love was eternal.

How very different from what she'd ever thought when she heard the word "love."

In that moment, she didn't mind that she liked his version a whole lot better.

"My father met my mother when she was sixteen, and he'd just turned eighteen," he murmured. "Her parents pitched a fit because he was older and had a reputation around town for being a bit wild."

"Like you?"

His deep chuckle rumbled against her breast.

"Worse. He'd actually been caught in the act a few times—haylofts in barns not being all that soundproof and everything. Anyway, her parents forbade her to see him. But my mom and dad found a way to sneak around so they could be together.

They did that for two full years until she turned eighteen. Then they went down to the courthouse and got married. Her parents disowned her. They sat back and waited for everything to fall apart. Waited for my mom to come running back and tell them my father was no good just like they'd said. They wanted justification."

"That's awful."

He gave a slow nod and drew their clasped hands against his chest. "They moved in with my dad's parents for a time until Jared was born. Then they built the house we all grew up in. They worked side by side building that ranch and a commitment to the community that's still strong today. They adopted Reno when his drug-addict mother abandoned him. And they raised five boys with equal love and attention. I never heard my parents argue. I only remember them being loving toward each other and doing silly things that would make us boys cringe."

"Like what?"

"They'd dance, just like this, in the kitchen, or on the veranda during a thunderstorm, or anywhere the mood struck. My father always sang low in my mother's ear, and she'd giggle like a schoolgirl."

"Obviously, they loved each other very much," she said, wishing her parents had shared that same kind of relationship.

"It wasn't always easy. Money was tight. My father often worked for others to make enough to put food on the table. My mom took in laundry or baked goods for Bud's Diner. Sometimes, she babysat other kids, which often created even more chaos than what already went on in our house."

"That's very admirable."

His big shoulders and the incredible chest beneath that light blue shirt expanded on an intake of air. "They just did what needed to be done. They worked together. They were committed to each other. Until the day my brother was killed. On that day, the laughter and the singing stopped. My father never recovered from the loss, and it broke my mother's heart."

"You don't need to convince me that your mother's a good person."

"Darlin'?" He eased back and looked her in the eye. "I'm not trying to convince you my mother's a good person. I'm trying to tell you how I was raised. Why I think the way I do. Why I believe that not only does true love exist and the tradition of marriage work, I believe it's an incredible gift."

He eased her back into his arms, and she could feel the strong thump of his heart against her breast.

"Then if you feel that strongly, why aren't you married?"

"It's not my turn."

"Come on, there's more than that."

"Just haven't found the right woman."

"You certainly seem to be making your way through enough to find one."

"Like I said, don't believe everything you hear."

Later, when Jesse walked Allison back to the truck, he found himself fighting a losing battle.

He wasn't naïve enough to believe that everyone had amazing parents and wonderful role models. But he did feel sad for those who'd not lived with the familial security he'd had growing up. He knew too well the anguish of loss, but at least he'd never lost his faith that all things were possible.

In the past few days, it had become clear that Allison might very well be incapable of sharing those same principles. And that made him want to work all the harder to get her to believe.

Why?

Not a clue.

Other than he was wildly attracted to her. And that he cared. And maybe also that he was unable to act on any of the surprising feelings he'd quickly developed. He had a sense he was getting in too deep. But for whatever reason, he couldn't stop.

When they reached his truck, he opened the door for her. She turned at the last second and looked up at him through the shadows. His gaze swept over her face and lingered on her luscious mouth.

"Did your mother's parents ever apologize for misjudging your father and disowning your mother?" she asked.

He shook his head, and her hopeful smile slipped away.

"They stuck to their beliefs and waited for the moment they'd be able to say "I told you so.""

"That's awful."

"My parents were married for thirty-six years, until my father died of a broken heart. My mother's parents are still alive. After Jared was born, they moved to Missouri. They've never spent one minute with any of us. I know everyone says it's their loss, but I find it sad that they've missed out on our lives, and we've been cheated getting to know them. All because they were too stubborn to change their minds."

He could tell the statement struck home when she lowered her eyes.

"Sometimes change is not as easy as people think," she said.

That smoky gaze came back up, and he found himself drawn into the flashes of silver and gold, the heat and the passion that lingered in those dark depths. Before he could stop himself he cupped her face in his hands and leaned in.

"It's always worth a try," he said, wanting to kiss her so bad he ached. Their lips were a breath away when sanity slammed into him like a runaway train. He dropped his hands. Tried to catch his breath. And cursed the circumstances.

"What's wrong?" she asked.

"*That* can't happen."

"But you want it to?"

Words tangled up on his tongue, so he just nodded.

"Me too." She reached up, slid her hand to the back of his neck, and lifted to her toes.

Before he knew it, her lips were pressed against his, and he was absolutely helpless to do anything but pull her into his arms.

The kiss was slow and sweet, and it knocked his heart into unfamiliar territory. But it was wrong, and he had to remember that she wasn't just someone passing through. She wasn't someone to have a good time with, then not bother to call the next day. She was his mother's fiancé's daughter. She was someone who didn't hold to his beliefs. And no matter how much his body ached to have her, he could not.

He took one last taste of her. Let her flavor linger on his tongue. Then he let her go and stepped back.

"New rule," he murmured. "In the future, I think it would be wise if we kept a good distance between the two of us."

She gave a slow blink. "Are you sure about that?"

No. He nodded. "Get in the truck, Allison. Before I do something really, really stupid."

Chapter 8

As a rule, Allison made it a priority not to crawl out of bed until the hands on the clock hovered somewhere around 6 A.M. This morning, however, she'd been up before the crack of dawn, and it didn't even have anything to do with Wee Man using her bed as a springboard.

Sleep had evaded her since Jesse had brought her home last night, walked her to her father's door, and said a hasty good night. His abrupt "See ya later" had been a complete 180 from earlier in the evening, when he'd held her in his arms and kissed her. She didn't wonder if she'd ever been kissed like that before. She hadn't. But that had been before he'd backed off like she had some terrible disease.

Hours later, she sat at her father's kitchen table as the sun peeked up over the hilltops, and she tried to put the finishing touches on her blog. She'd spent the greater part of the night attempting to put her thoughts into words and had kept going until she'd literally fallen asleep with her fingers on the keyboard. While her typical posts might run two to five hundred words, the dilemma *de* Jesse ended up over three thousand.

A huge red flag waved before her eyes.

As cathartic as writing the post had been, nothing in the piece could ever be shared. It was a total outpouring of emotion that included her confusion over her own feelings as well as Jesse's intentions and his artistic style of backpedaling once he'd kissed her.

He'd kissed her.

When the intensity of that memory fluttered through her stomach, she set down her coffee cup and touched her fingers to her lips. She could still imagine the sensation of his soft, masculine lips. The tingles the kiss had invoked and left in its wake. And then, like a dark shadow, the truth of what had actually taken place last night slammed into her brain.

He hadn't kissed her.

She'd kissed *him*.

And he'd soundly rejected her.

After he'd kissed her back.

Crap. Now she was more confused than ever.

What the hell was going on between the two of them? She had no business allowing herself to give in to a whim like that.

But had it really been a whim?

Hadn't she been thinking of him day and night since she'd arrived in Sweet? If she was the fanciful type, she might think some kind of love potion had been dropped into her drink that first night.

Not a love potion.

A hot-to-trot potion.

Facts were facts. Jesse Wilder made her mouth water, and she wanted him. She wanted to feel her hands on him. To taste him. To feel his hands on her. To feel him deep inside her while he made her moan like a crazy woman. That was it. That was all she felt for him. He just turned her on, and she wanted a piece of that action.

Liar.

A glance at the words on the screen of her laptop revealed the truth. Not a single damn one of them had anything to do with sex.

Without mentioning him by name, all those words spoke of matters of the heart. Hers. They spoke of the way she viewed him as a strong, caring man who, on the outside, appeared to live life in the fast lane without a care in the world, yet on the inside took life very seriously. And he loved deeply. Which was even a bigger turn-on than his incredible body.

And that really said something.

Her words had to do with her own desire to hope that there could possibly be a man out there who might dare to love her with the same devoted passion that she knew lived deep in Jesse Wilder's heart.

Pure fantasy.

A man like Jesse could never love someone like her that way.

Proof?

He'd barely contained his panic when she'd thrown herself at him last night.

Some things she knew to be true. *She* was a walking, talking relationship nightmare. Any man who'd willingly choose to get involved with her would have to have a screw loose.

With a simple click of the mouse, she highlighted all the emotionally charged words she'd written. Words that unlocked the overflowing vault of confusion, desire, and her ridiculous hope.

As her finger hovered over the delete key, her phone vibrated on the table next to her, and a text from Danielle popped up.

U up?

Allison poked at the touch screen. *Yeah. Y r u?*

Lily has flu. Need u back here now.

No can do. Allison sighed. *Promised to fix things for wedding next week.*

Please don't do this 2 me. I have mommy guilt.

Apologies. Do what you need 2 do. Reschedule appts. Work from home. Whatever it takes. Don't worry.

EZ 4 u 2 say.

When the icon on her phone continued to blink, she knew her sister had moved on to freak out another day. Allison picked up her coffee cup. She sipped at the tepid brew while reading over her highlighted post again. Once upon a time, she'd created the blog to allow herself an anonymous place to vent. A place to question things about relationships she didn't understand. A place to listen to her followers, who often offered sensible words of advice she couldn't ignore. She'd never held back before. She shouldn't start now. Especially when she could really use some words of advice. So what could it hurt?

Instead of hitting the delete key, she opened up her blog and added her long missive to NEW POSTS. Before she chickened out, she clicked PUBLISH and shut down her laptop.

Too late now.

Time to move on.

She poured herself a fresh cup of coffee and grabbed the notepad where she'd doodled out possible solutions for Charli and Reno's wedding. Next item on the list—a florist to replace the one who'd had to temporarily close up shop.

Yesterday, she'd called florists in both San Antonio and Austin, but at this late notice no one was able to take on the job. Tapping her pen against her chin, several ideas sprouted in her head. In the end, there was really only one *fabulous* solution. She grabbed her phone and hit her contact list. Even knowing he wouldn't be up at this hour, she pressed CALL. Antoine, Seattle's *super* florist, picked up almost immediately.

"Allie boo! Where are you?"

She nearly groaned at the ridiculous name he chose to call her. It didn't even make sense. "I'm still in Texas."

"Oooh, have you seen any hot cowboys yet?"

Had she ever. "A few."

"Care to bring one home for me?"

"I thought you were in love with Garrett."

"Oh, sweetie, Garrett is so last week. I've moved on."

"To who?"

"Benny. He's a new performer at Gaybaret. His stage name is Cherry DeVine. Isn't that precious?"

"Adorable." Some gay men fell in love and entered into committed relationships. Antoine entered therapy. Often. But he was a great friend, and his floral skills couldn't be beat. If the truth were told, she held a very special place in her heart for him because they were both so much alike. They both loved men, yet neither of them seemed to have the stick-to-it gene in their blood. "I need a favor. How booked are you for the weekend after next?"

"Uno momento . . ." His singsong response made her smile.

Allison waited while he tapped out scheduling info on his ever-present MacBook.

"We have four events."

"Can you squeeze in a fifth?"

"For you, anything."

"Can you bring your badass self to Texas to make it happen?"

"Hmmm. What gives, Allie Boo?"

"Are you familiar with makeover show host Charlotte Brooks?"

"Love her. Was so disappointed when she quit the show."

"She's getting married to the cowboy she met during the Sweet, Texas, episodes. Her local florist had a family emergency, and—"

"Sweetie! Say no more. You had me at cowboy."

"Thank you. I'll e-mail you the specifics. Charge it all to my account, including your airfare and whichever assistant you bring. I'll arrange your lodging."

"Where do I have everything shipped to?"

"Wilder and Sons Hardware and Feed." She rattled off the address.

"Seriously?"

"Would I kid you?"

"It sounds like you're out in the boondocks."

"I am. And you know what?" She smiled. "It's kinda awesome."

"Then count me in." Antoine gave a long sigh. "I want a slice of that."

Allison ended the call just as her father came into the kitchen.

"Good morning, little girl." He kissed her forehead, and, once again, she realized how much she'd missed him. "You're up early."

She poured them both a cup of coffee. "I've been striking out with all the florists in the area, so I called in a favor."

"Antoine?"

"Yeah. He's flying in."

"That's going to cost a pretty penny."

"Not for Charli and Reno. I'm covering it."

He lowered his cup and looked at her. "You are?"

She nodded. "I couldn't stand to see them disappointed if their special day didn't turn out as they'd envisioned."

A slow smile lifted her father's entire face. "You never cease to surprise me."

"What can I say?" She shrugged. "I like them. They deserve a chance."

"I'm so proud of you." Fatherly arms wrapped around her. "And I hope you understand that *you* deserve a chance too."

When it came to finding true love, she had a better probability of winning the lottery she never played.

As Allison parked Jared Wilder's big-ass truck near Jana Wilder's barn and opened the door, Wee Man sprang to the ground. Miss Giddy, who sported a pretty pink satin ribbon around her long brown neck, greeted them.

"Meh-eh-eh."

At the goat's cheerful hello, Allison laughed. Wee Man got down on his front legs and playfully wiggled his back end. Seconds later, the two of them took off like old friends. Never in her wildest imagination would she have imagined her dog would be BFFs with a farm animal. And never would she have imagined she'd think that was pretty cool.

"Good morning," Jana called from the veranda.

Last night, when Allison had been dancing with Jesse, it became clear how much he respected his mother, how much his parents had loved each other, and how the death of his brother and father had brought his mother to her knees. During that conversation, Allison had gained a new respect for Jana. For all the Wilders.

"If you're game for some several-hours-old coffee," Jana said, "come on in, and I'll pour you a cup."

Allison closed the truck door and walked across the gravel drive to meet up with her future stepmother. The woman never failed to delight with her untethered enthusiasm and Southern hospitality. It didn't matter how many chinks Allison tried to find in Jana's armor, she always came up empty.

"Actually, I came over here to ask a favor."

A smile that closely resembled Jesse's flashed. "Whatever you need."

"You don't even know what I'm going to ask."

"Doesn't matter. At one time or other we all need something. It's just good if there's always someone on the other end to help out."

Tempted to shake her head in disbelief, Allison returned her smile. She knew if she asked a favor of her own mother, the immediate response would be quite different.

"After my shameless prompting, Charli and Reno have decided that Jesse's backyard will be the perfect spot for their reception. Change-of-venue notices will go out to guests in the mail tomorrow," Allison said. "I've contacted the party-rental store, and everything Charli previously ordered, plus the addition of a portable dance floor, will now be delivered to Jesse's house."

"Oh, that's wonderful." Jana clapped her hands together. "My son has done a beautiful job with his house and yard, and he's never been able to show it off to anyone but the family."

"He must have worked with a wonderful land-scaper."

"With the exception of pouring the plaster for the pool, he did everything himself. Including the backhoe to dig the pool and spa."

"He did everything?" Why that surprised her she didn't know. He seemed quite capable of accomplishing whatever he put his mind to.

"Every tree. Every shrub. The pavers and tile. You name it."

"Impressive. But then I have to wonder why he's left the inside of his house such a blank slate."

"Maybe doing all that work outside just wore him out."

Or maybe he was afraid to make it too inviting so the women who *visited* wouldn't get any commitment ideas in their marriage-minded heads.

"Well, the favor I want to ask involves that very subject," Allison said. "I've heard whispers of the treasure trove you have up in the barn, and I wondered if I could borrow a few items to add a little personality to the interior of his house for the reception. Just so it looks a smidge more complete in case anyone wanders inside. And also . . ."

"What?"

"I think he deserves to be able to come to a house that feels like a home and not just a temporary landing place."

"That's an excellent and very thoughtful idea." Jana tucked her arm through Allison's and led her inside the huge wooden structure that apparently not only housed some livestock but an entire antiques store.

"If he doesn't like it, or you need them for the

shop you and Charli are opening, I promise to put everything back in your barn the following day. If he does like it, I'm more than willing to pay for the items. It would be my gift to him for allowing us to take over his house for the event."

"I'm very moved that you'd want to do that for him. Don't worry about anything you use. Charli and I aren't opening our store for several more months, and we haven't even taken a look yet at what we want to include. You're welcome to take whatever strikes your fancy. If my son will allow everything to stay, it's all his for the asking."

Allison stopped at the bottom of the stairs inside the barn and looked at the woman's gentle features and ever-present smile. "You have a very generous heart, Jana."

"That's kind of you to say so. And I'll allow you to retract the statement whenever I meddle in your life."

Allison laughed. "Are you a meddler?"

"Oh, you have no idea." Janna patted her on the back. "But I'm sure you'll learn. And hopefully you'll forgive. Now come on, let's go see what I've got that you might be interested in."

When she opened the locked door with an old skeleton key, Allison stepped inside. One look around the collection of antiques and collectibles that were packed to the rafters and all she could say was, "Wow."

*J*esse barely made it home from the clinic before he collapsed in his favorite chair and kicked off his boots. Even Dinks's and Rango's usual silly escapades couldn't hinder the exhaustion that grabbed him by the throat or the sadness that lay heavy in his heart. Most days, he loved what he did for a living. Other days simply broke his spirit.

Today had not been one of his favorites.

He wanted a shower to unwind but didn't even know if he could make it to the other room. He needed to eat, but the thought of another microwave dinner or frozen pizza left him cold. Even the refrigerator was too far away to grab a beer to relax. So he remained glued to the plush leather chair with his feet kicked up on the ottoman while he closed his eyes.

He'd just cleared his mind and drifted off when someone knocked on the door. Briefly, he opened his eyes, saw the lock was open, and said "Come in" in the strongest voice he could muster. At that moment, he didn't care if an army of thieves came through the door, he was just too tired and too down to care.

When the door cautiously opened, he couldn't have been more surprised to see Allison standing there looking like something he'd dreamed up in a white sundress with strappy little sandals, which were, to his surprise, flat. Her long hair floated around her shoulders in big loose curls. That toffee-colored streak was tucked behind her ear, revealing hoop earrings that matched the silver chain around her ankle.

She gave him a cautious smile. "Hey."

Without warning, her little dog bounded into the house. Rango hissed and darted upstairs.

Dinks gave a happy bark. The little terrier took off, and the chase commenced.

Allison stepped through the entry, shut the door, and came around to stand in front of him with a worried wrinkle to her brow. "Are you okay?"

"Bad day."

She sat on the edge of the ottoman, so he didn't have to move his feet. "Want to talk about it?"

"Not really." Air pushed from his lungs as he laid his head back and closed his eyes. He wanted to keep looking at her, but he was just so tired.

"You look exhausted."

"Bingo."

"And upset."

"Daily double."

"And hungry."

"Triple play."

"Is it work-related?"

He gave her a slow nod.

"You ever have anybody you can talk to at the end of a particularly bad day?"

Eyes still closed, he shook his head.

"Then talk to *me*," she said in a tone that was soft, sweet, and compassionate. She reached out and gently rubbed her hand over the top of his and sealed the deal.

"Can't tell you the details," he said. "You'll cry."

"I'm tougher than I look."

"You're a marshmallow."

"I'm pretty sure no one has ever called me a marshmallow before." She chuckled. "Most names I've been called have started with *B* and ended with *itch*."

He opened his eyes and drank her in. "Well I think you're kinda soft and wonderful."

"And I think *you're* kinda evading the subject."

"Kittens," he said, remembering he'd previously told her about the kitten incident that had made him want to be a vet.

"Oh no. What happened?"

"Something that made me determined to lobby for stricter animal-protection laws." She held his hand while he told her the story of the mother cat that had been mistreated and malnourished. In his office that afternoon, she'd delivered three adorable kittens. And though he hadn't thought any of them would survive, by some miracle they were hanging on. Abby had immediately found them a loving foster home. And though it was a threat to the loss of his man card, he admitted to Allison that when he handed them over to their foster family, he'd cried like a baby.

Allison didn't seem to think any less of him. Tears filled her eyes as she squeezed his hand and gave him a smile of encouragement.

"I don't know how you manage to deal with that," she said. "But I thank God you do. At least those animals found some compassion."

"I wish I could give them more."

"Because of you, they'll survive, and they'll find homes." She squeezed his hand again. "I kind of like that you're just a big softy beneath that alpha-male exterior."

He lifted his head from the back of the chair. "I'm an alpha male?"

"Oh yeah." A laugh that lifted his heavy heart

bubbled from her luscious lips. "And from the grumbling in your stomach, you're a very hungry alpha male."

Before he could grab her, she was gone. The sound of the refrigerator door's opening came next, followed by the freezer door.

"What are you doing?" he called out, closing his eyes again.

"Making you something to eat." A short pause was followed up with a long sigh. "You are such a bachelor. All I see in here are beans, weenies, beer, and . . . jalapenos."

"And the problem with that is?"

No response. He cracked open one eye when he heard the patio door open, then close.

"Good to know you keep the good stuff in the outside fridge."

"I spend more time out there."

"Apparently."

She came back into the living room and poked him with a finger. "Eat this while I scrounge up something relatively healthful for you to eat."

In her hand she held a small plate piled with crackers and slices of sharp cheddar cheese.

"You don't have to do that," he said, taking the plate before she changed her mind. "But it's appreciated."

"No worries. I'm actually trying to butter you up."

"Mmmm." The wheat crackers and cheddar roused his taste buds. "I've done vegetable oil but never butter."

She came out of the kitchen with a cooking utensil in her hand.

"Or a spatula," he said around a mouthful of cracker.

"What are you talking about?" she asked with half a smile curling those lips he very badly wanted to kiss.

He lifted his head and stopped midchew. "Weren't you talking about sex?"

She laughed. "No."

"Oh." He dropped his head to the chair again. "My bad."

"*Vegetable oil?*" He heard the curiosity in her voice, and he smiled.

"I've got all kinds of tricks up my sleeve. You should give me a test drive."

"Right now, I don't think you could even manage to start the engine."

"You'd be surprised." His eyes drifted closed again.

"How about you hold that thought while I whip up something."

"Not into whips," he muttered. "Or chains. But I'll give some thought to silk ropes while you go to work."

Just before he dozed off, he thought he heard her low chuckle and a sigh. He was exhausted, but that sexy sound was enough to send him off to dreamland with a smile.

*N*ot only did the man not have any home décor accents, he barely had enough in his kitchen to get by. How someone could spend so much time and money on the candy-coated shell of a house but not the essential core was beyond her. Lucky for him, she'd stopped by with a truckful of most everything this place needed—with the exception of groceries and some serving fundamentals.

When the dogs ended their chase and collapsed on the floor by her feet—just in case she dropped a juicy morsel, the living room grew silent. She peeked around the corner and found Jesse fast asleep. His big bare feet were crossed at the ankles on top of the leather ottoman. His large hands were folded together on top of those rippled abs currently hidden by a blue plaid shirt. And his jeans were worn in places that made her go hmmm.

No question the man was a complete knock-out. And while she could stand there all day and just gawk at him, she realized that her feelings for him went deeper than just the amazing exterior. She really wanted to wipe away the troubles that marred his forehead and compressed his lips.

He may have a very large family, but it seemed he kept a lot to himself. And for a man who appeared to have it all, she could tell there was something deep inside that needed letting out.

She went back into the kitchen and pulled together a reasonably healthy stir-fry with a frozen pack of vegetables, some chicken strips she'd found in the back of the freezer, and thank heaven for five-minute rice. She stuck his plate in the preheated oven to keep it warm while she faced the challenge of waking him up.

Tiptoeing into the living room, she stood there and watched him for a moment. Unfair, she knew, and didn't care. Allowing her eyes to roam over him again was like looking at a decadent chocolate window display. Unfortunately, the same problem existed. Just as she couldn't reach through glass to touch all those forbidden sweets, neither could she reach out and touch him.

She called his name in a quiet voice and got no response. After several seconds, she moved a little closer and called him again. With still no response, she bent down and whispered close to his ear, so as not to startle him.

Somehow, she ended up in his lap, looking up into those dark blue eyes that made her stomach do a masterful flip. A squeak bubbled from her throat, and he smiled.

"You should have checked with my mother first. I'm great at playing possum."

"You were awake?"

"Not the entire time."

"That's not very nice," she said from the comfy spot on his lap. Pressed against all that hard muscle and warm, masculine skin, she had to have a little tête-à-tête with her girl parts, who were singing *"Girls Just Want to Have Fun."*

"I beg to differ." He stroked a finger slowly down her arm. "I think it's *very* nice."

"What about your rule?" she asked.

"My rule?"

"Short-term memory loss?"

His brows dipped together. "Apparently."

"After the movie, you invoked the *keeping a good distance* rule."

His gaze lowered to her mouth, then slowly

climbed back up to her eyes. "Proof that you should never listen to me when I won't even listen to myself."

"So you're revoking the rule?"

"Revoking?" His big strong hand came up and gently caressed her cheek. Then those long fingers curled over the back of her neck and drew her face closer to his. "I'm blasting it all to hell."

His mouth brushed across hers, then he pulled back, just slightly, as though giving her a chance to push him away and run like hell.

She did neither.

Heat and desire licked over her as she curled her fingers into his shirt, leaned in, and inhaled his warm, masculine scent. He spoke her name in a rough whisper, then covered her mouth with his and took possession.

A hot flame of urgency burned at her core, but Jesse didn't seem to be in as big a hurry. His kiss was tender. Slow and languid, like he had all day and just wanted to take his time to explore. He tasted like passion and sex as his tongue stroked hers in a hot, sensuous rhythm that verified he'd never be a selfish lover. While one of his large hands gently caressed the sensitive skin along her neck, the fingers of his other slid beneath the strap of her dress and slipped it off her shoulder.

Yes.

A storm of need and lust whipped through her body. She wanted him to touch her. To strip her down and take control. She wanted to lose herself in him. Wrap herself around him. She wanted to touch all those firm muscles. To find out exactly how he liked those muscles to be touched. She wanted her greedy mouth and hands on all that warm, sexy skin. More than she wanted air, she wanted him deep inside her body, giving and receiving pleasure.

Hunger danced up her spine as his warm fingers dipped below the edge of her dress and covered her breast. Her nipples peaked against his palm, and liquid heat pooled between her thighs.

Someone moaned.

Her?

Him?

Both?

And then the oven timer dinged.

When he broke the kiss and lifted his head, she'd never felt a greater loss.

"Time's up?" he murmured against her lips.

Somehow, she managed to maintain a semblance of composure as she sat up and he withdrew the warmth of his hand from her breast. She cleared her throat. Licked the taste of him from her lips. "Are you ready to eat?"

The smile that curved his mouth left no doubt about the type of meal he had in mind—one where eating utensils weren't necessary. And while she was about two seconds away from stripping off his clothes and climbing on top of him in that leather easy chair, she forced herself to reason that he'd had a long day, was tired, and needed nourishment.

Especially if there was any chance she could

put her hot-and-bothered ideas into action later.

"Let me rephrase that," she said. "Your dinner's ready."

His long, dark eyelashes swept down in a slow blink. "Other than my mom or the local restaurants, I can't remember the last person who cooked for me. I appreciate it."

Adding to the sexual chaos in her body, the sincerity in his tone made her heart do a little flip. "It's just a quick stir-fry. Nothing special."

"It is to me." He captured her hand and kissed the backs of her fingers.

Well, what did a girl say to that?

She wiggled off his lap and held out her hand to help him from the chair. "Come on. It's getting cold."

"Not from where I'm sitting."

Not from where she was standing either.

Before she climbed back into his lap, she wiggled the fingers of her extended hand. "You're tired and hungry. And I plan to put you to work before you pass out."

"Exactly what did you have in mind?" With a cocky grin, he let her pull him to his feet, which put them breast to pecs. Her skin tingled, her nipples hardened again, and the entire front half of her body went into meltdown mode.

He followed her into the kitchen, pulled out a barstool, and sat down. She removed a steaming bowl of stir-fry from the oven and set it on the kitchen bar in front of him. His eyes widened. "Is this all for me?"

"Yes. You're going to need your strength."

He dug his fork into the meal, took a bite, and moaned with pleasure. "Damn that's good." He dug his fork in again as though he hadn't eaten in days. "So now *you're* going to throw out the innuendoes? Not fair."

Completely aware she was giving him an eyeful of cleavage; she leaned into the island and rested her forearms on the cool granite. "No innuendo intended."

"Damn."

"Your mother allowed me up into her barn loft today."

"Uh-oh."

"I brought over a few things to spice up your house for the reception, so it doesn't look so barren."

He lowered his fork. "You mean the lack of artwork and knickknacks and all that girly kind of stuff? Darlin', this is a man's house. You're lucky I didn't grab my dad's old black velvet John Wayne painting when my mom tossed it out. It would look great over the fireplace mantel."

"She didn't toss it out. It was in the loft."

"Are you shitting me?" At the shake of her head, he dropped his fork in the bowl. "We'd better get over there and grab it before the brothers find out."

"Actually . . . now it's in the truck outside."

He stared as though she'd spoken Martian.

"I think with a different frame, it might be kind of fun to put it somewhere," she said. "Do you have a family room? Or an extra bedroom?"

"You mean you wouldn't want to burn it like

every other woman who's ever seen it—including my mom?"

"Wouldn't that be sacrilegious? I mean, it is *the Duke* after all."

"I think I may love you," he said.

"You won't say that after I've had you drag in all the other stuff I found." She looked again at the exhaustion that slumped his shoulders. "I'm sorry. I had no idea you'd be so tired."

"No problem." He took another bite and grinned. "You don't look like a John-Wayne-loving kind of girl."

She folded her arms. "And exactly what kind do I look like?"

The way his gaze roamed her face, then traveled slowly down the front of her white eyelet sundress sent a tingle through those wild-and-crazy girl parts. His heavy-lidded eyes said she looked like the kind he'd like to take to bed.

"You look like a sunshine, fresh daisies, and bubble-bath kind of girl," he said.

"Well I do like all of the above, but that doesn't mean I don't love Westerns too. I used to sit on the sofa with my dad on Saturday afternoons and watch reruns of the Duke or Clint Eastwood."

"Yep. Me." He pointed to himself. "In love."

Knowing his comment was a joke, she laughed. Even as some crazy part of her soul wished it wasn't. "How about I let you finish eating while I go out and start bringing stuff in?"

"Care to join me?" He pointed his fork at the stir-fry. "There's plenty here for both of us."

"I must confess that I grabbed a pulled pork sandwich at Sweet Pickens earlier."

He pulled out the stool next to him. "Then how about I pour you a glass of wine, and you sit right here beside me while I eat? I don't get much company at mealtime. It's kind of nice."

The sincerity in his tone left her no choice but to grab a glass of the Riesling she'd found in the fridge and join him at the island.

"You ever tell anyone your deepest, darkest secrets?" she asked.

The fork halted halfway to his mouth. Brows pulled tight, he turned his head to look at her. "What do you mean?"

She shrugged and sipped her wine. "I get the feeling that, aside from the sad things that happen with your job, there's something else troubling you."

Expression shuttered, he looked away.

Allison waited. Watched while he took a long drink from his bottle of Shiner and swiped a drop from his bottom lip with his tongue. As she watched him struggle with the nerve she knew she'd hit, she wanted to reach out and wrap in him her arms. To take away whatever it was that seemed to stop him cold.

He brought his head back around to look at her. "You're a very perceptive woman."

"Sometimes one troubled soul just recognizes another."

"I appreciate that. But it's nothing I can talk about."

"Because I'm a stranger?"

Slowly he shook his head. "Because I made a promise."

"To who?"

His broad chest expanded on a sigh, then he dug back into his stir-fry as though they were merely discussing the weather.

"Jared."

"If you can't tell me," she said, "tell someone you trust. I know how much you love your brother. And I'm sure at the time he asked you to keep whatever it was secret, it was appropriate. But it's obvious that whatever it is, it is tying you up in knots. And if your brother is half the man I think he was, he'd never want that."

He studied her face. Then a small smile tilted his lips.

"As I said, you're a perceptive woman."

"I'll drink to that." She lifted her wine, and he tapped his bottle of ale against the glass.

While Allison would love nothing more than to know what it was that Jared had asked Jesse to keep in his confidence, she knew it was time to let him figure out what he needed to do about it.

They sat at the kitchen bar long after his meal, discussing their favorite movies. While he typically favored *The Transporter* and the *Mission Impossible* series, she naturally preferred anything where Meg Ryan and Tom Hanks shared the screen. Their favorite TV shows were equally diverse, with him loving *Dexter* and *Boardwalk Empire* and her adoring anything HGTV or Food Network. Music? Their tastes didn't even float in the same genre. As a wild-eyed Southern boy, he fancied Lynyrd Skynyrd, the Zac Brown Band, and Luke Bryan. She leaned more toward Katy Perry, Aerosmith, and Nora Jones.

However, their tastes came together as they discussed Charli and Reno's upcoming wedding and the reception that would take place in his backyard. Their chat flowed effortlessly, as if they were old friends instead of new acquaintances.

They finally brought in all the items she'd snagged from his mother's loft, and together they worked to put the shine on the empty rooms. They'd added some very eclectic boxes, baskets, a rusted Texas star, and a collection of old clocks that went in the living room. They'd also found a home for her favorite piece—a folk art chest Jana had rescued from an old barn about to be torn down. They'd even hung the black velvet John Wayne.

Before she knew it, the clock had ticked past midnight, and by the time she headed toward the door, Jesse looked as exhausted as she felt. Still, the Southern gentleman in him wouldn't let her walk out to his brother's truck alone.

She opened the truck door.

When Jesse glanced inside the cab at all the paraphernalia Jared had left behind, he gave an audible sigh.

"Damn I miss him."

"I can only imagine." Emotion welled up. "Riding around in his truck has given me a little bit of a sense of who he was. I can tell he was fun-loving and sweet."

"He was the best of us."

"I really am sorry for your loss. But as far as the best? I think you may be selling yourself too short." She stepped closer and laid a hand on his broad chest. Beneath her palm, his heart beat steady and strong. "You think about what I said about talking to someone. Okay? The last thing Jared would want to do would be to make you suffer."

He nodded as he drew her into his arms. For a moment, as they stood in that wordless embrace, something powerful materialized in her heart. Something that said this was more than just sexual attraction. Something that felt very much like a warning that she was getting too close. Too involved. Something that said if she stayed another second, she'd be irrevocably lost.

"I have to go." She broke the embrace and quickly climbed into the driver's seat. Before she could change her mind, she closed the door and turned the key in the ignition.

He clapped his hands over the open window. "What's your hurry?"

"It's late."

The furrow between his dark brows was so endearing she almost turned the truck off. Instead, she stuck her arm out the window, grabbed a handful of his shirt and tugged him close. Before she could think or stop herself, she kissed him. She'd meant it to just be a quick *I've-come-to-my-senses, see-you-later* peck on the lips. But everyone knew what they said about good intentions.

His long fingers threaded through her hair, and his grip tightened as if he didn't plan to let her go.

Earlier, the kiss had started out gentle and almost sweet. Now, with his lips pressed against hers, coaxing her to open to him, he moaned a sound of want and need that made her want to crawl through the window to get closer. She succumbed to the slick glide of his tongue and the warmth that spread through her limbs like honey.

Before she threw caution and her sanity out the window, she broke the kiss.

Came up for air.

And immediately regretted her decision.

"You are a dangerous man, Jesse Wilder."

With a sigh, she put pedal to the metal and roared down the driveway with a spew of gravel. In the rearview mirror she could see him still standing there, hands on those slim hips, looking hotter than hell and very much like a man she could love.

It took everything she had to keep her foot on the gas and keep going.

Chapter 9

On a good day, Bud's Nothing Finer Diner was a busy spot for the breakfast bunch. On a great day, it became standing room only. When Jesse stepped inside to meet up with his brothers, the place was packed with the senior citizens who never failed to liven things up.

As he made his way toward the back booth where Reno, Jackson, and Jake all sat sipping cups of Bud's smooth dark brew, he was stopped by Gladys Lewis and Arlene Potter. The ladies sat at one of the big round tables in the center of the restaurant with six other golden girls. To say that after their unorthodox visit the other night he was a bit apprehensive to stop and chat was an understatement.

"Sit yourself down and join us," Arlene said, patting the empty chair between her and Gladys.

"As much as that would be a pleasure . . ." *Not to mention entertaining and scary as hell.* "I've come to meet with my brothers for some last-minute wedding instructions."

Gladys tossed a look toward Reno. Her painted red lips lifted in a snarl. "Can't believe we're losing another good one to a younger woman. It's all your fault for chasing *him* away the other night," she said with a smack on Arlene's arm.

"Me?" Arlene pointed to herself.

"Yeah *you* with all your talk about X-rated stuff. And I told you, you spiked the tea too hard."

"So . . . ladies." Panic slithered up Jesse's back. "Gotta go." When he reached his brothers' table, they were snickering.

"What in the hell were you talking about with those two to get them so riled up?" Jackson laughed so hard, Jesse could swear he snorted the maple syrup off his pancakes.

"Not going there." Jesse slid into the booth next to Reno and shuddered at the thought.

Jake stuffed a forkful of waffle in his mouth and spoke around the bite. "This wouldn't have anything to do with the lovely Allison Lane, would it?"

Jesse held up a finger so the server would know to bring him a cup of coffee. "Not going there either."

"You suck," Jackson said.

"Yeah," Reno added. "You made us talk to you about Charli and Abby. What makes you think you get to be tight-lipped?"

"Because I'm better at it than any of you." *They all had no idea just how good.*

"Bullshit." This was said from all three of his brothers in a united grunt.

When their waitress showed up, he ordered the Cattleman's Special, then leaned back in the padded seat to await the huge platter of sausage, bacon, and eggs.

"That shit's gonna give you a heart attack." Jake grabbed the creamer from the center of the table and poured a big splash in his coffee. "Then who's going to escort the fair maiden Allison around town and dance with her in the dark at the Blue Armadillo?"

Jesse gave his little brother the stink eye. "Who told you about that?"

"I did." Chester Banks wandered over to their table on bowed legs. His straw cowboy hat sat at a jaunty angle on his bald head but did nothing to disguise the size of his schnozzola. Somewhere in his eighty-plus years on earth, Chester's eyeballs had shrunk, and his nose had grown to a magnanimous proportion. This, to everyone's amusement, did not eliminate or lessen Chester's amorous intentions toward any female over the age of thirty.

"And I come to talk to ya about it." Chester leaned a skinny jeans-clad hip against the side of the booth. "Don't think it's fair that every time we get a new girl in town, you boys snatch her up before any of the rest of us get a chance."

"Yeah," Jake agreed with a huge grin. "What's up with that?"

For some reason, everyone looked at Jesse. Not that he felt the need to explain, but he explained just the same. "I was just showing her around town. Being a good tour guide."

His evil brothers had the gall to snort.

"Boy?" Chester's forehead wrinkled up like tissue paper. "Them wandering hands of yours have a bigger reputation than any line of BS that mouth can spout. All the rest of us are asking is for a chance at an opportunity before you swing in like Tarzan and whisk her away."

Apparently, no one had informed Chester that the chances of a woman under the age of seventy being interested in a man with more snow on his roof than fire in his engine were hardly likely. Still, Jesse had never been one to intentionally hurt anyone's feelings.

When the diner door swung open, and Allison walked in, sunglasses atop her head pulling that silky hair back and wearing a flirty little yellow sundress, Jesse decided to give Chester his opportunity. Even as his primal instincts told him to grab her up, take her home, and finish what they'd started the night before.

"Have at it." He nodded toward Allison, standing at the door surveying the diner.

Chester turned, and his expression lit up like an aluminum Christmas tree. "Now *that's* what I'm talking about."

Jesse and his brothers watched with shock and awe as Chester found a new giddyup to his getalong and shuffled off to put his best wooing skills to work.

"Think we should go rescue her?" Jackson asked.

"Naw." Jesse grinned as the plate of his Cattleman's Special was set down in front of him. He picked up his fork and dug in. "Believe me, that girl can handle herself just fine." She certainly managed to keep him at bay.

As Chester gave his magic a go with a visibly reluctant Allison, Jesse tried to remain focused on his perfectly cooked eggs and not the woman who just last night had opened his eyes to something he'd tried to ignore for a long time. Something his baby brother had quickly pointed out. He'd built an enormous house that was far too quiet, and he'd been too busy to notice that when he came home at night, there was no one to talk to except Dinks and Rango. And unless you had a treat in your hand, their conversation skills were sorely lacking.

He hadn't noticed he was lonely until Allison had popped in, made him dinner, then sat by his side chatting about what had happened during their day. He'd been pleasantly surprised how in just a few minutes, she'd brought an appealing level of hominess to his four walls with her infusion of décor, not to mention her warmth and laughter. The extraordinary sensation of holding her in his arms had made him want to keep her there forever. It wasn't a feeling he was accustomed to. And he honestly didn't know what the hell to do about it.

A quick glance across the restaurant made his heart wobble funny in a way that had nothing to do with the gut-bomb breakfast he'd been shoveling in. As she and her short little sundress made their way to the counter, Chester was hot on the heels of her wedge sandals.

With the flash of a smile and some pretty good evasion tactics, Allison seemed to be holding her own. When she sat down at the only available seat at the old-fashioned counter, Chester gave up and rejoined his cronies at the table in the corner.

"We should ask her to join us," Jackson said.

Entertained, Jesse murmured over a bit of bacon, "She looks like she's doing fine on her own."

"Mom will kick our asses if we don't display our Southern hospitality." Jake slid out of the booth and headed toward the counter. Moments later, he returned sans Allison but wearing a big grin.

Jackson glanced over his shoulder. "She didn't want to join us?"

"Nope."

"What the hell's so funny?" Jesse asked.

Jake gave him a look. "She thanked me for the offer then said she decided to play it safe today. Said *you'd* understand."

Great.

While she was trying to play it safe, he was trying to break down barriers.

Guess the crux of the matter was, who would succeed?

$\mathcal{F}$or two days, Allison managed to keep her distance from Jesse. Though she'd driven past the pet clinic several times on her way here or there, she'd ignored the temptation to stop in unannounced, tear his clothes off, and have her way with him.

It had been a huge undertaking.

She didn't know what was wrong with her that she couldn't control the massive quantities of estrogen that pumped through her blood at just the sight of him; she only knew that where he was concerned, she had a major issue. Somewhere along the way, she'd discovered that there was a lot more to Jesse Wilder than met the ever-appreciative eye. He had a gigantic heart that made that six-foot-plus package of muscle even more appealing.

And that was just a huge turn-on.

In the meantime, she'd dodged offers of romance from a bowlegged cowboy named Chester and several of his good-time buddies who, despite their advanced ages, clearly intended to give the handsome Wilder brothers a run for their money.

With two wedding catastrophes resolved, Allison now had a solution to finding someone to replace the incarcerated reception deejay. Her quick trip to Austin had spotlighted two possibilities—a nice country cover band that specialized in tunes ranging from Luke Bryan to Carrie Underwood, and a deejay with his own dance floor and lighting system. The only issue was the deejay mainly spun Elvis tunes and insisted on dressing in full Elvis garb.

Once Charli and Reno made their choice, Allison would book their selection, then head back to Seattle. Obligation complete. She was sure Danielle would be relieved to have her back.

When late afternoon rolled around, she headed toward Charli and Reno's quaint ranch-style home. After she parked near the barn behind an SUV and an economy car, she made her way up the front walkway. She couldn't help admiring the inviting veranda, with its rocking chairs and flowerpots with brightly colored geraniums spilling over the sides. It seemed all the Wilders shared the love of a homey porch.

In the back of Charli and Reno's home there was a nice yard and a lush vegetable garden. While Allison had never been raised in such an environment, she could definitely understand its appeal. And at this home, much like the main house at Wilder Ranch, she could see the traditions that seemed to breathe in every nook and cranny.

The only ritual her mother had ever taught her and Danielle had been to make sure they served ham on Thanksgiving because turkey was so troublesome, and black-eyed peas for good luck on New Year's Day. Allison knew if she ever had the opportunity to cook a real Thanksgiving dinner, she'd go old school. Because even though her mother had no regard for traditional values, Allison was quickly learning to have a great appreciation.

As soon as she knocked on the door, it whipped open, and Charli stood there in a calico-print apron with what appeared to be smears of cherries down the front. Her little orange poodle Pumpkin and Reno's dog Bear danced at her bare feet.

"Hey!" Charli's face lit up. "You're just in time."

"For?"

"Canning." Charli grabbed her by the arm and hauled her into the house.

"I don't know anything about canning," she said, prepared to back the hell out of there.

"Me either. Thus the numerous smears down the apron. But we're starting to catch on."

"We?"

"Me and the girls. Minus Izzy, who's hanging with her Uncle Jesse for some swim time." Charli dragged her into the kitchen, where Jana, Abby, Fiona, and Annie all stood at what appeared to be specific workstations.

While her pregnant belly peeked from beneath a snug T-shirt, Annie sat on a stool popping cherry pits into a bowl. Abby stirred a huge pot on the stove. Jana had the food processor going. And Fiona was measuring out large portions from the biggest bag of sugar Allison had ever seen. Everyone stopped what they were doing and came over to give her a welcome hug. Their efforts definitely helped to overcome the awkwardness of walking into a room of women who all knew each other and you were the only stranger.

"We're making jars of jam for wedding favors." Charli thrust a pair of pinking shears in her hand and pulled out a chair. "You can cut the fabric squares we're using to decorate the tops of the Mason jars. We're tying them with raffia and putting these little tags on them. Aren't they adorable?"

Love is Sweet.
Reno and Charlotte
Thank You for Sharing Our Happiness.

"I've seen these jars filled with candies before but never jam. That's a lot of work," Allison said.

"Especially the week before your wedding. Most brides would sit back and take advantage of being catered to before the big day."

"Hang around her long enough," Jana said, "and you'll see that the girl never stops."

"I'll stop tomorrow night. And most likely the next day, when I'm hungover." Charli patted the chair for Allison, then she returned to tying the tags to the raffia. "You're coming, aren't you?"

"To . . . ?"

"Oh for land sakes." Jana turned and thrust her fists onto her hips. "Didn't your daddy give you and your sister the invitation to the bridal shower/ bachelorette party? I gave it to him to mail to you before you got here."

"It might have arrived after I was already en route. Danielle didn't mention anything. But she's pretty busy trying to hold down the chaos while I'm gone." The notion that they'd thought to include her and Danielle before they'd even met made Allison's heart feel all warm and fuzzy.

"Well, you're coming," Abby said. "We're going to need an extra body to lug the bride-to-be back home."

"No presents are necessary," Charli added.

"Especially lingerie." Annie laughed. "*Big* waste of money."

"And why is that?" Charli asked with a playful flutter of her eyelashes.

"Because there's no way Reno will leave it on long enough to appreciate it," Fiona added.

Allison shot a look to Jana, wondering how she felt about the topic of conversation. Jana laughed.

Comfortably. Allison couldn't imagine her own mother sitting idly by while people talked about *her* sex life. Then again, as the mother of five good-looking sons, Jana had probably heard it all. Especially when at least one of them had a *romantic* reputation a mile long.

"I'd love to come," Allison said. "But there's no way I'm coming empty-handed."

"There won't be male strippers," Fiona added.

"Thank God," Jana said.

"Because really, what's the point?" Abby said. "It would be impossible to find guys hotter than—"

"Lalalalala." Jana covered her ears with her hands and laughed.

"You get my meaning?" Abby winked.

"I get it." Allison had to agree. If there were better-looking men in the area than the Wilder brothers, she hadn't seen them. Although she had to admit—if only to herself—that she wouldn't mind a private performance of Jesse doing a slow, naughty, cowboy strip.

When the pot of cherry jam began to boil, the activity in the kitchen picked up, and all hands and bodies flew into motion. Allison picked up the pinking shears, and while she cut squares of fabric, she told Charli of the reception entertainment choices. Fake Elvis was out, the country band was in.

The camaraderie in the room was remarkable, and Allison found herself wishing Danielle was there to join in the fun. At the same time, as Allison began to relax a little and not feel like such an outsider, she realized that, were the shoe on the other foot, her own mother would never participate in this kind of down-home activity. She'd simply hire someone like Allison to put everything together, so she didn't have to get her hands dirty. At the end, she'd write out a hefty check to cover all the expenses and the hassle.

Sadly, Allison realized that as an event planner, while she enjoyed putting things together and seeing the outcome, she also had a good amount of her mother's DNA floating in her system. And as much as it pained her to admit, her biggest fear was becoming a replica of the woman who'd given her life. Most days, she fought to keep that from happening. Other days, she'd forget her boxing gloves.

She glanced across the room, where Jana stood next to Annie with her hands stretched over the young woman's expanded belly. The smile that spread across Jana's face reaffirmed that this was a woman who loved life and people. She was probably the most accepting person Allison had ever met. Her father might very well have struck gold.

There was no doubt Jana would take care of him and be there whenever he needed her. She'd listen to his troubles, hug him, and when he stumbled, she'd encourage him to get up and try again. She'd love him unconditionally. And when times got tough, Jana would put on her boots and kick the shit out of whatever was in the way of their happiness.

Allison craved that kind of connection with someone as deeply as she feared it.

Why that particular yearning brought Jesse Wilder to mind was something she didn't want to examine too closely. The feelings developing for him were extraordinary. Unlike anything she'd ever felt before. Those feelings made her honestly dare to hope for the first time in her life.

The pinking shears in her hand stilled as the inkling of that desire froze her solid in her tracks.

How could she dare to hope when, time and time again, she'd witnessed the heartbreaking disappointment when hope was crushed?

Coward.

The word slithered through her heart even as she knew it to be true.

When her thoughts and desires became too much to bear, she went back to focusing on something still out of reach but definitely more pleasurable.

Those thoughts were of Jesse Wilder wearing a cowboy hat, a smile, and absolutely nothing else.

Chapter 10

Seven Devils was the spot where all bachelor and bachelorette parties ended. Didn't matter where they began or whether the events started out prim and proper or down and dirty. Everybody ended up slamming shooters and draft brews until they were swimming in alcohol and stomping out a two-step on the battered dance floor.

Reno's good-bye-to-bachelorhood party followed suit.

Everyone from Deputy Brady Bennett—their designated driver, to Charli's brother Nick—a Marine sergeant who seemed quite popular with the women, and Aiden and Ben Marshall were there. Even creaky old Chester Banks had come out to celebrate the upcoming nuptials of the first Wilder brother to be taken off the market.

The females in the saloon lamented their loss.

Especially Lila Ridenbaugh, who'd tried her

damnedest to sweet-talk Reno into becoming baby daddy number five. Or six. Or maybe she was on number seven now. Hard to say. Jesse just did his best to keep his distance.

While the cover band on stage cranked into "Boys 'Round Here," the boys around the biggest table they could find raised their Shiners, Jack, and Wells in a toast. Most of what was said couldn't be repeated in the company of ladies.

The later it got, the louder the band played, and the more people tried to talk over the music. Jesse tried not to make a habit of frequenting the saloon if only for his hearing's sake. But once in a while a guy just had to say what the hell. He leaned back against the old barn-wood wall, kicked a booted foot up on the bench, and took a pull from his fresh bottle of Shiner. The ale went down crisp and cool. To his right, the saloon door opened and red neon light spilled inside the bar along with a giggling group of bachelorette party girls.

Charli came through the door first, decked out in a pink satin sash and a pink straw hat. Both proclaimed her the "Bride-to-Be." Fiona, Abby, Annie, Paige, and Sarah Randall followed, along with several other ladies from town. By the blush on their cheeks, it was apparent someone had spiked the punch. Not that there was anything wrong with that. It was a night for celebration. It just appeared the girls had gotten quite the head start.

Grinning, Jackson elbowed Jesse in the side. "I think my fiancée's trashed."

Jesse glanced at Abby, who'd obviously smiled

a while back, and it stuck. "No *thinking* about it."

"I should probably take her home so I can get lucky before she passes out." When Jackson moved to get off his chair, Jesse clamped a hand over his brother's arm.

"They just got here. Let her have a little fun."

"I can give her *big* fun."

"You're such a jackass."

Jake leaned in. "What are you two whispering about?"

"The girls are . . ." Jesse's words stopped along with his eyes when Allison stepped from behind the pack wearing tight, slightly ragged jeans, high-heeled boots, and a Pistol Annies "Hell on Heels" tank that hugged her glorious curves. A little slice of bare belly peeked out from the space between the top of her jeans and the hem of her shirt. "Damn."

"I believe the word you were looking for was 'tipsy,'" Jake said.

"Yeah. Sure." Whatever. Jesse couldn't take his eyes off her. Lucky for him, the girls spotted the bachelor party in the corner and made their way over. While Charli launched herself into Reno's arms, Jesse stood. Allison looked up and gave him a big smile.

"Heeeeeey, handsome!"

Yep.

Tipsy.

"What are you guys doing here?" she asked as though it was some kind of oddity that a bachelor party would end up in the only honky-tonk in town.

"This is pretty much where everybody ends up at the end of the night."

"Is that so? Last call doesn't happen for . . ." She glanced at her rhinestone watch. "Four more hours."

"Guess that means we still have some time to enjoy ourselves." He smiled as she settled her hand on his chest to steady herself. "You want to sit down?"

"I didn't come here to sit." When the band eased into Florida Georgia Line's "Cruise," she curled her fingers into the front of his shirt, whipped the Stetson off his head, and popped it on top of her long, silky curls. "Come dance with me, cowboy."

He ignored the catcalls some at the table made as she took him by the hand and pulled him onto the dance floor. At that moment, he'd let her take him just about anywhere.

After she'd burned rubber out of his driveway, he'd lain awake half the night thinking about her and wondering why he kept thinking about her. He didn't have the time. Didn't need the complication. He really needed to quit screwing around and stick to business, both of the four-legged *and* the two-legged varieties that bore the same last name as him.

With Allison, he'd tried to impose a *keep your distance* rule he'd shot down in flames about two seconds after she'd walked into his house. He had to keep his hands to himself. He had to keep his mind from straying to things like wondering what color panties she wore under those tight jeans. Or how badly he wanted to touch that bared midriff and caress her soft skin. He needed to get focused and stay focused.

All day he felt like he'd walked around in a daze. The one thing he realized as he'd stared up at his ceiling for hours was as hot as she made him for her body, something else ranked even higher.

Her heart.

She tried hard to hide the fact that she even owned one, but it didn't take an Einstein to know her heart was big, warm, and generous. He also knew it had been broken almost beyond repair. Which was only one of the reasons why it meant so much for him to help her believe that anything was possible. That a forever kind of love was not only imaginable but achievable if she'd only open herself up to the possibilities.

From restoring old cars with his dad to taking care of family issues, he'd always been a Mr. Fix-it kind of guy. With Allison, he just might have come up against the ultimate challenge.

Through the haze, he noted the stubborn tilt of her chin.

Yeah.

He was totally screwed.

Instead of leading him to the center of the dance floor, where most couples went, she led him to the edge, where the lights were dim. With any other country tune, he could have simply held her hand and kept his distance by leading her into a two-step or swing. But the rhythm of the song practically insisted he take her in his arms and hold her close.

At least that's what he told himself.

She came into his arms easily, with a smile that settled in right next to the slight buzz vibrating in his bloodstream. With his thigh pressed between hers and the heat of her warming him up, they swayed together. He couldn't deny his attraction. He inhaled and captured that same, sweet, cotton-candy scent she'd worn the first night they met. And like that night, he wanted to lean in and bury his nose right in the soft curve of her neck and inhale her tastiness. His fingers caressed the smooth skin at the small of her back. As he tucked her against him a little tighter, he could swear he felt a quiver down her spine.

With a smile playing on her luscious lips, she looked up. "Where'd you learn to dance?"

"Here and there."

"You move well," she said, sounding surprised.

Not sure if he should take that as an insult, he just said, "Thanks."

She chuckled, and the sound vibrated against his chest.

"What's so funny?"

"That's not what I expected you to say," she said.

"Which is?"

"Mmmm . . . maybe something like, 'I move better in the bedroom' or a number of any other boastful bad-boy remarks."

"Well, darlin', men who do don't need to brag."

That luscious mouth dropped open just slightly.

If you listened to the ridiculous talk on the street, he was a legend. If you were looking for the truth, he'd admit that since puberty, he'd simply paid attention to women. He'd noticed the idio-syncrasies they revealed about themselves—their likes, their dislikes.

Whatever opportunity had come his way, he'd carefully explored his partners. Did she like this? What about if he did that? It had never been all about his own pleasure. And though the women he'd been with had been as unique as snowflakes, he'd studied their ways like a hungry student.

Even as an image of Allison—eyes closed and moaning in pleasure—dropped into his mind then hit farther south like a Rockeye bomb, he realized he couldn't pin down her type.

And that just intrigued the hell out of him.

"Huh," she said.

He chuckled. "What kind of a response is that?"

"Well . . ." A flirty smile brushed her lips. "A girl can't help but wonder, can she?"

He'd done enough wondering in the past forty-eight hours for the both of them. "That kind of speculation can get you in trouble."

"Really?" She pressed herself a little closer and grinned up at him. "Exactly what kind of trouble are we talking about? Handcuffs? Silk ties? Satin sheets?"

Holy shit.

"You're killing me," he managed to say past the lump in his throat.

"Well that would spoil all the fun, wouldn't it?"

While his lusty imagination traveled in all directions, she asked, "So what's next?"

"Next? I don't follow."

"Right. Because you're a guy. You lead."

Aside from the ache in his groin, he felt a head-ache coming on. "Exactly how much have you had to drink?"

"Why? Am I not making sense?"

"Not even close."

"Perfect! Women are supposed to remain a mystery, right?"

"Unfortunately."

"I meant . . . what's the next thing you have up your sleeve to show me that all roads of love lead to a happy forever?"

"Obviously, I haven't done a very good job so far."

"Oh, don't be so hard on yourself."

Her hand smoothed down the buttons on his shirt, completely distracting him from what he'd been about to say.

"I enjoyed the movie," she said. "And really, watching you try to avoid the amorous attentions of Lucy and Ethel—I mean, Gladys and Arlene—was priceless."

"Yeah. They're a barrel of fun."

"Or . . . they'd like to be in a barrel with *you*."

Her smile sent a tingling sensation through the center of his chest.

"So what's next?" she asked.

"Persistent, aren't you?"

"If you talk to anyone who's ever worked with me," she said, "I usually get what I want."

"And exactly what is it you want?"

While the adolescent, horny devil inside him rubbed its gleeful hands together and thought *please say me*, Jesse amazingly managed to behave like an adult.

As if it had been planned, the song ended. Without giving him a response, she slipped from his arms, turned on the heels of her boots, and, still wearing his hat, headed back to the group of party revelers.

Following Allison was no chore. In fact, it was a pleasure he could do all day. She moved like a confident woman who knew she had the sexy on but didn't need to do a damn thing to advertise. He, unfortunately, had a whole lot of advertising going on below the belt.

In order to keep the catcalls and jokes to a minimum as he returned to the table, he stuck his hands into the pockets of his jeans. An action he'd learned years ago that helped disguise any evidence of uncontrollable physical attraction.

He hadn't had an issue with keeping himself in check since all those years ago when he'd first discovered that girls smelled pretty, wore skimpy underwear, and had body parts under that silky underwear that were infinitely more interesting than his own. He shook his head. With Allison, all those uncontrollable urges came back full force.

And on top of everything else, she hadn't answered his question.

So what was it that Allison really wanted? And why was she so evasive?

"What's up?" Jackson asked, as Jesse came back to the table, grabbed his ale, and sat down.

"Ever feel like you're back in the battle?"

His brother's gaze slid to the attractive focus of Jesse's attention. "Know exactly what you're talking about. She know you've got a thing for her?"

"Never said I had a *thing*."

Jackson leaned his head back and laughed. "Hell, you were both heating up that dance floor so bad everyone else had to move away or get singed."

He knew that. He could feel it in every pore in his body. The lasting effects had made his damned jeans uncomfortable. He glanced across the table, where Allison had tipped his Stetson back on her head and plopped her luscious behind between Brady and Charli's brother Nick. Judging by their smiles, neither man was oblivious to her charms. Jesse tilted his bottle and took a long drink to cool his ever-increasing awareness.

"You're imagining things, little brother," he said.

"Ha! I love how you're so good at handing out the advice—no matter in what wayward manner it's delivered—and yet you suck at taking it."

Jesse knew the reference was made to the way he'd tricked Jackson into thinking he was interested in Abby. His plan had been to get Jackson up off his ass and admit he'd been in love with her since they'd barely learned to tie their shoes. His strategy had worked.

"Maybe it's time for you to step back and do exactly what you preached to both me and Reno," Jackson said.

"Which is?" Not that he didn't know exactly where this convo was headed.

"Go for it." Jackson's familiar frown appeared. "Don't lose what's right in front of you because you're too damned stubborn to grab hold of what you want."

"Have you ever known me to *not* grab hold?"

"Yeah. *Now*."

Jesse slid his gaze across the table and noticed the attention Brady and Nick were pouring on Allison. They were both good-humoredly competing. And from what he could tell, she didn't mind their efforts.

"In case you've forgotten," Jesse told Jackson, "she's the daughter of the man our mother is about to marry."

Jackson's broad shoulders lifted. "So?"

"So that means we're about to be related."

"Before you go inserting any eeew factor . . . you will be related by marriage, not blood. And if you're thinking along the lines of putting a ring on—"

"Whoa." Jesse leaned back and tossed Jackson a look that said he was about to step into bat-shit-crazy territory. "Don't even go there."

"Okay." His little brother smiled. "But when *you* go there, I promise I won't say I told you so."

At that moment, Jake—who looked to be about two and a half sheets to the wind—stood, and announced "Pool party."

Before Jesse could summon the strength to say "Not tonight" and handle the disappointed party-goers, the designated drivers had keys in hand and everyone headed toward the door.

Chapter 11

The ride to Jesse's house became a lesson in Girl Talk 101 Allison was positive she'd never even had with her own sister. Apparently, men couldn't claim ownership or sole bragging rights when it came to sexual escapades.

These women weren't shy about speaking their minds. They made her laugh with stories of their sexual adventures *and* misadventures. Abby had a story about her and Jackson and a staircase, while Charli and Reno had a close encounter that got busted up by Deputy Brady Bennett. And Paige Marshall described how as an *Army of One*, she'd taken down her new former Army Ranger husband, Aiden, creek side.

Danielle—who'd held on to her virtue for a long time in order to snag the best-looking guy in school—had never talked about *doing the deed*.

To Danielle, giving a guy her virginity equaled a marriage proposal. Of course, in Danielle's perfect world, *waiting* had worked out in her favor and she'd married her knight in shining armor. Allison had lost hers to Bobby Richards over Christmas break during her junior year of high school. By Valentine's Day, he'd moved on to charm another girl or two out of their bikini briefs.

The women crammed together in Abby's SUV with a sober and pregnant Annie at the wheel, had a completely different take on finding their princes.

It seemed Charli had dated every slug in the garden before she accidentally came upon Reno. But even then, as she told the story, things hadn't gone smoothly until the night of the Wilder Barbecue Extravaganza. When she thought she finally had Reno on the line, she dropped the bait by telling him she'd forgotten to put on panties under her dress.

Allison admired her creative thinking.

Abby had been in love with Jackson since she'd been about five years old, but other than the few times he'd let his guard down, he'd never looked her way other than friendship. So she'd left Sweet and married a dog of a man who had money but no class. When she finally came back to Sweet, she'd had to *buy* Jackson at an auction to finally get what she wanted.

And Annie, well, God bless the girl. She'd moved all the way to Seattle to find what she'd thought to be her Prince Charming. Only to discover after he abandoned her and their unborn baby that he'd been a toad all along.

Allison's past relationships had been all over

the board. Since she'd never planned to look for the man of her dreams, let alone anyone even semipermanent, she'd taken the outlook that variety was the spice of life. She'd never had visions of sugarplums, or having babies, or a man to take care of when he grew old. Other than her career, she'd tried to never look farther than the day she happened to be living.

The image of Jesse holding her in his arms flashed through her head. For the first time in her life, she thought it might be a good idea to get a broader perspective. Maybe Forest Gump was right. Maybe her usual box of chocolates had gone way past the expiration date.

Annie parked in Jesse's long driveway, and they all stumbled out of the SUV. Giggling, Abby led the way to the back of Jesse's house. There they found a door that opened into a large bathroom—a very user-friendly bathroom, where beach towels were stuffed into cubbies. Spray cans of sunscreen and bug spray filled an entire shelf. And an organizer box was stuffed with women's bathing suits in every color imaginable. Abby grabbed a second box filled with men's swim trunks and shoved it outside the door.

"We've all left our suits over here. Some of us have left several," Abby said. "Jesse washes everything and puts it back for the next time."

"Oh. Good." Allison almost sighed with relief. "I was hoping this wasn't going to be a skinny-dipping extravaganza."

"We're close." Charli laughed. "But not *that* close."

"Here." Fiona grabbed a yellow-and-white string bikini from the pile and handed it to Allison. "This should fit you, and it will look better on you than it ever did me." Then she turned to Annie. "How about we give you bottoms and you just wear one of Jesse's T-shirts for a top."

Annie laughed. "Good idea. Because I don't think any of those bikinis has a tie long enough to wrap around *this* middle."

Curiosity tugged at Allison. "Can you feel the baby move yet?"

"For a long time now." Annie took Allison's hand and placed it on her big belly. As if on cue, the baby stretched out a foot or a hand or something, and Allison felt it press against her palm. She gasped and smiled at the wonderment.

"Haven't you ever felt that before?" Annie asked.

Allison shook her head. "My sister wouldn't let me or anyone else touch her stomach when she was pregnant. She always said it was private property."

"That's a shame. A baby's a wonderful thing. Even if the father happens to be a jerkwad."

"I'm guessing after what you've been through, you don't believe in happily-ever-afters anymore," Allison said.

"Oh, I still believe. And I'll find mine one day. But right now, I've got this little one to worry about."

Why Allison found it hard to believe that Annie wouldn't give up on the dream every girl had, she didn't know. She only found it fascinating. She didn't know what they put in the water here in Sweet, but it seemed as though everyone was steeped in tradition.

Having led a life with such a clouded view of almost folkloric traditions, she'd wondered for years what all the hoopla was about. But as she looked around at the women laughing and enjoying life to the hilt, she had no choice but to believe that her views might have been harshly skewed.

More than anything, she wanted to believe there were people on this earth who were truly meant to be together till death did them part.

Danielle might just be the perfect example. She'd grown up in Dysfunction Junction too. Yet she'd found the perfect man with whom to share her life. She had two amazing little girls who seemed untouched by all the negatives their surrounding family members and society wanted to cast on them.

Danielle truly seemed to be living the dream.

Maybe their father would too. Maybe he and Jana had been meant to be all these years, but it took them this long to find each other.

"Thank you," she said to Annie.

"For?"

"Letting me feel your baby."

Annie laughed out loud and grabbed her in a hug that was slightly thwarted by the burgeoning belly between them. "Anytime Auntie Allison wants to touch, hold, *or* babysit, you just say the word."

Something fluttered around Allison's heart. She liked being an auntie. But for the first time in her life, she had an inkling that someday she might want something more.

As the women began to undress like they were in a high-school locker room, chattering like cartoon mice and with no modesty whatsoever, Allison smiled. She was an outsider. Yet without any effort, they'd somehow made her feel like a part of the family. It didn't take much imagination to sense that in *this* family if you argued or got mad it all worked out. No one left in a huff or took to their bed for days pouting and whining until they got what they wanted.

She sensed that *this* family would yell, maybe cry, then they'd hug it out and go on like nothing had ever happened. She didn't understand that world, but she was eager to find out how and if she might fit in.

Once they were all down to bikinis, they opened the door and went outside. Allison had never felt the need to hide her body, but she'd never been much of an exhibitionist either. For some reason, knowing Jesse would be looking at her filled her with an odd sort of energy and more than a little trepidation.

Would he like what he saw?

Did it even matter?

Because at the end of the day, she was only here on a temporary basis.

The pool area was aglow with tiki torches, colorful patio lights, and white fairy lights that dotted the trees around the pool and waterfall. All that mixed with the vibrant landscaping lights amongst the bushes set a magical mood. A stereo had been turned on, and the band coming through the speakers sang a song about motorboating on the Pontoon. Water splashed high in the pool as Jake Wilder performed a perfect cannonball off the diving board.

Allison immediately got caught up in the party atmosphere. The camaraderie. The close-knit relationships within the group. Her gaze scanned those in and around the pool and came to a screeching halt when she found Jesse standing at the edge.

In a pair of baby blue board shorts with droplets of water running off his unbound hair onto his shoulders and sliding slowly off those broad shoulders and down that amazing chest, he looked . . . wow. The wings-of-freedom eagle tattoo on his left biceps and the words NO REGRETS on his inner forearm flashed as he lifted a longneck bottle to his mouth and took a drink. He laughed at something Nick Brooks said, then he lowered that amber glass and licked a droplet off his bottom lip.

Whew.

Her girl parts shimmied while her heart simply tried to stay in control.

Her imagination?

That took off into forbidden Fantasyland.

As if he sensed her standing there, he turned and gave her a slow smile. On a sigh, she realized she would have stood there forever and waited for those chiseled masculine lips to curl, if only for the responding shiver it sent through her core.

"You swim?" he asked.

She stepped closer while the other girls did various leaps off the side of the pool and into the water. "I'm no Michael Phelps, but I frog paddle pretty good."

"And you look much better in a bikini than Phelps ever could." His smile lingered as his eyes took an appreciative ride down her body. "You want something to drink?"

She shook her head, knowing that all her mouth was thirsty for was the water dripping off his body.

"Well then, jump on in and enjoy yourself." He gave a nod toward the pool. "You might want to try going off the deep end. See how that feels."

"I'm not much of a deep-end jumper."

"Sometimes you just have to let it all go." His broad shoulders came up in a shrug. "Take a chance. See where it will take you."

"Are we talking about swimming?"

He moved toward her until they were practically toe-to-toe. All the other sights and sounds around them blurred as if they didn't exist. His eyes darkened, and her entire body reacted to his unmistakable desire.

She tried to remember the last time she'd had sex, and the answer took a while to come to her. She could use deprivation as an excuse for her peaked nipples and the warm ache between her thighs. Looking at him could be equaled to oohing and aahing over Brad Pitt in *Troy* or Chris Hemsworth in *Thor* or even Channing Tatum in *Magic Mike*. He was a good-looking guy with a mouthwatering physique and a killer smile. But she knew it was more than his looks that struck her in the solar plexus. She didn't know exactly what it meant or where it would take her, but for the moment, she planned to enjoy the ride. Because as with everything else, whatever it became wouldn't last.

"Swimming? Sure." A quick grin lit up his face. "Enjoy." Before she could blink, he gave her a little push, and in she went. The cool water sluiced over her head, and the shock of what he'd done floated up as she broke through the surface.

"What did you do that for?" she sputtered.

Grin still in place, he hunkered down at the edge of the pool and pointed at her with his bottle of ale. "Sometimes it's good to remember that the unexpected things in life can be fun and exciting."

She swept her wet hair from her face and frog paddled to the edge.

He gave her a wink. "Have a nice swim, darlin'."

As he rose to leave, something devious that felt really good sparked inside her. Before he got too far she reached up, grabbed his arm, and gave a good yank. He and his bottle of ale tumbled into the water beside her. When his head broke the surface his cocky grin had vanished. Hers emerged.

"Wasn't that *fun and exciting*?" She laughed at the shocked expression on his face, then quickly swam away to join the others in the shallow end, where a game of pool volleyball was in full swing.

After a time of laughter and good-hearted competition—at least on the girls' side—the boys won. Apparently, when it came to water games, chivalry was dead.

Eventually, everyone got out of the pool, refreshed their drinks, and assembled around the fire pit, where flames snapped and danced and warmed their chilled bodies. The gathering reminded Allison of the first night she'd arrived at Wilder Ranch. Yet unlike that night, when she'd been unprepared for the barrage of questions the family had tossed her way, tonight's conversation was about the Texas Rangers and where everyone thought they stood to win the pennant.

All through the lively discussion, Allison could feel the heat of Jesse's gaze. The several times she'd looked up and caught him, he hadn't bothered to look away. He'd offered no smile— especially when she'd been engaged in conversation with the handsome and witty Nick Brooks. She didn't know why, but she couldn't remember a time she'd felt more alive or alert.

Each time she caught his gaze, she wondered what was going on inside his head.

On her end, there was no thinking going on at all.

With those intense blue eyes of his sending all kinds of crazy tingles down into her bikini bottoms, her body was doing the talking.

How did she feel about that?

The flickering light from the tiki torches reflected in his hair as her gaze licked over him.

She felt stimulated.

Curious.

Impatient.

And exactly like her veins had been pumped with kerosene.

*J*esse stood beside Jake and gave his best shot at listening to the conversation around his fire pit. On any given day, he'd be fully engaged because the current topic—the Rangers—were his team. He'd been a die-hard fan for as long as he could remember. But tonight, everything had changed, and the Rangers came in second place to Allison, who looked unbelievably hot in her yellow bikini. All that thick, luscious hair falling over her shoulders and down her back made his chest tingle as if the feathery tips danced across his skin.

He still didn't know what was so different about her from any other woman he'd met or dated. She had something undefinable that reached out and grabbed him—not only by certain body parts, but by the heart. When she'd first set foot on Wilder Ranch, she'd had a tough-chick attitude. But it hadn't taken him long to see through that façade. She was a marshmallow. A sweet, hot, and sticky marshmallow he was dying to devour.

While the baseball discussion flew, she nibbled at her bottom lip. He could tell she wanted to fit in. He longed to tell her she didn't have to try so hard. Most everyone gathered had already accepted her. Not just because she was the daughter of the man his mother intended to marry. Acceptance had been granted because she'd stepped outside her boundaries to go above and beyond doing the right thing when no one even asked. The girls had taken her under their wing and included her in whatever it was they were doing, whether it be canning jars of jam or whooping it up at Seven Devils. In a short time, she'd become one of them.

And that made him smile.

The only thing that currently had has hackles

up was Nick Brooks's obvious attraction. It seemed every time Jesse turned around, Nick was there getting her a towel, helping her from the pool, getting her a drink. Worse? Allison didn't seem to mind Nick's attention. She smiled, touched his arm, and yeah, leaned into him with a laugh like she was doing right now.

Jesse had never been a jealous kind of guy. He had no reason to be jealous now.

But the hell if he wasn't.

So what to do? Move in like some overgrown caveman and claim his woman?

Hardly.

Because she wasn't his woman.

Ignore it like it wasn't happening? Fat chance. Because it was, and he didn't like it.

He lifted his beer and took a long, thoughtful drink.

"I'd give you a penny for your thoughts," Reno said. "But they're pretty much written all over your face."

"Not thinking at all. I'm just tired," Jesse said to throw the dog off his scent. "These beers knocked me back."

Reno clamped a brotherly hand over his shoulder. "If that's what you're telling yourself, then we may need to stage an intervention."

Jesse didn't like being *read*. Even if it was by someone he loved and admired. Especially when they were honing in on what had him hot and ready to explode like a heat-seeking missile. "You need another beer? I was just going to get one for myself."

"I'll go with you."

"No need."

"Try and stop me." Reno's dimples flashed, letting Jesse know that he was the bigger brother and couldn't be shaken.

"Shouldn't you be spending time with your bride-to-be?"

"Yep. Plan on doing just that as soon as we get home. If she doesn't pass out first."

Jesse ignored the tingle at the back of his neck that said his brother was about to pull rank and give him a talking-to. Not that Reno didn't give out great advice. Jesse just wasn't always good about being on the receiving end. Of course, invited or not, Reno followed him over to the outdoor kitchen, where they were away from the lively conversation and the tune of Hunter Hayes singing "I Want Crazy," to which Jesse vehemently disagreed.

"So . . . about that River of Denial you're rowing." Reno glanced over his shoulder at the revelers gathered around the fire pit. "I've seen you *with* women before, Jess. I've seen you *look* at women. *That* look"—he pointed at Jesse's face—"is different."

"Don't know what you're talking about. It's the same face I wear every day."

"Yeah." Reno laughed. "I remember saying that very thing not so long ago. Doesn't mean the look isn't there. No matter how loudly you might disagree."

Jesse reached into the outdoor refrigerator and shoved a fresh bottle of Shiner in Reno's hand.

"I'm sure you remember the advice you so happily handed out to me just a few months back." Reno paused only long enough to sip the cold beer.

"I'm sure I can't recall."

"Then I'd be only too happy to remind you and toss it right back in your face. Because that's what big brothers do." Reno grinned. "Where Allison is concerned, you've been throwing out 'Back the fuck off' signals all night. Especially to Nick."

"You've got a hell of an imagination on you." Jesse took the opportunity to step around Reno, only to have a huge hand grab him by the arm and stop him.

"Yeah, that was part of the conversation too," Reno said. "But here's the new part. Where the hell did you get this idea that it was up to you to make sure everyone else was happy?"

"Again. Don't know what you're talking about."

"Bullshit." Reno pointed the bottle of Shiner at him. "Somewhere after Jared was killed, you got it into that pretty-boy head of yours that it was your responsibility to make sure everyone was happy, settled, and on their way to a happily-ever-after."

"Delusional. That's you."

"Accurate. That's me." Reno shook his head the way he always had when one or the other of them was too screwed up to notice they were up to their necks in a dilemma they refused to acknowledge. "Look, your efforts are appreciated, but not necessary. There isn't a single one of us who doesn't want to see *you* happy. So take a chance, will you?"

Jesse glanced away from the intensity in his brother's dark eyes. "It's not my turn."

Reno stepped in front of him and grasped his shoulders. Made it impossible to look away. "What did you say?"

"Not. My. Turn."

"What the fuck, Jess? You think we're taking *turns*? At what? Finding happiness?"

Jesse could deny it all day long, but Reno had uncanny perception. He'd lived a horrifying life before he'd come into their family that made him far more insightful than anyone Jesse had ever known. Reno had always worked hard to feel like he belonged when he hadn't needed to work at all. He was one of them. He'd completed them. And now, with Jared gone, he was the one they all looked up to. It was Reno's turn at being happy. Jackson came next. Their mom. Then Jake.

"Yeah," he said.

Reno's eyes narrowed. "Why?"

Jesse shrugged. Tonight was a night of celebration, not a night of sinking into the past and dwelling on what could never be. He needed to end this conversation ASAFP.

"Why?" Reno asked again, unwilling to let it go.

"Because Jared never found his happiness." Emotion clogged his throat. Threatened to cut off his air. "And I want to make damn sure the rest of you do."

"Fuck." Without another word, Reno pulled him into a bear hug. For any other man, that embrace might have been uncomfortably long. Too unmanly. But the Wilders were a demonstrative bunch. Jesse had long ago grown used to the shouting, the arguing, and the passion that dripped thick through their Texan veins. To him the hug simply said, "I care."

When they finally parted, Reno asked again, "Why?"

Jesse glanced at the crowd, who seemed to be having the time of their lives. As a man about to be happily married to the love of his life, Reno should be smack-dab in the middle of party central, not standing here talking about something so deep and intense.

Gut clenched, he thought back to the conversation with Jared that had started his crusade. Allison had told him Jared would never want him to bear a burden that would make him miserable.

Maybe she was right.

Maybe it was time to share the burden. To let someone who'd understand know the catalyst for his concerns.

"If I tell you this, I'll ask that you keep it to yourself until the whole thing is thought through."

Reno shrugged. "Not an issue."

A long sigh drifted from Jesse's chest. "The last time Jared and I were together at Camp Leatherneck, we sat outside the tents, looking up into the sky, counting stars, and shooting the shit. For whatever reason, the conversation got serious. Almost like he knew something would happen to him. During our chat he told me . . ."

"He told you what?" Reno folded his arms.

"That he'd fallen in love." Jesse pulled air into his lungs, not sure if he should or would overstep what Jared had told him in confidence. What followed shortly after that exchange between him and Jared drowned him in pain. He glanced away. "And . . . he told me he was gay."

Jesse jerked his gaze back to gauge Reno's silent reaction. To his surprise, his brother's expression remained blank.

"Jared was gay?"

"Yeah."

"Wow." Reno ran a hand through his hair. "How did I not know that?"

"You don't get to be the lone soldier on that. None of us knew."

"I wonder how long he'd been hiding it."

"Since as far back as he could remember." Jesse recalled the relief in Jared's eyes when he'd finally let go of the secret. "He was finally ready to tell everyone. He wasn't ashamed. But it troubled him that he'd continued to live a lie for so long."

"I can't even imagine." Reno rubbed his hand over center of his chest. "God, I wished he'd said something."

"Me too. Then again, I guess he did. He said the last time he was home on leave, he told dad—not only that he was gay, but that he'd fallen in love with another military officer."

"How did that go?" A worry line creased Reno's forehead. "Obviously, Dad kept that to himself."

"You know Dad. He didn't care what color, religion, or sexual preference a person had. Jared was his firstborn, and he loved him like crazy. But Jared said Dad was worried about the repercussions he and the other officer might face."

"With good reason."

"Yeah. Dad asked Jared to keep his silence until

they could discuss it further and figure out how Jared could *come out* with the least amount of fall-out to his career and private life."

Personally, Jesse didn't understand why a person had to hide who they were anymore. It's not like they were living in the dark ages. But not everyone was so accepting. Whether his big brother had fallen in love with a man, or a woman, or a damned polka-dotted squirrel didn't matter. All Jesse had ever wanted was for Jared to be happy.

But Jared's chance at happiness had been cut short, and their father's grief had taken him to the grave. His broken heart had extended far beyond the loss of his firstborn child. Guilt had eaten him alive. In asking his son to keep his sexual orientation a secret—even though the request had been intended to be temporary and had come from affection and concern—he felt he'd denied his son the ultimate happiness.

Love.

Jesse shared the guilt that had sucked the life from their father. He remembered the day he'd stood alone on the hilltop at Wilder Ranch looking down at his father's and brother's headstones. He'd been overwhelmed with the guilt that he should have done something more to help his father heal. Instead of talking with his dad, he'd kept Jared's secret to himself. Maybe if there had been someone to talk to, it would have eased his father's pain and guilt. Maybe the outcome would have been different.

"So how do you feel about all that?" Jesse asked.

Reno released a slow leak of breath. "I don't give

a damn who our brother chose to love. I miss him. And Dad." Reno glanced away. When his gaze came back around, he asked, "Did Jared tell you who?"

Jesse shook his head. "I asked. He said he wanted to keep it to himself until we met in person." Jesse absently ran his thumb over the label on the bottle of ale. "But I can tell you when he talked about him, his whole damn face lit up like Christmas morning."

"Fuck."

"Amen to that." Jesse took a long pull from the bottle of beer. "So maybe now you can understand why I feel as I do about everybody's finding their happy place."

"It's not your job to see that the rest of us find personal satisfaction, little brother. It's your job to find your own." Reno glanced over his shoulder again. "Whether you find it today, tomorrow, or next week; with Allison, or John, Paul, George, or Ringo, none of us give a shit. We just want you to find it."

Jesse turned his head, and his gaze landed smack-dab on the brunette sitting amongst the people he cared about the most. She smiled at something Charli said, then looked up as if she knew he was looking.

Their eyes connected, and he felt the heat and power of it right down into the center of his chest.

The people he cared about.

Like it or not, Allison currently topped that category.

Chapter 12

As a few sleepy yawns began to pass through the crowd, Allison realized she didn't even know the time.

The party had kicked into gear early that afternoon at Abby's house, with a fun bridal shower attended by old and young alike. The bride-to-be received everything from crocheted place mats to edible underwear. Because Allison didn't know Charli well enough to purchase naughty lingerie, she stuck with a traditional crystal vase.

Allison had put together many bridal and baby showers, but she rarely had the privilege to attend as a guest. In fact, in the past she'd thought the events were often hokey or, as in the case of a current Seattle Mariners' wife, trying too hard to be elegant just to raise their societal clout.

Charli's shower had proven to be laid-back and entertaining, exactly what Allison would want should she ever fall down the rabbit hole.

Once Fiona's delicious lemon cupcakes topped with handmade candy Gerber daisies were depleted, the golden-age group went home. The remaining attendees then took the party over the top with Jana's freshly blended strawberry and peach margaritas. Though Charli warned everyone that Jana had a tendency to hit the drinks hard with tequila, no one flinched. Eventually, the tipsy troupe had made its way to Seven Devils for a little dancing and maybe a smidge of hell-raising.

Had Allison known Jesse would be there, she might have gone straight home. The man affected her in ways she didn't want to acknowledge. He made her head spin until all her thoughts became a jumbled mess, and she started thinking ridiculous things like "What if" and "Maybe." But the moment she'd strolled into the bar, and her eyes had landed on him, she couldn't have torn herself away with the jaws of life.

From where she sat near the fire pit, she glanced across the patio to where he stood talking with Reno. A serious conversation, judging by the frown pulling his brows together. Maybe he was finally telling someone what had been bothering him. She hoped so.

On a personal note, she understood the ramifications of keeping things bottled up.

On a selfish note, she let her eyes skim over that tanned, tall, muscular body. Not for the first time that night, her body hummed with desire.

As she'd told him, he was a dangerous man. Somehow, she needed to escape the inexplicable pull toward him. Unfortunately, she was at the mercy of their designated driver to get home. And as Annie seemed engaged in a lighthearted argument with Jake, who insisted that men were more romantic-minded than women, it didn't appear getting home soon was likely.

For a few moments, Allison tried to focus on the lively conversation and the attentions of Nick Brooks, a stunning man though far from her type. If she even had a type. But hard as she tried, she could not break her attention away from Sweet's favorite playboy veterinarian. The only solution she could come up with to get herself back in check was to escape.

"Would you excuse me for a minute?" she said to Nick. "I need to use the little girl's room."

"You want me to refresh your drink?" Nick asked.

"No, thank you." She didn't need to encourage all those loosey-goosey sensations she had floating through her veins. "I've probably had enough." She headed toward the bathroom adjacent to the pool area, but the door was locked.

Having previously been in the house, she knew where the rest of the bathrooms were located, and she headed indoors. The one facility downstairs was busy too, so she headed upstairs and ended up in the master suite. Though furnished with elegant Spanish Revival furniture and an enormous bed, the bedroom was as sparse as the living room had been before she'd added the accent pieces from Jana's treasure trove. Still, she could imagine with Jesse lying naked on that big bed, she wouldn't care if there were pictures on the walls or knickknacks on the dresser.

The door to the massive master bath was closed but unlocked. After she'd taken care of business, she came out to wash her hands. She looked up into the mirror and gasped. No wonder Jesse had been giving her such strange looks all night. Her eyeliner and mascara had not only slipped and smudged, she looked like a rabid raccoon.

Grabbing a tissue, she scrubbed beneath her eyes until she looked less goth and somewhat human. Then, with another quick glance to the mirror, she realized how little the yellow bikini left to the imagination. She'd never been ashamed of her body, but no matter which way she tugged, she couldn't seem to cover everything to her satisfaction. Thank God for all those hours she'd spent beneath the hair-removal laser.

As she turned to go, something grabbed her leg. A shriek slipped out. She looked down to find Jesse's cat Rango upside down, both paws wrapped around her ankle, teeth bared. She scooped up the gray-striped feline and received an unhappy yowl in response.

"Listen you. I look bad enough. I don't need to go back out there with tiny vampire marks on my leg thank you very much." Rango blinked and looked away as though totally bored. She'd never been much of a cat person, and the animal's obvious disregard didn't help matters. Still, she pulled him close and stroked his fluffy head between his pointy ears. "So do you think we can just agree to disagree on this one?"

Surprisingly, instead of launching another attack, he purred.

After a few more gentle strokes, Allison set him down. As soon as she turned her back, he pounced. "Traitor."

Shaking him loose of her ankle with minimal damage, she opened the bathroom door and immediately went down on her ass with an "Oof."

Dinks, Jesse's giant black Lab, ran her over like she was in his way to the dinner bowl. He did an "Oh crap" slide on the slippery floor and biffed it into the wall. Undeterred, he did a quick spin, then came back for a second attack. Only this time it was with long slurps of his tongue up the side of her face.

It took a few moments before she could regain control and untangle herself from his affection. Another glance to the mirror sent her back to the sink to remove the dog drool.

Finally put back together—or at least looking somewhat less like a chew toy—she went downstairs and out into the backyard.

The very *vacant* backyard.

Though the music still played softly, a quick glance verified both bachelor and bachelorette parties had departed.

Without her.

The pool and patio lights had been turned off. All that remained aglow were the landscape and twinkling tree lights. With a little hint of panic, Allison realized Jesse must be in the process of shutting down for the night.

She'd been forgotten.

So much for feeling like a part of the crowd.

Without a car, phone, or money for a taxi—not that Sweet actually had such a thing—she'd have to call her father to come pick her up. At this late hour, she really hated to disturb him, but walking home was out of the question. It was too far, and she really didn't want to end up as a coyote snack. Hoping Jesse had a landline, she turned to go back into the house.

"Where you going?"

Immersed in the shadows, Jesse's deep voice reached out to her. She turned, walked back out to the edge of the pool, and found him neck deep in the water.

"It seems everyone's gone home. I was going to see if you had a house phone I could use to call my father to come pick me up."

"What's your hurry?"

"Well . . ." She folded her arms. "Judging by the dimming of the lights and the sudden disappearance of everyone, my guess is that last call came while I was using your restroom."

He came up out of the water until it hit him waist high. Droplets of water shimmered in the moonlight as they slowly slid down his broad, sculpted chest and abs. As he moved to the edge of the pool, he looked like a Nordic god. But even deities could be sneaky.

Remembering how earlier he'd tricked her and pulled her into the pool, she moved out of reach.

"So you think the night is over?" he asked.

"It would appear so."

"Darlin', the party's just getting started."

"Then why did everyone leave?"

"Because I told them to."

"Why?"

"So I could get you alone." He held out his hand. "Come join me."

So he could get her alone?

Run.

Everything sane and logical said to ignore that big hand reaching out to her and the amazing man attached.

Instead, her heart did some fancy two-stepping, her feet developed a mind of their own, and she walked toward him. "Does that tactic usually work when you bring your fan club here?"

"I've never brought anyone here."

"Right. I've heard the stories."

His smile slipped, and sincerity darkened his eyes. A strange little thrill tickled her stomach.

"Are you serious?" she asked.

He nodded. "I told you not to believe everything you heard." His hand reached out to her again, and like a magnet, she was drawn. "I'll see you get home safe when you're ready to go."

"What if I want to go now?"

"Then I'll make the call. But I hope you'll stay."

Yeah, like she really intended to go anywhere with a half-naked hunk she was wildly attracted to right in front of her? Nope. Not gonna happen. Still, she didn't plan to make it easy.

She lowered herself to the edge of the pool and dangled her legs in the warm water. He found his way between them, and she did absolutely nothing to stop him.

When they were face-to-face, he gave her a smile that smacked of confidence, promise, and satisfaction. She had no doubt he could deliver on everything that hot, hard body advertised. But she sensed something else hidden in the depths of those blue eyes.

She might not have come to Texas for romance, sex, or anything other than checking on her father's well-being. But the look in Jesse's eyes told her that if she'd just reach out, she'd find something sweeter than anything she'd ever imagined.

The enormity of that terrified her.

His big hands settled on the tops of her bare thighs. Despite the heat, a shiver danced up her spine. One touch was all it took for her to feel the snap that signaled her absolute surrender. It was more than the fact that she hadn't been with a man in a very long time. That snap told her that she belonged to *him* no matter how hard she might try to fight the truth.

"So you're saying you don't come with references?" she asked, trying to maintain an ounce of the control slowly slipping away.

"You know . . ." His smile said she didn't fool him for one second. "You've got that tough-chick thing going on that makes me want to grab you with both hands, strip you naked, and find your sweet, gooey center."

Oh. My.

Though everything between her neck and her thighs tingled like she'd stuck her finger in a light socket, she managed a laugh. "I'm afraid all you'll find with me is a hard-candy core."

"Hmmm. So the choice is to lick or suck?" He moved closer until the crotch of her bikini bottoms was pressed against his rippled abs. He looked directly into her eyes. Trailed a wet finger across her shoulder and down between her breasts. "Pretty sure you'll taste good either way."

With a cool smile, Allison managed to scoop up the estrogen pouring from her like a chocolate fountain. "Maybe I'm not interested."

"Really?" The corners of his sinfully delicious mouth lifted.

"Really."

"Then you might want to relay that message to the rest of your body."

She didn't need to look down to know he referred to her erect nipples pressing against the yellow fabric. She could feel them react to him and that seductive male mouth—all swollen and achy like they were willing to be the topping on his dessert.

"The air is cool," she said.

"Uh-huh." Moonlight danced in his eyes as his hands moved up her thighs and her waist. Those long fingers kept moving until they trailed over her shoulders. Then achingly slow, both hands slid down her chest, lightly grazing her hardened nipples.

She looked him over, tried to put a big "Whoa" on all the heat zipping through her system. "Has any woman ever denied that Southern charm that flows from you like honey?"

He grinned.

She'd take that as a no.

"Maybe I'll be the first."

His head tilted, and a lock of his hair slipped from behind his ear. "Is that so?"

She tucked the silky strands back in place. "Don't forget . . . I'm the tough chick."

"Got news for you, darlin'." He leaned in and whispered in her ear. "*I'm* the one going down in flames."

The heat of his breath warmed her, and she tried not to melt. She gripped the concrete edge of the pool like a lifeline. Tried not to focus on the delicious masculine scent that rose from him like a party invitation.

"I can't get you out of my head, Allison." He nuzzled the side of her throat and murmured in her ear. "Not during the day, when I'm working. Not at night, when I'm alone in bed."

Because his mouth felt so good on her skin, she tilted her head slightly to give him better access. "Why?"

"I don't know." He drew back and cupped her face in his hands. His thumbs gently stroked her cheeks. As he looked into her eyes, his breathing was unsteady. "But I'm willing to take a chance and figure it out. How about you?"

Admittedly, she'd been turned on by him since the moment he'd pulled her into his arms to dance that first night at Seven Devils. She could deny all day long that she wasn't interested. And she'd be a great, big, fat liar.

Plain and simple, her body wanted him.

Her heart wanted him too. And that had her a little more than worried. Even with all his pretty words, she wasn't sure she had enough experience to deal with such a heartbreaker.

"I've never been good at games of chance," she said, even as her hands lifted to his smooth, hardmuscled chest, and her fingers played across his wet skin.

"This isn't a competition. I think we both want the same results."

She wasn't sure about that. But when his lips pressed against hers, she responded in the same way as she had that first night when she hadn't known him at all. This time, instead of fighting the hot ache spreading through her belly, she gave in. His mouth opened over hers in a slow, soft, sexy kiss that sent the message he was in no hurry.

The beat of desire pulsed through her blood while his tongue caressed and coaxed. Promised and delivered. She leaned into him and curled her arms around his neck. The aching tips of her breasts pressed into his chest. With a moan, he wrapped his arms around her and drew her down into the water with him. Those big hands slid down the small of her back, cupped her rear, and pulled her up against a long, thick erection he couldn't hide beneath those wet board shorts.

A groan of pure male need rumbled deep in his chest. "Wrap your legs around me."

She did without hesitation. The heat and contact of her sex against his erection shot a tingling ache right through her core. With her back braced against the cool blue tile, he kissed her again, leaned into her, and rocked his hips. His erection thrust tantalizingly against her, making her ache and need with a ferocity she couldn't control. She didn't think there was anything she'd ever wanted more than him.

A warm rush tightened her chest, flooded the apex of her thighs, and sent her into a crazy whirlwind of desire. Her heart pounded, and her blood pumped through her veins in hot, pulsating waves.

She drew her head back, missing his mouth on hers the moment it left. "You don't have to go slow."

"Are you kidding?" He pressed his forehead against hers and murmured in a deep husky voice. "I've wanted you since the moment I laid eyes on you. I'm going to take my time enjoying you. Even if it kills me. And it just might. But I'm willing to take that risk."

With a provocative smile, he lowered his head again. This time, his hot mouth found the sensitive spot beneath her ear, where he gently kissed, licked, and sucked the flesh until the stimulated vibrations in her body made it impossible to remain still.

His long fingers reached up and untied her bikini top. When the yellow fabric floated away, he tossed it onto the concrete, where it landed with a splat. Then her bared nipples were pressed against his warm, wet chest. She couldn't stop the long "Oh God" that moaned through her lips.

"You make me crazy with wanting you," he murmured in a husky voice that sent a shiver through her chest.

Under his intense gaze, she might have felt shy. Embarrassed. But the heat in those blue depths did just the opposite, and when his hands slid up between them to hold and caress her breasts, she closed her eyes only because of the sheer pleasure.

His warm breath whispered across her puckered flesh as he gently cupped her breast, then lowered his head and smoothly sucked in her nipple. When his tongue flattened and stroked, a groan rose from his chest and vibrated against her flesh.

She gasped in response.

Fantasies didn't come close to reality as water lapped between them, and he took his leisure tasting her. Her hands wandered over him, enjoying the feel of his tight skin on top of all that muscle. Soon, it wasn't enough.

She wanted to taste him too.

"Jesse?"

He lifted his head, his heavy-lidded eyes burned with lust. "Yeah?"

"Did I ever tell you how much I love tattoos?"

A slow smile curled his lips. "I don't believe you have."

"Maybe I should show you instead." She grabbed hold of those broad shoulders and turned him so they switched places. Now *he* was the one backed against the wall of the pool, and she fully intended to take advantage for as long as he allowed.

She kissed his jaw, his mouth, his chest, the wings-of-freedom tribal ink on his biceps. She applied the same sensuous torture to his pebbled nipples as he had to hers. While she tasted him, she lowered her hand into the front of those baby blue board shorts, wrapped her fingers around his long, thick erection, and slowly stroked.

"Oh. God." His head dropped back. "That feels . . ."

"Good?"

"Amazing." He allowed her to touch him. To explore. To find what caused him to moan, shudder, or push his smooth, rigid cock into her hand. But he allowed it only for a brief time before he took control again. While he kissed her, his hands slid down her body in a sensual caress, then he touched her through the bikini bottoms. "My turn."

Everything about this man moved something deep inside her, and she was sure she'd never felt such a hot, aching need for anyone before. He wrapped her in his scent. His warmth. He had a body that knocked her out. But his heart was the sexiest thing about him. Even as those long fingers slipped beneath the bikini fabric and touched her slick, hot flesh. Even as he explored, circled, and stroked until she thought she'd go mad from the sweet fire pooling between her thighs.

He kissed the curve of her neck, drew that flesh between his lips, and flicked his tongue over the sensitive surface. His fingers made the same magic between her legs.

It would be so easy to let go. To find that ultimate release with him simply touching her. But she wanted more.

She wanted all of him.

Every single inch.

Every single drop.

Everything he had to give.

"Off." That single word burst through her lips rough and choppy.

"Damn." He backed off like he'd been burned.

"Not you." She pulled him back. Pressed her mouth to his. Wrapped her body around him. "The clothes."

"Thank God." His hands smoothed down her waist until his thumbs hooked into the edge of the bikini bottoms, and he pulled them down her legs. With a wet splat, they joined the string top on the concrete. The water felt amazing against her naked body, and she now knew why skinny-dipping was such a popular sport.

"Now you." When he reached for his waistband, she pushed his hands away. "Let me." As tall as he was, there was only one way to completely remove the board shorts.

Might as well make the process interesting.

He stood like a good and happy soldier while she took hold of the Velcro opening and separated it. She worked the fabric down his hips. When his erection jutted free, she ducked beneath the water and took him in her mouth. His groan vibrated through his body as she enjoyed him for as long as she could hold her breath. When she broke the surface of the water, she had his shorts in her hand, and she'd put a smile on his face.

"You never cease to surprise me," he said.

"Well"—she dipped her hand below the surface of the water, wrapped her fingers around his hard, thick length, and began a slow head-to-base stroke that made him close his eyes and smile— "let's not let it end there."

She tossed the shorts up over the edge of the pool.

"Not a chance." He reached for her, smoothed his hands down to her bottom, and lifted her.

Anticipation shivered down her spine as she wrapped her legs around his waist and her arms around his neck. The thick head of his penis nudged her slick opening, and her heart took off in a race. But instead of his pushing inside, where she really wanted him, he carried her toward the steps.

"Where are you going?"

"Condoms aren't safe in a pool." He held up a foil packet that must have been in the pocket of his shorts. She didn't dare wonder why or for whom he'd put it there.

"I'm on birth control."

He sighed. "And I have a reputation."

"Do you?"

"You've heard the talk."

"And you've told me not to believe everything I hear."

"Indeed I have." He kept moving toward the steps.

"I trust you."

He stopped. Tightened his embrace. And kissed her. "Thank you."

"So can we . . ."

"You may have enough regrets come morning. I'm not going to add to them." He carried her out of the pool and over to the day bed beneath the pergola. He laid her on the cool canvas cover and followed her down.

"But . . ."

"Sssh." He silenced her with a kiss. "I'm busy."

That firm, masculine mouth went to work kissing the curve of her neck, her breasts, and her stomach until he inched his way down between her legs. His big hands cupped her bare bottom, and, softly, he kissed the inside of her thighs. Then he parted her slick folds and found her with his warm tongue. Every bone in her body liquefied. Her core heated and tingled as he licked across her sensitive flesh as if she were a yummy scoop of ice cream.

Every nerve in her body sizzled and snapped like she was riding an electrical current. Nothing on earth could have stopped the climax that curled her toes and shot like liquid fire through her body.

Before the sensation died out, he moved back up her body and nudged her legs apart to accommodate his hips. The head of his long, thick penis nudged her opening and, this time, she knew he wouldn't retreat.

"You're so beautiful," he said. "So damned beautiful." He tilted her hips and entered her slow and deep. The penetration sent a second set of electric shocks through her system and stole her breath. He paused and shuddered.

"Are you okay?"

He shook his head as her body stretched and adjusted, then begged for more. "Give me a second."

"Jesse?"

"You feel so good, I could come right now. But I won't. I want this to last."

"So do I." She rolled her hips and elicited a groan from him.

"If that's true, you're not playing fair."

"And I'm about to play dirty." Somehow she managed to shift him to his back. She'd never wanted like this before. Meeting him was completely unexpected. And while she had him all to herself, she planned to take full advantage. She straddled his hips, then raised and lowered herself over his upward thrusts in a rhythm that set a leisurely pace so she could touch him. Kiss him. Lick him. Explore him. Find out what made him close his eyes in ecstasy or clench his jaw when the pleasure intensified.

Playtime ended when he growled. "While I love your particular form of torture"—he rolled her to her back and thrust so possessively, so deep, she felt it all the way into her heart—"it's time to get down to business."

He reached down and hooked her leg up over his hip. With his next deep thrust, a slow, rolling blaze spread throughout her body and burned her from the inside out.

"I'd complain . . ." She sucked in a breath and moaned as he pulled out and plunged deep again. Rocked his hips. Teased and stroked that special spot inside like she was a Stradivarius and he a virtuoso. "But not when you move like that."

"I aim to please." His breathing was harsh. Choppy.

"Then please . . . don't stop."

"Not even an option." His thrusts came harder, faster. His muscles tightened and flexed with each powerful drive of his hips.

She wrapped her legs around his hips so he could go deeper still. She became consumed with the intensity of the pleasure, the focus of where their bodies were joined. He pushed her toward another intense climax that finally exploded and shattered. Flames scorched her insides and sizzled through her veins. Her interior muscles throbbed, contracted, and pulled him in tight. She cried out his name, and in a frenzy of kisses and moans, he finally unleashed his passion and drove into her one last time.

The decadence of hearing her name on his long groan—feeling that powerful body stiffen as he found his own release—might live in her heart forever.

Face buried in the curve of her neck, he stayed embedded deep in her body while they rode out the throbbing pulsations. And then he kissed his way to her mouth.

She felt his smile against her lips.

"Satisfied?" she asked in a tone that came out much more like a purr.

"For round one."

"Round one?"

He pressed his forehead to hers and nodded. "Haven't you heard? We do everything bigger in Texas."

Still buried deep inside her, she felt him come to life again, and she laughed. "Yeeha."

Chapter 13

$\mathcal{J}$esse had never *spooned* with anyone before. Hell, he'd rarely spent an entire night in a woman's bed. But with Allison's sweet behind nestled against his groin, his arms wrapped around her waist, and his palm curved around the warmth of her breast, he'd be happy to stay right there all damned day.

Last night had been a lesson in listening to and taking his big brother's advice to finally let go. A few weeks ago, Allison hadn't even been on his radar. Now she'd become his number one focus.

How had that happened?

When had that happened?

And did any of that really matter?

He remembered the look on Jared's face that last night in Afghanistan before they'd hugged and parted. He remembered the passion behind his brother's horribly prophetic words. *"When you search for something, chances are you'll never find it.*

Be open to the surprises that come your way because you never know how quickly they might end."

Though he hadn't been looking or expecting, everything he'd ever dreamed or hoped for could very well be right in his arms.

Now all he had to do was convince her.

They'd made love several times last night. Each had given him the opportunity to get to know her better. Not just her body. Not just her desires. They'd talked until dawn broke across the sky. They'd talked about everything—from their favorite flavors of ice cream to their preferred sports. From the age they'd been when they'd lost their virginity to the theme of their senior proms.

When morning rolled around, he had a better understanding of what made her tick. Though there were parts she was obviously still reluctant to share, he hoped that in the coming days and weeks, she'd open up and divulge those important missing pieces. He wanted to help her overcome the issues that were holding her back from believing in a happily-ever-after.

I trust you.

Her words from last night came back to him, and they touched him as deeply now as they had then. He'd repeatedly told her that she shouldn't believe everything she heard about him. Last night, when he'd wanted to make love to her, she let him know with those three little words that gossip was just something people with boring lives engaged in when they had nothing better to do.

She believed him.

She trusted him.

That settled nicely around his heart as he felt her come awake. He enjoyed the little sigh she hummed as she nestled closer.

"Your cat hates me," she murmured.

He glanced up at Rango, who'd perched on the dresser and was giving her a Grumpy Cat glare. Jesse laughed. "You've stolen his spot."

She rolled to her back and looked up at him with several slow blinks before he tucked her beneath him.

"Your cat sleeps with you?"

He nodded. "Dinks too if there's a thunderstorm."

"No wonder you have such a big bed."

He nuzzled her neck. "I can think of better uses."

"Mmmm." She ran her hand down his back and gripped his buttocks. He complied with a hip roll that pressed his growing erection into the softness of her thighs.

"I thought you showed me all you had last night," she said.

"Are you serious?" He raised his head and looked at her like surely she was joking. "Darlin', I'm just getting started."

Allison smiled as his hands slipped beneath the covers and between them. As her body started to hum under the attention of those magic fingers, she glanced over his shoulder at the clock radio that read 9:00 in glowing red numbers. She'd never had such a decadent morning. Hadn't had the pleasure of sleeping in for ages. Usually there was too much . . . business.

"Crap!" She pushed him off her and leaped from the bed. She dropped to her knees on the carpet and searched for her clothes. "I've got to go."

"What's your rush?" He sat up. The expression on his face clearly conveyed his displeasure at her sudden retreat. "I thought we could make some breakfast and—"

"I have a plane to catch."

"You what?" His brows pulled together. At that moment, Rango arched his back and hissed. Dinks came running into the room and did an encore of knocking her on her ass, then he slurped his long tongue up the side of her face.

Still naked, she managed to push the black Lab off and climbed to her feet—watching him carefully so that he didn't get any ideas about sniffing delicate, naked parts.

"Where are my clothes?" she asked, while Jesse just sat there in bed looking at her like she'd flown over the cuckoo's nest.

"A plane?"

"Yes." She glanced around the huge bedroom searching for her jeans, her tank top, anything that would make her feel less exposed and vulnerable. "It leaves in three hours. Before that, I have to go back to Abby's and grab my purse. Then I have to go to my dad's and pack. And then I have to get to the airport at least two hours early because, God forbid, the TSA doesn't like the way I look."

"Last night you didn't mention you were leaving."

The expression on his face hovered somewhere between bewildered and righteously pissed off. She sat down on the edge of the bed and pulled the sheet up to cover herself. Explaining to the guy you'd just spent the night having amazing sex with that you were bailing like a cheap whore was awkward enough. Add doing it while you were naked? Yeah. Not pretty.

"I have a business to run," she explained. "I've depended on Danielle for too long as it is. She's been toughing it out even while her youngest daughter has the flu. I can't—"

"When?"

"When what?" she asked. The dark shift in his eyes slammed into her like a fist.

"When did you buy the airline ticket?"

"Yesterday."

"Seems hard to forget something that quickly," he said, his tone tight and accusatory.

"It was a crazy day. And night. And I—"

He lifted his hand, a clear sign he'd heard enough.

"Your clothes are probably still downstairs in the pool bathroom." He threw off the covers and got out of bed—clearly more comfortable with nudity. He reached down, snapped a pair of jeans up off the floor, and stuck his legs in one at a time. "I'll get my keys and take you home."

"Jesse." She reached for him, but he stepped out of the way. "Don't be mad."

"Why would I be mad?" When he looked up a caustic smile twisted his lips. It was *not* an attractive look. "We just had a night of great sex. You've got things to do. I've got things to do. And my reputation stands. Thanks for a good time."

When he walked from the room, he left a chill in his wake, and her mother's words clanged in her head. *"You're just like me, Allie."*

Last night when she'd walked into Seven Devils with the rest of the bachelorette party, she hadn't intended to go to Jesse's house. She hadn't intended to get naked. She hadn't intended to have all-night amazing sex. She hadn't intended to hurt him.

Above all, she hadn't intended to fall just a little bit more in love.

But she was afraid she'd done just that.

*L*ast damn time he'd ever listen to Reno.

Jesse glanced across the cab of his truck at Allison, who was doing her best to act like her jumping on an airplane was no big deal.

Maybe for her it wasn't.

Didn't mean he had to feel the same.

"My sister will be really glad to have me back. We still haven't found a white horse we can make into a unicorn for Jenny Curran's princess party. The costume shop didn't have a large enough inventory to choose from for the Schweinberg/Elliott medieval wedding. And . . ."

She rambled on about things he didn't give a rat's ass about.

She didn't owe him anything.

But that didn't stop the sense of betrayal that squeezed his chest.

"Don't make excuses to try to make me feel better that you *forgot* to mention you were bailing out today," he said, sounding much more like an asshole than he intended.

"I'm not."

"Okay."

"I'm telling you the truth, Jesse."

"Okay."

As he pulled his truck to the curb in front of Abby's house, she folded her arms across the front of that snug Pistol Annie's HELL ON HEELS tank top and glared at him. "Are you always this stubborn?"

"Pretty much."

Her hands came up, showing her frustration. "Why is that not a surprise?"

"I don't know." He pulled the key from the ignition, turned to look at her, and fought the desire to pull her into his arms. "But it's probably only *half* the surprise of your *suddenly* leaving town."

"Are we having our first fight?" she asked.

"And last." He got out of the truck, went around to her side, and opened the door for her. She sat there with those smoky gray eyes and a look that hit him below the belt.

Jesus.

They'd just spent an amazing night together. Just because he had expectations she hadn't lived up to didn't give him a right to behave like a petulant child.

Didn't stop him either.

"Sorry." He popped his fists onto his hips and

exhaled a harsh breath of air. "It's not like me to be a total jackass."

For an awkward, silent moment, she just sat there like she was thinking things over. Deciding if she should belt him a good one or just get out of the truck and walk away. Instead of doing either, she unfolded her arms and wrapped them around his neck.

"I'm sorry. I should have said something. I just got so caught up in everything . . . in you . . . that I really did forget." She pressed a soft kiss to his lips. "Can we call a truce?"

Instead of pushing her away, he kissed her back. He didn't want this to be a one-night stand. He was growing to care for her and was more than willing to figure out where their relationship could go. How they could make it work. He just wasn't sure how she saw the whole picture. Then again, maybe she did. Maybe to her he was just a one-time fling.

For the first time in his life, he felt unsure and unsteady where a woman was concerned, and he didn't like it. At all.

"I'm not sure when I'll be back." Her eyes searched his. "But I don't want this to be good-bye."

"I guess that's up to you."

A slip of air pushed from her lungs. "I guess so."

An unusual ache hit him center mass as he held out his hand and helped her down to the sidewalk. In reality, he'd like nothing more than to just roll her back up in his truck, take her home, and back to bed. But she had an agenda that would take her thousands of miles away, and it was pretty hard to snuggle at that distance.

Things got more awkward as, apparently at a loss for words, they walked up to Abby's door together in silence. Other than the faint, distant whir of a vacuum cleaner, the echo of their boot heels tapping the concrete path became the only sound.

He knocked. The door swung open.

"Oh, thank God." Abby pushed out a huge sigh of relief. "Crisis averted," she called out to whoever was inside the house. "Allie's here."

$\mathcal{T}$en minutes later, Allison found herself, once again, at Jana Wilder's big kitchen table. This time she was surrounded by her dad and what seemed like the entire Wilder family. The clock ticked away the countdown on her flight back to Seattle, and all eyes were on her.

No pressure.

As coffee pumped through Jana's ancient coffeemaker, the Wilders had all gathered to do whatever was necessary to eliminate yet another wedding-related disaster. To see a family pull together like this gave Allison an amazing insight to what kept this family glued together. And she was awed.

The old saying that everything happened in threes had certainly come to life with Charli and Reno's wedding, which was to take place in just six days. The biggest of the current catastrophes included an early-morning phone call from Charli's Marine general father, who was set to arrive in three days. It seemed the man had chosen his daughter's wedding as the perfect time and place to introduce his new girlfriend. A *woman*, he informed Charli, who was barely above the legal drinking age.

As an event planner, Allison was accustomed to the occasional kinks a family could insert into a family affair. It was her job to avert disasters, which in more than one case had included hiring someone to babysit the troublemaker until it was too late for them to destroy the festivities.

She could still remember the inventive names she'd once been called when an ex-girlfriend had decided to crash a high-profile wedding she'd spent months planning. The interesting curve to the story had been because the ex belonged to the bride. Apparently, the groom had no idea the bride had ever dipped her toes in lesbian waters. Sadly, the dishonesty had led to the couple's ending up as just another divorce statistic.

While Charli held back tears over her father's newly added stress to the happiest day of her life, she didn't manage to hold them back upon the news that the Austin bakery she'd chosen to make their wedding cake had burned down the previous night or that the caterer had overbooked.

With now a whopping six glitches racked up for Charli and Reno's wedding, one could easily scratch their head and look at it as a sign that it wasn't meant to be. But even a hard-core cynic like Allison knew retreat was not an option. Even she had to admit that Charli and Reno had something special.

Soul mates.

There was no other explanation for the incredible love that shone in their eyes when they looked at each other. If she was honest, she'd admit their love ignited a new spark of hope and opened the door to new possibilities.

From the corner of the kitchen, Jesse leaned against the counter and gave her a look that practically defied her to get up and walk away. To get on that plane and fly back to Seattle. To ignore the avalanche that threatened his brother's and Charli's happiness.

Murmurings of ideas on how to fix the problems flew around the kitchen as Charli dabbed her eyes with a tissue. Reno cupped Charli's face in his hands and looked at her with such love it stole Allison's breath. Though Allison was confident her brother-in-law was crazy in love with her sister, she was equally sure even Andrew had never looked at Dani the way Reno looked at Charli.

"I'll do anything you want," Reno said to Charli. "I'll fly everyone off to Vegas or Tahoe. I'll marry you in the courthouse. In jeans, a bathing suit, or your fluffy pink robe. It doesn't matter where or how. It only matters that you become my wife."

Knowing the tragedy that had stolen the first woman Reno planned to marry just a week before the wedding, Allison couldn't stop the tears that floated into her eyes.

"At this point"—Charli gave him a beautiful

smile—"I just want to marry you surrounded by the people we love. If that means no cake or flowers, I don't care."

The collective awwwww in the room twisted like a knife in Allison's conscience.

"I can help." The words burst from her mouth, not for the first time. As she reprised the vow she'd made upon the very first wedding she'd successfully planned—*never let a bride go down in flames*—she reached out and settled a reassuring hand over Charli's. "I know that on your design show, you must have hit some walls and had to change tactics. Was the outcome as good or even better?"

"Always," Charli said.

"Then trust me," Allison said. "This will happen. And your wedding day will be the one you've always dreamed of."

"You've done so much already." Charli turned her hand over and clasped Allison's. "You have a business to get back to. We can't ask—"

"And you're not," she said. "I'm offering." A surge of bravado jolted her veins that she knew she could back up with results. "This is what I do. And I'm good at it. I may be in foreign territory, but I've been known to sweet-talk a caterer or baker. And when it comes to your father's new *friend*, well, no worries. I've tackled that dragon a time or two as well. He may be a Marine general, but I'm a wedding planner. I'll trump his stripes with little bottles of bubbles and personalized candy tins any day."

When Charli gave her a relieved smile, and

Reno closed his eyes in relief, Allison darted a quick glance at Jesse, who now stood with his arms folded. She tried not to notice when her heart gave a happy leap as he too smiled.

"Daddy?" She looked up at her father, who stood with his arm around Jana's shoulders. "Think you can put up with me for a few more days?"

"Thought you had a plane to catch."

"Looks like it will be taking off without me."

He gave her a prideful nod. "Your sister's not going to be happy."

No big news there.

"She'll survive."

Hopefully.

"We appreciate all you're doing," Charli said. "But—"

"No *buts*," Allison said. And don't you worry, whatever happens between now and Saturday, we can fix it."

Jana leaned down and gave her a big hug. "Now you're talking like a Texan, sugarplum."

The show of affection felt genuine, and Allison hugged her back. Whatever chinks in the woman's armor she'd thought she'd find were nonexistent. Allison acknowledged the relief. Her father really couldn't have found a more remarkable woman to share his life with. She could have stayed back in Seattle and never made this long journey.

But she wouldn't have missed it for the world.

"So . . . Dad, can you spare that extra room until after the wedding?"

"It's yours for as long as you want it."

She grabbed her purse and pushed away from the table. Then she glanced around the kitchen that seemed to be the nucleus of everything Wilder. A tiny little fire lit deep in her heart. How wonderful it must be to have all that love and support whenever you needed it.

"I know it's Sunday," she said. "But I need to get banging on some doors. *You*." She pointed to Jesse. "Come with me."

He didn't hesitate to follow her outside and open his truck door for her. After she climbed up into the cab, she blew out a long breath. When he got up behind the wheel and stuck the key in the ignition, she looked at him and noticed the smile playing about that sexy mouth she'd kissed so fervently last night.

"What?" she asked.

"I can't figure you out." The motor turned over with a low rumble.

In the last couple of weeks, she couldn't figure her out either. "And that makes you smile?"

He nodded. "Fifteen minutes ago you were hell-bent to get on that airplane and fly out of here. What changed?"

"I like Charli and your brother."

"You could have easily given them a few tips on how to handle things and still made your flight." He turned in his seat to look at her. "So what made you offer to stay and personally handle another crisis?"

"When I first started planning weddings for a living, I initiated a motto that I'd never let a bride go down in flames." She pulled the seat belt over her lap and clicked the buckle. "I'll admit, with six major elements of a wedding all crashing within the span of a week I thought maybe it was a sign that this wedding is not meant to be. But I really like those two, and . . ."

He grinned. "You want to see them get their happily-ever-after?"

"I'd like them at least to have the chance."

"You know what I think?"

"I'm afraid to ask."

He leaned over and grabbed her by the front of her Pistol Annie's HELL ON HEELS tank top. Then he brought her face up to his and kissed the living daylights out of her.

When he let go, that grin returned. "I think your hard-candy core just melted into your sweet, gooey center. And *that* makes me smile."

Yeah.

She had to get out of Sweet fast.

Before she turned into a total cream puff.

Chapter 14

They'd made a pit stop at Allison's father's house, so she could shower and change clothes. Also they needed to kill a little time. Since it was a Sunday morning, they needed to wait until whoever it was she wanted to talk to got home from church.

Jesse made his way to church once in a while. But the bother of trying to fight off the elderlies who wanted to save his wicked, fornicating soul, often ruined his experience.

Before she'd gone down the hall to shower, Allison made them a breakfast comprised of something she called a messy scramble. The contents of the egg mix included everything from onions and mushrooms to bacon and cheese. It looked a mess but tasted like heaven. She'd now cooked two delicious meals for him and had sat down to share. He thought maybe he'd like to have her in his kitchen—and his life—on a more regular basis.

While he sat there finishing the meal and deny-

ing Buddy aka Wee Man a tasty bite, he couldn't
drag his mind off Allison naked in the shower.
He'd lost count of the times he'd been tempted to
walk down that hall and join her. Out of respect
for her father, who could walk in at any time, he
kept his clothes on.

Sometimes being respectful was just a big pain
in the ass. Or in his case, a big ache elsewhere.

"How do you like it?" Allison's voice sounded
fresh and energetic as she came back into the
kitchen.

He looked up and let his eyes skim all the way
down the front of her floral sundress to her cus-
tomary high wedge sandals and lavender-painted
toes. She looked good enough to eat. "You have
my full attention."

"I meant the breakfast."

"That's good too."

Her delightful laughter washed over him like an
invigorating waterfall, and he couldn't help notice
that she seemed a lot more relaxed and vibrant
now than before the shower. Something changed.

"The shower seems to have agreed with you,"
he said, sipping his cup of lukewarm coffee.

On the way to the counter, she bent down and
did a quick nose rub and baby talk with Buddy.
Then she picked up the freshly brewed pot and,
with a smile, refilled his cup. "The shower last
night was even better."

"Oooh, is that a confession?"

She sat in the chair beside him. "Probably the
most you'll get from me."

"Actually . . ." He pulled her chair closer, leaned

in, and snuck a kiss she didn't contest. "I hoped for more."

"I'm not sure that's wise." She wrinkled her small nose. "As soon as I get things settled with the wedding, I really do have to go back to Seattle. I just talked to Danielle and told her I was staying longer, and she is *not* happy. Plus there's your whole playboy reputation you have to live up to. What would people think if you were seen with the same woman for more than a day?"

"I really don't give a shit about what people think. But I understand this isn't easy for your sister. Maybe we could just enjoy whatever time we have together and have . . ." Before he could lock himself into thinking of possibilities and good times, he held up the NO REGRETS tattoo on his arm. He smiled, though every ounce of him knew his carefree manner was just a cover-up for how he'd really begun to feel.

"Maybe." Her slender shoulders lifted in a way that let him know her heart wasn't in her words.

That intrigued him.

"In the meantime"—her smoky eyes peered at him across her coffee cup as she sipped—"I'm putting you to work."

He leaned back. "Is that so?"

"Yes." She set her cup down. "I need you to call your girlfriends."

"My *what*?"

She laughed. "I don't mean the whole laundry list. Just Gladys and Arlene."

"Those two are a handful. They scare the hell out of me."

She grabbed the front of his shirt and planted a kiss on his mouth that had him thinking of anything but picking up a phone.

"Then maybe you need to make yourself a little less hotter."

She thought he was hot? Sweet.

"Darlin', the only way that's going to happen is if you put out the fire."

She gave a sexy little hum that shot straight into his jeans. "Hold on to that thought."

Oh, he was holding on all right.

To the hopes that she'd never get back on that plane to Seattle.

Wow.

In awe, Allison looked out over the sea of elderly citizens crammed into the senior center's activity room. The audience included the man who—with one phone call—had brought them all together. Jesse continued to surprise her way above and beyond what he did with her baser instincts. She'd judged him wrong that first and maybe even the second time they'd met.

She looked at the people he'd helped assemble. Some were obviously single. Most were couples who looked as though they'd been together for a very long time.

Maybe Jesse was right about the whole *forever* thing.

Sadly, today she didn't have time to evaluate the meaning of life, let alone what made some couples stay together and others fall apart.

Today was about making things happen.

Getting results.

Saving her new friends' chance at happiness.

Maybe later tonight she could further explore what all those crazy tingles Jesse created in her heart actually meant.

"Thank you all for coming," she said to the attentive group, hoping all that *attentiveness* was due to interest in what she had to say and not the high-caliber contents of the fifty-cup coffeepot percolating in the kitchen.

"As I look around this beautiful senior center, I can see all the heart and soul Charli Brooks put into making such a nice space available for you all to enjoy yourselves. And I'm here because she needs a little of that heart back right now. This morning, she received news that the caterer for her and Reno's wedding overbooked. I know there are a lot of you out there who make delicious dishes. And I wondered if—"

"If you're looking for a down-home menu," Hazel Calhoun said, "I can make my brisket sliders."

"You haven't lived till you had my shrimp macaroni and cheese," Gertie West announced.

"Gotta have my killer guacamole," Flirty Chester Banks said with a wink.

"And my sweet corn cupcakes," said another senior.

"And my sun-dried cranberry, sweet and spicy cashew, bleu cheese salad," someone else added.

One after another these amazing people popped up from their seats to volunteer their services. Allison's heart rolled over with admiration.

She knew how much *she* adored Charli and Reno, but to see the outpouring of love from the community just sealed the deal. The reception menu might be diverse, but it would definitely be tasty.

She turned to Gladys and Arlene—Jesse's biggest and maybe spunkiest admirers. "Could I put you two in charge of getting it all together and making sure it arrives to the reception venue on time?"

"You betcha," Gladys said through her red-painted lips.

Arlene nodded her agreement, then tossed her rheumy gaze in Jesse's direction. "Can we get Mr. Hot Stuff over there to help out?"

Allison held back a laugh. "I'll see to it that you get some very personal attention from Mr. Hot Stuff."

The wide grin on Arlene's face told Allison one thing—you never got too old for a good-looking man to rev up your engine. Even as he sat in a corner and rolled his eyes.

Later, after several cups of high-octane coffee, Mr. Hot Stuff walked her out to his truck.

"Pretty clever idea calling on the community to help out," he said, taking her hand and helping her up into the cab.

"It seemed an obvious solution. Especially since Charli put so much into helping them out. Plus, I've noticed that the elderly set here in Sweet seem happiest when they're involved in something. Or, for some of them, drooling over a guy a third of their age."

Chuckling, he reached across her, took hold of the

seat belt, and clicked it in place. His hands lingered at her waist. His mouth hovered near her own.

"Only one woman I'm interested in making drool."

And then he kissed her.

Right there on Main Street.

In front of anyone who walked by or came out of the senior center.

And she totally let him.

𝒞risis stop number two took them all the way into San Antonio and Fiona and Izzy's cozy apartment. Jesse had wondered why Allison hadn't just made a phone call, but now that he saw her in action, all his questions were answered.

The day was sunny but not too hot. Allison had suggested they go down to the apartment complex's playground so Izzy could play while they chatted. For a while Allison, immersed herself in his niece—pushing her on the swing, following her down the slide, and holding her up so she could use the monkey bars. He and Fiona sat off to the side on a park bench sipping glasses of pink lemonade.

"So . . ." His former sister-in-law's blond hair shone in the sunlight. Her impish grin was even brighter. "What's going on between the two of you?"

He glanced across the playground, where Allison pushed his loudly giggling niece on the colorful merry-go-round. "Not sure."

"You like her."

"No doubt about that."

"But you're afraid of her."

He chuckled. "Have you ever known me to be afraid of anything?"

"Yeah. I have."

"Seriously?"

"You Wilder boys all think you're so tough," she said. "But when it comes to love, you're all a bunch of scaredy-cats."

"Love!"

"See." Fiona laughed. "Just the word freaks you out."

"I've only known Allison for a couple of weeks. It takes a long time to fall in love. And frankly, I'm not in the market."

"Yeah. Because you need to keep up that whole *love 'em and leave 'em* thing you have going on. 'Cause that's working so good for you, right?"

"It works."

"Ah, Jesse." She leaned in and hugged him. "You've always been the one to rescue your bull-headed brothers when they've treaded treacherous waters. Yet you resist that same pull to shelter."

"When did you start talking in rhyme?" *And, unfortunately, making so much sense?*

"Silly boy." She gave him a playful punch in the arm. "You've got that same look—the one Reno wore when he met Charli. The one Jackson wore when Abby came back to Sweet."

"Don't know what you're talking about."

"Well, then, you'd better find a different face because here she comes. Oh. And by the way, she's looking at you? *She* gets it even if *you* don't."

Jesse looked up, and his heart did a wobbly

sidestep thing as Allison walked toward him holding Izzy's little hand. For a crazy moment he could picture her holding the hand of their own little boy or girl. The image warned him he was in deep.

"All you need is one woman to change your world. One you can give your heart to." Fiona gave Allison and Izzy a little wave. "Maybe she's the one."

His gaze shot back to Allison. First Reno. Now Fiona was encouraging him to move ahead. It wasn't a deed he was accustomed to. He didn't want to think about that funny feeling in his chest. He wouldn't try to deny he had feelings for Allison. But as soon as Reno and Charli said *I do*, she'd be gone. Her life was in Seattle, his was in Sweet. There were a whole lot of miles between here and there.

Maybe he'd do better to back off. Let things between them simmer instead of come to a full boil. It couldn't be good for either of them to get involved. Nobody liked to be on the receiving end of heartache.

He took a deep breath, acknowledging he'd made the right decision.

And then, she flashed him a smile that turned all that sensible rationale into a big pile of goo.

"Those lemon cupcakes you made for Charli's shower were delicious," Allison said as she and Fiona sat on the park bench while Jesse took a turn entertaining his niece on the playground equipment. "The frosting was so light and fluffy. And the Gerber daisy decorations were so charming."

"Thank you." Fiona was clearly appreciative of the compliment. "The lemon recipe came from my Grandma Grady. It's one I plan to use when I open the cupcake shop."

"You should. It's fabulous, and I'm sure your grandma will love that."

"She's passed."

Allison had barely known either of her grandmothers before they passed on, and she'd regretted not knowing them better. "I'm so sorry."

"It's okay." Fiona gave her a smile of sincerity. "She was a real live wire and lived an amazing life. At the age of sixty, she even learned to fly a plane. When she passed two weeks after her ninetieth birthday and we all gathered, it was a true celebration."

"I never knew my grandparents. They'd all passed before or shortly after I was born."

"I'm so sorry." Fiona patted her hand. "Grandparents are so special. My parents live on the East Coast. That's why I'm so glad Izzy has Jana. She's the best."

Allison nodded. With each passing day, Allison's respect for the woman grew in leaps and bounds.

"But I don't think you came all the way to San Antonio to talk about my grandmother," Fiona said. "Even as wonderful as she was. So what's on your mind?"

"You're very astute."

"I like to think so."

For whatever reason, Fiona gave Jesse a curious glance, and Allison had to wonder why. What had they been discussing before she'd joined them at the bench?

She reminded herself that she'd come here to help out a friend. Not to worry about what Jesse and Fiona talked about when she wasn't around.

"I know you plan to open your cupcake shop soon," she said. "How do you feel about making cakes?"

Fiona pushed her hair behind her ear and shrugged. "I work in a bakery, so I make them all the time. Why?"

"I need you to create the most beautiful wedding cake you can imagine."

"For who?"

"Charli and Reno."

"What?" Fiona leaned back, a look of astonishment on her face. "They ordered their cake over a month ago from a baker in Austin. Charli asked me first, but I declined. I was too afraid I wouldn't give her a cake that was good enough. She's my friend but . . . she's a *designer*. It was too intimidating."

"The bakery in Austin burned down last night."

"Are you serious?"

At Allison's nod, Fiona's blue eyes widened. Her hand lifted to cover her mouth. "My gosh, what else can go wrong with this wedding?"

Allison didn't even want to think about that. "Your friend needs you, Fiona. She needs you to make her a cake to celebrate the love she found with Reno."

"Of course." Fiona glanced away. "Whatever it takes, I'll make it happen."

Allison hugged her. "Thank you."

"Charli deserves a happily-ever-after," Fiona said as she glanced wistfully at Jesse, who was busy pushing Izzy on the swing. The little girl's delighted giggles carried like music across the playground. Then Fiona's insightful gaze came back to Allison. "We all do."

Late that evening, Allison held the phone away from her ear as her sister unleashed a few F-bombs and more than one threat of bodily harm.

"I promise, Danielle. I'll be on a plane next Sunday. The wedding will be over, and all catastrophes will have been resolved." After a few more rants and implosions, Allison grabbed the bottle of pain reliever.

Danielle also expressed her discontent with the long hours her husband Andrew had been working on the massage-parlor-prostitution-ring case. Apparently, he came home too exhausted to do anything more than shower and go to bed. And now that Lily had recovered from the flu, it was Angeline's turn.

Allison loved her nieces and felt horrible that their mother had to work so hard while they were sick. But Danielle had Andrew's mother to help out and a load of friends who shared playdates and were always watching each other's kids. So as much as guilt tightened around Allison's neck, it wasn't like Danielle was on an island.

By the time Allison got her to calm down, they went over the details for Benjamin Braunstein's bar mitzvah, which, though an entire three months away, was turning out to be a huge shindig with a celebrity guest list. The original and fun candy buffet table and human hamster balls at the Seattle Center were now being relegated to a more traditional dinner at the posh Sunset Club.

Once they'd put that discussion to bed, Allison hung up with another promise of *no more delays to go home*. With her father at dinner with Jana and some friends, Allison had the house all to herself. And while it was difficult to focus on anything other than Jesse or Charli and Reno's wedding, she changed into her sleep tee and boy shorts, then grabbed her laptop to write her blog for the following day.

She tried to coerce Wee Man up onto the sofa with her, but he was more interested in sniffing corners he'd already sniffed a hundred times. With a glass of milk and a package of Oreo Double Stufs nearby, just in case she got writer's block, she got down to work. Cookies always helped her think. And do housework. And plan events. Cookies helped pretty much anything that exerted her brain or her muscles. Sometimes, just trying on shoes brought on a cookie attack. So writing an entire blog? Definitely necessary to have them nearby.

After she read the comments on her last gut-spilling blog, she felt encouraged. No one slammed what she thought, and they all seemed to relate to how she felt. Not that she needed her readers' permission to live her life, but it was always help-ful when they didn't tell her she needed to get her head examined.

With only one thing on her mind, she typed in her new headline.

FINDING HOPE IN A WORLD OF WHAT-IFS

Time—and the Oreo Double Stufs—dwindled as her fingers tapped at the keyboard. The content of the blog had her questioning the possibility of being wrong about her previous observations. It included her thoughts on meeting a family like the Wilders and how they all seemed to stick together through the proverbial thick and thin without anyone's running off to indulge in retail therapy as her own mother would do. The concept was unique but one she found highly attractive.

Describing her feelings for Jesse was much more complicated. How did a woman who'd spent the greater part of her life in denial about love suddenly look at the possibility of a forever kind of relationship through different eyes? The answer might not be clear, but she knew it had happened. She knew that the more time she spent with Jesse, he opened her eyes and made her want things she'd never wanted before. At least not consciously.

She lifted her hands from the keyboard.

The power and the fragility of those newfound feelings stole her breath.

Even so, she had to face the truth.

Jesse Wilder made her dare to hope that the fantasy of a happily-ever-after could actually come true.

A knock on the front door sent Wee Man into a barking fit that shattered her concentration. She saved her file and closed the laptop before she went to see who thought to come knocking so late at night.

She opened the door and found every woman's fantasy leaning against the front porch post—a hot cowboy in a hat, jeans, and boots with spurs. Not to mention the snug white T-shirt he wore beneath an open plaid button-down that matched those bedroom eyes.

"Evening, ma'am." Jesse tipped his straw hat and grinned.

"Oh. My. God. Get in here." She grabbed him by the shirt and pulled him inside.

"Happy to oblige," he said, maintaining the whole cowboy thing that was sending her girl parts into an absolute quivering mass of tingles.

"What are you doing?"

Before he could answer, Wee Man leaped into his arms and began furiously licking the whisker shadow on his chin. He gave the dog a rub over the top of his head and back. To her amusement, he called her dog "Buddy" the entire time.

"You're going to give him an identity crisis by calling him a different name," she told him, suddenly aware that his eyes were focused on the front of her skimpy little sleep tee.

"Better than a masculinity complex." He set

her dog down and stepped closer. "I'll bet you call him all kinds of girly names when nobody's around."

She couldn't stop a grin. "Such as?"

"Baby boy, snookums, sweetie pie . . . shall I continue?"

"I have never called him *baby boy.*"

He glanced down at the little dog tap-dancing at his feet, and said with disgust, "She calls you snookums, doesn't she?"

Wee Man barked.

"I knew it. You'd better bring him into my office, so I can do a full psychological exam. Probably why he's so pudgy. He's eating away his emotional issues."

"You're ridiculous." And why did she like that so much? "Did you come over here just to evaluate my dog's mental health? Or was there another reason?"

"Actually, I came over to take you for a ride."

And didn't that just set off all kinds of wicked thoughts.

"No offense," she said, "but it's late, and I've already been in your truck all day."

His head tilted just slightly. "Now, did I say anything about my truck? And would I wear these"—he pointed to the silver spurs on his boots—"if I were going to climb up into a four-wheel drive?"

Good point.

"So what are you saying? That you have a horse parked outside?"

Crickets.

"Oh my God! You have a horse parked outside?" She rushed to the door and yanked it open.

"*Two* horses, darlin'. I brought you your very own."

"I've never been on a horse in my entire life." She whipped around and speared him with an "Are you out of your mind?" glare.

"Now's a good time to start."

"Are you crazy? It's dark out there. And those animals are huge. And—"

Arms with expanded biceps folded across his muscular chest. "Do you honestly think I'd do anything to put you in danger?"

"I don't know. You've looked like you wanted to kill me a time or two."

He chuckled with three low huh-huh-huhs. "You're imagining things." He led her outside, where, untethered, two horses munched her father's front lawn.

"This is Bonnie," he said, sliding his big hand down the blond horse's long neck. "She's as gentle as they come. She's the horse Izzy rides, so she's plenty safe enough for you. And this is Sonny. He's a Tovero paint." He made the same smooth motion of his hand down the big black-and-white horse's neck. The animal tossed his head, and Allison took a step backward.

"He's new to the ranch and still a little green," Jesse said. "But he won't hurt you."

"Green?"

"Means he's still learning the ropes. Doesn't have much training."

"Is he safe to ride?"

"For me. I've been riding since I was about two years old. For you? He'd be risky."

"I don't like taking risks."

"Yeah. I got that."

"What's that supposed to mean?"

"That you don't like taking risks."

"Avoidance of the question only makes me more curious."

He moved closer. Warmth, desire, and promise rolled off him in waves. "I'm sure I can take your mind off all those pesky questions."

The implications of that sent some really interesting signals down into the crotch of her boy shorts. "Oh really?"

He nodded. "How about you go put on some jeans and take a little ride with me? I promise to keep the risks at a minimum."

"Are you making fun of me?" Her hands went to her hips. "Because I guarantee that is no way to get me to go with you."

"Is this better?" Before she could blink he swept her into his arms and planted a kiss to her mouth that made her bones just completely disappear.

When he released her, she nearly fell. "That's a better start," she said.

"Good." He gave her a little pat on the rump. "Now go change."

"Are you sure? It's really dark out here." She glanced at the horses and hoped that would be enough to deter him from making her get up on that huge, scary animal.

He pointed toward the sky. "Full moon is about

to come out from behind those clouds. That will be enough to show us the way. You might want to bring a hoodie or something in case it's cool by the creek."

"The creek?"

"The one that runs through Wilder Ranch."

"Well you're just full of surprises, aren't you?"

He opened his arms, and that white T-shirt settled nicely against the ripple of muscle down his stomach. "I'm willing to give it all I've got."

She knew that. He'd made love to her. And she could verify that he gave it all he had times ten.

When Allison came back into the living room a few minutes later dressed in what she thought might be appropriate riding attire, she found Jesse sitting on the sofa with Wee Man in his lap, looking at her computer.

She'd turned it off, right? She couldn't remember.

"Looks like you were busy before I got here," he said.

"Have you been snooping?" Panic tossed a bag of butterflies into her stomach. She grabbed the laptop and shoved it into the bag on the floor.

"That's not my style," he said. "I just didn't think you might be working or that I'd interrupt."

"Not a problem. I was done."

"You sure?"

"That I'm petrified about riding a horse out into the dark forest?"

"Trust me. I'll keep you safe." He held out his hand, and after she placed her palm in his, she realized she did trust him. And trust was not something she readily gave to anyone.

"You promise you're not taking me off somewhere so I'll get lost and never find my way home?"

"I promise." He chuckled. "In any case, I contacted your father earlier and told him my plan. I also told him you might be home very, very late."

"Quite an assumption that I'd agree to go with you."

"Well, I'm just all hopeful these days."

Oddly, so was she.

After Wee Man took a triple-whiz tour of the yard, they locked him up in the house. Jesse gave her quick instructions on how to ride, and before she knew it—or was ready—they took off at a slow clop through the meadow that met up with the Wilder Ranch property line.

It took a while to feel comfortable up on the big horse, but she quickly learned that Jesse had told the truth. All she had to do was hold on to the reins, and Bonnie would take her wherever she wanted to go. Her fear subsided, and her admiration grew as she watched Jesse ride and school his frisky young horse along the way.

Moonlight illuminated a path as long as they stayed out of the shadows of the trees. Jesse kept up a conversation about growing up on the ranch and how he and his brothers gave their parents a run for their money. She'd met four of the five brothers, and she had to acknowledge that they probably did a good job of keeping their folks on their toes.

What seemed like hours later—at least to her rear end, which was not used to riding in a saddle—he finally pulled his horse up beneath a cover of trees. Allison heard water splashing over rocks and figured they'd reached their destination. When he helped her down, she tumbled from the saddle into his arms.

Not a bad place to be. Still . . . "You planned that."

"Nope." His chuckle vibrated against her breasts. "Just reaping the rewards."

She could barely see him through the dark of the trees, but judging by all the tingling going on in her lips, she would swear his gaze lingered on her mouth. Yet he did not kiss her.

"You stand right here, and I'll make us some light." He let her go and walked away.

Even in the darkness, he was sure-footed and comfortable in his elements. Her? She was imagining hungry coyotes creeping up from behind. When an owl hooted nearby, she about came out of her skin.

Jesse gave a low chuckle from a distance. "No worries there, darlin', I'll protect you."

She hugged herself and was glad she'd brought a hoodie. At least the coyotes would get a mouthful of cotton first. "You don't get scared out here?"

"Scared? Not much scares me."

Of course not. He was too alpha for that.

"Being out here is like second nature to me," he said. "Once the brothers and I got old enough, we'd pack up the horses and camp out for a couple of days at a time. We ended up building a tree house down a ways. That's where Jackson and Abby are building their new house, so I didn't take you there."

"That's okay. Regardless of what you think, I'm always willing to experience new things. As long as I don't get eaten by bears."

"You're safe from the bears," he said, then he was right in front of her again, his warm breath tickling her chest. "No guarantees about me though."

She heard the smile in his voice, and her thoughts went back to their night out by the pool, in the shower, and in the bed. She could attest to a great appreciation for his appetite, and she quivered at the memory of all that passion.

His big hands clasped her arms and rubbed briskly. "Cold?"

Turned on would be more accurate. "A little."

"Give me a second." With that, he was gone again. Moments later, a small campfire roared to life. Golden light reflected off the ring of river-washed rock and bathed him in a warm glow. She held back an appreciative sigh as he made a quick trip over to the horses, then returned to the fire with several blankets, a bottle of wine, and paper cups. You had to love a man who came fully prepared.

He waved her over. "Cocktails by campfire. Cowboy style."

When he spread out the blankets and encouraged her to sit down with the promise that he'd keep away spiders, snakes, and other crawly critters, she realized how much trouble he'd gone through to bring her out here.

Why?

She could only guess. But if he'd just wanted sex, he could have gotten that back at the house. So something else was on his mind as he poured deep red cabernet into the cups and handed her one.

Curiosity peaked when he lifted his cup in a toast.

"Just wanted to say thank you for jumping in and rescuing my brother's wedding when I know you were set on getting out of town."

"It's no big deal. It's what I do for a living."

"It's a big deal, Allison."

The expression that darkened his face was serious, and she knew exactly why that stung just a little. She didn't want to do something nice for someone only to have it seen as a *big deal*. She wanted to do something nice for someone and have them think it was just an everyday thing for her to be so thoughtful. She didn't want to be like her mother, who rarely showed consideration for others. She wanted to be like Jana, whose compassion went without question.

"I know you question how so many things could go wrong and why they'd want to go through with it," Jesse said. "I know you think Reno and Charli's marriage will probably be cursed and that they'll end up in divorce court along with hordes of other married couples. But I can tell you that will never happen."

"How can you be so sure?"

He took a moment to compose his thoughts. She was completely captivated.

"Because I believe that true love doesn't come around every day," he said. "I believe that some people meet, have a few things in common, maybe some great sex, and think that's enough to base a lifetime when they really should have moved on and discovered the person they were really meant to be with. How many times have you seen someone get divorced after a short run, then marry someone they call their soul mate, and that marriage lasts forever?"

She didn't have an answer for those statistics and shrugged.

"Haven't thought that far, have you?"

"I guess not."

"Some people marry for the wrong reasons, Allison." His big warm hand covered hers on top of the blanket. "I believe true love is tested. It doesn't come easy because it's a gift, and it has to be treated with respect. You don't walk out on someone just because you're having a bad day, or the kids are cranky, or you don't get the TV remote enough."

His strong fingers curled around her hand. "Reno and Charli have been tested. They respect each other. And I guarantee neither of them would ever run out on the other. They're meant to be."

"But how do they know?" The million-dollar question. "How does anyone know?"

"You feel it in here." He lifted his hand and settled his warm palm above her heart. "Once you get past the butterflies that come with the newness of a relationship—the infatuation—you listen with the most important tool in your body."

"I thought that was your head."

"Uh-uh. Your head will tell you someone's good-looking and would be easy to wake up to every day. Or that they make a good living and can provide you with the lifestyle you want. There are usually warning signs when it's not right. Most people ignore them. Or they think they can change someone. Your head will fool you. Your heart never will."

A smile tweaked the corners of his mouth. "My mom always says that if you listen carefully, your heart will help you find that one person whose hand you want to hold until they take their last breath."

"Your mom is really grounded." And wonderful. And so unlike her own mother.

"She is."

"So that must be how *you*—renowned playboy of Sweet, Texas—got so smart about relationships."

"Maybe." His broad shoulders lifted. "I just pay attention to what I see. And I allow myself the right to believe that my heart won't steer me wrong."

She pulled a deep breath into her lungs and wondered what his heart said about *her*. Most likely, there were flashing red lights and sirens warning him off.

"Enough about me." He took a drink of wine and firelight danced in his eyes. "Your turn."

"For what?"

"In case you haven't noticed, this is called sharing time." He gave her a hopeful look. "So this is where you get to reveal something about yourself you wouldn't normally share."

She set her paper cup down on the ground, crossed her legs, then held her hands up to catch the warmth of the fire.

"You're stalling," he said.

"You *do* pay attention."

"Which means I'm a good listener. Believe me; as the middle child in a family of five brothers, I've pretty much heard it all. Nothing you say is going to make me judge you. But it might help clear things up a little. So tell me something new. Something you might not share with others."

She studied his face as flickering highlights and shadows leaped up from the flames.

"So reluctant." He trailed his index finger over the top of her hand. "Would it make you feel better if I shared something first?"

"I don't want to know how many lovers you've had if that's where you're going."

His face grew serious. "I'm going to tell you something because I feel safe telling you. Even though telling you is wrong. There are others who should know first."

"You don't have to."

"I know. But when two people care about each other, they share."

She swallowed down her fear and opened her heart.

"The last time Jared and I met up at Camp Leatherneck, he told me he'd fallen in love."

"That's wonderful."

"With a man."

"Did it matter who he fell in love with?"

"No. But he made me promise not to tell anyone. He'd told our dad, who, in turn told him to keep it quiet until they could figure things out."

"So your father was against homosexuality? From everything I've heard about him, that doesn't sound right."

"He wasn't against it at all. He was only concerned for Jared's and his partner's well-being. For their safety. The military isn't always accepting of homosexuals, and Jared had always had his sights set on a military career. But my dad asked Jared to keep it private, then Jared was killed. The guilt my father felt for denying his son love ate at his conscience until his heart just . . . broke."

"Oh my . . ." She pulled him into a hug and stroked her hand down his back. "I'm so sorry. Your mom told me he'd died of a broken heart. I had no idea just how broken."

He leaned back, and his long fingers framed her face. "After my dad died, all I wanted was to make sure everyone found happiness."

"Oh, Jesse." She touched his face. "And so you've been denying yourself that very thing?"

"Apparently."

Her heart expanded. She could not love this man more if she tried.

"I'm sure neither Jared nor your father would ever want or expect you to give up so much."

"The only other person I've spoken to about this is Reno."

"How did he take the news?"

His broad shoulders lifted with the weight of the secret he'd held on to for so long. "The same as me. Don't care who Jared loved, just wished it could have all been out in the open, so he could have enjoyed his life more."

"I guess in situations like this, life really is too short."

He nodded. "Thanks for listening and not judging."

A smile touched her lips. "I've spent a lot of time in your brother's truck. I only wish I'd had the chance to know him. If only to tell him to quit smoking."

A chuckle rumbled deep in his chest. "You wouldn't have been the first to nag at him for that nasty habit."

"I'm sure I wouldn't." She reached up and combed his hair back with her fingers. "He was lucky to have you, you know."

"I was the lucky one."

The way she saw it, all the Wilders were lucky to have each other.

"Thank you for trusting me," she said.

"Ditto." He gave her a quick kiss. "Your turn."

"I . . ." She blew out a slow breath. "Have a blog."

"A blog?"

She nodded.

"Tell me more."

Clearly, she'd stepped off the cliff, so at this point she had no choice but to spread her wings and fly.

Even if she crashed and burned.

"I started it after my parents' divorce because I needed somewhere I could release all my frustrations. All my life, my mom and dad fought and argued. I heard more yelling than I did laughter."

The nightmares of her parents' battles still haunted her. She captured a breath in her lungs. Jesse smoothed a hand down her back. Only because of the compassion he offered was she able to continue.

"I have memories of my mother's ripping me and Danielle from our beds in the middle of the night and forcing us to stay in a hotel away from my dad. Sometimes for days. My father did his best to keep us out of their battles. My mother preferred to drag us right into the core. She took us away, not because she wanted us with her, but because she knew it would hurt my dad."

"I'm sorry." His hand gently rubbed up and down her back. "That must have been really hard for you and your sister."

"It wasn't easy. But it also explains a lot about me." She glanced away because the truth stole the breath from her lungs. "You only get to see things as they're presented to you. From my observation, marriage seems to bring out the worst in people."

"I guess from your standpoint, in a very cynical way, that makes sense," he said.

"It's not that I like being cynical." She hesitated, surprised at how badly she wanted to look at life through less skeptical eyes. "But it's been pounded into my head since I can remember. Guess even though you become an adult, and you think you're your own person, you're just fooling yourself."

"What do you mean?"

"My mother has always told me I'm just like her. That I'm unsuitable for being with just one person for the rest of my life."

"Bullshit."

"It's probably true." She shifted her gaze to where the horses stood beneath the trees because she couldn't handle the disappointment darkening Jesse's eyes. "Settling down has never even entered my mind."

"Never?"

Lately, something *had* changed, and the truth of it made her snap her gaze back to the man who sat beside her.

In the past weeks, she'd found herself surrounded by loving couples she couldn't help but admire. People she was learning to respect and aspire to be.

When she looked at Jesse, a funny tickle in her heart whispered, "What if he's *the one*?"

She'd been taught from early on that there was no such thing. But it appeared her heart wasn't listening.

Maybe Jesse was right. Maybe a person needed to listen to their heart, not all the nonsense that had been shoved into their head.

"Well, maybe not never," she said, going for a smile that probably wavered with her uncertainty.

"Allison, I'm glad you found an outlet for dealing with your past and your doubts. I'm a strong believer that if you have too much weight on your shoulders, there's always someone to help you through. Next time?" He cupped her face in his hands. "I've got your back. Talk to *me*. Okay?"

His willingness to step up and take on her issues brought tears to her eyes. "I've never had anyone I could talk to about this before," she admitted. "My dad couldn't handle it. My sister was too busy building her own life. And my mother didn't want to hear it."

"Not trying to talk smack about your mother," Jesse said, "but I'm pretty sure her reasons for getting married and divorced so many times are a major personality flaw."

"Well, she does have that," she agreed. "But no matter how many times I try to find my way around everything, it all comes right back to my mother's DNA and her insistence that I'm just like her."

"That might be wishful thinking on her part. Misery loves company, right?" He plucked a long blade of grass from the ground and twirled it between his fingers. "Look, if everyone thought that way, then Reno would be a drug-addict dealer who'd abandon his own kid. Can you imagine him that way?"

"No! He's one of the finest people I've ever met."

"Exactly. But that's his past. That's who his birth mother was. So maybe instead of focusing on your past, you should look toward the future. Find the things that outshine your mother's misguided prophecy." He tickled the blade of grass across the top of her hand. "What about your sister's marriage?"

"Danielle and Andrew truly are my one hope,"

she admitted. "Their relationship has always been perfect in every way. They've never had a fight. They *communicate*—something I don't think my parents ever managed to do. Andrew has always been so supportive of my sister. Especially when our parents went through their divorce. She could call on him at any time, day or night. He's always been so understanding and compassionate."

Allison took a breath. In her eyes as well as her sister's, Andrew walked on water. "Danielle had morning sickness the entire nine months she was pregnant with Lily. Andrew would hold her head when she got sick. He'd rub her back, legs, and feet. One time, in the middle of the night, he even went to the store in the pouring rain to buy crackers and ginger ale because they'd run out.

"Danielle is equally devoted to him. When he went through the police academy, the hours were long and hard. Danielle stood by him and took care of everything, so all he had to do was focus on his career. Though he works in such a violent profession, he's never lost his warm and generous heart. When you see him with his wife and his little girls, there's no question he can block out the horrible things he deals with in his job."

She smiled, knowing that her brother-in-law was a man to be admired and a man you could trust. And though she'd occasionally found herself a little jealous of the prince her sister had found, she was pleased that at least someone in her family had found utopia.

"If anyone can go the distance, it's them," she said with confidence.

"That's great." He leaned in and cupped her cheek in his hand. His smile warmed her from the inside out. "It's better to have *one* hope than *no* hope. Because that means there's room to grow."

The ache in her chest lifted, and her heart seemed to float like a happy-face balloon. "Jesse Wilder, you never cease to surprise me."

"Darlin', I've only just begun."

*J*esse didn't need more unpleasant details to figure out the pattern that had been Allison's childhood. It was now clear why she was so afraid to let go of her beliefs. It crushed him that she'd lived such a complicated life, one with so little love and affection. Right now, he just wanted to reach out. Touch her. Feel her. And give to her. To find that connection they shared. Hopefully, she'd come to realize there was more to life than the bad stuff she'd been dealt.

Regardless of the way she'd been raised by an obviously heartless woman, Allison had an amazing heart. The way she quickly jumped in to rescue Reno and Charli's wedding spoke volumes about her. She might want to believe that it was the knowledge of her profession that made her volunteer, but he believed it was more. Helping out, making things happen, making people happy was as much a part of who she was as those amazing gray eyes.

While her cynical side might assume the prewedding disasters were a sign the marriage shouldn't take place, he believed the disasters happened in order to keep her here. To show her the other side of the coin. And maybe that *they* were meant to be together.

As the middle child, he'd spent most of his life trying to figure out where he fit. When it came to Allison, all questions stopped.

He fit with *her.*

As he drew her into his arms, the heavy pull of desire spread in a hot flush across his chest and down his abdomen. He drowned in the heavy lust that beat through his veins, pounded in his chest, and rasped through his groin. He inhaled that sweet scent that was hers alone as a sliver of air separated their mouths. Firelight danced across her face as he lowered his head.

Her mouth tasted like sweet wine and passion. As his hand dipped beneath the hem of her shirt and his fingers grazed her bare flesh, she moaned her approval into his mouth.

They came to their knees, and their hands got busy removing clothes. From the waist up they were skin to skin. Her fingers slipped across his shoulders, down his chest, and explored all that was bared to her. Her touch spread fire across his skin. And then, with her satiny hair falling across him in a curtain of soft caramel, she lowered her head and licked her warm, slick tongue up his throat. Desire shot white-hot pleasure into his groin.

He slid his palms down the small of her back, tucked his fingertips between her jeans and warm, soft skin, and pulled her tight against his ache. She reached for the band holding back his hair and pulled it free. Then she tangled her fingers in the strands at his nape.

She leaned back and smiled up at him. Firelight reflected in her eyes and shimmered within the flecks of silver and gold. "I never knew I was such an outdoorsy kind of girl," she said through a ragged breath. "Until I met you."

"Stick with me . . ." His fingers skimmed down to caress her plump, luscious breasts. "I'll be happy to take you places you never had on your radar."

"Such as?"

Love, he wanted to say. But that would only scare the hell out of both of them.

"How about we start right . . . here?" With his palms, he held her by the waist while he licked and suckled her nipples until they were wet and erect. Until she moaned, and squirmed, and reached for him.

He didn't let her.

Tonight was all about her. No matter how badly he wanted to sink deep inside her warmth. He wouldn't let that happen until she'd been satisfied over and over. Until he'd tasted her. Devoured her. And let her know that in this relationship, he was more than willing to give her whatever she needed. Wanted. Desired. He didn't mean just sex although that was about to happen. He meant everything he had, body, mind, heart, and soul.

He'd never felt so strongly about a woman. It was new and exhilarating, and he was ready to explore whatever it was and wherever it took them.

It *was* his turn.

And he planned to enjoy every second.

He pushed the jeans down her legs, tossed them aside on the blanket, and positioned himself between her soft thighs. Leaving her ice-cream-colored panties on, he laid her back, slid his fingers into her long, silky hair, and lost himself in her heat. Her scent. And the exhilaration surging through his veins.

When he moved his mouth down the slender column of her neck, she let go a long, seductive sigh. Moonlight peeked through the leaves of the oaks and splashed her skin with highlights and shadows. Beneath his tongue, her pulse throbbed.

"Take your pants off, Jesse." She reached for him. Tangled her fingers in his hair. "I want to feel you."

He didn't dare. If he so much as came in direct contact with all her warm, sweet-scented flesh, his good intentions would shatter. He wanted her, in the worst way. But he wanted her moaning with pleasure and release before he allowed his own. Right now, nothing else mattered but her and this time they had together.

"You're so beautiful." He looked at her lying there bathed in moonlight. His fingertips tingled to life as they met her warm skin. "Just let me love you."

He pressed his lips between her breasts, and her throaty moan vibrated through him. She arched against him, her response to his request. He took his time sweeping his lips and tongue over the sweetness of her flesh, working his way down her body until he reached that tiny little patch of lace. He'd never thought a scrap of material could be sexier than a woman's naked body. But on Allison, the sheer fabric was like whipped cream on top of the most delicious dessert.

Her moist heat greeted him as he slipped his fingers beneath the elastic band and moved the material aside. When he pressed his lips to the inside of her silky thighs, she moaned. Whispered his name on a sigh. She wanted him. And that knowledge swelled in his heart.

A sense of pleasure washed over him. With her in his arms, there was no place on earth he'd rather be. He vowed to take his time and love her thoroughly. He wanted her to connect. Bond. And remember this night even if she was thousands of miles away.

A smile brushed his mouth as he lowered his head and proceeded to take her to those places she'd never been.

Including heaven.

Chapter 15

$\mathcal{I}$f the actual wedding day and reception were a high point of stress for a bride, the rehearsal dinner rated top with the groom's family. As Jesse was once more relegated to manning the enormous BBQ grill, he smiled at the flurry of activity. While tending to a multiple of chores, his mother barked out instructions. The rest of the family scurried about with their assigned tasks.

Though the guest list was comprised of mostly family, there were several out-of-towners such as Charli's father and his new barely-over-the-legal-age girlfriend. This, according to Reno, had Charli more stressed out than all the other prewedding disasters put together. Jesse had never crossed paths with General Brooks during his time in the Marines, but he knew of his tough reputation, and he knew the man had used that same method in raising his children.

Weddings and funerals always seemed to bring out the worst in some people. Which was probably what had both Charli and Nick on edge.

With all the high stress levels and fuss, Jesse was happy to mind the brisket. And while he slathered the tender beef with more sauce, he promised himself that if he should ever marry, he'd prefer a quick and easy ceremony. Something more about the bond than cake and flowers.

Dead center of all the activity, Allison flashed him a smile as she rushed by with her arms full of Mason-jar centerpieces blooming with daisies. Since the night he'd taken her riding—in more ways than one—they hadn't had much time together. She'd been focused on helping Charli and his mother, and he'd been swamped at the clinic with spays and neuters. Seems she'd gotten the brighter end of the spectrum.

But when he'd dropped her back off at her father's house in the glow of the morning sun, he knew they'd found something together neither of them had expected.

He wasn't surprised to find that as she passed by him now, his body hit full alert. Her sweet scent wafted by as if he'd walked into a cupcake shop, and his appetite increased for more than barbecue.

That she fit in so well with the others in his life spoke volumes. Not everyone could manage to keep up with the high-velocity lifestyle they lived. Yet in the past weeks, she'd proven not only that she could keep up, she could soar past them and not even blink. He'd never thought about finding the right woman or what she might even be like. He knew now Allison was perfect for him. In every way.

Something warm fluttered in the center of his chest as Izzy, in a pretty pink polka-dotted dress, came running up and threw herself into his arms.

"Hey there, little darlin'." He gave her a kiss on her chubby cheek. "What are you up to?"

"Stayin' outta gwanma's way."

He laughed. "Is grandma getting grumpy?"

Izzy nodded, and her springy blond curls bounced.

"You want to hang out here with me?"

"Yeth."

"Are you giving me that big smile, so I'll tell you where grandma's stash of candy is hidden?"

"No, Unca Jethe." She planted her little hands on his cheeks and batted her eyelashes. "I wub you."

He laughed. Even at three years old, a female knew how to use her wiles to get what she wanted. He opened his mouth to give away the secret location of the jar of lollipops his mother kept hidden only to be sidelined by the woman herself.

"I know I've said it before, but I'll say it again. You look good holding a baby, son."

"Don't go getting any ideas, Mom."

"I not a baby, gwanma."

His mother reached out and took his niece, placing loud squeaky kisses on her cheeks and making her giggle. It was nice to have a little one in the family. Hopefully, his soon-to-be-married brothers would do their part to add to the clan. He wouldn't mind having a few of his own someday, but he didn't plan to advertise that to anyone. Especially his meddling, crafty mother.

"Go get your daddy to give you a lollipop, sugarplum." His mother set Izzy down. "And y'all tell him to hurry up with getting those chairs out to the tables."

"Mom, she's three. You think she's going to remember anything past *lollipop*?"

"Probably not." A chuckle slipped past her smile. "But I'm trying to train her early. Unlike you and your brothers, who had selective hearing when it came to chores until . . . well, you still do. Guess that's the difference in boys and girls." She turned and gestured toward Allison, who was now helping Fiona put tablecloths on the picnic tables. "The girls are already on top of things without any prompting."

"This conversation leading somewhere?" he asked. "Or have you been tipping the cooking wine?"

"Oh so perceptive." She patted his cheek. "Things seem to be going well between you and Allison. Her daddy told me you kept her out practically till dawn with an impromptu trail ride the other night."

"Just thought she might like to learn a little horsemanship before she went back to the concrete jungle."

"So y'all were riding all night?"

So to speak. "No. We stopped by the creek and had a chat."

"Jesse, sugarplum–"

"Wait." He held up his BBQ tongs. "Is this going to lead into a lecture with a football analogy?"

"You know me too well." She grinned. "How about I leave out the football?"

"How about you leave out the lecture?"

"Now where's the fun in that?" She patted his

biceps the way she had when he was a kid about to get a vaccination. "I'm not pushing for details. Just make my heart happy and tell me you're interested in the girl."

He glanced across the lawn to the subject matter, who looked appetizing as hell in a low-cut floral sundress and cowgirl boots. "She's a beautiful woman."

"And you're interested?"

"And you're butting in because?"

"Not butting in. Just verifying that the smile you've been toting around lately is because of her and that I haven't just been imagining things. Starts happening when you get older, you know."

"Bull. You're too insightful for your own good," was all he'd admit to.

"Why is it so hard for you to admit you've got a thing for her?"

"Look, it took me years to build my wicked reputation. Why would I want to destroy it over one woman who is ready to pack up and leave any day?"

"Your reputation is plum embarrassing." She folded her arms across the front of her yellow print blouse. "And because sometimes the heart can't help where it lands."

"My heart is right in the center of my chest where it belongs."

"All y'all are so much alike, it makes my head hurt. I don't know what I did wrong to raise such a hardheaded bunch of boys."

Jesse leaned down and kissed her cheek. "We're just taking after you."

"Nonsense." Her voice came out a gruff expression of disappointment. "The moment your daddy and I met, that was it. We knew we belonged together. Neither of us was perfect. Neither of us expected perfection. We worked together. We loved each other. And until your brother . . ."

Jesse wanted to ask what she was referring to—that his brother had died or that his brother was homosexual. Had his mother known?

"We had a very good life." Eyes filled with unshed tears, she reached up and stroked his cheek. "I just want each of you boys to find that one person in your life that makes you happy. Before it's too late."

Yeah. She knew. She had to. The woman was more intuitive than the woman in Comfort who told fortunes for a living.

Still, he needed to have that talk with her and the rest of the boys. Especially now that he'd opened up to Allison.

"I promise you . . ." He took her hand and kissed it. Clasped it to his heart. "If the love of my life comes dancing before my eyes, I will reach out, grab her, and make her mine."

His mother gave him a watery smile.

"Now," he said, "make those happy tears and go help my brother get married."

She opened her mouth, and before she spoke, he knew exactly what she would say.

"One Wilder at a time, Mom."

"Hardheaded or not, you're a good boy, son."

"Now, don't go starting rumors."

With a laugh, she went off to wrap up the rehearsal-dinner preparations. He looked up, searching out the small brunette who'd somehow landed an unexpected wallop to his heart. When he found her, she had little Izzy in her arms. They were dancing cheek to cheek to an imaginary song. As though she felt his gaze on her, she looked up and smiled.

Keep your promise.

Reach out.

Make her yours.

*T*here were few things in life Allison craved. But as she wandered among those gathered at the rehearsal dinner for Charli and Reno, she realized she'd always craved this kind of close-knit family.

The conversation was lively. The food delicious. And the genuine affection of those assembled— including her father—was too much to deny. She glanced across the lawn at her dad, who stood talking with a protective arm around Annie's shoulders. She couldn't blame him for moving to Sweet. Couldn't blame him for wanting to stay. And as her gaze fell upon Jana, she couldn't blame him for wanting to be a part of the family Jana had created and nurtured.

Heck, *she* wanted to be a part.

"It's all a bit tacky, isn't it?"

Allison looked up to find Lauren, the very young, very unsophisticated, very leggy blonde General Brooks had shown up with on his arm. "Excuse me?"

"This." She waved an arm. "It's nothing like the parties back in DC. It's just so . . . hillbilly. I mean, there's a goat walking around wearing a ribbon around its neck. It doesn't get more redneck than that, does it? I know the bride was in show business although I have no idea who she is. Supposedly, she's a designer. So you think she'd have better taste."

"You have no idea who your boyfriend's daughter is?"

Lauren shrugged a bony shoulder. "You'd think she'd at least try to class things up a little. I can't even imagine what kind of gown she'll wear. Hopefully, it won't be camo like the one Honey Boo Boo's mom wore."

Charli's gown was understated elegance. And she'd look like a princess wearing it. But whether Charli wore a beaded fit-and-flair gown or Daisy Dukes to her wedding, she'd have more class in one strand of hair than this after-market boobed creature.

It wasn't often Allison allowed rage to overtake her good sense. At that moment, she didn't bother to hold it back.

"I've been in the wedding business for a long time."

"Oh? Then maybe I can call you for advice when the general and I get married. And we will. He just hasn't asked yet."

"Right." Allison had a feeling General Brooks's bimbo would be waiting a long time for the man to put a ring on her finger. Men like him didn't marry women like her. They made great playthings but rarely made good wives.

"In any case," Allison said, "you might want to keep in mind that *tacky* is in the eye of the beholder.

Sometimes the things one chooses to wear"—she dropped her gaze to the woman's dress, which seemed more appropriate for a swing shift on Sunset Boulevard than a family gathering—"just reek of desperation."

Lauren's overly glossed mouth dropped open with a soundless gasp.

"So tomorrow when you show up for the general's daughter's very classy and poignant wedding," Allison said, "maybe you could show up in something that doesn't look like it should be worn on *Pimp My Ride*. And maybe you could pretend to appreciate being invited to this wedding. Because it's an *honor* to be here."

Lauren stomped off, hooker stilettos teetering in the gravel. Allison was delighted to see that the sausage-casing dress she wore was stuffed up into the crack of her skinny ass. No doubt a souvenir from sitting on those *tacky* picnic benches.

Someone chuckled from behind, and Allison turned to find Jesse there with the biggest grin she'd ever seen.

"You sure y'all don't have *Southern* in your blood?" he drawled. "Because that sure was a powerful Texas tornado I just witnessed."

Allison threw another glare in the escaping Lauren's direction. "She said mean things about my friends."

"Remind me not to get on your bad side."

His smile melted away her anger. "I'm not sure you could."

"Does that mean I get a free pass?"

She leaned into him and turned on the flirt.

"Depends on what you're offering to stay on my good side."

"Right now . . ." He gave her a look and slowly trailed his fingers down her arm. A slew of tingles shot right through the center of her heart and down into her core. "You could have just about anything you asked for."

"That's a lot of options."

A smile spread over those masculine lips she'd kissed and was tempted to taste again right then and there. No matter who watched.

"I'm all yours," he said.

She wished.

"Thank you." He took her hand and locked their fingers together.

"For?"

His gaze searched her face, and he made her feel like they were the only ones on the face of the earth. "Looking out for my family."

"Family always comes first."

He nodded. "Looks like you've been paying attention."

"More closely than you can imagine," she said. And then she rose to her toes and kissed the corner of his mouth. "But if you tell anyone, I'll have to turn on the tornado and take you down."

"Darlin', you keep using words like 'take me,' and we've got a deal."

Her heart fluttered. For the first time, she began to believe that anything was possible.

Even finding the elusive soul mate and falling in love.

Chapter 16

$\mathcal{E}$veryone had an opinion on the best time of day to hold a wedding. As an event planner, Allison believed there were certain factors to consider: season, honeymoon destination, and the time of day the bride always looked her best. In certain situations, that factor could also include such anomalies as when the mother of the bride might be sober or how long they had before the bouncing-baby shotgun reason for the wedding made its appearance.

During her final inspection of the wedding venue before the ceremony began, she moved past the gallery of white folding chairs. Charli and Reno had chosen dusk in the Town Square gazebo for their special day. Each row had been accented with small votive lanterns to welcome the arrival of the wedding party and their guests.

Allison stopped at the front row of the groom's side and looked down at the chair where earlier she'd placed an eight-by-ten photograph of Jared Wilder in his Marine dress blues. The elaborate midnight blue jacket emblazoned with ribbons and medals had been draped over the back of the chair, while Jared's crisp white hat with its eagle, globe, and anchor ornament sat on the seat next to his photo. Charli had insisted Jared be included in the wedding in spirit even if he couldn't be there in person. A touching tribute to the man so many people loved and admired. Whether they knew he was gay or not.

Allison sighed and walked up the gazebo steps to make sure no further disasters lurked. As she looked out over Town Square, she knew there couldn't have been a better venue for the radiant bride and her handsome cowboy to exchange their vows.

During her days on the cable TV show *My New Town*, Charli had taken a run-down piece of grass smack-dab in the center of Sweet and turned it into something spectacular for the entire community to enjoy. She'd designed the new Victorian-style gazebo that now stood within the glow of thousands of tiny white lights. Thanks to the very talented Antoine, the gazebo was also draped with gorgeous garlands of hydrangea, roses, iris, and lilies.

A month ago, Allison would have explained away the tingles skipping through her system as anxiety over the preparation for the ceremony. This evening those vibrations were created by sheer happiness.

And someone very special.

Everything had changed since she'd come to Sweet, all because of Jesse and his insistence on showing her a glass-half-full life instead of half-empty. She'd dared to hope, to take a chance, and the rewards, so far, had been incredible. Though she didn't exactly know where or how everything would go, she realized Jesse had opened doors to possibilities she'd never imagined.

When she briefly closed her eyes and pictured him in her mind, her heart openly admitted that she'd fallen in love for the first time in her life.

Hopefully, if miraculously he felt the same, the last.

For her, Jesse Wilder was *the one*.

"Everything looks just beautiful."

Allison turned to find Jana standing at the head of the aisle.

"Charli has amazing taste."

"I agree. She's marrying my son." Jana smiled as she walked toward her in a pretty but simple royal blue tea-length dress and a corsage pinned at her shoulder. "But the compliment was for you."

"Me?"

"Yes. You." Jana took her hand and clutched it tight. "Without your help, Charli and Reno's dream wedding wouldn't have come true. The flowers, the music, the cake, and the reception. No one else would have ever thought of using Jesse's house."

"It's actually the perfect place."

"It is. I have no doubt the wedding would still have taken place, but you've given Charli and my son a beautiful beginning to their life together."

"They deserve to be happy."

"And they will be." She tucked her hand beneath Allison's chin. "You deserve that same happiness, sugarplum."

A sigh slipped past Allison's lips. "I didn't used to think so, but . . ."

"Things change."

Allison nodded. "They do."

"I'm glad." Jana gave her cheek a gentle pat. "You and Jesse are so good for each other."

Allison wasn't surprised Jana was aware of their relationship. They were, after all, a close family. Even if Jesse hadn't said anything, the sparks between them were pretty obvious.

"I know he's good for me," she said. "I'm not so sure he thinks I'm good for him. *Or* that reputation he worked so hard to build."

"Oh that boy. So misguided." Jana chuckled, then the hint of a frown pulled her blond brows together. "You do realize it's all myth, right?"

"I wouldn't say *all*. But yes, I do realize his *exploits* took on a life of their own."

"I'm so glad. I've told him over and over that someday those stories were going to ruin everything for him when he found the right woman and fell in love. I'm glad you can look past all that silliness."

When he fell in love?

Had he mentioned that to Jana, or was it merely wishful thinking?

Was she the right woman?

Allison didn't know. She had to admit the idea frightened her a little. There was a whole lot of responsibility in being the right woman. Or even the maybe-kinda-sorta woman. But with Jesse, she'd be willing to take that chance. With him, she'd be willing to push aside her fears. To just allow herself to dream of a possible future spent in his arms gave her shivers of anticipation.

"Well," Jana said, "guess I'd best go check on Reno. He's as nervous as a cat in a bathtub. Who'd have ever thought he'd be preparing for his wedding in the back room of the hardware store."

Allison laughed. "Maybe we should have decorated the aisles with little hammers and wrenches."

"I'm sure they'd come in handy in the future, when Charli needs to give his stubborn head a good whack." With a smile, she turned to leave.

"Jana?"

Jesse's mom turned and tilted her head just slightly. Her big, blond, Texas-sized hairdo never wobbled.

"I think you're just wonderful. And I'm sorry it took me so long to come around," Allison said. "I think my father is very lucky to have found you. And I truly wish you both a lifetime of happiness."

"We're lucky to have found each other." Jana's smile was so genuine, Allison's heart clenched. "Just remember, sugarplum, it doesn't matter what road you travel, or how far, or *when* you come around. When love is meant to be, there's nothing that will stop it. Not time. Not place. Not circumstance. You remember that."

A sigh stuck in Allison's chest as she watched

Jana walk across the street and disappear into the hardware store.

Who knew when she stepped off that plane in San Antonio that everything she'd thought, dreamed, or imagined would change.

Life was looking really good.

*N*o one in their right mind would choose to be stuck inside a monkey suit on a sultry Texas night, but to see his brother happy, Jesse would have worn a suit of molten lava.

Alongside his brothers, he stood inside the Victorian gazebo his soon-to-be sister-in-law had created. A shiver that had nothing to do with the weather and everything to do with the elation in his brother's eyes, danced down his back as he watched that effervescent woman walk down the aisle. Jesse had seen radiant brides before, but none glowed quite as dazzlingly as Charlotte Brooks. In a strapless dress that was a little lacy, a little ruffly, and a whole lot Charli, she had her eyes focused on the man she was about to marry. Her smile was wide and steadfast, and Jesse knew he could only hope to be so fortunate as to have a woman look at him that way.

Beside him, his brother sighed. While that same almost silly grin was planted on Reno's face, his dark eyes were lit with a "hurry up" brightness that left no question he was anxious to make Charli his wife.

Thanks to Allison's help and her creative friend from Seattle, Town Square had become a floral fantasyland with twinkling lights and even candlelit lanterns at the end of each row of pristine white chairs. Yet as spectacular as the twilight setting might be, Jesse didn't understand all the fuss. It wouldn't have mattered if there had been one flower or a million. A single ribbon or a truckload. Because as sure as he was standing there, neither Reno nor Charli noticed.

They only had eyes for each other.

Jesse swept his gaze across the friends and family gathered together and zeroed in on Allison at the back of the crowd. Earlier, she'd flitted about like a hummingbird, fluffing out the petticoats on Izzy's little dress, straightening boutonnieres on tuxes, calming nerves. She was a pro. Yet the whole time she'd been doing her job, she'd been unable to hide her excitement over *these* nuptials. And he hadn't been able to stop himself from kissing the smile that never left those pretty lips.

Even in front of an audience.

He no longer felt a need to hide what was growing with velocity between them. And by the way she'd wrapped her arms around his waist and kissed him back, neither did she.

Now, as Charli and her father, in full-dress uniform, stepped up into the gazebo, Allison stood at the back, watching and smiling with pride. She'd helped rescue this moment in time, and Jesse could almost see her chest rise on a happy sigh.

His respect and appreciation for her selfless deeds created a huge lump in his throat. When she caught him looking at her, a smile blossomed on her face, and she gave him a pinkie wave.

Pleasure rolled over him with just that small gesture. In that moment, he realized the connection they shared was rare and wonderful. No doubt the journey on which they were about to embark would be an adventure.

He couldn't wait to get started.

With reluctance, he pulled his attention away from Allison and back to the ceremony just as General Brooks handed off his daughter to Reno. The about-to-be-marrieds didn't even wait for the vows or exchange of rings to kiss and whisper I love yous. Even as the audience chuckled, and the ceremony began, Jesse noticed there wasn't a dry eye in Town Square.

After traditional vows were exchanged, Reno and Charli also spoke the personal vows they'd written. Charli's version comically included promises of no décor changes without prior notice, and ignoring Reno's grumpiness after a long day of counting nails and bucking hay bales. But it was her whispered promise of at least one barn dance per year where she'd forget her "you-know-whats" that got Jesse and his brothers laughing.

Annie might have gotten her gun; but Charli had gotten her man by conveniently *forgetting* to don underwear beneath her party dress.

Reno's promises had been to continue to call her Fancy Pants even though she mostly wore jeans, to finally paint a mural in their home just for her, and to love her even when she wore bunny slippers and a big fuzzy robe.

The ceremony ended with a kiss that made everyone go "Awwwwww." As the preacher introduced them as Mr. and Mrs. Reno Wilder, Charli lifted the hem of her wedding gown in a cancan dancer fashion to show off her hot pink rhinestone-covered cowgirl boots. With the crowd chuckling, the newlyweds walked up the aisle arm in arm.

Heart content, Jesse's gaze drifted to the empty chair in the front row that held his brother's Marine photo, cap, and medal-and-ribbon-studded jacket. Briefly, Jesse closed his eyes. In his mind, he pictured Jared sitting there, nodding his approval in that stubborn-ass big-brother know-it-all way.

Amid a skipped heartbeat, that vision altered as the image of Jared's blue-eyed gaze locked with his own.

The smile on Jared's face faded, but his nod lingered in a slow up-and-down motion that flashed a ray of sunlight across his pale hair. Jesse's heart clenched as he received the meaning of Jared's unspoken message.

It's time to tell them all.

Was it possible to float on air? Because surely, as Allison watched Charli and Reno come up the aisle arm in arm and grinning like there was no tomorrow, that's what was going on. She'd witnessed hundreds of weddings before, but she'd never seen anything quite like this one. And she was sure she'd never before required a tissue for anything other than touching up a bride's smudged lipstick or lending it to a guest who'd forgotten their own. But as her new friends had spoken their vows, Allison had felt the need to blow her nose in goose-honking fashion.

As they passed her by, Reno gave her a wink, and Charli mouthed a thank-you. They didn't need to thank her. In her newly awakened eyes, it was vice versa.

While the crowd dispersed, Allison stayed behind to make sure the chairs and florals were transported to Jesse's house for the reception.

"Hey, darlin'."

Before she even turned, she smiled. There was only one Southern drawl that deep, that smooth, and that sexy that could send her heart dancing in a million directions.

"Hey yourself, handsome."

A smile brushed his mouth. Then those sexy lips came down and met hers in a kiss that started out soft and ended up removing her lipstick. The scent of warm, clean male and an aftershave that hinted of vanilla and cedar drifted on the night air and wrapped around her in sensuous tendrils.

"I had a few minutes while they take photos of the bride and groom," he said. "And I wanted to see how you were holding up."

"I'm holding up just fine." She brushed a microscopic piece of lint from his lapel near the small rose boutonniere just for an opportunity to touch him again.

"That was a bold-faced lie I just told," he said. "I didn't just want to see how you were holding up. I wanted to *see you*. Up close. But I guess the *and personal* part will have to wait for later."

"Probably." *Darn it.* "I think there's a city ordinance against nudity in the park."

"At least until after sundown."

A laugh tickled her lips. She liked that he just said what he thought. And that he'd been thinking about her at all was quite . . . thrilling. "The ceremony was perfect."

"True." He glanced over his shoulder at the rest of the wedding party. "But those two could have gotten married in a cave, and they wouldn't have noticed."

"It's just like you said. They're meant to be."

His smile broadened as he took her hand and kissed the backs of her fingers. "You're such a brilliant pupil."

"Does that mean you still have more lessons to teach me?"

"More?" He lifted his large hand and gently brushed a lock of her hair away from her face. "Darlin', I have an endless supply. Though I can't guarantee the studying will require you to wear clothes."

Even as her girl parts raised a toast to his attention to academic detail, she chuckled. "Promises. Promises."

"I deliver too. Just like the pizza guy."

"The pizza guys who come to my door are always fast and only interested in the tip."

"Guess the comparison stops there. I take it slow." He leaned in and spoke close to her ear. "And I'm interested in the whole thing."

"I can verify that you aim to please."

"Several times a night." He winked.

From the corner of her eye, she caught movement and saw the wedding party headed toward the horse-drawn carriage she'd hired at the last minute. Jackson was waving Jesse over. "Guess you'd better go. I'm sure they want to include you in the photos."

"Guess there's no time to pull you behind the bushes."

A sigh of disappointment pushed past her lips. "Guess not."

"Maybe later?" His smile was so hopeful, there was no way she'd even consider turning him down. Not to mention her girl parts, which had swung into the chorus of "Hot In Herre."

"Count on it."

He curled his arm around her waist and pulled her against him for a soft, slow kiss that melted her from the inside out.

When Jake shouted, "Get a room," Jesse withdrew, and Allison immediately missed the connection that made more than just her heart flutter.

After another quick kiss, he said, "See you back at the house."

Watching Jesse walk away created a mix of emotions. While she didn't want him to leave, she loved to watch him go. With broad shoulders squared, his long legs ate up the distance between them. The man looked great in a tux, jeans, and board shorts. But he looked best in nothing at all. Allison knew she'd be counting the minutes until she could get her hands on his smooth skin and firm muscles.

As she watched him clamp a hand over Jackson's shoulder, her phone vibrated from the pocket of her jacket. When she saw Danielle's name, she tapped ANSWER. "Hey, sis. What's up?"

"That son of a bitch Andrew, that's what."

Whoa. She'd never heard her sister so angry before. Not even when their mother had tried to sabotage her lovely wedding reception by getting drunk and hitting on Andrew's best man.

What could her brother-in-law have possibly done so wrong that would inspire so much rage? Forgotten to pay the cable bill, and the girls were pitching a hissy fit over missing SpongeBob? Gotten a parking ticket he couldn't get out of—even being a cop? Whatever it was, it couldn't be that bad.

"What's going on?" she asked.

"All these months that son of a bitch has been telling me he's working overtime on a prostitution ring? He was *screwing* a confidential informant."

"What?" Allison felt like she'd just stepped into another dimension. Her world wobbled on its axis, and she sank down in the nearest chair.

"He was caught with his pants down. Literally. It's over, Allie." When Danielle's voice shattered like glass, a shiver knifed down Allison's spine. "I don't understand. We never fought. Not once. He never acted like anything was wrong. I mean, yeah, sure, things have changed over the years, and we weren't jumping each other's bones every minute of the day, but I thought that was just the natural progression of being married."

Allison swallowed. She was still stuck on the words "It's over."

How could this happen?

How could the two people she'd counted on most to show her the way to relationship nirvana just . . . implode?

"Are you sure?" she asked. Her sister's shriek a moment later gave earsplitting verification.

"Of course I'm sure! Just as I'm sure I made up all the *wonderfulness* about my marriage in my head," Danielle cried. "It was probably shit right from the start, and I was just too stupid to notice. How is it we can become so blind? Huh? Tell me."

"Well, I—"

"I mean, when we were in our twenties, everything was so passionate. We couldn't stand being away from each other for even a minute. But then you have kids, and it seems like your time with each other becomes less in regularity and less important. And when you hit the sheets at night, all you can think is about falling into a deep sleep. Maybe the *wonderfulness* really was just about the sex. Because, obviously, a *hooker* can give him what he really wants. Forget about the woman at home cooking his dinner and washing his dirty underwear."

"Don't be ridiculous." Allison wanted to defend her sister's right to retain the fantasy that her marriage had been wonderful, but it was beyond her how to make that happen when the *perfect* Andrew Schafer was a big fat undercover fraud. Devastation strangled her, and for a moment, speaking became impossible.

"How am I going to tell the girls?" Danielle sobbed. "What am I going to do? I thought we'd be together forever. Now I'm just supposed to come up with a whole new way of life?"

Words spun like a hamster wheel inside Allison's head. She searched to pull the right ones out of the whirling mass and offer comfort. "Dani, I—"

"What did I do wrong?" Danielle wailed. "What did I do to make him do this? I watch my weight. I put on makeup every day. I fixed my hair. I never walk around in stained sweatpants. I mean sure, I collapse exhausted at night, and maybe I haven't performed a striptease for him in a while, but . . . what the hell did I do wrong?"

Wait.

What?

"Stop." Allison pushed aside her feelings of despair, cleared her throat, and got her temper under control.

Now was not the time to sink into her own shattered illusions. Now was the time for understanding and reassurance. When that was done, then and only then, could she plot Andrew's slow, torturous death.

"Danielle, *you* have done nothing wrong. This might affect your entire life, but as crazy as it sounds, it's not *about* you. This is about Andrew and whatever egomaniacal selfishness that crawled into his head to make this happen. Sometimes good people do stupid things."

"This isn't stupid. It's . . . shattering. And unforgivable. He was my heart and my soul. And now he's . . ."

The fact that her sister couldn't find the words to describe the man to whom she'd pledged her life spoke volumes. For Allison's entire life, Danielle had been her rock. Her friend. Her mentor.

Her shining example. Her light at the end of an emotional tunnel.

Now it was time for the tables to turn.

Allison took a deep breath and continued the conversation with patience, love, and as much understanding as she could find. The more she kept her tone calm and her words reasonable, the more Dani's sniffing on the other end of the phone tapered off. It would have been so easy to jump on the *bash Andrew* wagon, but she'd have to deal with that side of the issue another day. Right now she was only concerned with her sister and her nieces' well-being.

"Please don't tell Dad," Danielle pleaded. "Please don't tell him until I figure out what to do. It's so . . . embarrassing."

"Embarrassing?"

"My husband had an affair with a *hooker*, Allie. A prostitute. What does that say about me? Our sex life? Our personal relationship? I'll never trust anybody after this. Never. Mom was right. There's no such thing as a happily-ever-after."

Shit. "Don't you dare go near those waters, Dani. Aside from being a damned good sister, you're an incredible mother and wife."

"Obviously, I'm a shitty and easy-to-forget wife." A loud nose blowing followed that awful statement. "Maybe I should have shown an interest in whips and chains. You know that whole dominatrix thing is wildly popular. There has to be something behind that, right?"

Yikes.

This was going from bad to worse.

Time for a detour.

"Where are the girls?"

"They're spending the night at Sheila Brisby's house. She offered a sleepover with Courtney before the shit hit the fan. Sheila doesn't know what happened; only that something did. She's offered to keep the girls until I can come pick them up tomorrow."

"Can you call someone to stay with you tonight? I promise I'll be on the next plane home."

"That's what you said a few weeks ago. And now . . . when I need you . . ."

Though she had nothing to do with Andrew's recklessness, guilt slipped a noose around Allison's neck.

"He'll lose his job," Danielle announced with an abrupt sidestep in the conversation that had Allison shaking her head. "At the very least, they'll force him to resign. Plus there will be an investigation, and he could go to jail."

Oh God.

"Have you talked to him?"

"No. And I don't want to. His chief came by the office just a few hours ago and personally delivered the information. I asked him to please relay a message to Andrew that he is *never* welcome in this house again. The chief seemed to understand, but then he delivered another punch by telling me that the SPD has handed the investigation over to an impartial department. They're holding him until the FBI questions him."

"The FBI!"

"Because of the nature of some of the investigations he was involved in. They said they may have to overturn some of the convictions on his previous cases if this . . . *affair* was in any way involved."

"Dani, I am so sorry. I promise I will be there as soon as possible. We'll figure this out together, okay?"

"Okay." *Sniff.* "Allie? I'm serious. Please don't tell *anyone* about this yet. Especially not Mom or Dad. It's quiet here for now, but the media are going to get wind of this, and as soon as they release the story . . ."

All hell will break loose.

And then some.

"I need time to figure out how to do damage control with our kids, and our friends, and . . ."

"I won't tell a soul," Allison promised. "I'm about to wrap up this wedding, but if you need to talk more, call me. You come first."

"Okay." Her sister's voice sounded so vulnerable. So devastated. So very lost.

"I love you, Sis. Hold on. I'll be there soon." Allison tapped END CALL, held the phone to her chest, and fought back tears. It would be so easy to dive into her own feelings. Her own misgivings about life, relationships, and trust. About the fact that her one hope had just gone into a death spiral and exploded on impact.

But this wasn't about her.

For a moment, she'd allowed herself to have fun.

To dream.

To hope.

In the end, she'd been taught another nasty lesson.

Happily-ever-after was just an illusion.

End of story.

With a satisfied sigh, Jesse took a look around him and smiled. The night air had cooled to a comfortable seventy degrees. The wedding had gone off without any further hitches. Even General Brooks's hoochie girlfriend behaved herself.

The whirlwind of activities for the event were a done deal. Now, at the reception being held in his completely transformed backyard, the party had busted out with free-flowing champagne for the ladies and Gentleman Jack for the men. The rented dance floor was alive with a country line dance to a cover of Kip Moore's "Beer Money."

As best man, for a time he'd been relegated to certain duties. But once the cake had been cut, and he'd raised a toast to the bride and groom, he'd passed the baton to Jackson and Jake to put in their two cents. Now he was free to spend a little time with Allison.

He'd caught sight of her now and again as she kept the flow of the reception moving forward. He could tell she was in her element, doing a job she wasn't being paid for. He respected that. And he'd be damned sure to personally thank her when he got her alone.

And naked.

A tug on the bottom of his jacket made him look down. There he found Izzy rubbing her sleepy eyes. He swept her up into his arms and kissed her forehead. "You sleepy, little darlin'?"

"Nuh-uh." She rubbed her eyes again and yawned. "Need mo cake."

He chuckled, then caught Jackson's eye as he twirled Abby on the dance floor. Since Fiona was busy dancing with one of Jackson's firemen buddies, Jack and Abby headed in his direction.

"I think someone's ready to pass out," Jesse said, handing his niece over to her father. Izzy promptly laid her head on Jackson's shoulder. Her body went limp, and Jesse would swear she'd instantly fallen asleep.

"Annie just mentioned that she's exhausted and ready to go home," Abby said, gently stroking the toddler's tired little brow. "She can take Izzy home with her."

Something powerful caught in Jesse's chest as he watched his brother and his brother's future wife look lovingly at each other. A few months ago, their destiny had been uncertain. Yet here they were now, acting as a couple, as parents, who were obviously deeply in love.

Envy.

Perhaps a not-so-pretty mistress. But that just encouraged Jesse to do something about his own path in life. He didn't want to spend it alone. He wanted someone to look at him the way Abby looked at his little brother. He wanted to hold the warmth of that woman—the warmth of his own child—in his arms.

He was ready to take that step.

As Jack and Abby walked away with their precious cargo, Jesse spotted Allison coming toward him with a tray of cake slices. The music changed to the ballad "Hey Pretty Girl." Without a word, Jesse caught her by the hand, relieved her of her tray by placing it on a nearby table, and led her out onto the dance floor.

Filled with surprise, her smoky eyes looked up at him as he pulled her close. She didn't fight him. Instead, she sank against him and with a long exhale laid her head on his chest.

He breathed in her sweet scent and wrapped his arms around her waist. Hampered only slightly by the layered skirt of her peach-colored dress, his thigh pressed between hers as they swayed together. He wasn't sure they were keeping time with the music. He didn't care. She was in his arms after a long day, and that's all that mattered.

Too soon, the song ended, and his body went cold as she stepped away.

A smile that was a lot more edgy than sweet curled her glossy lips as she looked up at him, and said, "Meet me upstairs in five minutes." Then, with a gentle swish of her dress, she picked up the tray of cake slices and offered them to the guests at a nearby table on her way back toward the house.

He supposed it was ridiculous and pathetic that for the next five minutes he checked his watch approximately every fifteen seconds. Eventually, the hands on the Bulova blessed him with the allotted five minutes.

Once inside the house, he passed through the kitchen and thanked the seniors who'd cooked, helped serve, and stayed to clean up. Then he took the stairs two at a time. When he reached his bedroom, Allison was nowhere to be found.

He closed the door and went into the master bath. She wasn't there either. As he passed by the walk-in closet the door opened. A hand reached out, grabbed him, and pulled him inside.

"God." She shut the door, pushed him against it, and grabbed him by the lapels. "I thought you'd never get here."

Anticipation and lust pulled him in a million different directions. "Allison, I—"

"Sssh." She pressed a finger to his lips. "No talk." Her hand headed south, cupped his erection, and squeezed. "Just sex."

God, he loved this woman.

He groaned. "Yes, ma'am."

The next seconds flew by in a flurry of hands, lips, and tongues. Clothes flew off and sailed to the carpet. Before he knew it, he was buried deep inside her with her back to the door and her legs wrapped around his waist. His hands gripped her bottom as her warm skin and pebbled nipples pressed into his chest. The slick, hot, intense friction where their bodies were connected nearly drove him mad as she kissed him with hunger and desperate need.

He tried to control his thrusts, but she wasn't having any of it.

"Harder, Jesse." Her tongue plunged into his mouth, and the heat of her almost made him come right then and there. She pulled her head back. "Faster."

Oh God.

He shifted his hips, dove in, and gave her what she wanted. Intense pleasure grabbed hold and nearly twisted him inside out. Her breathing broke into little pants. Her moans grew louder. Against his palms, her butt tensed. When her inner muscles contracted and pulled him in tight, she cried out his name. Fire flashed across his skin, and an almost violent burst of heat shot up his legs and into his groin. With a long groan he joined her in that free fall into oblivion.

Once their racing hearts slowed, and they were able to catch their breath, he eased her feet to the ground.

"Are you okay?" he asked when she continued to pant.

She nodded, reached up, and slipped her hand behind his neck and pulled his head down for a kiss. "That was amazing."

"*You're* amazing." He kissed her again. "Guess we'd better put ourselves back together and rejoin the party."

"You go ahead. It will take me a few minutes longer to pull myself together."

He reached for his pants. "You sure?"

"Yeah." A slow blink fanned her thick, dark lashes. "Go ahead without me."

A while later, Jesse found himself stuck in a conversation about ground squirrels that couldn't have held his interest even if he hadn't just had hot closet sex. He glanced up to see where she'd gone off to but couldn't find her. When Charli walked by on her way to another glass of champagne, he caught her hand. "Have you seen Allison?"

She looked around. "Not for a while. She might be in the house helping clean up. You know how she is."

Jesse nodded, but something ominous tickled the back of his neck, and he excused himself from the table of elderly squirrel lovers. Inside the house, the seniors were still busy washing up and packing things away.

"Have you seen Allison?" he asked them. His only response came from Gertie West, who thought she'd seen her go upstairs earlier. Surely it couldn't take her this long to put herself back together. Before he'd left the room, she'd looked mussed but still amazing, with a warm flush to her cheeks and lips.

He took the stairs two at a time, opened his bedroom door, and glanced around at the empty room. The door to the bathroom was open, and the light was off. He opened the closet door, but there was nothing there except the sweet aroma of her perfume and the heady scent of their lovemaking. When he turned to leave the room, he noticed the piece of paper propped up on his pillow.

Nausea burned his throat as he walked across the room and picked it up.

Jesse,

> *I'm sorry.*
> *I have to go.*
> *It's been fun.*
> *Thanks.*

A.

Fun?

Thanks?

He reread the brusque, quickly scrawled words.

Her references didn't mean what they had was *fun*.

They meant it was over.

His heart sank deep in his chest as sat down on the bed and pulled his cell phone from his jacket pocket. He swept his thumb across the screen, tapped her name in his contact list, and wasn't at all surprised when his call went straight to her voice mail.

Memories of the past weeks tumbled through his heart and dropped into his stomach like a lead ball. Apparently, everything he'd been feeling for her had not been reciprocated. While he'd been foolishly imagining their future, she'd been booking a flight out of his life.

He felt like a fool.

Maybe he should have taken her at her word when she said she didn't believe in long-term relationships, marriage, or happily-ever-afters. She'd barely made it with him a couple of weeks.

Sure, he knew she'd go back to Seattle. She had a career. Friends. Family. But he'd thought they'd had something worth working on. He hadn't dreamed she'd dump him on his ass without at least a face-to-face good-bye.

Tempted to try to call her again, he tossed the phone on the bed.

She'd made herself clear. And he'd never begged a woman for anything.

The hell if he'd start now.

*S*unday passed in the dregs of a hangover. Once Jesse returned to the reception, he allowed himself a personal pity party. No need to involve anyone else. He didn't need lectures. Didn't need sympathy. Only time to lick his wounds and find his way back to the life he'd led before Allison had sauntered in.

A less-than-complete life to be sure. But one in which he'd find a way to survive.

He always did.

Twice, he'd broken down and tried to call her. Each call had gone straight to her voice mail. A clear signal she didn't want to talk. In a morbidly humorous way, he thought of how awkward future holiday gatherings would be if she ever came back to Sweet. Surely, she'd come for their parents' wedding. But who knew. She didn't believe in true love, soul mates, or forevers. Maybe she'd just send a gift.

By Monday morning, he'd helped the party-rental store load up the tables and chairs. Reno and Charli were happily off on their Caribbean honeymoon, and life went on as usual. Marcy Pettifer brought her cocker spaniel, Buttons, into the clinic for her yearly checkup, and Abby came in with a crate full of kittens that needed exams before she took them to her rescue center to await their forever homes. After quitting time, he had a couple of farm calls on his schedule that would keep him and his wandering mind busy the rest of the day.

The problem was going to be come nightfall.

With the wedding complete, he'd looked forward to seeing Allison at the end of the day. He'd imagined bringing her home, sitting out back with a glass of wine, and getting to know her even better. He'd liked that she fit so well into the family, and he'd been eager to finally focus on them as a couple.

Apparently, all that had been a fantasy on his part.

He didn't know what had happened to make him fall for her so hard. He only knew that he now needed to rewind and come up with a new plan that didn't include her smoky eyes, soft skin, witty comebacks, and easy laugh.

By mid Monday afternoon, he closed his office door, sat down at his desk, and grabbed the stack of mail he'd overlooked for too long. He half-ass skimmed a brochure for exam tables. After the Great Pyrenees disaster last fall, he'd needed to replace the table in room two even though most of the time he just got down on the floor with the animals. They didn't like high places, and he believed in a gentler method of seeing to their health and welfare. No need to terrify the little guys more than necessary.

He raised an eyebrow at the outrageous pricing and tossed the brochure in the round filing cabinet at his feet. Maybe next year. Till then, he'd just have to tolerate the creaking and groaning that sounded like something out of a *Paranormal Activity* movie.

The knock on his door didn't surprise him. Abby usually took a break around this time to run over and check on things at her rescue center. When the door opened, he was surprised to see his mother standing there.

"Hey, sugarplum. Looks like you've got a busy day ahead of you."

He leaned back, sensing something more than a casual visit was at hand. "No busier than usual."

The door opened wider, and in walked Jackson and Jake.

"Reinforcements?" Jesse asked, eyeing the stubborn expressions on their faces. "This must be good."

"We told her she could handle this on her own, but she seemed to believe you might need some ass-kicking," Jackson said.

Jake grinned. "Couldn't miss that opportunity."

Jesse ignored the somersault his heart turned, and he held up his hands. "Look, I know Brandy Huckabee was a little tipsy at the reception and at the end of the night she was hanging all over me, but I did *not* take advantage of her. I can assure you of that. I respect her position as Miss Rodeo Texas."

"This isn't about Brandy Huckabee, jackass." This from Jake, who was heading back to his troops at the end of the week.

A chill zapped his spine. "Are Reno and Charli okay?"

"They're fine."

Relief settled in his stomach.

And then Jake's image and unspoken message floated through his mind.

It's time to tell them all.

"I'm glad you're all here," he said. "There's something I need to talk to you about."

"Oh?" His mother planted herself in the chair opposite his desk. Wearing twin scowls, Jackson and Jake leaned against the wall, arms folded.

"It's about Jared." He took a deep breath, cleansing his soul, looking for courage. "And Dad."

Lines of concern pulled at his mother's forehead. "Go ahead."

Jesse set the scene regarding the night he and his brother had talked. Right down to the Snickers bar Jared had pulled from his pocket and munched while pointing up at the stars. Avoidance tactics were always so obvious to his mother, and her brows pulled tighter.

"Jared told me he—"

"Was gay?" his mother said.

"What?" Jackson and Jake said, their shoulders abruptly coming off the wall.

Jesse nodded.

"Oh, sugarplum." His mother reached across the desk and patted his hand. "Is that the secret that's tied you up in knots for so long?"

"Jared was gay?" Jake said.

Jackson remained quiet as he dropped down into a chair.

"There's more." Jesse relayed the rest of what his brother had revealed about finding love, and the promise Jared had asked him to keep. He told them of the conversation Jared had shared with his dad, to which his mother's eyes welled up with tears.

"I wasn't sure you knew," he said to his mom.

"But I was determined to uphold my end of the bargain."

"And now you believe that had you spoken up sooner," she said, "your daddy would still be alive."

He nodded.

"It wouldn't have changed a thing, son. I'm only sorry you didn't say something sooner, so you didn't have to bear this burden alone."

"I'd have done anything for him." The emotional clog in his throat made it difficult to speak. "He was my big brother."

His mom reached across the desk and covered his hand with her own. "He looked after all of you like you belonged to him. And I know he'd never want you to be so miserable about his path in life that you'd give up your own."

"It doesn't matter."

"It does," she insisted. "And I bear as much responsibility as anyone."

Jackson finally spoke. Quietly. "Why didn't he tell us?"

"He wasn't sure how all y'all would feel," their mom said.

"Yet you've known all along?" Jesse asked.

"Of course. He was my firstborn. I knew when he'd have a stomachache before he'd reach for the Pepto. We were thick as fleas on a dog. But I respected him enough to allow him the right to let everyone know when he felt comfortable. Your daddy didn't know until Jared told him. To him it didn't make a lick of difference. He just wanted Jared to be careful moving forward. Especially if he wanted a military career. Your daddy would never deny any of you happiness. But that's what he felt like he'd done with your brother. And that's the guilt that broke his heart."

Silence hovered in the office before Jackson finally lifted his head and spoke again. "I wish he'd told us."

"Would it have mattered?" Jesse asked.

Jackson's blue eyes narrowed. "Only in the fact that he would have been able to lead a fuller life. It sucks when you have to hide your love for someone."

Jesse nodded. Jackson had done exactly that. But now he'd found happiness with her. Jared would never have the opportunity to spend his life with whoever it was he'd loved.

"Jared had a lot of love to give, that was for sure." Jake ran a hand over his buzz cut. "Does anyone know who his partner was?"

They all looked at their mother, who shook her head. "I hope he'll come forward. If he loved Jared, he must be a special man. And, like us, he must be devastated at the loss."

"Then let's keep our fingers crossed that he'll step forward someday," Jake said. "So we can welcome him into the family."

"Fuck yes, we would," Jackson agreed.

Jesse leaned back in his chair and felt a sense of pride. He should have known his brothers would never judge Jared for whom he'd chosen to love. For who he was. And he hoped his big brother was looking down right now and knew that they all loved him without question. And that should his partner ever show up, they'd love him too.

Relief flowed through him, even as he realized Allison had been right. He should have told them all sooner. But now it was time to let all that go.

Time to move forward.

Even with a broken heart.

His mother patted Jackson's knee and verbalized what Jesse felt.

"Y'all make me so proud. All I ever want for any of you is for you to live your lives to the fullest." Her smile turned into the evil eye as she zeroed in on Jesse. "Which is exactly what brings us here."

"It's about Allison," Jackson said.

A horde of butterflies hit his stomach at Mach speed as he looked at his mother's grim expression. "Is she okay?"

"She's fine," his mother reassured him.

"Then, she's made her feelings pretty clear. And I'm not enough of a glutton for punishment to be interested in anything else you might have to say in her direction."

"Oh, stop being such a stubborn ass," his mother said.

"Look, Mom, I—"

"We know she took off on you and that you might be a bit miffed about that," his mother said.

Miffed?

The emptiness in his soul went way beyond miffed.

"Fact is she had a good reason for taking off."

"Really not interested," he said.

"Just shut up and listen," Jackson said. "You forced me to take a good look at the truth with Abby. Now it's your turn with Allison."

Resigned, Jesse leaned back in his chair and did the proverbial la-la-la-la in his head.

Childish?

Maybe.

Self-preservation?

Absolutely.

"Martin received a call early this morning," his mother said over the la-la-la's. "Apparently Danielle's husband has been involved in . . . some very bad stuff."

"Such as?" Jesse asked, knowing if the man had been injured—or worse—Allison would be devastated.

"It appears he was doing undercover work and was caught in a compromising position with a confidential informant."

"No shit?"

"No shit. And stop cussing."

"Sorry."

"Danielle called Allison just after the wedding and broke the news. Danielle is devastated and embarrassed and didn't want anyone to know until the local media turned it into a circus, which has now happened. She made Allison promise not to tell a soul—not even their father—until she figured out how to handle it with her two little girls."

"What a jackass, right?" Jake said, referring to the husband.

"Clearly."

"That's why Allison took off without a word," his mother said. "She'd made a promise to her sister—just like you did with Jared. Then she grabbed the last flight out Saturday night, so she could get back to Seattle."

Family first.

A conviction both he and Allison had in common.

He'd vowed to put his own life on hold until those he loved had found happiness. Could it be that in Danielle's time of need, Allison had put her own happiness on hold to be a supportive sister?

Possibly.

Did he understand why she'd leave so abruptly?

Yes.

Would he have likely done the same thing were he in her situation?

Hell yes.

Family first.

Was he unhappy that she'd left him an impersonal note instead of telling him face-to-face that she had to leave?

Undeniably.

But he knew there was more involved than just her going back to help her sister.

Allison had put her sister and her brother-in-law up on a pedestal. Their marriage had been her *one hope* in believing in a forever kind of relationship. And then she'd discovered it had shattered right before her eyes. So why would she believe that *their* relationship, which was so fresh and new, wouldn't eventually fall by the wayside?

She'd lost her one hope.

No wonder she'd bailed.

"I know you boys well enough to know when you're in love even when you don't." His mother sat at the edge of her seat and planted her doubled-up fist on his desktop. "And I'm not the kind of mama who will stand by and watch you let that love slip through your stubborn fingers. At least not ever again."

Jaw clenched, his mother got up out of her chair, came around to his side of the desk, and dropped her fingers to the keyboard of his computer. She typed out a URL and hit ENTER.

The blog that popped up on the screen had a white background with a broken-heart design that made a powerful statement. *Project Happy Ending* was obviously a blog where love did not triumph.

"I could stand here all day barking at you," his mom said. "But if you're the smart man I think you are, you'll read every word on that Web site. The girl makes her feelings pretty clear. If after that, you still have questions . . . well then, you're dumber than I thought."

When his mom went back around the desk, Jackson stood, and he and Jake followed her out the door.

Jesse returned his gaze to the computer monitor and scrolled over some of the headings. Then he dropped to a post written on the same night Allison had been introduced to the Wilder family.

An image flashed in his mind of her sitting beside the creek campfire while the flickering highlights and shadows of the flames danced across her face.

"*I have a blog,*" she'd said.

Holy shit.

His eyes jumped back to the words on the screen. He scanned words like *love,* and *trust, hope,* and *forever.* All were used in a promising manner that made his heart skip a beat.

This was Allison's blog.

She'd used it to express her fears and doubts, her hopes and dreams. But mostly she'd used it in a way that let him know she understood there was more to finding happiness than living in the past. Her most recent entry had him picking up the phone.

As a man of action, he jumped in and did what he did best.

Chapter 17

Three days into catastrophe and damage control, Allison dropped into the chair behind her desk and laid her head down. Exhaustion had managed to fill every nook and cranny in her mind and every pore in her body. She was currently surviving on a high-octane caramel macchiato and was seriously highly considering the Starbucks next door for a refill.

When she'd arrived back home on Sunday morning, she'd gone straight to Danielle's. Her sister had answered the door in stained sweats, a blotchy face, and a red, drippy nose. Her perfect marriage had not only disintegrated, so had her fashion sense. The nose had gotten redder as they sat together on the couch, her big sister curled into her looking for comfort and bawling her eyes out. Later, after a long shower, Danielle had somewhat pulled herself together. Allison picked up the girls from school and took them to Mickey D's while

Danielle responded to some follow-up phone calls from the Seattle PD and the FBI.

As Allison had sat across the table from her two precious and adorable nieces, her heart sank. She'd hoped they really could live the perfect life with a happy mom and dad. She'd wanted that for them more than anything she'd ever wished for herself.

Somewhere in her life, she'd heard the phrase "life isn't fair." No shit. At the moment, it sucked for everyone.

Including her.

In a moment of pure panic and an obvious loss of brain cells, she'd walked away from the best thing that had ever come into her life. There wasn't a chance in hell he'd ever understand why she'd left behind a stupid heartless note to explain her sudden disappearance.

She should have stayed. She should have told him in person. She should have asked him to understand. To give her time to figure things out. That night at the campfire, he'd told her if she ever needed to talk, to go to him instead of spilling her guts as an anonymous person on a blog. So what had she done? She'd spilled her guts on her blog instead of talking to him.

Dumb. Dumb. Dumb.

One of these days, she'd figure out the whole behaving-like-an-adult thing. Until then, she'd pull her usual hiding-behind-her-cowardice trick and bury her head in the sand, so she didn't have to face her stupid mistakes.

After Lily and Angeline had picked all the

breading off their Chicken McNuggets and devoured their Oreo McFlurries, she took them home. Danielle had tiptoed around the truth and simply told them that their daddy's work was going to keep him away for quite a while. The girls asked few questions and seemed more interested in the Happy Meal toys they'd received than anything their father might be up to. Fortunately, they had no idea their comfortable little world had just blown apart.

On Tuesday morning, Allison had awakened in Danielle's guest room with a crick in her neck and a headache the size of Texas, which only served to remind her of the mess she'd left behind in the little town of Sweet. Danielle's crisis had forced her to put a stop on all her intentions to further explore what she'd found with Jesse.

Though they'd only shared a few weeks together, she knew he was special. She felt something very different than ever before. He gave her a sense of belonging, a sense of home. He made her laugh. Made her think. And Lord knows he brought a level of sensuality to the table she'd never imagined even though a table had never actually been involved. As a woman, he made her feel loved and wanted. As a human, he made her feel admired and respected.

Where on earth would she ever be lucky enough to find that again?

Before Danielle's urgent call, she hadn't intended to leave Sweet no matter how many events were piled up on her calendar. She loved being a part of the Wilder chaos. They were like a ray of

sunshine on a cloudy day. You wanted them all at
full volume: laughing, loving, and caring for each
other with every breath they took. But with Danielle's devastating news, life took a sharp left turn.

At the time, so many confusing thoughts had
clouded Allison's clear thinking. Before she'd
come to Sweet, Jesse had a reputation a mile long
as the love 'em and leave 'em type. What if all
those oogly-googly feelings that danced through
her heart were only on her side? What if he didn't
share them? What if he'd been ready to toss her
aside for the next brunette or blonde who sauntered into Seven Devils?

Now, as she gave thought to those questions,
she knew they were ridiculous.

In a very short time, they'd come to share something special. She knew it. And now she had to
live with the regret that she might never have the
chance to really know if happily-ever-after could
come true.

On Tuesday afternoon, she'd face-planted with
exhaustion on her desk. Exhaustion begged her
to keep her eyes closed, but her heart pushed
that option away. She'd never considered herself
a slow learner. She'd always been the top in any
class she'd ever taken. But when it came to life, it
appeared she was quite sluggish.

Why was she just now realizing that whatever
her parents had done with their marriage, whatever Danielle and Andrew had done with theirs,
had nothing to do with *her*?

Happiness wasn't an illusion.

Life was what you made it.

She glanced at her watch.

Maybe it wasn't too late.

Maybe if she called Jesse and explained, he'd understand. Or maybe not. She at least had to give it a try.

Flexibility. Determination. Heart. That's what it took to make a relationship work. If you were willing, it was never too late.

With a quick call, she told her assistant to re-schedule her remaining appointments for the week. She was on a mission to face the fear factor in her life. Because the biggest risk in life was not taking a risk at all.

Chapter 18

He'd caught Seattle on a good day.

As Jesse maneuvered the busy and sometimes rolling streets in his rental car, he admired the glimpses of ocean, islands, mountains, and the snowcapped Mt. Rainier against a cloudless blue sky. Allison had once mentioned how many days of rain the city received a year. Jesse couldn't imagine living in all that gloom. But looking at it now, he had to admit it did have its perks.

The most likely was the sole reason he'd traveled so many miles.

Living in a town with a population far below an average day at Disneyland, he'd never needed to have supersleuth skills before. Since she still wasn't answering his calls, he'd gratefully accepted all the help he could get from her father in tracking Allison down.

After parking his rental car on the narrow street, he approached the typical, boxy-looking condominium complex. A cypress hedge in front of the building did little to add to the charm. Knowing Allison as he did now, he couldn't imagine her living in such an uninteresting place. She belonged with him in charismatic Sweet. Which didn't mean he wasn't willing to compromise. Hell, to be with her, he'd pack up and make Seattle his home too.

He passed through the building's glass entry and headed upstairs. Before he knocked on her door, he smoothed his hand over his newly cut and much shorter style hair. The long hair had simply been an image he'd presented. Time now to step up to the plate and be the man his parents had raised him to be.

Moments after he knocked, the door swung open, and he had to catch his breath. Even in sweatpants, with her hair pulled up in a wild tangle on her head and not an ounce of makeup on her face, she made his heart explode.

Her sensuous mouth dropped open, and her smoky eyes widened.

His fingers tingled to touch her. To inhale that sweet scent that belonged to only her. He longed to take her in his arms and keep her there.

At that moment, it was all he could do to keep his hands tucked into the pockets of his jeans.

There was still the possibility she didn't want *him*.

*A*llison had been expecting someone to knock on her door. She'd just never imagined that someone would be Jesse.

"You cut your hair!"

The corners of his mouth lifted into a grin, and her heart felt like it had been hit with a blowtorch.

"I fly two thousand miles to see you, and you want to talk about my hair?"

"No. I'm just . . ."

"Surprised to see me?"

"That's . . . an understatement."

"Guess it's my turn to catch *you* off guard."

At that moment, Wee Man bounced into the room and did his best rabbit impersonation until Jesse reached down and picked him up.

"Hey, Buddy. Miss me?"

Allison hated to admit it, but she believed that's exactly why Wee Man had been so restless since they came back to Seattle. Of course, he could also be missing Pumpkin, or Reno's dog Bear, or Miss Giddy, or the gazillion acres he'd grown to love to roam. His affection was noted by a long slurp up Jesse's clean-shaven chin. The resounding deep chuckle Jesse gave sent a little quiver up her middle.

With a final stroke of affection over the top of her dog's head, Jesse put him back down on the floor and chuckled as Wee Man happily trotted away. Then those inquisitive blue eyes zeroed in on her.

"So . . ." Larger-than-life and a teensy bit intimidating, he stepped inside her condo. Somehow, she managed to maintain control of her breathing as she stepped back. "About this disappearing act of yours."

"I'm sorry." She closed the door, hesitating to

turn. Guilt pricked at the back of her neck. The night of the wedding, Danielle's bombshell and all Allison's reasons to run had dog piled. It hadn't been until she'd come back to Seattle that she'd gained clarity. "I had no choice."

"Sure you did." He folded his arms. "You could have told me what was going on."

"I promised Danielle I wouldn't tell anyone. Not even Dad."

"Not talking about Danielle," he said.

"Then what?"

He glanced away. When he swung his gaze back, she could sense his exasperation.

She'd told him she trusted him.

But she hadn't.

"You should have told me you were scared of what was happening between us," he said.

She'd said it. Just not to him.

Hello, my name is Allison, and I'm a cowardly blogo-holic.

"Want some coffee?" In an obvious stall tactic, she headed toward the kitchen. "I just made fresh."

He followed her into the kitchen. "I didn't come all this way for a caffeine fix, Allison. I came to discuss why, aside from your sister's situation, you felt the need to run."

Her hands shook as she grabbed two cups from the cabinet and set them on the granite-topped island. Then she braced her hands on the edge of the counter and dropped her head.

"You're right. I *was* scared. Danielle and Andrew were my—"

"One hope." He braced a hip against her counter and folded his arms again. "I get that. But don't you think you'd be better off putting all that energy into finding your own happiness instead of *hoping* someone else will show you the way?"

"Yes. And I know that now."

His eyes narrowed just slightly. "Do you?"

Stunned by the intensity in his eyes, she could only nod.

"What changed?"

"Everything."

"The truth, Allison."

She lifted her hands. "The truth is, with you I caught a glimpse of how my life *could* be. And that made me realize I had to quit hiding behind excuses. I had to let go of my fears and the past. The only way I'm truly going to be happy is if I reach for the future."

"How does it make you feel?"

"Scared. But hopeful."

"That's a good start." He moved closer. Finally within touching distance, he reached out and rubbed his hands over her cold fingers. "So what's your future?"

"Depends." Their eyes locked. "Why did you come here, Jesse?"

"You wouldn't answer my calls."

"I had a lot to think about. Plus there was that whole trying to deal with my sister while she was trying to deal with the collapse of her marriage thing."

"I'm impressed that in the middle of the crisis, you realized that her happiness, or lack thereof, had nothing to do with yours."

"*You* helped me realize that, Jesse."

"I'm glad."

"So why did you come here?" she asked him again.

"I'll admit, initially you weren't on my radar. I had a list of things I needed to do. People I needed to take care of. To make sure they were happy. You made your way onto that list. No matter how many times I heard you deny the possibility of true love, *I* knew it existed. And no matter how indignant you got when I forced you to see another point of view, I also heard that little whisper in your voice that said you really wanted to believe."

"I do."

His responding smile sent a warm tingle down into her heart.

"To answer your original question, I came here for you, Allison," he admitted. "For us. I love you."

When she gasped, he pressed a finger to her lips.

"I've come a long way. In more ways than one. So please let me just say what's in my head. What's in my heart."

"Okay," she said in a shaky voice.

"Regardless of what everyone back in Sweet thinks of me, I've never been reckless *or* impulsive. I'm not now. I realize what I just said might sound crazy because we've only known each other a short time. Believe me, I've thought long and hard about everything. I love that you love my crazy family. I love that you make me want to be a better person. I love that you don't buy in to all the crap I spew and that you make me want to be honest. And I love that you pushed aside all the lies that were told about me and just saw me for yourself."

"I love that about you too."

"I've never believed in love at first sight, but you proved me wrong." He kissed her fingers, then clasped her hands to his chest. "I knew I'd fallen hard that night at the movies when you doused your popcorn in butter, then licked it off your fingers."

"That's lust. Not love."

"Yeah. The love part came when you were bawling your eyes out and wiping your nose on my shirt, and I didn't mind."

Laughter danced in her chest. "I'm sure I've never heard a man say that to a woman before."

"I told you, darlin'"—he grinned—"stick with me, and I'll take you places you've never been."

"Then consider me glue."

"Back in Texas," he said, "I didn't tell you I loved you because I was afraid you'd think I was crazy. I knew how you felt about relationships, and I didn't want to scare you away. I was willing to do whatever it took and however long it took to keep you. Even if that meant finding a way to make a long-distance relationship work."

Emotion floated from her heart and up into her eyes and made it impossible to see his handsome face.

"I love you, Allison. And when I look at you, I see my future. *Our* future. When I see you holding Izzy, I picture you holding our own baby. When I watched my brother marry the woman he loves, I knew that's what I wanted too. I know that might be too much for you to take in right now, and I know your life is here in Seattle, but—"

"I'm packed."

His head came up sharply. His brows drew together. "What?"

"My suitcases are in the bedroom crammed full of everything I could fit." She nodded, and tears spilled down her cheeks. "I've already made arrangements for movers to pick up everything at the end of the week and haul it to Sweet. Without you, there's nothing."

"What about your business? Your sister?"

"Danielle wants to buy the company. She said she needs something to focus on, so she doesn't become a bitter divorcee like our mother." She touched his face with trembling fingers. "I love you, Jesse. And I'm not afraid of that. Not anymore. Just promise me something."

"You bet."

"It took me a while to realize that love and a lasting relationship don't just happen because you want them to. I'd always seen Danielle and Andrew as the golden couple. Like nothing could ever go wrong just because they seemed so perfect. But as time went on, they hadn't grown together. They grew apart. Promise me we'll always work together on our relationship. I want to be more than just your girl. I want us to be more than just a couple. I want us to be best friends as well as lovers."

"I couldn't agree more. And you have my solemn promise."

Her heart pounded while he cupped her face

in his hands and kissed her. If she'd had a flurry of fairy godmothers fluttering around, Allison knew she could not have felt more loved. Without words, the look in Jesse's eyes said it all.

He loved her.

And she loved him.

It might not always be easy, but their life together would be amazing. She didn't know what she'd done right to find such a man, but hoping others would prove her either wrong or right about love hadn't been it. She'd taken a chance and completely lost her heart to a man who would cherish it for as long as they both lived.

Truth dawned in that fairy-tale fashion of birds chirping and flowers singing.

"Jesse?" She looked up into his handsome face and found tenderness brightening his blue eyes. "As long as I'm taking a leap, I'm going to do it without a net."

His head tilted. "What are you talking about?"

"I love you." Three little words had never felt more right.

"And I love you."

"Then . . ." She took a deep breath. "Will you marry me?"

The smile that pushed up the corners of those masculine lips came slow and steady. "I was going to wait for someplace more romantic than your kitchen but . . ." He reached into his pocket and pulled out a little black box. "It looks like we think alike."

He flipped open the lid to reveal a stunning natural pink diamond ring. "I wanted something as unique and special as you." He slipped the ring on her finger.

It was a perfect fit.

Just like them.

She was speechless.

Almost.

"So . . . you're saying yes?"

He laughed, and the happy sound fluttered through her heart. "I'm saying yes."

"Are you sure you're ready to give up your hard-earned playboy status?"

"More than ready."

"What about all those female hearts you'll break? Especially Gladys's and Arlene's."

"There's still another Wilder brother left. I'm sure Jake can give them a run for their money."

"I love you, Jesse Wilder." She touched his face, unable to believe her good fortune the night she'd stopped in that rowdy honky-tonk. "When I came to Texas, I was looking for any reason to believe love didn't exist. But I found something sweeter."

"And what's that, darlin'?"

"I found *you*. My happily-ever-after."

Can't get enough of the wild Wilders?

Well, get ready because next winter Candis Terry and her sparkling, sexy Sweet, Texas, series return with . . .

Sweet Surprise

Fiona Wilder's past is a road rife with heart-wrenching twists and life-changing turns. But now she's trying to make things right. Be a good single mom. Take charge of her life. And never, ever repeat her mistakes of falling in lust, not love. This includes keeping her cool when it comes to a red-hot fireman who openly admits his heart is locked up tight ... even if he might turn out to be a real knight in shining armor.

Firefighter Mike Halsey learned the hard way that life throws curves that aren't always fair, are sometimes destructive, and occasionally irresistible. Guy code dictates that one never goes after his best friend's ex. But what's a guy to do when he meets a damsel in distress and their attraction is an unstoppable force as well as a danger to his guarded heart?

Coming February 2015

From Avon Books